I0574514

A HERO
OF A DIFFERENT STRIPE

LTUE BENEFIT ANTHOLOGIES

OTHER WORKS BY JALETA CLEGG

Dark Dancer
Autumn Visions (collection)
Brain Candy (collection)
Llama Tell You a Story . . . (collection)
Soul Windows (with Frances Pauli)

Altairan Empire series

Nexus Point

Priestess of the Eggstone

Poisoned Pawn

Kumadai Run

Cold Revenge

Jericho Falling

Obsidian Tears

Chain of Secrets

An Indecent Proposal

Phoenix in Flames

Redemption

As Editor

Wandering Weeds: Tales of Rabid Vegetation (with Frances Pauli)

OTHER WORKS BY JOE MONSON

Anthologies (as editor)

A Universe of Stories
The Horror at Pooh Corner (forthcoming)

Legacy of the Corridor publication series (as editor)

The Florilegium of Madness (D. J. Butler) (with Callie Butler)
Dragon Soup for the Soul (Emily Martha Sorensen)
Down the Arches of the Years (Lee Allred)
Sharks in an Inland Sea (Lehua Parker)
The Bacillus of Beauty (Harriet Stark)
In the Haunting Darkness (Michael R. Collings)
Interplanetary Edition and Other Tales of Tomorrow (Emily Martha Sorensen)
All the Monoliths in the Universe (Michael C. Goodwin)

Other Collections (as editor)

Thin Air: The Cosmic Crime Fiction of Gustavo Bondoni (forthcoming, 2023)

A HERO
OF A DIFFERENT STRIPE

EDITED BY

JALETA CLEGG AND JOE MONSON

HEMELEIN PUBLICATIONS

A Hero of a Different Stripe
LTUE Benefit Anthologies, volume 5.

A Hemelein Publications Original. Copyright © 2023 by Jaleta Clegg and Joe Monson. Individual stories copyright their respective authors. Copyright and first appearance information for individual stories is found at the end of the book. All rights reserved.

Except for brief excerpts in the case of reviews, this book may not be reproduced in any form without prior written permission of the publisher. All stories and essays published by permission of the authors.

The works in this book are fiction. Any names, characters, people, places, entities, or events in these stories are products of the authors' imaginations, and any resemblance to actual people, places, entities, or events is entirely coincidental.

Cover artist: Kevin Wasden. Cover image copyright © 2023 by Kevin Wasden. Used under license.
Cover and interior layout and design: Joe Monson

"Spark" icon is by Alexander Skowalsky and is used under a CC-by-3.0 license See https://commons.wikimedia.org/wiki/File:Spark_By_Alexander_Skowalsky_756341.svg for details.

Edited by Jaleta Clegg and Joe Monson
Proofreaders, for whom we are eternally grateful: Marny Parkin, Amanda Rodriguez, and Stephan Fassmann

Managing Editor: Joe Monson
Publisher: Heather B. Monson
Published by Hemelein Publications, LLC.
http://hemelein.com/

First Edition
First Hemelein printing, February 2023
10 9 8 7 6 5 4 3 2 1

ISBN:
978-1-64278-019-2 (trade paperback)
978-1-64278-036-9 (ebook)

Library of Congress Control Number: 2022949990

To Tom:
You were, and continue to be, an inspiration to us all,
even those of us you never met in this life.
Thank you.

CONTENTS

A QUIET
AND UNASSUMING HERO

JOE MONSON

Here we are!

This is the fifth LTUE Benefit Anthology! It's hard to believe that this project was started six and a half years ago and it's still going strong! My coeditor, Jaleta Clegg, has stoically stuck with me the entire time, and we've put together some pretty solid anthologies. Thank you so much for sticking with us!

Now, onto this year's theme!

Life, the Universe, & Everything was created by volunteers. Outside of the faculty advisors when it was first organized, all of the work in creating, organizing, and running the symposium has been done by volunteers. Unless you've been on the inside, you have no idea how many hours are spent getting everything ready for the annual event each February. I've never tried to calculate it, but I suspect that, by the time the event itself winds down and everything is done, there have been thousands of hours of volunteer work put into it. Even the faculty advisors put in far more unpaid hours on it than they do paid. It's a true labor of love.

Tom Grover was much like the other early volunteers at LTUE. He showed up to meetings, offered to help where he could, and put in many, many hours making sure everything that needed doing was done. He was a member of The Association (and later, Quark), the science fiction and fantasy club on the campus of Brigham Young University, and was involved in countless activities related to that.

However, the thing people remember about him is just how much he helped out with everything. If something needed doing, he was there. If more help was needed, he volunteered. The comment I've heard over and over again from everyone who knew him was that he was *always* ready and willing to help. And he didn't do it for the recognition. He was a genuinely friendly and helpful person. His death in 1988 was a shock to the community, and a great loss.

In honor of his tireless volunteering, LTUE created the Tom Grover Award several years ago, periodically giving it to a volunteer for LTUE that goes above and beyond the call to help everything run smoothly, especially behind the scenes. I don't think it's given out every year, either (I'm not part of that bit of planning).

This anthology collects stories of ordinary, non-traditionally heroic individuals who step up when something needs doing, when they see someone in need. You'll find shapeshifting detectives, amazing sidekicks, romance-novel readers who face down an alien menace (that's the cover story, by the way), and even lunar garbage collectors! These stories truly capture the spirit of Tom as these ordinary people make themselves available when it counts, and often with little fanfare.

As you enjoy the stories here, consider ways in which you can be the quiet difference in the lives of those around you, in organizations to which you belong, at work, at play, and wherever. Everyone can be a hero of a different stripe and make a huge difference, even if you can't see the difference yourself. You, too can be an unsung hero in someone's life. Let's be about it!

Joe Monson
February 2023

OLIVE GARDEN

TRISTAN A. GILMORE

"HERE ARE YOUR MENUS, and your server will be right with you!"

I groaned inwardly as I leaned against the divider separating the kitchen from the dining floor. That was definitely Jess's voice seating them, and if Jess was the hostess tonight, then I was in for a long night of soups, salads, and fifty-cent tips.

Jess was my ex, and she hated me with more passion than she had ever invested in our actual relationship. The breakup hadn't even been my idea, but apparently I wasn't supposed to have agreed with her when she said we didn't work. Oops.

I get it, hurt feelings and such. I wasn't perfect, but I really hated that the hard feelings hit my wallet so directly.

I sighed, letting my sour stomach unclench and chalking the inevitable loss up to some perverse form of relationship alimony before bracing myself to begin my shift for the night. I lifted my face into a smile, rolled my shoulders, and slapped my apron pocket to make sure my pen was still there before walking around the divider into Merlot. (Each of the seating areas was named after a wine, and tonight that was my section to cater.)

Just as I turned the corner, my radio crackled and announced that a table had, indeed, been seated in Merlot. I twisted the dial to decrease the volume as I approached the guests.

"Hello, my name is Scott and I'll be your server. How are we doing tonight?" I asked, blinking to make sure that my smile reached up and into my eyes convincingly enough. There were four of them, and they had been seated in the corner booth, which was convenient because it meant I could see all of them eye-to-eye without having to hummingbird around the table all night. Oddly, it wasn't the usual date-night setup of two couples, but a group of three men who were all sitting opposite a woman in a sleek, surprisingly pragmatic-looking red dress. Also strange was the way that the three large, leather-clad men did not move their eyes from the face of the woman while she looked up at me and smiled.

"It's been a good evening, thanks," she said, sounding calm and genuine. As for the men, I might have been invisible for all the reaction they had.

"Great!" I said, eyes darting across the group again for more context. Normally, I could pin a group within the first few seconds: a business meeting, a double date, a new, awkward couple . . . but the men were large, serious looking, and struck me as hiding a lot of pent-up frustration with their posture. The middle one had a series of rings on his knuckles so large that they could have been a set of brass knuckles. The juxtaposition they offered in contrast to the woman's relaxed smile was both unnerving, and incredibly intriguing.

Evidently, the woman intuited the reason for my hesitation, as I was about to leap into a more general greeting and presentation of specials when she winked and said, "We're just old friends, catching up. Could you get us all some water while we look at the menu?"

I was so caught off guard that instead of maneuvering the conversation like I usually would, I just nodded and said, "Of course," before walking away. A moment later, I was scooping ice and pouring water as I shook my head, already feeling off my game for the night.

Smile, check. Water, check. I walked back into Merlot, determined not to trip myself up this time around.

"I think we know what we'd like," the woman said, this time before I could open my mouth. "Do you have salad and breadsticks?"

I placed the waters down in front of each and gave a wry glance toward the men, who appeared unchanged since I had been there last. "This is Olive Garden," I replied sardonically.

The woman chuckled and said, "Perfect. House salads all around, and I'll have a strawberry daiquiri as well. Virgin."

"Fantastic," I said. I didn't even bother taking notes. I turned to the men and asked, "Would you like anything else to drink?"

The man furthest left shook his head slightly and raised his palm toward me, as though annoyed. I nodded and said, "Then I'll be right back," before turning and making my escape to enter their order and head to the kitchens.

"Who are they?"

I jumped as Jess confronted me around the corner of the kitchen door. Damn, when had I become so jumpy?

"No clue, just another table," I said, trying to shrug it off. "Why? What are you doing back here?"

Jess's lips tightened as her snark-levels leapt in response.

"Because I work here, doofus, and I was looking for you."

"Me? Why?" I asked.

"Not because of you!" Jess snapped, each syllable sounding like the crack of a whip. "Because there are four other tables asking to be seated in your section, and I need to know if you can handle it."

"Four other . . . what?" I replied intelligently.

Jess huffed out a calming breath and said, in a slightly less agitated tone, "There are four more tables—about twelve men—all asking to be seated in your section. It's . . . kinda freaky."

I just stared and blinked, and then mechanically moved past her to begin prepping a tray. I couldn't just stand there in the doorway, and my mind was having trouble comprehending what she was telling me, so it instead counted olives into the salad. "So, they all need to be in my section? Are they family or something? Someone I know?"

"No," Jess said, arms folded. "They all look like those guys in there with the woman. They're creeping us out up front."

I paused, frowning. "Are they, like, mobsters?" I asked.

"How the hell should I know?" Jess retorted before her voice softened. "But, yeah. Maybe."

"Well, tell them to sit somewhere else," I said, shrugging. "You know Harvey would have a fit if you messed up his seating pattern. Just tell them it's policy or something."

"I did, and they said they'd wait for the same section as the other men and the woman. No exceptions."

I turned to look at her and saw that there was real concern on her face. She was afraid something was going to happen tonight.

We were bad for each other, but I couldn't help but feel a pang of . . . something, seeing her like that. I looked down at my salad dish and sighed.

"Well, go ahead and seat them. I'll figure it out."

Jess watched me for a moment, and then seemed to revert her nervous energies back into being annoyed by me.

"Idiot," she mumbled as she moved out the other side of the kitchen and up toward the front.

What was I supposed to do, though?

What a way to start the night, I thought, loading the breadsticks onto the tray and lifting it up to head back out to Merlot.

Usually, when a table is seated, there is conversation. You can at least hear the people shuffling in their seats or whispering something at each other as you enter from the kitchens, but the woman and the men were silent as I returned. The traditional elevator-style music humming in the background provided the only sound outside of the clacking dishes I set on the table. The men hadn't moved, and the woman was pleasantly examining the painted glass pattern in the chandelier above them.

"Here's everything but the daiquiri!" I announced, placing things onto the table with my smile as fixed as before. "It should only take a minute though. I'll bring it straight out. Cheese?" I asked, brandishing the wedge shredder before them like a Holy Grail.

Not a peep. Nobody made a sound. The woman simply shook her head in the negative and raised an eyebrow as she watched a procession of large men in leather jackets begin to filter into the dining area led by a flustered-looking Jess. Each of them took a seat that allowed them to see the booth, and none of them looked relaxed as they watched the woman intently. Several of them jostled their elbows in the traditional fashion of "yep, my gun's still there," and my stomach dropped a few inches lower than usual.

Jess shot me an exasperated look as she passed back up toward the front, and I looked around at the dozen men seated throughout the section, all watching the woman and apparently oblivious to my existence. I turned back to look at the woman, and she just smiled, offering the smallest of glances toward me as explanation.

I licked my lips and turned back to the dozen men. "Uh, hello!" I said loudly, "since you all seem to be together, perhaps I can take your orders all at once? What would you like to drink?"

"Water," a man with a shaved head barked from beside me, causing me to flinch. A few others nodded in agreement, and I soon found myself carrying a tray of a dozen waters on my shoulder, depositing them at each of the tables.

Almost as soon as I opened my mouth while depositing the water glasses, the same man said, "Salads," with a seriousness that dried my mouth instantly. Aside from being the scariest, they were also going to be the

4

easiest party I'd ever catered. I swallowed and returned to the kitchen without saying anything.

"What is going on?"

I jumped again. This time it was my co-server, Douglas, who was watching the edge of Merlot from the door's window over my shoulder.

"Beats me," I shook my head. "All I know is I just hope they don't stick around for desserts."

"Are they, like, with the government?" Doug asked.

"I don't know," I said curtly. "Just let me get them their salad so they can get out. I really don't want any trouble around here."

"Why would there be trouble?"

I jumped for the fourth time that night as Harvey, our manager, came out of his office into the operations area. He was only just reaching middle age, but his hair hadn't heard the memo that people had lifespans beyond forty in the twenty-first century and had turned completely white already, including his eyebrows. It gave him the look of someone who was constantly surprised, and Harvey was simple enough that it probably was accurate most of the time.

I had to take a breath before turning to speak with him.

"Nothing, sir. Just a weird group over in Merlot; a bunch of guys in black leather jackets. But they've been fine, just . . . kinda serious."

"Oh?" said Harvey, his white eyebrows up near his hairline. He walked over to the kitchen door and peered through the window. Then shrugged and said, "Well, I'll give them a quick walk-through and see how it goes!" He smiled and pushed open the kitchen door, moving out to Merlot.

A few minutes later, while I was counting olives and peppers for the series of salads, Harvey came back into the kitchen with eyes wider than usual.

"You weren't kidding, Scott!" he said. "They're a tough crowd! I told that story I always tell about the breadstick we used as a doorstop, and they didn't make a sound." He mopped his forehead on his sleeve and shrugged. "Don't let them start anything in here, but otherwise just keep them happy, I guess. Let me know if there's any problem."

I nodded and plated the last of my salad trays. Two silent trips later, all of them had salad on the tables, and no one was eating aside from the woman.

I wasn't the anxious type, but I couldn't help but pace as I waited before my obligatory return to ask how the food was. The good thing about having everyone in the section—and none of them eating—was that I was markedly less busy than usual.

I was also much more stressed than usual.

"Let me just walk out and see 'em," my co-servers began asking. They all had heard or passed by my section and seen the odd situation, and now they were all curious. Some of them joked, others were just excited for gossip and a change of pace, but I couldn't seem to settle myself. I felt on edge, and struggled not to snap at anyone to leave me alone.

What were those people doing here? They obviously weren't eating, and they all seemed far too focused on the woman for it to mean anything good. I kept having to mop sweat from my brow, though it wasn't hot and I wasn't working that hard.

Eventually, I felt I had no choice but to return and check on our guests.

I walked back out into Merlot, and if I had thought it was tense before, it was nothing to the scene I now walked in on: the woman was still sitting, sipping her water, but several of the men around the room were now standing. They had hands in jackets and pockets, and it seemed to me as if they were on the verge of drawing firearms. Nothing but sheer force of habit moved me into the room, leaving behind my sense of self as I opened my mouth and asked, "Can I bring you your bills? And are they all together?"

My arrival must have offset something, because the men seemed to return to a more casual stance, and the woman smiled at me.

"Yes," said the man of single word requests.

"I'll . . . I'll be right back," I said, bowing awkwardly in a way I had never attempted before, and then stumbling over my own feet as I swung around and headed back to the kitchens. I had just collected a pocket full of chocolate mints and printed the receipts when I gasped.

The strawberry daiquiri!

I practically ran to the bar, where, sure enough, the virgin strawberry daiquiri was set atop the order receipt. It was somewhat melted, but I was too panicked to consider any other options. I grabbed it, sopped up the pooled condensation with my apron, and ran back toward Merlot.

I practically crashed through the door of the kitchens, waving the smoothie drunkenly above my head, just as a dozen men leveled handguns at me.

There was an extremely tense moment, in which my only thought was *Did I wet myself? No? No, I didn't, oh, good,* followed by an immediate self-reprimand of my psyche for being more concerned about embarrassment than the firearms pointed at my face.

"Uh," I said as the men continued to stare at me. "I, uh, I forgot—"

"My daiquiri!" the woman exclaimed, teeth shining as she came to her feet and walked up to take the drink from my hand. As soon as she stood, every gun in the room swiveled to follow her, but she paid them no mind.

"Thank you," she said politely, taking the drink. "Do you have a straw?"

Numbly, my mouth agape, I reached into my apron pocket and proffered a straw. She opened it with one hand and palmed the wrapper, slipping the straw into the drink and sipping it.

"Mmm, excellent," she said.

The bill book was still clutched in my other hand, and she gently tugged it out of my grasp and flipped it open. She retrieved two crisp hundred dollar bills from her sleeve, slipped them in beside the bill, and handed it back to me. I placed it into my apron mechanically. The men continued to watch with hard eyes and drawn weapons.

"Best you go back to the kitchens, I think," the woman said, turning her back on me with a wink and facing the men. "Now, shall we return to business?"

For a moment I was going to turn and run and prepare myself for the seemingly imminent rain of gunfire, but my brain was again on autopilot, and I found my mouth open before I could stop it.

"Uh, I'm sorry, but you can't be doing that kind of thing in here," I croaked. "I'm, I'm afraid I am going to have to ask you to leave the premises, or I'll, I'll, I'll have to call the police."

Regret immediately hit as about half of the weapons returned to point at me directly, and I flinched back a step. Again, I considered running, but now I felt too much like prey being cornered, and felt that running would just feed the predatory instinct in the men's eyes and start the hunt.

"Boy," said the speaking man, "don't chu think you might be lost or something?"

"No, sir," I stammered, unsure of what I was saying, "I, I work here. This is an Olive Garden."

The entire room was frozen for a long moment, and then the man began to shake. For a moment I just saw the muzzle of his gun shifting slightly, but then I realized that he was laughing. Deep, shaking, quiet laughter that brought slow tears to the man's eyes.

"Indeed," he said, a broad smile shaping over his lips. "This *is* an Olive Garden."

The man gestured to the men, and they slowly stored their firearms and turned to file out of the restaurant. The woman, still as calm and gentle as ever, turned and said "Scott, I have to hand it to you," she raised an eyebrow, "the salad was excellent."

She followed the rest of the men out, and I watched from the window of the restaurant as the men and the woman piled into a series of black cars and drove away.

Jess appeared at my shoulder, face white and tears in her eyes. "What in the *living hell* were you thinking?!" she exclaimed in barely more than a harsh whisper.

I knew I was in shock by the extreme lack of feeling I was experiencing, but I couldn't help but recognize that tonight would be one of those unbelievable stories that you told your friends, and that they never believed.

A slow—but steady—customer service smile slipped over my face. I blinked, to make sure it was reaching my eyes, and said, "Nothing. This is an Olive Garden."

THE JUSTICE BEACON

MARK SILCOX

I WAS STANDING near the back of the produce section squeezing a mango when I heard the crash. The lights inside the supermarket flickered and the ceiling quivered above us, dropping a curtain of dust and fiberglass particles onto the fresh fruits and vegetables.

Jimmy grabbed my free hand and looked up at me, eyes agoggle. "What was *that*, Mommy?"

"I dunno, J. I'm sure somebody will . . . "

Before I could finish, a frenzied unshaven geezer in overalls crashed in through the doors that faced the parking lot. "Oh my gawwwd," he bawled at us, "it's *Missile Man*! He's fightin' some villain up in the sky!"

Everybody around me gasped and dropped whatever they were carrying to rush outside.

I set my piece of fruit down carefully. Jimmy was already tugging on my arm.

"C'mon, Mommy, c'mon! Outside! We gotta see Missile Man!'

"Uh. Yeah, okay, I guess we do."

On that particular day, my main ambition had just been to grab a few dollars' worth of groceries and get home in time for a mayhem-free family dinner. But if there was some sort of Battle Royale going on nearby, it was probably safer out on the tarmac than it was inside the building. Plus, my kid would never forgive me if he missed his chance to glimpse the famous superhero.

By the time we stepped out into the cool autumn afternoon, several cars in the parking lot were already smoking husks. A couple of dozen other shoppers were out there with their heads tilted backward, examining the sky. Missile Man was, indeed, hovering about thirty feet straight upward, blasting the air above us with bright bolts of laser vision. But who or what was his target?

A teenaged girl pointed up at the airborne hero. "His cape looks different than on TV!"

Then we heard a maniacal cackle from the roof of the building we had all just abandoned.

"I've got you now, Missile Man! I knew I could trick you into coming here alone!"

The voice from above was reedy and petulant, but very insistent. I started to get a shivery feeling in my stomach.

"Your friends in the Corps of Protectors can't save you now!" A pot-bellied, bespectacled figure appeared at the edge of the roof, and there was a collective gasp from the crowd. It was Lord Graviton, right there in front of us!

"Oh no!" squealed Jimmy, "He musta broke out of prison!" He was clearly enjoying every minute of this little scene.

But some of the faces of the older people there went ashen. Ol' Lord G wasn't just any regular old supervillain: he had teleportation *and* telekinesis, both at fourth level. Anybody who ever watched the news knew he was rated close to the top of the government's list of Threats to Society. Last time I'd checked, he was just a little bit behind the Carnage Squad, and a few places ahead of the entire Middle East. More importantly from our current point of view, though, was the fact that he had a rep for being just a wee bit careless during these sorts of public brawls when it came to following the "no civilians" rule.

"You maniac!" bellowed Missile Man, shaking his massive fist—but also, to be honest, looking slightly ill-at-ease. "How dare you disturb the peace and threaten the safety of all these powerless citizens!"

A ragged round of applause broke out. I noticed a couple of people weren't clapping, though. One tall dude in a clingy muscle shirt looked like he maybe wasn't nuts about being referred to as "powerless". And there was a mournful old lady with a hearing aid who had probably only caught the general tone of angry male shouting.

Lord Graviton took a deep breath, looking as though he was about to treat us all to one of his famous Evil Monologues. But before he could get warmed up, Missile Man tagged him on the left shoulder with a pretty well-aimed eye-blast. The rest of the heat ray hit the roof beneath the villain, which immediately caught fire, then must have melted or something, because the chubby psychopath dropped through it like a rock to the floor of the checkout aisle. He gave out a hysterical shriek.

"Hooray!" Jimmy squealed. "*Finish* him, Missile Man!"

I was faintly surprised that my seven-year-old offspring could sound so bloodthirsty. "C'mon, J, we'd best get out of the way here before . . . "

But before we had time to move, Lord Graviton had stalked out of the supermarket doorway, kicking aside broken acoustic tile and smoking boxes of snack cakes as he approached. From up close he was even more repulsive than he usually looked on TV—his eyes bugged out of his oblong skull, his neck was covered in pimples, and two fat ankles poked out from the bottoms of his grey spandex leggings.

He sure did seem to be enjoying himself, though. "*Taste my wrath, Missile-moron!*" He made a vague gesture with his right hand. A row of maybe a dozen shopping carts reared up like a long metal snake from the middle of the lot, then surged up through the air toward the flying hero.

Missile Man made a rather graceless lurch to one side and managed to dodge the incoming carts. But before he could stabilize himself, Lord G had gotten a couple of Hyundais airborne, one of which made a sickening sound as it crunched against the hero's right shoulder. Our protector fell to the pavement and lay still for a few uncomfortable seconds.

"C'mon—you can take him, Missile Man!" shouted a bespectacled twenty-something in an Oakland Raiders T-shirt. Everyone else there stayed pretty silent.

"I'm fine, everyone, it was just a . . . *ooooooh!*"

We all held our breath as the caped champion got slowly up onto his feet then stumbled a few steps to the right. Lord Graviton gave a malicious cackle and elevated a couple more vehicles into the air between them. This did not look to me like it was going to end well.

But then, a lady in a purple business suit with long press-on nails pointed up toward the horizon. "Look, everyone!" she shrieked. "It's The Justice Beacon!"

And there it was, too, shining high up in the clouds at the end of a conical beam of mysterious light projected straight upward from a downtown skyscraper. A brilliant golden circle enclosing a cut-out image of the scales of justice.

"The Justice Squadron will be here any moment now!" squealed Ms. Purple.

It was still a couple of hours before sunset, and as I watched the great beam sweep through the air, I found myself wondering how the weird thing managed to be visible at all in broad daylight. Could something like that really be good for the ozone layer?

Just a few feet away from me, Lord Graviton muttered—I kid you not—"*Curses!*" He flailed his right arm around, and the two levitating cars spun wildly in the air above us.

It was just at that moment that I saw the chihuahua. The lop-eared, shoebox-sized critter started straight at me balefully through the side passenger window of one of the flying sedans. Then, when the car turned upside-down, I saw its poor scrambly little feet sliding all over the rear windshield.

"Hey!" I shouted at the crowd, pointing. "Whose dog is that?"

Totally silence. The owner must have either been embarrassed or too wrapped up in the drama of the battle to care about a defenseless pet. Sometimes the awfulness of other human beings just makes me want to hide in a hole.

Jimmy was gazing up at me now, eyes very wide. He's a bright kid, overall—maybe he had already figured out what was about to go down. As I dropped into a crouch, he shook his head violently. "Mommy," he whimpered, "don't do it! You can't . . . "

But I had already made up my mind. I sighed and shrugged, making a wavery attempt at a smile. Then I took a deep breath and launched myself toward the inverted Chevy.

Flying up to the car took less than a second, but using my magnetic touch to steady it in midair required some delicate adjustments. The poor dog was huddled on the backseat, wailing. I tapped on the glass to get its attention, then melted the window with a quick puff of microwaves from deep in my diaphragm so I could reach in and grab him by the scruff.

I already had the terrified little guy halfway liberated when I heard a booming voice from behind me.

"What do you suppose *you're* doing?"

I turned around slowly. I thought I recognized the voice, and sure enough, there was Mister Volcano, hovering a few feet behind me with his hands on his waist in the classic pose. Condor Girl and The Human Iceberg were swooping up behind him. The other members of the Justice Squadron were steadily approaching dots against the skyline.

I held up the chihuahua, which was licking at my inner wrist. "Had to save this little guy." I inwardly cursed my parents for their sentimental habit of taking in stray pups off the street. I had obviously inherited a fatal weakness.

"Please pass the creature to me," said Mr. V.

I sighed and placed the dog gently into his enormous, knuckly hands.

Down on the tarmac, Missile Man and Lord Graviton were standing shoulder to shoulder waiting for their peers to haul me out of the sky, their earlier disagreement apparently forgotten.

I drew in a deep lungful of the sweet, cool air from just below the clouds, then descended of my own volition. Police cruisers were already lining up along the street beside the parking lot. The crowd was mostly somber as I waited for the cops to pick me up.

But Missile Man stomped straight up toward me. He was still a little unsteady on his feet, but clearly in a huffy mood, wanting to compensate for his earlier embarrassment.

He jabbed an immaculately manicured finger against my sternum. "So tell me something, lady—when did *you* get your Heroism Permit? I sure didn't see you at the last Boosting Your Powers convention in Toledo! You really think there's nothing more to being one of us than just swooping around in the air and puffing out a few microwaves?"

From behind the blackened carcass of a Honda Civic, Lord Graviton nodded piously.

Up until that moment I had been willing to go quietly. But the sight of the two of them in their sweaty, virtually identical masks, suddenly all buddy-buddy with each other, was too much for me to take.

"I have no *idea* what it's like to belong to your little club!" I shook a finger at the preening hero. "How much did your rich daddy *pay* for your lousy permit—like, ten million dollars?" Condor Girl plopped onto the ground; I wheeled around to face her. "And everybody knows *you* only got onto the team because you're engaged to Doctor Petroleum! Yet you clowns all still pretend you're the *only ones* who have all these abilities! As if everybody didn't know that after that comet passed through the atmosphere . . ."

"Shut up! Shut *up!*" Missile Man was in full whiny teenager mode now. "Nobody's allowed to talk about the comet! Don't you know the law?"

Mr. Volcano thudded to the earth behind him, dropped the shivering dog onto a grassy knoll, then laid a hand on the younger hero's shoulder. "Shh, now, Gary," he said to his comrade. "This lady will pay her debt to society, never fear. And I'm sure she'll come to understand why we can't let just *anyone* use their powers." He glanced across at me and shook his head. "I mean, *really*, ma'am! Just think of the social chaos that would ensue!"

The other spectators in the parking lot all nodded as though this nonsense was some sort of timeless wisdom. For just a moment, it seemed like the guy in the muscle shirt looked faintly irritated on my behalf. But of course he didn't say anything. A couple of cops had gotten out of their cars and were walking purposefully toward me. I knew there was nothing left for me to do with so many people watching but hold out my wrists to be cuffed.

The last thing I saw from the back of the cruiser window was Jimmy cautiously holding hands with the woman in the purple suit. The dog had wobbled over toward him, and Jimmy leaned over to ruffle its ragged ears in a way that made me smile. I hoped that somebody there would get him to Child Protective Services, instead of just throwing him into the back of a van. But if something bad was going happen to him, I was at least pretty sure he would have the good sense to jump into the air and fly away.

GET ORGANISED

ROSS BAXTER

DYLAN ARRIVED at work an hour early, riding his bicycle right up to where his boss stood forlornly outside the small workshop.

"He's done it again," sighed Jenny, without even turning around to greet him. Instead, she continued to stare at the battered wreckage of the Wonder Car piled up in the small yard.

"I thought as much," answered the young mechanic sadly, dismounting and taking off his cycle helmet. "I caught the early news on BBC London. Seems like he had a dust up with the Count around the docks at Limehouse Basin. It's pandemonium down there, the Rotherhithe Tunnel is blocked, and it seems one of them even shot down a press helicopter by mistake."

Jenny shook her head, having a good idea exactly which of the so-called superheroes would have taken out the chopper. "I'll check how many Stinger missiles are left in the magazine."

"Seems like the mayor of London is majorly pissed off again," continued Dylan. "She said on the early news that the Count and Lord Flash have done more damage to London over the past few months than the Germans did over the whole of 1940."

Jenny continued to stare at the smoking remains of the Wonder Car laying outside the workshop. Every panel not missing appeared badly damaged, with either dents, bullet holes, or both. Coolant and oil pooled under the wrecked vehicle, and only one window remained intact. Only five of the six wheels looked to be present, the thick tires all shredded and ruined.

"This is going to need a total rebuild," she muttered.

"We won't be able to get the Wonder Quadbike fixed by the end of the shift either," said Dylan. "We're still waiting on parts for the gearbox."

"I know," frowned Jenny. "With the Wonder Copter still grounded, I'm not sure what transport we can get ready for tonight."

"The boat is still serviceable. Maybe he can patrol the river?"

Jenny made no reply, running her calloused hands through her short grey hair as she tried to think of the options they had.

"I know this is bad timing," ventured Dylan, "but am I still okay to take the holiday I booked tomorrow? For my sister's wedding?"

Jenny looked at him for the first time since he arrived, seeing the earnest look in his youthful face. "Sure. Of course."

"Thanks," said Dylan. "I'll work late again tonight, maybe I can get one of His Lordship's spare vehicles running again."

"He won't be happy using one of his father's mounts. The old man preferred old-school sleuthing and fists, not Lord Flash's showmanship and firepower."

"I miss him," mused Dylan, pocketing his cycle clips. "He always treated us with respect, and he never brought any of his vehicles back like this."

Jenny nodded silently, turning to walk sullenly back into the workshops. Not knowing where to start was something she had never experienced in her twenty years' service with Lord Flash's father, but ever since the son had taken over when his father retired six months previously, chaos was the new norm. Each day felt worse that the last, and she knew she was getting to the end of her tether. Despite her frequent pleas for more resources, Lord Flash never listened. Instead, he seemed to actually take pleasure from putting his staff under duress. He reveled in creating mayhem and destruction, justifying everything he did by being a superhero crime-buster, upholding law and order, dedicated to fighting crime wherever it could be found.

With her small team of four at the absolute limit of what they could do and an uncaring employer unwilling to be reasonable, she had to think outside of the box. Instead of picking up her tools as usual, she went into the small workshop office and closed the door firmly behind her.

LORD FLASH APPEARED at seven in the evening as usual. Instead of being busy at work preparing and arming the various vehicles and weaponry, Jenny and the four technicians sat drinking coffee on the odd assortment of battered chairs at the back of the workshops.

"Is the Wonder Car repaired?" demanded Lord Flash, his first words on arrival.

Jenny put her chipped mug down and stood. "It has a broken axle, and we've used all the supplier's stock of armored door panels."

Lord Flash gave a malicious grin, showing off his perfect teeth. "Well, you should have seen the damage I did to the Count's mob! I mangled two of his staff cars, and even shot down one of his helicopters!"

"It seems from the news that it was a *London News* press helicopter," said Jenny coldly.

"Well, serves them bloody right! The press hasn't been onside for months now, they seem to have forgotten that I'm the good guy and the Count is the bad guy. I never get the credit my father did," sneered Lord Flash.

"Well, your father never shot down a press helicopter, nor closed the Rotherhithe Tunnel. And since you destroyed Nelson's Column and blasted the head off one of the lions in Piccadilly Circus last month, people are starting to wonder if you really are the good guy," said Jenny.

Lord Flash looked at her in surprise. "How dare you! I've never heard such impertinence from staff. Let me remind you that crime has fallen in London since my father retired, and the streets of London are now a much safer place!"

"Not if you're a helicopter pilot or work the toll booths on the Rother-hithe Tunnel," retorted Jenny hotly.

Lord Flash's face turned crimson. "Your job is to run this workshop, not lecture me on how to fight crime! Now, when will the car be ready?"

"Not till next week at the earliest."

"What?" Lord Flash cried. "How can that be?"

"Every time you take it out, it requires substantial repairs. It's a one-off superhero car, spare parts are not readily available, and we've been working flat out for months," explained Jenny, repeating the message she had given him dozens of times over the past months.

"Spare parts were always available for my father!" he challenged.

"Your father rarely damaged it. He preferred stealth to show and calm to chaos."

"You just need to work harder and get organized!" hissed Lord Flash.

"It's impossible to work any harder, but we did get organized. So the answer is no," said Jenny flatly.

"What!" roared Lord Flash. "Have you lost your mind? I'll fire the lot of you!"

"You can't. Today we got organised. We formed a union. We have rights, and now, you have responsibilities."

"So, you cripple the capitol's crime fighter, letting the Count have free reign over the city. How do you think that will go down with the Lord Mayor?" Lord Flash scoffed.

"We've formed a union with the Count's workshop staff. They're having the same discussion with him right now. We've agreed that neither party will work over their contracted hours and will only release a vehicle if the other party's vehicle is also roadworthy. We contacted the Lord Mayor, and she gave her full backing to the union and signed the articles of agreement. She said it was the break London needed. From now on, you and the Count need to abide by the rules, or we all down tools."

Lord Flash looked at Jenny and her team in astonishment.

"So, because the Wonder Car is off the road for repairs, the Count is grounded until we get it back working. Maybe next week, maybe later."

"But, that's not fair!" stammered Lord Flash. "What's this damn union called?"

"S.H.I.E.L.D," smiled Jenny. "Super Hero Initiative for Employee and Londoner's Defence. You'd better get used to it."

MASTERPIECE

JESSICA GUERNSEY

THE HERO WON. The entire kingdom felt the moment of the Tyrant's downfall as a subtle shift that brought in fresher air, a lightening of burdens piled on over the decades of mistreatment. For Harun, it was a day with a different meaning. This day his son was born. This day his wife died. Cella's labor had been too hard and she had only a few heartbeats to hold her tiny son, gaze at him and Harun with a face lit by pure joy.

"Baylan," she'd said. "After your father."

His father. The greatest man Harun had ever known. Surely the new Baylan would be as great.

Harun smiled. But something was wrong with Cella's smile. Not as joyful or bright and fading fast. Then her lovely blue eyes closed forever. Harun's smile faded, possibly forever.

With the Hero's victory, Harun was nearly lifted to hero status himself. It was his forge and hammer that had crafted the Hero's Sword. Once the blade was finished, Crismon, the enigmatic wizard whose magic never faded no matter how the metal was reworked, enchanted the rune-carved sword Harun had crafted so that the blade would be stopped by nothing tainted with evil. The dark Tyrant's bespelled armor could not withstand the Hero's blows. Through their efforts, Crismon and Harun had handed the kingdom's salvation to the Hero.

Now, every orphaned farm boy who could come up with the coin wanted a sword from Harun. Not all were worthy of Crismon's attentions so remained as ordinary weapons, not the stuff of legends.

After the burial of his precious Cella, stoic Harun handed off the boy to be cared for by their neighbor, Old Marya, and returned to his forge. He could do nothing for the boy now that Cella was gone.

And the world would need more swords to sweep away the Tyrant's left-over army, now that he was defeated.

THE HAMMER SANG across the anvil, singing the song of strength as Harun belted the metal into shape. So intent was he on his work that he no longer smelled the smoke from the blazing forge beside him. And he didn't hear the tiny cries from the room beyond, where his small son lay. It wasn't until Old Marya all but yanked the hammer from his hands. He turned on the woman who measured less than a third of his bulk.

"Do not interrupt me, woman," Harun snarled.

But the heat seeped from his anger when he saw Marya's face, already worn and weathered, but now drained of color and wet with tears.

"Your son," she began but shook her head and hurried from the hot space and back toward the portion of the building that held the living quarters.

Harun hardly looked where he set the hammer down and followed.

The dark room was heavy with sick and sweat but Harun inhaled sharply when he saw the tiny form of his son, his only child, sprawled on a pallet closest to the fire. Already walking and getting underfoot, the boy had been healthy and round just days before. Now he was a sickly gray color, blue eyes sunken into dark circles, his soft blond hair slick with sweat and matted to his head.

"What happened?" Harun turned to Marya as she dabbed a cloth on the boy's brow.

Marya's gray eyes shot him a look with enough heat to light his forge. "It is the wasting sickness. You have been away too long. I told you I had a birth to attend and would be away. You were supposed to be here."

"I have work to do." Harun kept his distance, not knowing what he was meant to do. He was no good with tending children, especially sick ones.

"This is your son," she hissed, then quieted when the boy's tiny form flinched. "You should have been here to check on him."

Harun wanted to argue, saying that he had been in this room very recently and the boy had been sleeping soundly. But a quick glance at the window showed the setting sun in a much different place than it was before. How long had he been away?

"You must summon Crismon." Marya wasn't suggesting.

Harun wanted to argue but knew he could not refuse her. Striding to the window, he opened the small cage and removed the bird inside, a dainty green songbird. Not the usual messenger bird, but Crismon was not the usual visitor.

No sooner had the bird disappeared into the distance than a man walked through the front door, the bird perched on his shoulder. His long, thick green robes did nothing to disguise his slight build and barely stooped shoulders. Harun had been told that Crismon had once been very handsome, but the last century or so had taken its toll on the old wizard. Even his once-glorious beard verged on scraggly. Still, the man's dark eyes remained clear and his grin broadened as he saw Harun, though just as quickly slipped from his face as his gaze dropped to the small form now clasped to Marya's bosom.

Crismon's thin hand pressed against the child's forehead, chest, and abdomen. Before he stood and faced Harun. "I shall require your good bronze basin."

Harun held it in front of the wizard as Crismon began removing various bottles and pouches from the folds of his robes, adding a portion of each to the basin.

A breath of fire from the wizard's mouth sent the mixture bubbling.

"The illness has progressed too far," the wizard held the boy in his lap, supported by one arm while the other held the bowl. "An exchange must be made for his restored health, as much as I am able to restore." Crismon cocked one bushy eyebrow at the bladesmith.

Harun didn't quite understand, but that was frequently the way with these magical folk. The bladesmith simply nodded vigorously, then pushed the heavy, dark locks away from his eyes, before twisting at his thick beard.

Tipping the bowl, the wizard held the boy's jaw open as the potion poured down his throat. The boy jerked and spasmed but Crismon's grip was firm and the entire contents of the bowl soon disappeared.

In a motion that spoke of his exhaustion, the boy swallowed, then collapsed further into Crismon's arms. Harun wondered at how the boy had gotten so much smaller in just a matter of days. He didn't know many things about children, having never spent time around them. Surely they were supposed to grow and not dwindle?

Crismon passed the now sleeping boy to Marya. After returning the bird back in its cage, he nodded to Harun and the old woman, then swept through the door and vanished.

There weren't the usual whimpers and cries as when the boy normally went to sleep. The old woman cradled the boy and rocked him, humming under her breath.

Harun's chest tightened. That should be Cella, holding the boy. But Cella was gone and the boy remained.

Soon enough, Marya laid the boy out on his pallet and covered him with a fine blanket. She then placed a bowl of food in front of Harun, who ate it mechanically, his mind already turning over how he would make up for the lost time during the next day.

The next morning, the boy appeared much improved, sitting up as Marya brought him a slice of bread spread with crushed fruit. He ate well enough as his father watched.

His tiny mouth opened but only the barest squeak came out. The boy wrapped his hand around his throat and motioned to Marya.

"What is it, Baylan?" Marya was immediately by the boy's side. "Do you want a drink?"

The small blond head nodded vigorously and Marya was quick to comply, pressing a cup into the boy's hand. He swallowed noisily. Handing back the cup, he opened his mouth, only to squeak again. This time Marya looked to Harun, her eyes wide and hand pressed to her own mouth.

"The exchange," was all she managed before tears overflowed.

Harun set down his bread and bent over the boy. With his large hands, he stood the boy up, noting that his legs were not unsteady. The dark circles had vanished and only those large blue eyes so much like his mother's stared back at Harun as he inspected the boy.

All seemed in working order.

Except the boy wasn't able to speak.

Even a shouted command from Harun sent the boy into tears but no sound came forth.

The exchange had been made. His health for his voice.

Harun released the boy, patted Marya's shoulder and stomped from the house back to the familiar heated air of the forge. There was nothing more he could do for the boy. His time was better spent making the world a better place with his swords and armaments. The Hero's Sword was magnificent. But was it the best Harun could produce? He insisted to his doubting voices that he could do better.

HARUN HATED FESTIVAL DAYS, and not just in the fifteen years that Cella had been gone. She had loved these special days. For every one, she somehow managed to coax her husband to attend and buy her something pretty from the visiting merchants. Now, he'd rather spend the time grinding a sword to a fine edge or crafting a pommel for perfect balance. The festival crowds brought other problems. He didn't have time for all the awkward young men who huddled around the shop, hoping he'd let him purchase one of his swords.

The boy, now not much younger than these lads, was the one that ran the front end of the bladesmith's shop, handled new orders and haggled over pricing. New visitors were rather startled when Baylan pulled out his board with numbers and carefully drawn images, pointing to the necessary areas to convey his meaning. The boy even provided sketches of the desired blades with fine enough detail that no request was rejected for inaccuracy. Harun hadn't noticed when the boy had made the board but he did notice the fewer interruptions. Bladesmithing was a lot about timing and he couldn't simply let the metal cool while he handled the latest lordling's eldest son demanding a new blade.

There were to be plenty of lordlings of late. Since the Tyrant fell, all manner of men attempted to exert their claims on lands formerly held with an iron fist. Skirmishes arose here and there. Hence, the need for swords.

Perhaps most concerning were the reports of the Hero himself. Ten years after the fall of the Tyrant and the Hero still roamed the land, dispensing justice. Though lately, these reports were frequently whispered down at the inn and tavern instead of touted. No one wanted to believe them at first. But with so many stories of the Hero destroying homes, shops, and even entire villages that had offended him, his mighty sword easily shattering stone supports or solid wood beams, there had to be truth in their words.

The innkeeper for their own small hamlet had a married daughter in a town across the river. She had recently returned home to work for her father once more, after the Hero had set fire to her former town's only merchant store. All because the merchant had lacked a suitable stock of footwear for the Hero to choose from.

Harun shook his head, flecks of sweat flying where they may, sizzling when they landed too near the coals. It did him no favors to listen to the stories in town. He had his own work cut out for him. Just this last new moon, when Crismon had come to inspect his latest collection of swords, the wizard had only selected three to imbue with special abilities, detailing the runes to be struck into their grips and pommels. Three! That was less than half the moon before. And the powers he gave them seemed lacking, in Harun's opinion. What good was the ability to purify water with a sword? Perhaps purifying blood was the better option, with the wasting disease that infested the land, now that their ruling class had time only for squabbles and not seeing to the needs of their people.

Only three swords. Harun swung his hammer a touch too hard, requiring more strikes to even out the metal around the new dent. Surely the small number of acceptable swords was due to Harun's slackening efforts. Though he was at the forge from sunrise to sunset, there was always more work to do, with no assistance from the runt of a boy in the front of the shop. His arms were far too thin to wield a hammer. Even considerable training as he grew saw no improvement. The boy had little interest in swords, preferring his papers and sketches instead.

Perhaps the potion that restored his health took more than his voice. Perhaps it took his potential also.

The blade before him now shaped to his satisfaction, he once again plunged it into the glowing heart of the forge, pumping the bellows to stoke the fury of the red coals as well as his own anger at having to tend to such a menial task.

"What is the good of having a child if the child is more hindrance than help?" Harun muttered as he stabbed the unfinished blade in deeper. "An apprentice is what I need, not a shopkeeper."

Hardy young men were in short supply these days. And even fewer were the ones seeking to learn the art of the blade.

A movement from the shop front caught his eye. Was that a *skirt*? What was a woman doing in his shop? Had things gotten so bad that women were seeking swords? Would the next hero be a heroine? Harun very nearly chuffed a furrow keeping one eye on the doorway.

There it was again. Most certainly a skirt. And . . . a giggle?

Harun tucked his hammer into his broad waistband and strode toward the shop. Pushing through the door he saw the woman. Just a girl really.

And the boy. He smiled at her.

Harun focused back on the girl. Brown eyes. Curly brown hair. Freckles. In his younger days, Harun would have found the girl cute, in a childlike way. But he was not younger. And she was in his shop.

He cocked one eyebrow at the boy.

The boy at least had the good sense to look abashed, turning his eyes to the sword on the table before him, adjusting its position so it was perfectly even with the edge of the table.

Harun knew this blade. It was a short sword, on the lighter, flexible side, like many of the fancier swords the soldiers from the coastal kingdom preferred. The hilt was tight, good for close combat.

The bladesmith turned his gaze on the girl. She blushed and glanced at the boy but then met Harun's eyes with a steady look. Perhaps she was Heroine material after all.

"You are seeking a blade?" Harun brought himself up to his full height, considerably taller than the other two, massive arms crossed over his broad chest.

"Oh, no," the girl shook her head vigorously and, widening her eyes, hastily added "sir."

But Harun had seen her hands as she brushed a curl from her eyes. Calluses only seen on those experienced in swordplay. Why would she want to hide her skill?

Harum shrugged. No business of his if she didn't want him to know. He turned back to the forge, head already filled with ideas for swords designed for smaller hands, lighter weight, but no less worthy of the next hero. Or heroine. Perhaps one would become his masterpiece.

"BLADESMITH." The boy was barely old enough to leave his mother's skirts and yet he raised his too-long nose to sniff disapprovingly at the forge air. "Can you design a blade to match my bracers?"

Harun crossed his immense arms over his considerable chest and looked down through one narrowed eye before the boy lost some of his haughtiness and took a step back from the bladesmith.

Harun then held out one hand.

The boy unclasped the bracer from his forearm and placed it in the waiting palm, immediately dwarfing the metal piece.

Harun turned the piece over in his hands, noting the shape like scales along the outer edge, a fair imitation of the fabled dragons. Nary a weak spot to be seen. The heavy leather straps looked to be long enough so if the boy managed to live long enough to reach his full height, the bracer would still fit him. Decent work, Harun begrudgingly admitted.

"Where did you get this?" Harun didn't look at the boy but from the way his narrow feet had shifted, this lordling's son was sufficiently cowed.

"Larek of Tortown," came the hesitant reply.

Harun looked up at that. "Larek? He's making armor now?"

Larek had been Harun's chief competition. Until Harun had crafted the Hero's Sword. Larek hadn't been able to compare after that.

"Has been for ages. He's considered the very best." The undersized chin came up a little at that.

Harun harrumphed and continued to study the design. Perhaps the flow of the design could have been angled in a more pleasing way. And that scale there was just ever so slightly smaller than the one next to it. Surely a mistake.

Reaching for the top sheet in the stack of parchment Baylan kept for him, Harun also snatched up a wedge of charcoal and began a sketch of the hilt. The hilt and pommel were all that mattered to these young types. Even the appreciation of a perfectly balanced blade only came with experience and the way this lad wore his dagger belt too high and too tight spoke volumes on his inexperience.

After a few more moments of the boy's nervous shifting, Harun slid the sketch across the work surface. No words necessary.

His potential customer's eyes went wide and his jaw dropped a little. Harun covered his smirk at the reaction. He'd work the pommel into a dragon's head, keeping the weight light enough so it didn't over balance a narrow blade. The twin curving quillons over the hilt guard would carry on the dragon motif by ending in pointed tails, hints of scales mirroring the bracers.

"It's perfect," the lordling breathed, then as if realizing he had given away any sort of bargaining power, quickly added. "Or at least it would be. If you can make it."

Harun's eyebrow ticked up. He resisted tossing the boy out on his head.

"If Larek is the best at armor," Harun began carefully, slowly, "then who do they say is the best at blades?"'

The boy's gaze dropped. "You are, Sir Bladesmith Harun."

Harun snorted at the title but nodded. "This sword will take three moons to complete to my satisfaction." No mention whatsoever of the customer's satisfaction. "Go and see the shop boy about the payment."

The young lordling brightened somewhat at the prospect of not having to haggle with Harun. But the bladesmith chuckled at his retreating back. Baylan would ask for far more coin than Harun would have considered. The boy was good with numbers. Much like his mother.

The thought of Cella drove the smile from Harun's face. Baylan may wear her looks, but he was not her.

THE GIRL WAS in the shop again. Harun heard her laugh as he sanded wood for a fine grip. Setting the wood aside, he moved quietly to the front. He arrived in the doorway with enough time to see the girl move through the midpoint of a rather graceful river form, the same blade in her hand as if it were a part of her.

A knock on the wood counter and the girl spun toward the sound. Baylan's hand rested on the counter. His father loomed over his shoulder.

The girl had the presence of mind to not drop the blade. Instead she shifted her grip to grasp the guard and offered the blade, hilt first to Harun.

"I had heard that Tefnor had a daughter." Harun strode forward to stand beside the counter as he examined the sword in his hand. "But I didn't know that the greatest swordsman this side of the Canalaba River was also training her."

"I trained alongside my brothers," she said, that steady gaze never leaving Harun.

"And I made all of their swords." Harun set the blade on the counter.

They stood facing each other. She, in a warrior stance. He, merely waiting.

Her gaze flicked to the boy. Harun could see the motion of his hands. The girl's shoulders relaxed.

She bent at the waist in a bow. "Jensa Tefnor."

"Pleasure." Harun returned the bow. "Now. Have you set a payment for this blade?"

Jensa's eyes widened yet again and Harun began to think that was her only response.

"I wouldn't dare to assume . . . "

Harun raised a hand. "You are clearly worthy. Is the payment too much? We can make arrangements."

Jensa cleared her throat, looking again at the boy before answering. "While this is a very fine blade," she paused and looked to the boy again, "it is not meant for me."

Harun tilted his head to one side.

"While the balance is impressive, it is meant for someone with a longer arm. The grip is a touch wide for a hand like mine." Her eyes flicked to the boy and back to Harun. "And the quillons, while expertly made, are much too broad to be comfortable on a belt at my waist. I've considered learning the craft so that I could make a blade that was truly meant for those like me." She licked her lips slightly. "Bladesmith Harun. Sir."

Harun's teeth that had clenched at her first criticism, were grinding by the end. Unlike her, he didn't bother to look at the boy before turning, heading back into his forge. Clearly the boy had enough time on his hands to watch the swordplay of others so perhaps he could be doing a bit more work instead. The lordling's dragon sword was nearly complete, awaiting only the runes that would hold the wizard's power. Should Crismon deem it worthy of such.

"Boy," he called toward the shop.

The slight form immediately appeared, framed in the doorway, and Harun motioned him forward, feeling the heat from the girl's words still building in his gut.

Harun pressed too hard with the charcoal, he knew. The dark marks on the paper were not as clean as he would like but the boy would be able to read them sure enough, having imprinted runes many times before. He rough-sketched the hilt around the runes to show positioning. Snatching up the paper he shoved it at Baylan, nearly knocking the boy down with what was not a harsh move, so frail he was. So slight in the shoulders. Much better suited to work in a merchant's shop than a smithy.

Harun didn't say anything. Baylan could figure out his father's commands without verbal instruction. For the next long while, whenever Harun stopped hammering, he could hear the smaller tinking of the detail hammer and chisel in the shop front.

Some time later, as he thrust the red hot metal into the water tank, breathing in the metallic steam, Harun became aware of a presence behind him.

Baylan stood, sword in hand, silently waiting for Harun to notice him rather than interrupt the work.

Once the thirst of the sword had been quenched, Harun looked down the edge of the blade. Still straight. Of course.

He set the sword aside and reached for the sword Baylan had finished. No sooner had he brushed a thumb over the pommel than he knew something was wrong. The runes carefully imprinted into the surface were not the ones Harun had sketched.

"Boy," Harun bellowed.

Baylan flinched.

"What have you done?" Harun tempered the heat in his voice. He'd have to remake the hilt. Reforge the metal in order to erase the mistake.

Baylan didn't attempt to speak. He had given up on forcing words through his squeaks long ago. Instead he held a hand out, bearing the parchment Harun had given him.

Harun snatched the paper. "Get out of my forge," Harun's voice had gone cold. "You do not deserve to be here."

Baylan turned and strode away, though he didn't run, not like he had when he was smaller and had run from his father's anger.

Harun crumpled the paper and was about to feed it to his forge when he noticed the thinner marks of the runes. Definitely not his handiwork. Careful not to smudge the lines further, he smoothed the paper as best he could, noticing that the paper was finer than the stock he kept. And the lines were drawn with a sharpened tip, not a block of charcoal.

Most certainly the same sword, with the dragon head and scaled quillon. But the runes were . . . out of order and slightly different. He recognized their shape; most certainly Crismon's hand. But why weren't these runes familiar to Harun?

He'd ask the wizard himself. Striding into the living area, Harun reached for the green bird's cage.

When he arrived, Crismon's typical grin held firm in the face of Harun's withering glare.

"Harun, my friend," Crismon began.

Harun held up the paper, now considerably more smudged. "Explain."

"Ah, it's finished? Good. Let's see it." Crismon slipped around Harun into the forge before the large man could turn himself about. By the time he arrived, Crismon already held the sword, purple and white light flickered along its length.

"You waste your power." Harun yanked the sword from the wizard's hands. "I cannot sell this sword. Not now. I will have to start over."

Crismon only smiled and inclined his head toward Harun. "Apologies for the misunderstanding. I am certain that this metal requires these magics."

"Using farsight, wizard?" Harun kept the sneer from his face but not entirely from his voice. "This lordling is to be a great hero, then?"

Crismon's smile faltered just a touch but Harun noticed.

"Did you think this sword was meant for someone greater? Maybe someone for which there is an ancient prophecy left to fulfil? The near child who ordered this sword has no more honor than all the other would-be royals before him. And what of these runes? What do they mean?"

Crismon nodded quietly, almost to himself. "These are counter runes. Meant to thwart the magic of others."

Harum blinked. That . . . was a rather useful piece of magic. It just might be the only hope now that the Hero took up where the Tyrant had left them. The stories of the Hero and those that rode with him grew in destruction, with slaughtered livestock and burning crops adding to the list of misdeeds.

Crismon tossed the paper onto the coal, watching as it caught fire immediately and was soon ash. "Perhaps I was too hasty in ascribing these spells to this blade. It's clearly not ready."

Just as his forge had flared, Harun's anger came up. "Not ready? Just as the dozens of others were not ready? Or perhaps they are not good enough? Their grips a touch too large? Perhaps it is time for you to take your skills to Larek and bestow all manner of blessings on his armor."

Harun's voice shook the forge but Crismon didn't flinch, only inclined his head in that infuriating manner he had when he refused to answer Harun's questions. Or give him direction on what he needed to do to be worthy of crafting another Hero's Sword.

"So it will be Larek, will it?" Harun strode to the bellows and pumped until the forge glowed and sweat dripped from his face to evaporate in the heat. "I'll ease your journey, old man."

With the dragon sword aglow, Harun went to work with his hammer, breaking the blade, the pommel, the quillons, into pieces and thrusting them into the heat. The metals melted and fused. With Crismon still standing watch, Harun beat the lumps into flat pieces. The shape wasn't as sure or as fine as Larek's but soon enough, he had the forms of two bracers. He tossed them at the feet of the wizard.

"There's your armor, wizard." Harun breathed heavily from the ceaseless work and his throat burned.

Crismon did not smile. He only nodded and picked up the bracers, tiny sparks of purple and white met his touch. The wizard handed the bracers to the bladesmith. Then with nothing more, he turned and disappeared through the door.

Harun moved to the shop, gaze roving over the displays. Many fine blades. Expertly crafted. Flawless. Music made metal. And none of them were good enough. Over a dozen blades not worthy of the wizard's magic lined the walls of the shop. Only metal. No power to change a man's fortune. Surely no power to aid a kingdom.

Perhaps Harun's days as *the* Bladesmith were at an end.

Over the next few days, Harun would neglect the other work, instead choosing to smooth the bracers, fitting them to his own forearms with soft leather linings and sturdy straps. Larek may laugh if he saw them but to Harun, they were a reminder that the wizard betrayed him. The strange man only ever worked for himself, not for Harun, and not for the kingdom.

THE NOISES of the festival outside still managed to squeeze their way through the forge, despite Harun's efforts to drown them out by grinding a sword edge relentlessly. Festivals served only to remind him of Cella and annoy him with needy customers demanding new swords. The day could not end soon enough.

Baylan waited behind him. Harun knew, but still gave the raw metal a few more swings from the hammer before resting it on the banked coals. He turned halfway toward the boy, his eyebrow raised.

The boy, which Harun was not ready to admit was quickly turning into a man, held a piece of paper out to Harun.

On it, instead of the sword sketch that Harun anticipated, there was a finely-detailed sketch of Jensa, holding the blade as she so often did. He had written her name at the bottom, as if Harun would mistake the image for some other curly-haired girl with a sword.

Not sure what he was supposed to do with this, Harun looked up at the boy, the question in his eyes. The boy motioned for him to turn the paper over.

Harun did so and revealed the words "Jensa is looking for an apprentice-ship and you need an apprentice."

The boy did not have the strength to bury a fist in Harun's gut but those words had the same effect.

"An apprentice?" Harun growled.

The boy handed over another paper, already prepared. "You work so hard. An apprentice will help. She is smart. She is strong."

Harun crumpled the papers in his fist. When one was a highly skilled craftsman, the first choice in apprentice was almost always the one that shared a roof with them. A child. A close relative. Just as Harun had helped in his father's forge. But Harun's child could not wield a hammer, got too winded even pumping the bellows. And now the same nearly worthless offspring was telling him how to run his shop. *His* shop, which had been his father's before him.

An apprentice. And a girl. Harun couldn't decide which was worse.

Harun strode forward, the boy backing up until they were in the front of the shop.

"Get out." Harun didn't shout but his voice was full of the fire of his forge. "You don't belong here. And neither does she."

As the boy's form disappeared down the street. Harun took a step back into his shop. His shop. It was his. And yet, it wasn't. There was the boy's board on the counter. A glance at the walls showed the available swords but how had they been arranged? Not by length. Not by weight. And where were the coins collected from sales? Harun looked behind the counter, shoving polishing rags, stacks of sketches, and broken charcoal sticks to the floor. There had to be coins here somewhere.

Running his hand along one of the shelves, he felt an edge in the board. His father had crafted this counter all those years ago. And a finely made counter should not have had an edge there. Harun pushed on the board, attempting to flatten it down. But when he released it, the board sprang up, revealing stacks of coins in a hidden compartment.

Harun stared at those coins for a long moment. The compartment was not there when it was Harun as a boy behind the counter. When had the boy done this? Had he commissioned the work? No. Harun had seen no other craftsmen working in his shop. Standing, Harun's attention was called to the boy's board. It had been repainted. Probably recently, in preparation for the crowds arriving for the festival. Numbers carefully written alongside images of the correct amount of coins, for those that did not know their numbers. The cycle of moons, so a time could be conveyed. Even parts of the sword so the customer could have concerns addressed. It was rather . . . clever.

That dark feeling that filled Harun's chest every time Crismon passed over a sword came again but this time, it was for something much greater. The shame of incomplete swords was nothing compared to the shame of never knowing his son. Baylan. Named for Harun's own father, a great and gentle man who would never have treated the boy as Harun had treated him.

Tears clouded his eyes and Harun let them come, falling on the perfectly polished counter and the fine fabric there for displaying swords. In his shame, it was as if the specter of his father stood beside him, shoulders and stature much smaller than Harun but no less commanding.

"I will do better, Father," Harun said with thick words. "I will treat him as he deserves."

Harun continued to promise his father, the humble blacksmith who allowed his son to take his own path and make swords instead of horse-shoes. Harun would do the same for Baylan. The boy had a talent for draw-ing. Perhaps he'd like to learn more under a master? Harun knew of one. He'd arrange an apprenticeship immediately.

Satisfied, the presence of the bladesmith's father dissipated.

His promises and tears silenced, Harun noticed a chorus of shouts coming from the streets. Not in the pleasant tones one would expect of a festival.

Jensa plunged through the open shop door.

"Sir Bladesmith!" she called breathlessly. "You must come! It's Baylan."

She hesitated one more moment, then snatched the blade she had so frequently admired from its place and rushed back out the door.

Harun paused long enough to claim a sword from the racks and followed her streaming hair through the gathering crowd. No music met his ears. The scent of sweetcakes and roasted meat should have coaxed smiles from the festival-goers but all faces he saw looked grim.

Most of the people cleared the way for Harun, especially as he held a sword in hand. Some called to him, hurrying him forward. Nearing a run, Harun, broke into an opening in the masses, the people kept back by a half dozen armored young men. In the center, with his own sword in hand, stood the Hero.

Even without the sword, Harun would have known who he was. Tall, broad shoulders, strong chin. Clearly the very image of legends. Lit by the sun at his back, his long, dark hair caught a breeze and waved gently. The Hero wore only a few pieces of armor over his fine, tightly-fitting leather clothes. Why would he need more protection? He was the Hero, after all.

But it was the eyes—hard black and flashing with anger—that ruined the image.

Kneeling at the Hero's feet was Baylan.

Harun focused on what the Hero shouted at the crowd. "—caught a thief! How dare one of you *peasants* take something from *me*? When I have given you so much!"

Baylan? A thief? Never. Impossible.

Jensa, so tiny in front of Harun, turned to him. "It's not true," she spat. "The Hero dropped a riding glove and Baylan picked it up to give it back. But the Hero demanded an explanation and . . . well . . . besides, who steals one riding glove? It's absurd!"

Jensa had gotten louder as she spoke.

The Hero faced her, those cold eyes narrowing. "Are you calling *me* a liar?"

Jensa squared her shoulders and stepped forward. Harun stepped with her.

"Hero, you do not know our town. If you did, you would know the boy before you is Baylan. He has no voice. He cannot answer your accusations with no voice. He did not steal the glove. He merely attempted to return it to you."

The Hero threw back his head and laughed. The armored men joined in. The crowd shifted uneasily beyond them.

"You would challenge me? Your Hero? What I *say* is the law. What I *do* is the law. I say thieves shall lose a hand. And this boy is a thief."

Gasps and mutters rolled through the crowd and they surged forward a few steps. The armored men shifted with them, no longer able to keep them back. These were the people that had cared for Baylan while Harun worked the forge. They knew the boy's heart better than his own father. They knew the Hero lied.

Jensa's stance moved into a ready position. Before she could bring her blade up, Harun's hand covered her shoulder. Gently, he pushed her behind him.

Harun bowed slightly to the Hero, who did not return the motion.

"As the boy . . . as Baylan's father, I will stand in for any punishment you require." Harun stood tall, dropping the sword he held into the dirt in front of him.

The Hero noticed the change in the people, his glower sliding along them before coming back to Harun.

"And who," the Hero flexed the sword blade in front of him, the light sparkling on the ruby Harun had so carefully laid in the pommel, "are you?"

"I am Harun."

The Hero didn't flinch but his face changed, becoming slightly less frosty. "The Bladesmith." It wasn't a question.

Harun copied Crismon's frustrating head tilt in response. By the further narrowing of the Hero's eyes, the motion had the same effect.

The Hero's chin dipped and his eyes bored into Harun's. "Fine. I'll take your hand instead of the boy's." He motioned to his men.

It took four of them to get Harun into position. Harun did not resist. He simply did not let them hurry him. With one hooligan hanging off each arm, Harun knelt before the Hero. A block of wood was placed in front of him.

One look from Harun and the goon attempting to heft his arm onto the block stopped, raised his hands, and backed away. Harun lifted his left hand and placed it on the block himself, the solid thunk of the bracer sounding loud in the near-silence around them.

Now so close, the Hero's Sword was lovely to behold. Clearly the work of a master. Harun's heart swelled with pride at again watching the light flicker down its perfectly straight length. The spiraling knuckle guard and hilt didn't shine as it had when Harun had polished it. Perhaps the Hero didn't spend the time to do so. Such a pity. It surely was a masterpiece.

Harun's gaze went to Baylan, who stood beside Jensa, a hand on her sword arm to keep her weapon down. Smart boy. So much smarter than Harun ever gave him credit for. What else had he missed about his son? The clenching of his heart told him that he had missed too much. He had missed what truly was his masterpiece.

Before his eyes could blur with tears that the Hero would no doubt misread, he offered Baylan a short nod, waited for him to return it, then turned back to the sword held before him. He'd keep his gaze locked on that.

Leaning down, the Hero also looked toward Baylan. "Your son has fine taste in women. Perhaps I shall have to try her." His face, which was most likely considered handsome by most, twisted into an ugly sneer.

Harun thought of the Hero and little Jensa, with her graceful river forms and her three older, very skilled brothers. And Harun laughed.

The Hero looked at him darkly. He'd probably wanted to make a speech, to show how he was the last word or the law or whatever such thing he felt inclined to claim. He would have wanted the crowd brought to heel, cowed by this show of dispensing of his brand of justice. But this crowd was moving, agitated. Harun saw several hands clutching farm tools in a manner that did not anticipate gardening. Even Old Marya clutched the handle of a frying pan. The Hero must have seen it, too. Because there was no speech.

Soundlessly, the Hero's Sword swept up and then down, with power enough to slice through the bone of a man's hand even without the enchantments placed on the blade.

Harun watched the blade, glinting in the sun, as it came down in the middle of his left bracer.

The blade shattered. As if Harun had crafted it in glass instead of the finest steel.

Holding only the broken hilt, the Hero stared for several poundings of Harun's heart. When the Hero looked up, it was to see his men pulling back, the crowd surging forward. He tossed the hilt into the dirt beside Harun. And with his men gathered around, they mounted their horses and raced from the town, the crowd roaring after them.

Harun, still kneeling, looked between the broken blade and the bracer, with nary a dent.

Plush green robes brushed his right arm and Harun looked up to Crismon, beard messy with crumbs as the wizard munched a sweetcake.

"Did I miss it?" The wizard said. "Oh, fiddlestrings. I really wanted to see his face when the sword shattered!" Crismon giggled then took a bite of cake.

"You . . . knew?" was all Harun could manage.

"Of course I knew!" The wizard's eyes narrowed slightly before crinkling at the edges. "You can't go giving powerfully enchanted swords to just any farm boy without good parents and expect there to be harmony ever after. The Hero would have to be brought back down to ordinary. Otherwise, you and I would forever be making greater and greater swords to take them on. You might be up for the challenge, clever Harun, but I'm getting old, you know."

Now that the thugs were run out of town, the crowd went back to a cheerful, festival air. Music played. Cakes were eaten. And Baylan put an arm around Jensa.

HARUN STOOD BEHIND BAYLAN, the boy's blond head bent over his work as his father tried to wait quietly. These last twelve moons, Baylan had been apprenticed to Master Bosal, an artisan of great renown, but still managed to find the time to run the front of Harun's shop with Jensa's help.

Baylan looked up, a grin on his face that made him look so much like sweet Cella that Harun could do nothing but return the grin.

Carefully, Baylan turned the board to face Harun, and with a flourish of his hand announced that the painting was finished.

The painting depicted the moment the Hero's Sword shattered, with the Hero depicted in dark colors while kneeling Harun was crowned in light. And it was magnificent! Though that could be the father in him, tainting his opinion.

Harun laughed and praised Baylan's work, while the blond smiled wider. Jensa came over from the counter where she'd been polishing a blade.

"Oh, Baylan!" she murmured, placing a hand on his shoulder. "It's perfect!"

Harun raised an eyebrow. "Perfect, eh? I wasn't sure your opinion went so high?"

Jensa didn't even blush, just laughed. "Well, Sir Bladesmith, perhaps it is time you took on an apprentice to pass on your skills. We wouldn't want such oversized quillons to fade into stories."

Harun grinned, clapped the girl on her shoulder. "I was thinking much the same thing. When would you like to begin, Jensa?"

THREE LITTLE PORCINIANS

HENRY HERZ

HENWYN'S REAR HOOVES clicked briskly on the narrow cobblestone streets of Castellum.

After a year of courtship, tonight's the big night, he thought, his whiskery chin held high and forelimbs clasped behind his back. He smiled, sneaking a peek at Gertrude striding beside him. The petite Porcinian wore a lavender-colored dress that flattered her figure. A matching feathered hat accentuated her pale snout fuzz and delicate facial features. *I hope she doesn't notice my worn jacket elbows or my faded waistcoat,* he thought, *though this is my best suit.*

They arrived at the tavern and were promptly seated at a prime window table for two, Henwyn having made the proper arrangements the day prior. He helped Gertrude take her seat. By tightening his belt this past month, he had saved enough to splurge on a modest bottle of red wine.

After polite but superficial dinner conversation, Henwyn took Gertrude's hand. "My dear Gertrude. You would make me the happiest Porcinian in Castellum if you would do me the honor of becoming my wife."

Gertrude sat up straighter and raised her eyebrows.

Is she waiting for something else?

"My dear Henwyn. You are kind, clever, hardworking, and a handsome fellow. But . . . "

Damn. Henwyn's stomach knotted.

Gertrude pursed her lips. " . . . a lady must have a husband who can provide for her and their litters. Where is the proposal ring?" She glanced at Henwyn's plaid waistcoat. "And I did not fail to note the sorry state of your wardrobe." Gertrude pushed away her dessert plate, which showed little evidence that it once held truffle cake. "I do have feelings for you. Please don't consider this a refusal, but rather an exhortation to better your station before asking again."

Suffice it to say that the walk home was devoid of conversation, and that Henwyn's roiling emotions kept his night devoid of sleep.

HENWYN DUTIFULLY REPORTED bleary-eyed for work at the weapon factory the following day. Unlike their enemies, the Porcinians had not yet mastered gunpowder. Only the Porcinian's vastly superior numbers kept them at rough parity with the militaristic and better-armed Lupinians.

Henwyn's innovative mind and clever hands had yielded several enhancements to weapon designs over the last year. But today, his normally nimble fingers lacked their customary skill. *If I am to win Gertrude's hand, how will I earn enough for a proposal ring?* The cough of a newly assembled steam engine from a reverse-engineered steamcar, captured during a Lupinian raid last autumn, loudly interrupted Henwyn's reverie.

Fortune further favored the Porcinians, as the only known source of firestone was their desert mine at Lapicidina. Firestone generated steam far more efficiently than burning coal, resulting in more powerful engines.

The Porcinians fortified their firestone mine as sturdily as they did their town at Castellum. A host of skilled stonemasons and laborers built mighty walls impregnable to Lupinian attack. Castellum depended upon Lapicidina for its firestone. But the miners depended on Castellum to provide ongoing supplies of food and water.

Eschewing fruitless attacks against high-walled strongholds, Lupinian corsairs focused their predations on convoys crossing the harsh desert separating Castellum and Lapicidina. The Lupinians had pirated the three most recent convoys, depleting Castellum's firestone stocks to perilously low levels.

"Attention," called the factory foreman. "Everyone stop working for a moment."

Workers put down their tools, wiped their sweaty brows, and gathered 'round in the now eerily silent factory.

The squat foreman frowned and put his hands on his hips. "As you know, our last convoy crew got chewed up pretty badly. We need more volunteers to man a cargo steamtruck and its escort. Given our dwindling supply of firestone, the mayor is offering a hazard pay bonus of ten silvers for participants in a successful round-trip convoy. That's ten to get a load of food to Lapicidina *and* a load of firestone back. Anyone interested, come see me now."

A few brave Porcinians followed the foreman as he hobbled back to his office. Henwyn stood stone-still. *I'm a pretty handy shot with a bow, but I'm no soldier. Still, ten silvers would buy Gertrude a lovely ring . . .*

Henwyn returned to his cluttered workbench. By the end of the day, he'd fashioned only a single longbow. But he had reached a decision.

AFTER TWO DAYS of hasty training for the new recruits, the massive front gates of Castellum lumbered open to disgorge an enormous cargo-carrying steamtruck escorted by half a dozen steamcycles with lance-armed drivers and an archer in each sidecar. Hauling a heavy load of food crates and water jugs, the steamtruck had a driver and navigator in the cab. Two weapon platforms menaced from atop the truck's cargo bay. Two soldiers on the fore platform serviced a steam-powered harpoon launcher. Two soldiers on the aft platform crewed a flamethrower. Armor plating protected the engine compartment, cab, and tires. Long steel spikes bristled from the front and side bumpers. The truck towed a spare steamcycle.

The sour smell of burning firestone filled Henwyn's nostrils. Goggles kept the wind out of his eyes, but the whine of steamcycles made it hard to hear his driver. *What have I gotten myself into?*

Once the convoy cleared the fortress gates, the steamcycles assumed a standard escort formation—a wedge of three in front of the steamtruck, one on either flank, and one to the rear. They scouted ahead to provide early warning of a Lupinian attack and use their superb mobility and high rate-of-fire to harass raiders attempting to engage the steamtruck.

After two hours of high speed eastward transit, the convoy passed the low stone wall marking the edge of cultivated land. The fresh breezes, paved road, and lush irrigated farmland gave way to scorched air and trackless sandy desolation. They wound over dusty, bumpy roads for another hour.

Curse this miserable combination of noise, vibration, and heat.

Although he didn't think it was possible, Henwyn's discomfort increased further when the archer in another steamcycle raised a red signal flag. *Lupinian corsairs!* The message repeated, followed by the driver pointing his lance. *A single raider to the south-southeast.*

His mouth suddenly dry, Henwyn double-checked his safety harness and drew an arrow as his driver swerved to the right. The four steamcycles closest to the enemy would engage, while the other two remained in reserve on either side of the steamtruck.

A tracked Lupinian land frigate crested a distant dune, a black skull painted near the bow beneath the name *Fangstorm.* Under the skull blazed red-painted crossbones, signifying that the frigate had one kill to its credit.

Henwyn couldn't feel his hooves.

As the four steamcycles neared the frigate, the crack of musket fire reached Henwyn's ears. His experienced driver jinked the steamcycle to make it a more difficult target for the low rate-of-fire muskets. Paralyzed with fear, Henwyn took no shots as they swept along the frigate's port side. He noted ten portholes from which the Lupinian corsairs fired.

"What're you waiting for?" screamed his driver. "Shoot next time."

"Aye," was all the response Henwyn could muster. *I just have to manage to shoot through a small porthole from a moving mount against a moving target.* He braced himself for their next pass, managing to get off three shots, though he couldn't tell if any found their mark.

The steamcycles swarmed the frigate like bees attacking a marauding bear. But their stings were equally ineffective. The frigate drew inexorably closer to the steamtruck.

With a clang, a harpoon fired from the steamtruck buried itself in the bow armor of the frigate. Exhibiting astonishing bravery, the Lupinian captain exposed herself to bow fire to assess the damage. The wind whipped her loose purple vest and black fur. She remained visible long enough to scan the steamcycles, making eye contact with Henwyn before ducking behind cover.

Lupinian muskets aimed at the truck's front right tire. Only a small section of tire was exposed below armor, but eventually the raiders punctured it.

Henwyn fired arrow after arrow, but all bounced off the frigate's armor.

"It's just a matter of time now," screamed Henwyn's driver. "We've got to save the crew."

The other steamcycle drivers drew the same conclusion. They rallied to the now-stationary truck on the side opposite the frigate to take on surviving crew. Last to abandon their vehicle, the driver and navigator scrambled into the steamcycle towed behind the truck, cut the rope, and raced back to Castellum.

I have nothing to show for risking my hide.

CASTELLUM'S CAPTAIN of the guard met the convoy survivors in the main courtyard to hear their report. "Blast you, you swine. Lapicidina needed that food!" the captain cursed unfairly.

After being dismissed, Henwyn limped home, still sore from the day of riding. *Should I tell Gertrude how the day went? Surely, she'd be impressed by my actions. But to what end? I'm no closer to those ten silvers.* He soaked in a long hot bath, then enjoyed a large, if plain, dinner of seasoned roasted vegetables and whole grain sourdough bread. His old mattress never felt more comfortable. He fell into a sound sleep as soon as his head hit the straw-filled pillow.

HENWYN RETURNED to work the following morning. He wasn't at his workbench for long before the foreman announced another convoy was to be organized. *Well, I need the silver as much as I did before.* Again he signed up.

Henwyn shuffled his hooves. "Excuse me sir, but I noticed something during yesterday's convoy. If we could increase the speed of the steamtruck, that might mean the difference between being intercepted and getting through."

The foreman raised his bushy eyebrows. "Go on."

"Well, sir. Could we reduce the weight of the truck? For example, a smaller payload? Some supplies are better than no supplies. And the flamethrower wasn't particularly effective because the corsairs' muskets outrange it. We could save weight by removing one platform and its crew."

The foreman nodded. "Those are clever ideas, but they'll take some doing. Let me see what I can do. Thank you, Henwyn."

AFTER TWO HOURS of the foreman conversing with the city guard captain, two days of steamtruck modifications began.

During that time, Henwyn sought out Gertrude. "I hope to become a good provider by serving with the convoy. There's generous hazard pay."

Her eyes widened.

"In fact, I was in the last convoy. But we couldn't stop the Lupinians from seizing the cargo. So I didn't earn the bonus."

Gertrude's mouth formed a thin line.

Henwyn pushed down his own dread. "I must try again with the next convoy. It leaves tomorrow."

Gertrude exhaled slowly. "Well, I hate to be mercenary, but if this second attempt doesn't turn out better, I may have to explore other options. I'm not getting any younger."

Does she not appreciate that I'm risking my life? Henwyn turned so she wouldn't see his face flush and strode off.

"Do be careful," she called after him.

THE CONVOY ASSEMBLED in the Castellum courtyard. Workers rushed to finish loading the modified steamtruck to three-quarters capacity.

The Porcinians set out. The steamtruck lumbered at its normal pace, keeping its newly enhanced speed as a surprise for any corsairs. They took a different turn than the previous convoy.

"We *are* going to Lapicidina, right?" Henwyn asked.

His steamcycle driver nodded. "Of course. We're just following a different route to avoid being predictable."

Henwyn's snout wrinkled. *When the destination is known, there is only so much subterfuge that can be employed.*

THREE LITTLE PORCINIANS

THE CONVOY PROCEEDED WITHOUT INCIDENT, Henwyn periodically wiping dust from his goggles. *We're nearly at Lapicidina.* A grin at the prospect of silvers in his pocket vanished when the lead steamcycle raised a red signal flag. Twice. *Two raiders to the north. Damn.*

The steamtruck accelerated to full speed as four escorts veered left to intercept the Lupinians. Henwyn's steamcycle and another stayed with the truck. He noted that their attackers included the same frigate as before, the *Fangstorm,* plus a smaller, faster steamcar.

The firm terrain, packed earth rather than sand, gave additional mobility to the wheeled steamcycles compared to the tracked frigate. The valiant Porcinians swooped and harried the *Fangstorm,* forcing it to alter its intercept course with the steamtruck.

Henwyn gazed east to the now-visible guard towers of Lapicidina. *Almost there. Once we get close, the harpoon launchers atop the fortress walls will keep the corsairs at bay.* He jerked his head left at an orange flash of light. *Damn.*

The Lupinian steamcar had a roof-mounted flamethrower—a devastating weapon against steamcycles. While the four escorts managed to distract the larger Lupinian vehicle, they dared not approach the steamcar, which used gouts of flame to keep its path clear of Porcinians.

"We must stop that steamcar!" Henwyn shouted to his driver.

His driver nodded and signaled the other escort guarding the truck. Both steamcycles raced toward the Lupinian.

Henwyn took shots from beyond the range of the enemy flamethrower. But his arrows bounced harmlessly off armor.

His driver weaved to the left of the steamcar while the other steamcycle split right, using maximum speed to reduce the chance of being turned into pork roast.

Henwyn shouted, "I have an idea. Get directly behind it where there's no armor plating."

He took aim as his driver lined up their vehicle behind the steamcar.

The other steamcycle crew screamed when flames engulfed their steamcycle. *Damn.* As the roof gunner roared and raised a clawed fist in victory, Henwyn loosed an arrow. The shaft pierced the unprotected gunner between his furry shoulder blades. Before the Lupinian driver could react, Henwyn put an arrow into the back of his head. The steamcar continued forward, the slain driver's paw still on the accelerator pedal.

Henwyn stowed his bow in the sidecar. "Get closer."

"Whatever you're going to do, be quick about it," replied the driver. "The frigate is headed our way."

Henwyn cursed and stood up in the sidecar. When they reached the steamcar's rear bumper, he leaped onto its rear deck. Nearly tumbling off, Henwyn regained his balance and glanced up. *The frigate is close.* Again, the *Fangstorm*'s captain caught his eyes. She dipped her whiskered chin in acknowledgement of his feat.

Henwyn clambered inside the steamcar. He shoved aside the dead Lupinian and took the blood-spattered steering wheel. His driver signaled the other steamcycles to disengage. Three loosed a final volley of arrows and peeled away from the frigate. The fourth remained motionless, its crew slumped over their vehicle.

Henwyn's steamcycle pulled alongside him to ensure the other escorts and the Porcinians on the fortress walls would not target the captured steamcar. He breathed a sigh of relief when the *Fangstorm* halted just outside the range of the fortress harpoon launchers. The escorts followed the steamtruck through the gates of Lapicidina to a chorus of cheers. Henwyn found himself whooping.

LAPICIDINA HAD RUN low on provisions, making even the partial cargo delivery welcome beyond measure. Henwyn received five silver pieces as a bonus for the capture of the steamcar. Accounts of his exploits, often magnified through retelling, won him guest of honor status at a celebratory banquet at which the incoming convoy crew mingled with the outgoing crew members.

One in particular caught Henwyn's eye—a female harpoon gunner with warm brown eyes and adorably shaped ears. As drink flowed and tongues wagged, he learned from others that the gunner, Ophelia, was a courageous veteran of five convoys. He introduced himself and soon learned that her beauty and heart were complimented by an irreverent sense of humor.

The following morning, Henwyn found himself at breakfast describing to Ophelia and others the enhancements he had suggested for Castellum's steamtruck. Ophelia's eyes glowed as she listened to his explanations, and Henwyn's heart warmed at her reaction.

The mine foreman asked Henwyn for recommendations for the fire-stone convoy that would soon leave for Castellum. The two explored ideas until lunchtime, after which the foreman raced off to make the arrangements.

As was customary, the Castellum survivors would recuperate at Lapicidina for a week. But when one of the Lapicidina crew suffered a broken arm working the mine, Henwyn volunteered to take his place.

The sooner I return to Castellum, the sooner I earn my ten silver and move on with my life, he thought. The Lapicidinans welcomed him, none more than Ophelia.

Two Porcinians took a day to learn how to operate the captured flamethrower steamcar. Henwyn received training as the replacement harpoon loader, the lessons made all the more interesting because Ophelia provided the instruction.

THE FIRESTONE CONVOY ASSEMBLED. The Lapicidinan steamtruck boasted full armor plating and three steam-powered harpoon launchers. The captured steamcar and two steamcycles would comprise the escort.

Friends and family offered farewell wishes. Without understanding what moved him to do so, Henwyn gave Ophelia one of the two smooth-bore pistols he'd despoiled from the dead steamcar crew.

"Be careful."

Ophelia surprised him with a hug. "Thanks. You, too."

With the steamcar at the head of their formation, the convoy departed Lapicidina amid cheers. It took the southernmost of the westerly routes toward Castellum.

Hours passed, though Henwyn's fears did not ease with time. The fierce sun beat down on him as he crewed the stern harpoon launcher. He had no seat, but at least standing atop the truck involved less sand in the face than sitting in a steamcycle sidecar.

AT THE HALFWAY point of their journey, Henwyn snuck a glance at the center harpoon launcher.

Ophelia offered him a subtle smile and dip of her chinny chin chin before dutifully returning her attention to the horizon.

As Henwyn contemplated the pulse quickening induced by Ophelia, a red flag from the steamcycle to port flashed a warning. *THREE corsair vehicles to the south. Damn.*

The harpoon launchers pivoted left. The steamcar and two steamcycles swung southward, plumes of sand in their wake. With three attackers, no vehicles could be kept in reserve.

Henwyn's eyes bulged. "That's the same frigate I fought before," he told his gunner. "But what are those other two vehicles?"

The gunner peered through his binoculars. "One's a rammer and one's a boarder." In response to Henwyn's blank stare, he continued. "The one with the wedge-shaped front is the rammer. They'll try to get in front of the truck for a head-on collision that will flip us onto our side. Taking them out will be the fore gunner's job. The boarder vehicle—the one with the open top—will try to pull alongside us. It carries a squad of Lupinian marines who will climb aboard. Ophelia and I have to prevent them from getting that close. We are no match for them in claw-to-hoof combat. Now, look smart."

Henwyn glanced down at the four metal quivers bolted to the platform, each holding ten harpoons. *Will that be enough?*

The Porcinian steamcar engaged the *Fangstorm*, setting the port forequarter of the frigate afire. The flames would not damage the metal armor but did suppress musket fire from that section of the vehicle.

One steamcycle harried the Lupinian rammer as it raced to intercept the steamtruck. The unarmed rammer could not directly threaten the steamcycle crew, but its cabin armor had no difficulty deflecting Porcinian arrows. The archer switched her aim to the tiny sliver of front tire exposed below the armor, but the rammer swerved periodically to make that a near-impossible shot.

In an act of breathtaking courage, the second steamcycle, grossly overmatched in terms of armor and firepower, drove resolutely straight at the boarder vehicle.

A lump formed in Henwyn's throat at the crew's valor. *They mean to disable it with a collision, killing themselves in the process!*

The archer took a shot, but the distance was too great. Not so for muskets. Ten marines stood up in the bed of the boarder and returned fire, hitting the archer. The driver leaned lower in his seat and accelerated toward the boarder. The marines reloaded and loosed another volley, knocking the driver off the steamcycle.

"Damn. Why aren't you firing at them?" demanded Henwyn.

"They're still too distant from us. Nor did I want to risk hitting our folk. Don't worry, they'll oblige us soon enough."

Whomp!

Henwyn spun his head as the fore launcher shot at the rammer. The first harpoon missed high. The steamcycle driver, wanting to give the harpoon gunner a clearer shot and observing that the boarder was now unopposed, turned sharply to intercept it.

Whomp!

The second harpoon flew true, punching through the rammer's side armor. The rammer rolled to a stop.

That shot must have killed the rammer driver! Henwyn and the other crew shouted with joy.

BOOM!

"By the gods, what was that?" cried Henwyn.

"A cannon."

"What? The *Fangstorm* had no cannon when we last met them."

"Apparently the Lupinians are just as capable of upgrading their vehicles as we are."

BOOM!

"Well, at least their aim is poor," observed Henwyn.

The gunner shook his head. "They're not shooting at us. They're aiming at the steamcar. See how our driver is staying so close to them. Clever. I don't think the cannon can depress low enough to hit them."

"Great news."

"Yes, for the steamcar . . . "

"Hells bells."

"Exactly. Now we become the target."

The cannon boomed in agreement with the gunner. A cannon shot whistled invisibly overhead.

Henwyn winced.

"There's nothing for it. Focus on the boarder," ordered the gunner. "We, too, will not be able to depress low enough to hit them once they get within a truck-length. We need to stop them before then."

The boarder advanced toward the port side of the steamtruck. When it drew within range, the harpoon launchers responded.

Whomp!

Whomp!

Whomp!

Two harpoons missed, but one punched through the left side of the cab's front armor.

"That probably killed their copilot," said the gunner. "Reload!" he yelled as Henwyn stood momentarily paralyzed.

The boarder did not slow, even as the second Porcinian steamcycle peppered it with arrows.

BOOM! WHAM!

The fore harpoon platform disintegrated into shards of metal and flesh. Blood painted the steamtruck roof.

Gods save us!

Whomp!

Whomp!

One harpoon missed again, but the other hit the bed of the boarder, killing or wounding some marines.

A gush of flame drew Henwyn's eye. The steamcar braved point-blank enemy musket fire to douse the *Fangstorm*'s foredeck in fire. The flames engulfed the cannon, but devastating return fire killed the steamcar crew.

Damn. Damn! They gave their lives to stop the cannon.

The gunner's shout, "Reload!" snapped Henwyn's attention back to the boarder vehicle.

Whomp!

Whomp!

A harpoon pierced two marines, knocking them off the back of the boarder.

The gunner sighed. "I think we took out six of the marines. But now they're too close to hit. They'll be boarding soon." He released the harpoon launcher and snatched a harpoon to use as a spear.

Crack! Crack! Crack!

Henwyn craned his neck "What's that?"

"The marines are probably shooting at our steamcycle."

Following the gunner's example, Henwyn grasped a harpoon. *No amount of silver is worth this.*

Grappling hooks clanged against the side of the steamtruck.

Henwyn and the gunner readied, bracing their feet and leveling their harpoons to port. The boarder vehicle drove off, having delivered its payload.

Where are the devils? Nothing. Henwyn risked a glance at Ophelia.

Two marines surged onto the middle harpoon platform and drew their cutlasses. Ophelia ducked under a horizontal slash and thrust with her harpoon, taking the Lupinian in the throat. He tumbled off the platform, dragging Ophelia's harpoon with him.

Holding his harpoon with two hands, Ophelia's loader blocked a downward cutlass chop from the other marine. Using his free hand, the Lupinian raked his razor-sharp claws across the loader's stomach, disemboweling him. The marine roared and turned toward Ophelia.

No! Henwyn dropped his harpoon and drew his pistol. He aimed with two hands.

Crack!

His shot took the marine in the back, knocking him forward into Ophelia.

"Henwyn," cried his gunner as two other marines scrambled onto their weapon platform. The gunner exchanged blows with a male marine, while a female swung at Henwyn.

Purely by instinct, Henwyn used his pistol to deflect a blow that would have parted his head from his shoulders. But the marine's stroke knocked the pistol out of Henwyn's grasp. She snarled and stabbed Henwyn in the gut.

Henwyn started. The stroke hurt, but no more than being punched. He felt to no blood oozing out of a deep wound. *The silver!* That morning, Henwyn had tucked a thick leather pouch holding five silver coins into his waistcoat pocket. *My silver foiled the Lupinian.*

The marine roared at the sky with frustrated bloodlust. She raised her cutlass to cleave the unarmed Henwyn in two.

Crack!

The marine's head shattered from the impact of Ophelia's large-bore musket ball, splattering blood on the face of the other marine.

Henwyn's gunner took advantage of the distraction, stabbing the remaining marine in the stomach. The marine gasped and toppled backward off the platform, but not before sinking his claws into the gunner's forearm and dragging him to his death.

The clacking of frigate treads drew Henwyn's attention to the approaching *Fangstorm*. He called to Ophelia. "Time to leave."

She nodded and scrambled with Henwyn to the towed steamcycle. They boarded and drove to the starboard side of the steamtruck cab to save the navigator. The driver would not leave his station. He would deliver his cargo or die trying.

Henwyn and Ophelia saluted the driver's courage and sped off toward

Castellum, accompanied by the other steamcycle, its archer bleeding from a shoulder wound.

THE CAPTAIN and first mate of the *Fangstorm* observed through binoculars the close quarters combat atop the steamtruck. "Signal the boarder to pursue the steamcycles," the first mate ordered.

"Belay that," huffed Cap'n Gevaudan. "Thrice now has that pig in a waistcoat demonstrated the heart of a Lupinian. Order the boarder to recover the rammer vehicle while we take the steamtruck."

"Aye, aye."

THE GATES of Castellum swung open for the two steamcycles. The four crew members received a somber welcome in the absence of the steamtruck. The wounded archer received medical attention, but the mayor stomped off grim-faced.

Henwyn spotted Gertrude in the crowd and rushed to her.

She frowned. "I'm pleased to see you alive, but less so that you arrived without the cargo. It would seem this day offers reward to neither of us." She turned and walked away.

Henwyn stood openmouthed. *Don't you want to hear my news? No? So be it. Good bye, Gertrude.* He returned to Ophelia and the steamcycle crew.

"You gunners took out all the marines," said the archer, his face wide with wonder and his arm now in a sling. "Incredible."

Henwyn smiled, finding comfort in the company of brave comrades who appreciated him. "Should we tell them now?"

Ophelia's eyes twinkled. "Let's not. I want to see the look on their faces."

Half an hour later, a steamtruck loaded with firestone arrived unescorted from Lapicidina. Amid the triumphant cheering, the mayor returned to the main courtyard. "How is this possible? Didn't the Lupinians capture the steamtruck?"

Henwyn smiled. "Well, milord. I suggested that we serve as a decoy convoy. The Lupinians captured a steamtruck filled with bricks packed with straw and sticks."

The mayor squealed with delight and summoned the city treasurer.

His leather pouch now bulging with fifteen silver pieces, Henwyn turned to Ophelia. "I'm so hungry I could wolf down dinner. Would you do me the honor of joining me?"

Ophelia curtsied. "I'd love to."

Thus it was that Henwyn collected two rewards that day.

SUBORDINATE

MELVA GIFFORD

Clerk Tudva tried to ignore the lieutenant's impatient tapping of a boot as the officer stood near his desk. Outside of the tent walls were the yells and orders from men settling for the night. They would face King Loraid's forces tomorrow. Thick dust filtered through the open tent flap.

The lieutenant thumped his desk, as if it would help him move faster. "You idiot, why are you so slow?"

The clerk's stomach rolled, but not from the officer's harassment. He continued writing in his clear, precise script. "I have been translating coded message from our forty-two scouts for the last two days, without sleep." He shifted in his hard wood chair. "I'm glad that I'm still conscious."

The other leaned forward. "King Naveed should get someone better and faster."

Tudva suppressed the snark in his response. The fact that he was such an essential spoke in the line of command appeared irrelevant. "It would be an enormous help to find someone. Someone else who can transcribe messages as efficiently as I." Tudva kept writing. "Please relay to the King that I support your recommendation."

The lieutenant opened his mouth to bellow when Tudva lifted the final paper and placed it on the pile. "I'm done."

The man cursed, grabbed the papers, and stomped off.

Once he left, Tudva promptly leaned over beside his desk and threw up in the bucket next to it. *Idiot wizards with potions.* The vial on his desk gave clarity of mind when tired but could made one sick to their stomach. He had not eaten for two days. *Stupid clappers!* The wizards gained that nickname from their ability to clap and create great thrusts of wind.

The clerk used a damp cloth to remove the spittle from his mouth. He lifted a whistle and blew it. A subordinate entered, replace the used bucket with a new one, and retreated.

Tudva glared at the empty vial at the front of his table. *Whose side are the clappers on anyway?* From his empty stomach, he was sure the vial had contained a toxin and not a potion. Had Tudva been the king or an officer, maybe they would have made an effort to add something to counter the side effects.

He leaned back. *Can I sleep now? Can we find spies with better penmanship?*

His back hurt. Oh, how his back hurt! There were indents on his fingers and thumb where he held the quill. Tudva imagined spending the rest of his life with furrowed fingers. Ink splotches covered his work vest. His butt . . . *I should have used a cushioned chair.* He hadn't dared. All Tudva would need is to be caught sleeping. King Naveed was more impatient than his officers. He had executed more than one person just because he was in a bad mood.

His Majesty demanded impossible results.

I haven't seen my family for two years. For those who dared to whisper, all the army, save for the king, wanted to abandon the war. The king's quest for power prevented them. Ransomed family members ensured obedience. Any criticism of the king would ensure dire consequences for them.

Maybe sensing a potential mutiny, the king took care to ensure that the men were well fed and rested prior to battle. But what of the treatment of those doing the paperwork? What of the workload of those feeding the troops or managing equipment and horses?

The king's motto of "All my army is essential" did not apply to clerks or other support staff.

A slight *thrum* vibrated the air, and the ground shook a little. For all the king's boasts of his army, he didn't trust them very much. The shaking earth was an integrity spell. It could sense a current act of betrayal of anyone standing. It also tended to put Tudva's feet to sleep. He didn't need the distraction during work. So he propped his feet on a mounting stool while decoding messages.

A young lieutenant tromped through the tent flap. "Requisitions," he said, fighting back a yawn. The officer dropped a pile of papers on the clerk's desk. The lad was furiously blinking as if he too was trying to stay conscious.

SUBORDINATE

Tudva raised his hands. "These are not for me. I work codes not—

"Blavouc is not in his tent. I was told to come to you."

"I am not responsible—"

The lad left the tent.

Clerks don't deserve such treatment. I must act, to give an example. We deserve respect.

Tudva leaned against the doorposts of his tent as he watched the army march past. King Naveed, leading his troops, glared at him. A set of three wizards rode in second position, chins raised. A row of loaded wineskins flopped against the flanks of their horses. Wizards worked best when drunk. They could ignore their bleeding hands a little longer and only stopped to prevent permanent disfigurement. The senior staff followed them, joking and sure of their victory.

Tudva kept his face neutral, gaze centered on his ruler.

I can stay behind, he thought gleefully.

Once the senior echelon marched past, the clerk could not resist a smile. One should appreciate those who process the paperwork more. Especially when one might have a tendency to lower a value in reports, such as an 8 to a 6, a 5 to 3, or a 7 to a 1. It would be hard to trace where the miscommunication occurred. It was common protocol to burn spy messages after processing.

His second sabotage wasn't planned. It became possible because of the absent Blavouc. Besides requisitions, he was responsible for management of the wizard's wine. Tudva redirected juice to the tents of the clappers and the spirits to the med tents. The clappers would face quite a surprise when they wanted to power up and encountered juice and not alcohol.

His Majesty would learn soon enough that the enemy severely outnumbered his army. Kill the king and someone would quickly rise up to replace him. Or, if the defeat was significant enough, the survivors could finally return home.

Maybe the new king would be more appreciative of—and attentive to—the silent cogs of his army.

WEREDODO SLEUTH

EMILY MARTHA SORENSEN

CHAPTER SOMETHING

THERE WAS A CRASH.

I woke up, my heart pounding. *Is somebody trying to rob me? Did the heater explode? Did I leave the TV on all night again?*

Quite naturally, I had to investigate. What self-respecting weredodo would leave such a thing unexplained?

I hopped out of bed, slipped my feet into my fuzzy slippers, pulled on my bathrobe, which had a rather odd smell I couldn't quite place, and shuffled downstairs. I checked the living room, and everything looked fine. I checked the water heater, and nothing looked different. I checked the kitchen, and everything seemed the same as I'd left it.

Except that my foot was cold. Why was my foot cold?

Ah. I had only put on one of my slippers, it seemed.

I stood there, puzzled, looking around the room. *Why did I come downstairs, again?*

I spun around in a slow circle, trying to figure it out. Surely there must be a clue somewhere.

The door! The door was ajar. I must have come downstairs to check the door!

Triumphantly, I headed to the kitchen door to close it.

Then I paused, puzzled.

Why had I left the door open? I didn't live in the safest neighborhood. I had forgotten to lock it before but didn't think I would have left it open.

I thought back carefully. I hadn't gone outside yesterday. My clan leader had come to visit me, but she'd left through the front door, as she usually did. I vaguely recalled the back door having been open last night . . .

Then my heart leapt in my throat. If I hadn't left the door open, then *somebody else must have.*

Sheer terror filled me, and I started to shake. Were they still in the house? Did they have a gun? I was only sixty-three! I was too young to be robbed at gunpoint!

No, no, I told myself. *Calm down. Calm down.*

I took deep breaths. All I needed to do was leave the house. If I told my neighbors what had happened, they would dial 911, and the police would come and take care of everything. They'd check my house to make sure the burglars were gone. I could go back to sleep, warm and secure and safe.

Or . . .

I looked around the room, my heart pounding with excitement. This was a genuine crime, wasn't it? I'd always wanted to be a sleuth. What self-respecting cozy mystery detective would let the police solve a mystery for them?

Oh, there were dangers, of course. I might be put in harm's way. On the other hand, my life had been so *boring* since I had been forced to retire early and my brother had started acting like an overprotective mother hen.

What self-respecting sister listens to her younger brother when he tries to act all authoritative?

My fear gone, replaced with glee, I pranced across the kitchen and flung open the back door. To my delight, there were footprints all over the snow outside, heading down the stoop and down the narrow path through my long-dead garden.

Let's see, I thought, squatting down and measuring one of them with my hand. *This is two and a half pointer finger lengths long.*

I should write this down. There was no way I'd remember. I reached into my pocket and pulled out a pen and a notebook. I scribbled down the measurement I'd taken from my first clue, made a carefully detailed sketch of the tread marks, and put the pen and notebook back.

I beamed as I stood up, my knees stiff from crouching. I was behaving like a real detective already!

There was a set of footprints heading clearly through the snow of my back yard. Not mine, I was certain, because my feet weren't as large as those. Besides, there hadn't been any snow on the ground when I'd gone to bed. The set of footprints made a detour to the kitchen window, and then over to the kitchen door, where I stood.

So the thief looked in the window before heading to the door, I deduced shrewdly. *That means he—or she—didn't come here knowing there was anything to steal. The thief just saw something he—or she—wanted and went for it.*

Of course, that begged the question of what the thief had seen. What was in view from my kitchen window?

I shapeshifted into my dodo form and waddled around the large footprints so that I didn't disturb any evidence, wading through the inches of snow to reach the kitchen window. I shifted into my half-form and craned my extra-long, feathery neck to see what the thief had been seeing from that position.

Aha! I thought. *The TV!* I could just make out the TV in the living room behind the kitchen table. That had to have been their target!

Oh, wait, I thought, ruffling my neck feathers in embarrassment. *The TV's still there. So what did they steal?*

Maybe I'd left my wallet on the kitchen table. Had I left my wallet on the kitchen table? I checked my pocket, and my wallet was there, where I usually kept it, so that was good.

Well, this was most puzzling. Maybe nothing had been stolen from my house at all. That would be good, I supposed, but awfully disappointing. Being robbed would have been such an interesting change of pace.

And then I saw him.

The door to my coat closet opened slowly, and a man with a ski mask over his face poked his head out. His head whipped first one way then the other, and he dashed for the kitchen door that I was standing beside.

I shrank until I was all-shifted and scuttled behind the box that belonged to the air conditioner's large outdoor fan, waiting with my heart pounding at triple the rate it should have.

I was little. I was tiny. I was only about three feet tall. He definitely wouldn't notice me here.

The man burst out of my kitchen door and ran down the path, snow flying as his boots churned it up.

One set of footprints, I realized with chagrin. *Of course he was still in my house. How could I miss such an obvious clue?*

Then the ski-masked man stopped abruptly. He looked around at the bird footprints I had left in the snow. He turned slowly to follow them to where I stood, frozen in place.

I'm a statue, I thought. *I'm just a statue in a little old lady's garden.*

"Oh, come on!" he burst out. "You're clearly alive!"

I waddled over, pecking at the snow with large, innocent eyes. *I'm just a pet. A pet in a little old lady's garden . . .*

"Dodos are extinct!" he exploded. "You're clearly a shapeshifter!"

Ah. Yes. I might have forgotten that one small detail.

Deciding that I'd be a little more imposing if I were more than three feet tall, I shapeshifted into my usual human form, holding my hands out menacingly. "What were you doing in my house, sir?"

The ski-masked man stared at me incredulously.

Hmm. Perhaps my human form was less imposing than my dodo form, after all. I was a sixty-three-year-old woman in a nightgown. Also, it was cold out here without feathers. I tied the bathrobe shut in front of me, shivering.

"Okay, lady," the man said in what he must have thought was a reasonable tone, holding out his hands. "I didn't take anything. Got it? You're not going to call the police. Right?"

"Of course I'm going to call the police!" I said indignantly.

"Okay, look," the man said defensively, edging off to the side, "I didn't take anything. Okay? I just went in on a dare. There was a guy who gave me fifty bucks to do it. I'm not a thief, okay? You can have the fifty bucks, okay? Stop looking at me like that!"

I gave the man a stern look. "Being an accomplice after the fact still makes you guilty. Unless, of course, you'd rather be a witness instead."

He paused, looking right and left nervously. "Witness?"

"That's right," I said proudly, drawing myself up to my full height. "I just so happen to be a sleuth. If you want to prove yourself not guilty, you can help me catch the person who did rob me."

"But I didn't steal anything!" he exploded.

"Ah, but somebody did," I said, raising my finger. I didn't know for sure if that was true, but I wanted it to be. "And so: who?"

He hesitated, looking one way or the other again, as if deciding whether to flee.

I folded my arms. "Are you familiar with my magical power?"

"Uh . . . ," he said, eyeing me. "No."

"Well!" I said grandly. "Weredodos have the ability to track people wherever they go. If you try to leave, I'll simply call the police and lead them straight to your hideout. Your only option to prove yourself innocent is to help me find the real criminal."

The man's hand jerked toward his pocket, and I flinched back, terrified that he'd pull out a gun. In retrospect, I realized that killing me would also be a way to make sure he didn't get caught.

But he didn't pull out a gun. He just pulled out a wallet and threw a fifty-dollar bill onto the snow. It lay there, fluttering slightly as a breeze drifted through.

"I got dared to do it," he said. "Just like I said. You can have the fifty dollars. Just don't call the police!"

For a moment, I considered it. Fifty dollars would be a reasonable reward for solving my first case, especially if no crime had actually been committed.

But if a crime *had* been committed and I let him go, I wouldn't be able to track my only witness. I'd been lying shamelessly about that. Weredodos had no magical abilities.

Come to think of it, perhaps that was one of the reasons my species was so rare.

"You can keep it," I said grandly. "Don't be so silly. Pick it up before the thing blows away. Then come inside and tell me all about the person who dared you to enter my house. That person is now my chief suspect."

Looking very uncomfortable, the man in the ski mask picked up the fifty-dollar bill and stuffed it into his pocket.

He headed back to the house with stiff shoulders as I followed after him.

I was about to interrogate my first witness. How exciting!

CHAPTER ?

MY RELUCTANT WITNESS settled down as he seated himself at the kitchen table, looking most uncomfortable. Personally, I was delighted by this whole situation. Who would have thought this morning that tonight I would be on my way to solving my very own mystery?

"Now, first of all," I said authoritatively, "you must tell me your name."

"Sebastian," he said reluctantly. "Sebastian Noclanhuman."

Oh, that poor boy! I thought, pity rising. *His turning failed!*

My own turning had gone wrong when I was close to his age. I had been turned at twenty-one, back in the days before it'd been determined that seventeen was the optimal age, and instead of becoming a werehawk like the rest of my family, I had become a weredodo.

It wasn't that I minded being what I'd become. I had long since gotten used to it, and when most of my extended family members called me "Aunt Dodo," I was quite philosophical about it. Still, there was a part of me that wondered wistfully what it would be like to fly. Dodos were flightless birds, after all.

My heart went out to this poor soul who had come to my house. A failed turning was a nightmare. He would never be a person.

"Stop it!" he shouted, banging his fists on the table. "Stop looking at me like that! I *chose* to stay human, all right? I've never been turned on purpose!"

I blinked and stared in bafflement at this impossible young person who apparently lacked common sense in every possible way.

"Why would you stay unturned?" I asked.

"What's wrong with staying unturned?" he asked defensively. "My parents have never been turned, or the rest of my family either, and we're all just fine that way!"

My eyebrows raised. I lived only a few streets away from a human ghetto, so I had met humans before, but never one that had chosen to be that way on purpose. To be eligible for almost any well-paying job required one to be a person, seeing as most specialty fields required a magical ability that was unique to a specific race or species. For instance, most doctors were draculas, since they could use their blood to heal their patients.

"I would argue that you are not 'just fine' if you are so desperate for money that you think trespassing in somebody else's home for fifty dollars is a superb idea," I said mildly. "Now, tell me about the man who dared you. Do you know him?"

"No," the ski-masked man said immediately. "We were complete strangers."

Liar, I determined, deciding to write that down. I checked the pockets of my bathrobe for my notebook and pen and found nothing. I checked my nightgown too, but there were no pockets within it. How puzzling. I could have sworn I'd put it in a pocket earlier.

No matter. This was why I had a junk drawer. I kept spare paper and Post-It Notes and several dozen pens there in case I needed to remind myself of things.

I stood up and headed across the kitchen.

"Where are you going?" the human named Spencer demanded.

"I'm getting a notebook to write down your testimony," I said, pulling open my junk drawer. For a moment, I stared at it in bafflement. Why was there silverware in my junk drawer?

Oh, wait. My junk drawer was the one next to it.

With relief, I opened the drawer to the right and collected a pad of Post-It Notes and several pens. I peeled off the top note, which said "Don't forget to pay phone b," and tossed it back in the drawer before heading back to the table.

"Now then," I said, sitting down with a purple pen posed over the block of sticky notes. "Do continue."

"Uh," the ski-masked man said, eyeing the Post-It Notes. "Uh, as I said, I have no idea who the guy was that dared me."

I wrote, *A likely story.* "Mm-hmm?" I asked encouragingly.

"I was just, like, out playing poker with my friends. I was on my way home, and . . . "

No-good gambling addict, I wrote. "Mm-hmm?"

"Oh, come on!" he exploded. "I can read what you're writing! I am not a gambling addict!"

"Well, then, I'd love you to explain why you were so desperate for money that you accepted a dare from a complete stranger to trespass in my house," I said severely.

He muttered something under his breath. "All right, my friends might've cleaned me out this week," he muttered. "Happy?"

I was, in fact. Interrogating a witness who was also a suspect was great fun. Not that I was sure what had been stolen, mind you, but I was certain there was something missing that was supposed to be in this room. Something . . .

I got up and headed to the wall.

"*Now* where are you going?" the man demanded.

"Nowhere," I said, adjusting the thermostat to 90 degrees. The vent was right behind the table. The heater immediately came on, and a wave of sweltering warmth gushed over us.

The man flinched and tugged the ski mask off his head.

"Aha!" I cried triumphantly, pointing at him. "Now I know what you look like!"

He froze, staring at the ski mask in his hand. Then he gave me an aggrieved look. "Lady, I told you, I haven't done anything wrong! I was just wearing that because it's cold outside!"

"Uh huh," I said gleefully.

He glared at me.

I studied his face, determined to be able to pick him out of a lineup if I had to. He had a thin nose, dark hair, no scars or freckles, a pasty white complexion . . .

I sighed. Okay, I had no chance of picking him out of a lineup. He looked terribly boring, and if I was being honest with myself, there was no chance that I'd be able to tell him apart from fifty other young men like him. Still, he didn't have to know that.

"Now, then," I said, settling back into my seat, "tell me again about the man who dared you to enter my house. The truth."

"I told you the truth!"

"Then tell me again."

He looked like he was grinding his teeth. "I was just walking by—"

"In the middle of the night?"

"I was coming from a poker game with my friends."

"High school students shouldn't be playing poker," I scolded.

"I'm not a high school student! I'm twenty-five!"

"And still unturned?" I asked archly. "You're clearly sixteen."

"I'm unturned on *purpose*, lady!"

Well, why hadn't he said that in the first place? He did look a little old to be sixteen. I wrote *Unturned on purpose* on the top Post-It Note.

"Very well," I said, adding *Makes poor life choices* underneath it. "Please continue."

"Well, a man appeared from behind a lamppost and asked me if I'd like fifty bucks."

"You say 'appeared,'" I said. "What does that mean? Did he do it magically?"

"I don't know," the boy shrugged. "He was wearing black. It might've been magical, or I might've just not seen him."

Wearing black, I wrote down, reaching the end of the Post-It.

Why was I using a sticky note again? I ought to be using my notebook. I checked the pockets of my bathrobe for my notebook and pen, but all I found was a half-eaten sandwich. I sniffed it, wrinkled my nose, and set it on the table.

"How old is that?" the boy named Stewart asked in horror.

"Not too old," I lied, though I had no idea. "But don't eat it."

He looked repulsed. "I wasn't going to."

Not always, I squeezed under the note that said *Makes poor life choices.*

"So the guy," Spencer said, "asked me, 'Hey, want fifty bucks?' I said,

'Sure. Why?' He said, 'I dare you to go into that house over there. The back door's unlocked.' I said, 'Why?' He said, 'My buddy bet me a hundred bucks I couldn't get someone to go into his house.' I said, 'Okay.' And I took the money and went."

I removed the top Post-It Note and wrote *Very stupid* on the next one. "Go on."

"Well, that's when I met you," he said defensively. "Can I go home now?"

No, he most certainly could not. Not until I knew what had been stolen, at least. Why did my kitchen look so wrong to me? Why did I feel like it was missing something?

I *knew* something had been stolen. And I had a feeling it had been something important. But what was it? What?

"What was the sound I heard?" I demanded. "The one that woke me up?"

"What sound?"

"The crashing one!"

"Ohhhh," Stuart said. "I dunno. I didn't make it."

"Did it come from outside?" I asked.

"I think so, maybe?" he hedged.

Maybe the crashing noise had something to do with what was missing from my kitchen. I stared around the room, focusing on each portion at a time, but nothing seemed to jump out at me. Everything was the same as usual.

This was maddening. I ought to be able to find out what was missing from my own house. I was a sleuth with the cleverness of a fox and a mind like a steel trap.

"Stanley, when you heard the noise—"

"It's Sebastian!"

Okay, like a sieve.

"—where did it sound like it was coming from?"

"I dunno," he said hesitantly. "Perhaps from . . . the right?"

My next door neighbor to the right were a childless couple from some sort of vampire clan. They weren't giants or specters. I could see no good reason why a crashing sound should have come from the direction of their home.

"Then we'll have to go speak to them," I said. "Come on."

"Come on where?!"

"To visit my neighbors," I said coolly.

"It's three in the morning!" he said shrilly.

"It doesn't matter," I said with great dignity. "They were most likely awakened, too. I am a sleuth and so must investigate all clues. After all, a sleuth without clues is like a test without a student. Like a doghouse without a dog. Like a cookie without sweetness. Like a clan without a turning stone—"

I stared at the table and gasped. It had just clicked.

"What's wrong?" the boy asked, looking alarmed.

"My clan's turning stone!" I wailed in horror. "It's gone!"

CHAPTER UM . . .

OH NO. Oh no, oh no, oh no no. I remembered yesterday now.

Victoria was going to kill me. She was definitely never going to trust me again.

"Your what?" the human named Stewart repeated, his brow wrinkled as if he didn't understand the significance.

"Our turning stone!" I exclaimed. How could he, of all people, who had been through the terrible tragedy of having his turning fail, underestimate the importance of that? "I promised Victoria I'd watch over it while she was out of town! How could this happen?! She'll never forgive me!"

"Where was it?" Spencer asked urgently.

"On the kitchen table," I said, distraught. "I . . . I promised her I'd put it somewhere safe . . . but I forgot . . . and I must have forgotten to lock the back door, too . . . "

There was a terrible silence.

"So you told your clan leader you'd watch over your clan's turning stone, and instead, you got it stolen?" Summer asked.

"Yessssssss!" I wailed, putting my face in my hands.

He walked over and patted me awkwardly on the back. It didn't help, but I supposed I appreciated the gesture.

"Anabel couldn't have taken it," I murmured frantically, "because her grandson's living with her, and she doesn't want it at her house. Charles wouldn't have taken it—he would just have woken me up and scolded me. Irma wouldn't have taken it—she would have just hidden it someplace and left a note for me."

Just in case, I checked the floor, but there was no note.

"Who are those people?" Stanley asked.

"Charles is my younger brother," I said, getting up and checking a cupboard, just in case I had hidden the turning stone there. "Irma's my older sister. Anabel's in my clan."

"How many people are in your clan?" he asked.

I checked another cupboard. "Three."

"Isn't that kind of . . . small?"

"Don't rub it in!" I snapped, slamming the door. "We haven't had a new turning in forty years. I was the last one."

He wrinkled his nose. "Okay, I'm not an expert in clans, since I don't have one, but . . . isn't it kind of pointless to have a turning stone if you never use it?"

I opened the oven door. No stone within. "Do you think we don't want new members? Of course we do! But Anabel and I both came from turnings that went wrong, so neither of us have relatives who are interested in being dodos. As for Victoria, she quarreled with her children, so they all live in a different state and belong to a weredodo clan there!"

"Yeah, but if you're not *using* it, you might as well just *sell* it," Sonny said.

I spun around and gave him a furious glare. "Nobody would sell their clan's turning stone! There's always the *hope* of new members!"

"What if they could get a lot of money for it?" Sonny asked.

"Of course they could get a lot of money for it," I said tightly. "But your own clan's turning stone is priceless. It could never be replaced. Especially with a rare species like dodos!"

"Because the stones have to be trained?" he asked.

"The word is 'programmed.' And yes. Our turning stone's been programmed over centuries to turn dodos. No one else could ever value it as much as we do."

I spun around, desperately seeking some other place I might have accidentally left it.

Aha! The dishwasher! I couldn't imagine why I might have put it there, but maybe . . . maybe . . .

No. There was no green, glowing stone.

A lump rose in my throat. This wasn't mere misplacing it. This wasn't like the car keys I'd lost two weeks ago and still not found. It really had been stolen. I really had carelessly allowed someone to steal it. I swallowed a sob—

No! No! I wouldn't let some selfish thief destroy my clan! I would stop them, and I'd find it!

I spied my phone on the countertop, and I seized it. I usually loathed my smartphone because I had a tendency to lose it, but right now, I was grateful for anything that could get me online.

"What are you doing?" Stewart asked, looking alarmed.

"Checking Wereconnection," I snarled. "Maybe there's a weredodo clan somewhere else in the country that is big enough that they want to split into two. They'd have a motive for stealing our turning stone—"

But there were too many clans when I searched for "dodo." There were hundreds, and at least five that had several hundred people in them. No suspects that would stand out to me.

Besides, was it really plausible that one of them had stolen my clan's turning stone? It was much more likely that it had been some common sneak thief who had simply walked by my house, seen the stone on the table, found the door unlocked, and walked off with it. Surely any turning stone could have value on the black market, even if it was programmed to an unwanted species . . .

I slammed my phone on the countertop. *An unwanted species!*

No. I would not let our turning stone be corrupted by another species. It was meant for turning dodos, and it would stay that way.

I had only one lead, and I would follow it. I'd solve the case, I'd save my clan, and I would show those no-good sneak thieves that crime never paid. That lead was . . .

Um . . .

That lead was . . .

What was that lead?

Maybe Skipper could help me remember.

"What else did you notice about the man who dared you to trespass in my house?" I asked him, turning around.

He stared at me, exasperated. "You mean, like the fact that he had a scar on his left cheek and he spoke with a heavy accent from south Paris and he was fairly obviously a dracula because he turned into a bat right in front of me?"

"Yes!" I exclaimed, diving for my Post-It Notes. "That will help immensely!"

"Do you know the meaning of 'sarcasm'?"

I paused, having gotten as far as "Almost certainly a dracula beca" in my notes. "What?"

"I was being sarcastic. I already told you everything I know."

I ripped the misleading Post-It Note off the top and wadded it up into a ball, preparing to throw it at him. The crinkling noise reminded me of . . . of . . .

"The noise!" I cried triumphantly. "We have to investigate that noise!"

Stanley looked less than enthusiastic. "There is no 'we.' I'm going home now."

"You most certainly are not," I said, fixing him with a stern glare. "You involved yourself in this crime, and now you have to help me solve it."

"I fail to see why," he said sourly.

I grabbed my phone from the countertop and held it up. "You want a reason why? I'll give you a reason why. If you leave now, I'll call the police and tell them that I caught you trespassing in my house right before I discovered my clan's turning stone had gone missing. Turning stones are worth hundreds of thousands of dollars, you know. Being involved in stealing one would be an automatic felony."

"C'mon, lady!" he cried. "You know I'm innocent!"

"I do not, in fact, know that," I said tartly. "But I do know your name, your face, and what neighborhood you likely live in."

He mumbled something under his breath.

"What was that?" I asked. "I didn't quite catch that."

"I said, 'Whatever,'" he muttered. "You could've used your tracking magic on me, no matter what."

What tracking magic? I didn't have tracking magic. I couldn't think where he'd gotten the impression I did. Still, it was a useful wrong assumption, so I wouldn't disillusion the boy.

"That's right," I said. "So let's not waste any more time. We need to go next door and interview my neighbors. Hopefully they saw something we've missed. Something that will crack this case wide open."

"Or maybe they were asleep. Like I want to be right now."

"Then we'll talk to everyone in this neighborhood!" I declared. "Someone must have seen something! We're going to find the thief if it's the last thing we ever do!"

Sonny looked dismayed.

"Well, come on," I said briskly, picking up my bathrobe. I pulled it on over my nightgown and tied it tight. "Let's go."

"You're going next door like *that*?"

"Indeed I am," I said. "I'm not letting you out of my sight. Unless you want to go upstairs with me while I change—"

"Please go next door dressed like that," he said immediately.

I smirked and went to the hall closet, where I retrieved a pair of snow boots. I put my phone in my pocket in case I would need it again, then shoved my feet into the rubber boots. I walked back to the kitchen, where Spenser was thankfully waiting for me.

"How are you planning to explain me to your neighbors?" he wanted to know.

"Well, I was thinking I would tell them the truth—"

"No."

"Why not? If you have nothing to hide—"

"Just tell them I'm your nephew!"

I gave the boy a doubtful stare. Quite apart from the fact that we had no facial features in common, my skin was dark brown and his was pasty white.

"I'll tell them you're my sidekick," I decided. "Every sleuth needs one, and I don't have a cat."

"How about assistant?" he asked.

"How about sidekick?"

"How about coworker?"

"How about sidekick?"

"I don't want to be a sidekick!"

"You'll do just fine," I assured him. "After all, you already have the perfect name for mystery solving."

"I what?" he asked, looking baffled.

"Sherlock," I said, shaking my head. How could he not know the name of the most famous detective of all time?

"My name is Sebastian!"

Chapter It's on the Tip of My Tongue

SKIPPER DID NOT LOOK enthusiastic as I banged on my neighbor's door.

There was a long silence as we waited for someone to answer. I took the time to look out over the silent stillness of a snow-fallen night. I could see our footprints in the blanket of whiteness, trailing from the front door of my house to our neighbor's. Shifting to half-form so that I could crane my extra-long neck, I looked back to see Sean's footprints heading behind my back yard toward the human ghetto, then turning to go into my house.

There was no sign of another pair of footprints back there.

I couldn't decide whether that made Sven seem more guilty, or whether that just meant the man he had talked to had been a specter. Specters could go insubstantial, after all.

But something was off about that . . . something . . .

Aha! I realized as the front door opened. *Specters can't talk while insubstantial! If the man were insubstantial, he wouldn't have been able to dare Sven!*

"H'lo?" the man asked in a bleary, grumbling voice.

I swallowed. I just realized that I couldn't remember my neighbor's name at all. Had it started with a P? Or a D?

"Hello, Mr. Vampireclandracula," I said, hedging my bets. "I'm your neighbor, Dorothy Wereclandodo."

"I'm not a dracula, I'm an aswang," the bearded man muttered, scratching his chin. "D'you know what time it is?"

"I believe it's three o'clock in the morning, but that's immaterial in light of the catastrophe," I said. "Did you hear a very loud crash about fifteen minutes ago?"

The neighbor's eyes opened beyond their sleepy squint. "What catastrophe?"

"The one in which my clan's turning stone was stolen," I said. "I very much need to get it back. Have you seen or heard anything?"

The man's eyes were now quite wide. "Your turning stone was stolen? There are turning stone thieves around?"

"Yes, I believe so," I said.

"Lily!" the man yelled, turning around to call up the stairs. "Check the safe! Check the safe now!"

So his wife was named Lily. That was helpful. I would have to remember that when I saw her.

"Mr. Vampireclanaswang," I said, "were either of you awakened by the crashing sound? I ask because I want to get right on—"

A woman screamed upstairs. Mr. Vampireclanaswang and I both bolted up there without hesitating.

At the end of the upstairs hallway was a safe. A safe that had been torn right out of the wall and flung on the ground. It looked like it had been punched open. And the safe was empty.

The neighbor woman, a forty-year-old showboat who tended to dress like she was twenty and wear layers of makeup so thick that they resembled a rock stratum, was now standing in the hallway in a silk nightgown and screaming.

I had a terrible misgiving that my turning stone had not been the only one stolen.

"What was in there?" I asked.

"Need you *ask?*" my neighbor shouted.

"Yes, I very well do!" I shot back. "I am a sleuth! I act on facts, not assumptions! Now: what was in your safe that is now missing?"

"What do you think?!" the man roared.

"Our—our turning stone," the woman sobbed, collapsing to the ground and staring at the empty safe. "Our clan's turning stone. How could this happen? Who would do such a thing?"

"I don't know," I said grimly, but a terrible fear rose in me. The last time there had been a rash of turning stone thefts, it had been because an underground organization had been stealing them to taint them, in order to blackmail the leaders of our city into . . . something. I didn't remember what offhand, but I knew my great-niece Lisette had done something to stop them.

What if my clan's turning stone has been tainted? I thought in terror. *It will have to be destroyed!*

That would be even worse than having it stolen and sold to become another clan's turning stone.

No. No, no, I told myself. *They fixed that problem, didn't they? They did. I'm certain they did. I would have remembered if they were still at large.*

"Bram, what'll we do?!" Lillian wailed.

"Yeah, looks really bad," Scooby commented from behind me. "That safe's totally busted."

I jumped. I hadn't even noticed that he'd followed me in, but of course he had. He was my sidekick.

"Who's that?" my neighbor snarled, pointing at Scooby.

"I'm her assistant," he said immediately.

"He means my sidekick," I corrected. "I am a sleuth, and he's helping me."

"Sleuth?" my neighbor asked sharply. I tried to remember what his wife had called him. Bran? Yes, it must have been Bran. "As in, detective?"

"Yes," I said firmly. "I'm here to solve the case, and I will do so. I'm quite certain the two crimes were perpetrated by the same people. Tell me everything you know or can surmise about what happened here."

"W-well," Lillian said in a wavering voice, "we keep the safe locked all the time. E-everybody in our clan knows we have the stone, but none of them would steal it."

"How often do you open the safe?" I asked.

"How often?" Bran repeated, as if I were speaking a foreign tongue.

"Yes," I said. "How often?"

"Whenever we have a turning," Lilith said in a shaky voice. "We have one in just a few days."

My mind hummed with that news. A turning in just a few days! Such a rare and special event, and they had one imminent. "So it's possible that it was someone was trying to prevent that particular turning. Your being about to use it in just a few days can't be coincidence—"

"Of course it can be a coincidence," Brian said brusquely. "We have a turning practically every week."

I gaped at him. "Every *week?*"

My clan hadn't had a new member in forty years. We were all over sixty. And they had a new turning every *week?*

I felt a stab of intense envy. It would be so nice to be part of a clan that was growing. Even a normal-sized clan, with a turning every year or so, would be terrific. I liked Anabel and Victoria, but our clan meetings were so desperately *boring.*

It was too bad Skyler's turning had failed, because I would have willingly invited him. Of course, I would have willingly invited anyone who could liven things up. If he'd at least been unturned, perhaps I could have persuaded him to be a dodo.

"Yes, we have nearly a thousand people in our clan," Lina said, rising. She stared down at the safe and let out a moan of dismay. "How are we going to explain this to them? We can't possibly merge with another clan. Our meetings are too crowded as it is!"

I tried to feel sorry for them, and failed. Perhaps it was uncharitable of me, but the fact that merging with another clan might even be an option for them made me jealous. Our tiny clan had never had an option to merge with another dodo clan because of distance. The other dodo clans were all at least an hour away.

Bryan was giving Shaun a suspicious stare. "What does it mean to be a 'sidekick,' anyway?"

"Oh, well, we met because—" I began breezily.

"I'm her nephew!" Shawn said quickly.

Brandon looked at him. He looked at me. He looked at him. He gave me a flat look.

"He isn't my nephew," I said.

"You don't say."

"We met because—" I began.

"Because I'm dating her niece!" Shaun interrupted. "That's why I said I'm her nephew. I'm going to *be* her nephew."

I stared at him in horror. I certainly hoped he was lying. I might have been willing to allow him in my clan, but to allow him to date one of my nieces or great-nieces? Absolutely not.

"It's not really that serious," I replied with great dignity, figuring that covered all my bases. "You can't call me your aunt when you aren't even engaged."

"Just give us time," Stewart shot back.

"Um, excuse me," Libby said, looking from one of us to the other with a confused look on her face. "What is your name?"

"Sebastian Noclanhuman."

Libby gasped. "Your turning failed? Oh, you poor boy!"

Stuart's face twitched.

"I hear there's a way to fix that now," Braeden said gruffly. "Some of the people in our clan have been talking about seeing if they can get work doing that if the process gets legalized."

"Which it shouldn't be!" his wife said indignantly. "It requires being tainted! Don't taunt the boy with things that can never be!"

"Those things very well *can* be," Bronson retorted. "There's a thriving black market now. I imagine that's why our turning stone got stolen—so it can be used for that!"

Lilith let out a thin wail.

Oh, if only I had my notebook with me! Both Bronson and Libby were terrific suspects, but I wasn't sure I would remember all the reasons for it.

Bronson, of course, might have sold the turning stone to the black market in order to cash in on a fortune. If he made it look like a robbery, he might have thought his wife and clan wouldn't ever know he'd been responsible.

Libby, of course, might have wanted to protect the stone from clan members using it in the wrong way.

The two of them might have colluded on the scheme together. Or one of them might be trying to spite the other. There were myriad possibilities, and while I was sure neither of them could have pulled the safe out of the wall in that way, there was no doubt that they could have hired someone to do that.

Three suspects, I thought. *Bronson, Libby, and Skipper.*

While it was satisfying to collect new suspects, it wasn't enough to solve the mystery. A sleuth needed to do more than collect suspects; they also needed to eliminate them. And regardless of whether one of those three was the true culprit, there was clearly somebody else involved. Somebody with incredible strength.

"I think a giant did this," Lillian said, looking down at the safe, which looked like it had a hole punched straight through it. "Nobody else could, could they?"

I glanced up at the ceiling. It looked unharmed.

"No," I said with certainty. "Not a giant. A basajaun."

Everyone stared at me.

CHAPTER 4

"A BASAJAUN?" Bruno repeated skeptically. "You mean the half-beasts?"

His wife elbowed him in the stomach.

"I mean the people whose physical appearance tends to resemble a were's half-form and whose racial magical ability is to become solider and tougher, yes," I said, ignoring the rude term. "A lot of giants could have done something like this, to be sure. But not without becoming taller than your ceiling. I see no cracks in it."

Everybody looked up.

"Now a basajaun," I said, "can become solider and tougher at any time. They do it without growing larger . . . because of course, they can't grow larger, that being the giants' racial ability."

"What if it's not a racial trait, though?" Lilith asked. "What if it's a species trait that allowed them to do this?"

"Like what?" Seamus asked.

"A weregorilla," I said, catching on. "They're strong, even in human form. It's their magical ability."

"Eww." Lina wrinkled her nose. "A gorilla in my house!"

"A haltija," Brandon suggested. "They're super strong while insubstantial. That's why they guard banks."

Seamus pointed at the busted safe. "That was not done by someone who was insubstantial."

"Ghouls are pretty strong, and they don't feel pain," Lina said.

"True," Bruno nodded. "For that matter, draculas have super strength."

I was starting to feel rather dismayed. My suspect list, which had seemed narrowed down as far as one of the eight races, was getting broader and broader. Yet I couldn't afford to overlook these exceptions. Any one of them might be vitally important.

I had to take notes. I simply had to. I checked the pockets of my bathrobe, but I couldn't find anything there. Where had I put my notebook?

Maybe I'd take notes in my phone. I'd installed a program to let me keep notes straight a few months ago. Except, where was my phone? It wasn't in my bathrobe pockets, either! I thought for sure I'd brought it with me!

"At least we know what the crash was now," Skipperdoo said, pointing at the safe.

I nodded slowly. It *did* seem safe to assume that the crashing sound had come from this house . . . except . . .

"Except the crash didn't wake up either of you," I said to Bradley and Lina. "It woke me up, and I wasn't in this house. Are you both sound sleepers?"

"We woke up when you rang the doorbell incessantly," Braeden said sourly.

Which means it didn't come from here, I thought, nodding. *Which means . . .*

"Which means we have to check the outside again!" I cried. "There might be clues there we've missed! Skipperdoo, come with me!"

"My name is Sebastian! And it's cold outside!"

I ignored his protests as I marched down the stairs, and the rest of them followed me.

"I'm going to call the police," Brady said with an edge of defensiveness in his voice as I reached the front door. "No offense to your detective skills, but . . . "

"No, no, please call them," I said, waving my hand. "If I can't solve the case before they get here, I'm not much of a sleuth. If they can find our turning stones before I can, then I welcome their help."

Bruno nodded sharply, looking mollified, and then shut the door as Sassafras and I stepped outside.

"It's c-c-cold," my sidekick complained, rubbing his arms.

"You have a ski mask," I reminded him.

"I'm not going to wear it when the cops are coming!" he declared. "They might think I'm a crook!"

And yet, you didn't think anything of wearing it into my house, I thought, shaking my head. *Or of going into a stranger's house in the first place.* This human boy had such strange priorities.

Well, Spenser's complaining notwithstanding, I commenced a diligent search for clues. I hadn't thought to bring a magnifying glass, so I shrank down to dodo form and held my face close to the ground as I waddled beside Spenser's footprints, watching for any sign that someone else might have been outside.

We were almost all the way back to my house before I found the clue I'd been looking for.

"Just because he didn't leave any footprints doesn't mean I was lying," Steven was saying defensively. "He might've been a specter or something. He wouldn't have left footprints if he was insubstantial."

I had already thought of that theory and dismissed it. Specters couldn't talk while insubstantial, much less hand over fifty-dollar bills. If the man had been insubstantial, he couldn't have dared Steven or paid him to go anywhere, and if Spencer had lied about that, I had no reason to believe that there had been a stranger involved in the first place.

My eyes fell on a tiny scrap of something that looked like a corner from a candy bar wrapper.

I let out a quack of delight and shifted to half-form so that I could seize it triumphantly. It had been half-buried in the compacted snow of one of Stephen's footprints, which must have been why it hadn't blown away.

This was proof that somebody had been here, perhaps eating a candy bar while waiting for a gullible sucker to wander by!

Unless of course it was Steven's litter.

"Do you like candy bars?" I demanded, interrupting my sidekick's defensive and wandering spiel.

"Huh?" He looked startled.

"It's important," I said sternly. "Do you like them?"

"Ye-esssssssss," he said slowly. "Everyone does."

"Do you like this kind?" I asked, shoving the tiny scrap at him.

Scotty stared at the corner of the semi-metallic wrapper, with its silver underside and brown top. "What kind is it?"

"A kind with a brown wrapper," I informed him. Was he blind? "Have you eaten a candy bar with a brown wrapper recently?"

"I—I have no idea," he said. "I might have. Why?"

"Because either this fell out of your pocket while you were walking . . . or . . . ," I said dramatically, "it's proof that somebody else was here before you. It was partly buried in your footprint, which means you stepped on it."

Siegfried's face brightened. "Then it belongs to the thief!"

"Only if it didn't fall out of your pocket."

"It didn't," he said immediately. "It definitely didn't."

That didn't really strike me as convincing, given that he had only declared himself sure that it wasn't his after I had told him it would prove his innocence if it wasn't, but never mind. It might still be useful. Any slight lead was better than nothing.

I shrank back to dodo, not bothering to pocket the clue because it would disappear inside me, like my clothes, while I was shifted. I found nothing else beside Spaghetti's footprints, so when they veered off toward my house, I kept heading straight forward.

"Hey. Hey!" Squirrel protested. "Where are you going? The warm house is that way!"

I turned around and shook my feathered dodo head in disbelief. Did he really think we were done searching for clues?

"Warm house!" he insisted again, pointing.

I shifted back into my human form, now holding the tiny scrap of clue in my left hand, where it had been before I'd shifted.

"Sheridan," I said patiently, "the crash might have come from the other side of my house. We need to talk to my other neighbors."

"Sebastian," he said. "It's Sebastian. How bad *is* your memory?"

I ignored that terribly rude question. "We probably don't have much more time before the police come, and I'd dearly like to solve this mystery before they get here. Come on."

I shrank to dodo and continued waddling forward through the freezing powder.

He grumbled vehemently as he stomped after me. I didn't know why he was the one complaining. I was the one wading through inches of snow wearing nothing but feathers and bare bird feet.

When we reached the side yard of my right neighbors' house, I spied something that presented a dreadfully disappointing solution to the mystery of the crash.

I shifted to my half-form so that I could sigh heavily.

"What?" Siegfried demanded. "What is it?"

"Their garbage cans are lying on their sides," I said, pointing. "With the trash scattered everywhere. The wind must have blown them down."

"So . . . the crash didn't have anything to do with the robbery?" he asked.

"Apparently not." It was most disappointing. "I suppose I should be grateful that the noise woke me."

"You should," Sheridan said. "You definitely should."

"I suppose so," I said desultorily. "But now one of my clues is gone."

"Not all of them," Sheldon said. "You still have . . . " He stopped and stared at my empty fingers. "You didn't drop the thing that proves my innocence, did you?!"

I laughed and shifted all the way back to human form. The clue reappeared in my fingers. Trust a human to be ignorant about how weres worked. "No, no. I just made it disappear inside me while I shifted. Weres can do that."

"Only with their clothes, though, right?" Shelly said.

"Of course not," I said. "We can do it with anything, within reason. For instance . . ."

I grabbed a loop of his jeans before he could stop me, and shifted to dodo. He was left standing in the snow in boxer shorts.

"HEY!" he shouted.

I snickered as I shifted back, and his pants reappeared. "It was just an example."

"A VERY COLD example!"

Spencer did not seem particularly happy. I, on the other hand, was quite impishly amused.

"Very well," I told him. "Let's go back to the house. I'll make you some ginseng tea to warm up."

"I want hot chocolate instead," he complained.

CHAPTER 4

Just because he wanted hot cocoa didn't mean I had any. My great-niece Annette had drunk all of it the last time she'd visited.

"You're going to love ginseng tea," I assured him, putting the kettle on the stove and heading back to the table. "It's delicious."

"Aren't you supposed to turn the stove on?" he asked.

I paused, then ran back to do so. "Of course. I was just testing to see how good your detective skills are. Sometimes I wonder why your parents named you Sherlock."

"They didn't!"

"In any case," I said, seating myself at the table, "we need to figure out how the man who left this clue did not leave any footprints. Was he hovering over the snow?"

"I dunno. I wasn't looking."

"Did he have wings?"

"He was wearing a jacket."

I sighed. Sherman was not being very helpful.

"How tall was he?" I asked.

"Average height?" Skipper hedged.

"Short end of average or tall end of average?"

"I wasn't paying that much attention! What does it matter?"

"If he was on the shorter end of average," I said reproachfully, "he could have been a very tall abatwa, such as a pixie or sprite."

"Well, I don't know," he snapped, "so it doesn't matter."

Another useful possibility occurred to me. "What color was his skin?"

"What does that matter?"

I stared at Sumner in exasperation. One might suspect him of being deliberately unhelpful. "Just answer the question."

"I dunno. Medium, I guess."

"Medium brown, or medium peach?" I asked, gesturing from my dark wrinkles to his pale pastiness.

"Medium peach?" he hazarded.

So that was another possibility eliminated. Tellems were a species of abatwa that could fly without wings, but they all had brown skin, even if they had been white before being turned.

"It might have been a kappa," I mused. "They can control water, including snow. If it was a kappa, he might've erased his footprints."

"What if it was a plain old, boring human?" Silas demanded, looking annoyed. "Why does it have to be someone with magical powers?"

"Oh, Sirius," I said, shaking my head. "You do realize that if I thought a human had done it, you'd be my prime suspect?"

"Why *couldn't* a human have done it?" he asked defensively. "We're smart, too!"

"Smart, yes, but capable of walking on snow without making any mark in it, no. It's possible the thief came to my house before the snow fell, but in that case, he couldn't have left the clue. The clue was only partly buried in your footprint, which means it was on top of the snow when you stepped on it."

"So maybe someone else left the clue," he said. "Maybe the thief came hours before the snow fell."

"Then why did someone dare you to come into my house?" I challenged. "If nothing else, the person who made that dare was standing out in the snow without having left footprints."

"Okay! Whatever!" he said, throwing up his hands. "At least my being human means I'm innocent, then!"

"Simon, you *did* leave footprints leading up to my house," I said with exasperation. "Your being human proves no innocence at all. Now, maybe if you were unturned as opposed to having had your turning fail . . ."

"Why would that make a difference? And I *am* unturned! I told you that before!"

Had he? I didn't remember.

"Well, in that case," I said, "I highly doubt that you would have stolen a turning stone, much less two of them. The very fact of what was stolen implies your innocence."

"Huh?" he asked.

"If an unturned human touches a turning stone, they turn immediately," I said. "If they do so without anyone else touching it at the same time to show the stone the desired form, the turning usually goes wrong or fails. That is, of course, why turning stones are rarely kept in the same house with small children. If you are unturned, I doubt you'd want to take the chance of stealing a turning stone and perhaps possibly touch it by mistake."

Samuel shuddered.

"Exactly," I said. "Now, a human whose turning had failed might be an excellent suspect, if only the evidence didn't imply magic being used. A human whose turning had failed might have a possible motive of wanting to spite people whose turnings had succeeded . . ."

My voice trailed off. What if Silas was lying about his unturned status? I had the sudden, uneasy feeling that I had forgotten the rather obvious possibility that more than one person could have been involved in this robbery.

I silently ran through the possibilities in my mind. If he was guilty, then he must have hidden the turning stone somewhere in my house. He couldn't have delivered it to anyone else, because I'd been watching him ever since I'd found him. He couldn't be carrying it on him, because turning stones were quite large—the size of a bowling ball.

As I was starting to worry extremely that perhaps I had made a dreadful miscalculation, I heard a knock on my front door.

I jumped, startled.

"Police!" a voice called. "Ms. Wereclandodo, may we speak with you?"

"Oh, good," I said with relief. I'd wanted to solve the case before they came, but now I was more worried about my safety. "Sherwood, come with me."

"What am I, Robin Hood?" he grumbled. But he got up from the table and followed me to the front door.

I opened it and let two police officers in. One of them, a man with a dog face, tipped his hat.

"I heard about your loss, ma'am. May we investigate your house to see if we can find anything of help?"

"Of course," I said.

He immediately became a tailless dog with a man's face and raced down the hallway, sniffing with his nose to the ground.

"What's *that?*" Stanford demanded, looking freaked out.

"He's a penghou," the other police officer said, chuckling. "He can sniff out turning stones, among other things."

"Is he some kind of weredog?" Stanford asked.

"No, it's a kapre. He can also turn into a camphor tree."

Kapres were like weres, except that they shifted into plants instead of animals.

"But he's a dog!" Stanford exclaimed.

The other police officer laughed heartily. "Well, in that case, I'm no more than a horse."

"What species are you?" I asked curiously.

"A nokk," he said. "I turn into a horse when touching water."

I couldn't quite remember which race they belonged to. "A specter?" I hedged.

"Lorelei."

I blinked. All loreleis could only breathe underwater during the full moon. "So you spend your full moons as a horse surrounded by fish and mermaids?"

"Yes, I do."

His partner ran back, tailless rear end wagging, and he turned into a human with a dog face again.

"Smell anything?" the nokk asked.

"No turning stones here," the penghou said.

"What about insubstantial ones?" I demanded. Because it had occurred to me that Simon might have been lying about being human. He could be a specter who had hidden my turning stone in a wall.

"I'm getting to that." The penghou cracked his knuckles, stretched, and shifted into a short, spindly camphor tree. A branch shook vigorously, and a leaf broke loose and fell onto my carpet. A second later, he was back to being a man with a dog face. He leaned over and picked up the leaf.

"Does the leaf help?" I asked in confusion.

"The smell of camphor makes it possible for me to sniff out insubstantial things," he explained, pulling a rubber band out of his pocket and stretching it around his head to fasten the leaf on top of his nose. "Be right back!"

And the man-faced dog raced off through my house again.

"While we're waiting, why don't you tell me how you figured out your turning stone was missing?" the nokk asked me, pulling a notebook and pen from his breast pocket.

I eyed the notebook enviously. If only I knew where I had put mine.

"Well, it all started when I heard a crashing sound," I began.

Come to think of it, we still hadn't found any explanation for that noise yet, had we? I would have to take Sirius to investigate. Maybe my neighbors to the right had heard it. I really should have thought to go there while we were still outside.

"And then I went downstairs, and I found—"

Severus let out a protesting sound.

I turned to give him a disapproving stare. If he was innocent, he shouldn't mind me telling the police the whole story. We had to catch the crook.

"Yes?" the nook police officer asked.

He was interrupted by a loud whistle from the tea kettle.

I jumped, my train of thought completely interrupted. What was that horrible noise?

"Oh, is that the teapot?" Saul broke in eagerly, looking relieved. "We're making ginseng tea. You want some?"

"No, thank you," the NOKK said.

"It was ginger tea," I corrected the boy.

"No, it was ginseng."

"Ginger!"

"Ginseng! She has a terrible memory," Stetson added in a confidential whisper to the police officer. "That's why I'm here. To help her. I'm her assistant."

I bristled. "The word is 'sidekick.'"

"The word's 'assistant.'"

"No, it's 'sidekick'!"

"See?" Stetson said, shaking his head. "Terrible memory."

I was very annoyed.

CHAPTER 4

WE HEADED BACK to the kitchen to check on the tea kettle. It was whistling quite shrilly as it waited for us.

"Hey," Sampson whispered as I lifted the kettle off the burner. He eyed the hallway where the nokk was standing. "Don't tell them about how you met me."

"I certainly will," I said, turning off the stove. "You should have nothing to hide."

"I don't wanna get thrown in jail for trespassing!" he hissed.

"Well, maybe you should have thought of that before you took that silly bet."

"It was a dare, and I regret it, okay?"

"I'm glad to hear that," I said. "But you're still the only witness who has seen the man who probably broke into my house. You need to tell them the whole story so that they can find him."

Sawyer ground his teeth. "I don't know anything useful."

"I imagine they'll be the judges of that."

"I don't want to get in trouble!"

"I'm delighted to hear that. I'm sure you'll behave with more wisdom in the future."

He glared at me.

"Is there a disagreement here?" the police officer from the hallway asked, wandering into the kitchen.

"Yes," I said. "Sawyer's being a little silly. If you don't like ginger, can I get you another kind of tea? I have ginseng and chamomile."

"No, thank you," the police officer said. "I'd rather not turn into a horse right now. Can you tell me about how you found your turning stone was stolen?"

I stared at him. Good gracious! A horse? Why would that happen?

"Hey, how come you guys aren't next door?" Sonny broke in. "Their turning stone was stolen, too."

"We have another unit over there," the man who had been inexplicably worried about turning into a horse said. "Right now, we're here to help you. Please tell me how you learned the stone was missing."

"Well, there was a crashing sound," I said, "and then—"

"I was here with her the whole night," Sawyer broke in. "Because I'm her assistant."

"You'll get your chance to talk, son," the police officer said, looking rather annoyed. "Let me hear from her first."

I blinked in startlement. "Is he your son?"

"What?" the police officer asked, looking baffled. "Oh, that. No. It's an expression. Please go on, ma'am."

I cleared my throat. "Well, it all began when there was a crashing sound from outside . . . "

I went on to explain everything else that had happened so far, stopping a few times to fill in parts I had forgotten. As I did so, I poured the water from the tea kettle into the mugs for me and Spencer, and I passed one to him. I sipped mine, which tasted rather flavorless for some reason, as I talked.

The police officer said nothing aside from "Mm-hmm" and "Uh huh" and "Go on" while he wrote down my words, and it wasn't long before his partner joined us, asking for permission to open anything that was currently shut.

"Of course," I said. "Please search everything."

By the time I finished my story, he was back, having searched everywhere thoroughly.

"No turning stones," he said, "substantial or insubstantial, though there was one on this table recently."

I sighed. So much for my last vestige of hope that I had simply hidden it somewhere I'd forgotten. Still, that also cleared Sherwin. It was a relief to know I hadn't been spending the last two or three hours with a criminal.

"Sorry, ma'am," the non-canine police officer said. "Quite often missing turning stones turn out to still be hidden insubstantially in the house they went missing from, but it seems this time that isn't the case."

"Quite often?" I asked. "Do turning stones get stolen a lot?"

"More often than you might think, given how careless people can be with them. That's why we have officers specially trained in hunting them down."

"Me," his dog-faced partner said, raising his hand cheerfully.

"But that wasn't even what I was taking about. It's far more common for a specter to accidentally turn one insubstantial and knock it inside a wall or under the ground. You'd be amazed how many times that's happened."

"So you thought it might be accidental?" I asked.

"Indeed," he said. "It happens all the time with senior citizens, especially specters."

I bristled. "I am not a specter! And I wouldn't misplace such an important thing!"

"Of course not," he soothed. "May I ask what you are?"

"A weredodo," I said.

He and his partner exchanged a glance.

"Are you in half-form, by any chance?" the dog-faced man asked delicately.

"No, I am not!" I said indignantly. "I couldn't disappear an entire turning stone inside myself without noticing! Do I *look* like I'm in half-form?"

"Half-forms aren't always obvious," the dog-faced officer said. "I have a sister who's a weredog. As long as she keeps her hair combed over her floppy ears and her paws in shoes while she's half-shifted, nobody notices."

"Well, *my* half-form is obvious," I said huffily, demonstrating. An enormously long feathered neck sprouted between my head and shoulders.

"No offense meant, ma'am," the non-canine assured me. "It's just that penghous can't sniff out turning stones that are hidden inside weres. And we've seen it happen before. Especially with senior citizens."

I was getting extremely irate with his use of that word. Some might think that knowing how age had degraded my memory would mean I wouldn't mind others assuming that fact. But no. That just made it even more of a touchy subject. Especially when there was any implication that I might not be competent enough to take care of myself.

"Well, I appreciate your checking every possibility," I said coldly. As far as I was concerned, the two police officers had worn out their welcome. Polite about it or not, I did not appreciate people questioning my judgment. I got enough of that from my brother. "Now that you're satisfied that I was not the accidental culprit, I hope you'll be able to find the thief before he gets much further away with my clan's turning stone."

"Just one last thing," the dog-faced man asked, eyeing Sherwin. "What species are you?"

"Human," he said with an edge in his voice.

"I don't smell a failed turning," he said suspiciously.

"You wouldn't! I'm unturned!"

"Hmm. That would explain it." The dog-faced man paused. "How old are you, kid?"

"Twenty-five."

"And still unturned?"

"Yes! I'm allowed to stay unturned if I want to!"

The dog-faced man scratched under his neck. "Sure, you're allowed to, kid, but it's pretty weird."

Sherwin looked very peeved.

"Oh, here's the clue we found outside," I said, remembering it for the first time. I picked it up from the table and handed it to them, explained where we'd gotten it from and what we'd deduced from it. "Perhaps you can check it for fingerprints!"

"Perhaps," the non-canine said, pulling out a plastic bag and gesturing for me to drop it in. He didn't seem to consider my clue particularly revelatory. "It might have been more helpful if you had left it where it was."

"She couldn't do that!" Sherwin said defensively. "The thief might have come back and picked it up to cover his tracks!"

"Uh huh." The police officer looked like he didn't believe for a second that would have happened. "Well, thank you very much your help. We'll get back to you as soon as we find your stone, or if we have any other questions."

"You *will* find it, right?" I asked anxiously.

The non-canine police officer paused. "I'm not going to lie to you, ma'am. In cases like this, where the object wasn't simply misplaced and we have no solid leads, the chances are only twenty, thirty percent that we'll find it eventually. We'll do our best, of course, but you might have to accept that it's gone."

That took the breath out of me. Even the police couldn't promise any more than thirty percent?

No. That wasn't acceptable. I couldn't let it be gone.

"Thanks very much for your time," the dog-faced police officer said to me, bobbing his head with his ears flopping.

The two of them got up and headed to the front door.

"You're welcome," I said quickly, following them, "but I can help much more than this. I'm a sleuth. I can find more clues—"

"Of course," the non-canine said. "Give us a call if you find any."

I had the nasty feeling he was only humoring me.

"I *can!*" I said angrily. "I can, and I *will!*"

"Well, then, remember to leave them where they were, so we can inspect them properly," the man said, tipping his hat. "Good day, ma'am."

As the front door shut, my blood was boiling. I wanted to be taken seriously, and I would be. I was certainly not going to trust the fate of my clan to the police's twenty percent. If they weren't going to find it, I would do it myself. I had wanted to do that, anyway.

I sipped my flavorless tea, fuming. Surely I had learned something earlier that would crack this case wide open. That was how mysteries worked. All I needed to do was put the pieces together in the right way, and the answer would emerge from a chrysalis, flapping its wings in brilliant obviousness. I just had to notice something . . .

Something . . .

Something . . .

Blast. Nothing was coming to mind.

"It's a shame about your turning stone," Shelby said.

I ignored him. This wasn't a time for my sidekick to distract me. I focused all my brainpower on sorting through tonight's clues.

"I know you wanted it," said Something. "But really, is this so bad? I mean, you weren't using it. If no one's joined your clan in forty-two years, it's highly unlikely that . . . "

Yammer, yammer, yammer. I wished Something would cut it out. Couldn't he see I was trying to think?

There was something about that safe that bothered me. The way it had been ripped out of the wall and punched through, with no noise being made. I was pretty sure I knew what species could do something like that, if only I could . . . remember . . .

That's it! The answer burst into bloom in my mind.

I stood up from the table, drank the rest of my lukewarm tea in one gulp, and slammed the mug on the table. "Come on, Shannon! We've off to investigate!"

"Off to investigate *what?*" he goggled.

I grinned ferociously. "The Vampireclanaswangs' safe. I'm about to blow this case wide open."

WASN'T THIS CHAPTER 4?

I MARCHED STEADILY FORWARD, heedless of the snow that I was kicking up as we went. I didn't even worry about the tiny flakes I saw drifting down from the sky. If I was right about my theory, and I was guessing I was, it wouldn't matter if it snowed more and the footprints were all erased.

Sheldon let out a steady stream of grumbling from behind me, mostly about the fact that I had refused to elucidate him before sending us back out into the cold.

"Just be patient!" I called, not turning around. "I can't explain until everybody is there at once!"

Honestly! Hadn't he ever read mysteries?

"But do you know who *did* it?" he yelled.

"All will be revealed!" I called back mysteriously.

We reached the front door of my neighbors' home, I pounded on it, the door was opened, and the Vampireclanaswangs were more than a little surprised to see us back.

"We have the police here," Lillian said. "We don't need you."

"There's where you're wrong," I said. "I've noticed something that everyone else overlooked."

"Are you all right?" Braden asked, glancing behind me. "You look a little ill."

"So c-cold outside," Stephan complained.

"Well, come in, then," Layla said, looking displeased to be forced into hospitality.

I didn't wait to be invited twice. I immediately bustled in and up the stairs, fairly relieved myself to be back in a warm house. In my excitement, I had found the flurries and the chill wind stimulating rather than upsetting, but there was no denying that my ears felt like two ice cubes hidden in an igloo and then packed with snow to keep a soda can cold.

Upstairs, I found four police officers pouring over the broken wall and the busted safe, talking to each other and taking notes. Two of them were the ones who had been at my house before.

"Hey!" the dog-faced man said, alarmed, as I headed toward them. "Stay away from the crime scene!"

I ignored this advice, though I stopped short of coming close enough to disturb anything they were photographing.

"Is everyone here?" I asked, looking over my shoulder.

The Vampireclanaswangs emerged from the top of the stairs. Sinclair was with them, shivering as he hunched into the scarf Lilith was draping over him.

"What is this regarding?" one of the police officers I didn't know asked, looking annoyed.

"It's regarding the fact that I know exactly what species did this," I said proudly, pointing at the safe and then the wall it came from. "It's a haltija."

The police officers didn't blink.

"You don't say," said one of the unfamiliar ones. He was a duergar and very ugly.

"You see, haltijas only have super strength while insubstantial," I said excitedly. "So we figured one of them couldn't have done this. But a specter can also make things they touch insubstantial at any time! Which means he could have made the safe and the wall insubstantial, ripped the safe out of the wall, punched it open, grabbed the turning stone, and escaped! It could all be done in complete silence, because insubstantial things don't emit sound waves!"

My brilliant theory was met by stormy silence.

"This is not our first haltija crime," the duergar said finally.

I blinked and stared at the four police officers. They all looked rather impatient.

"Is there anything else?" the non-canine who had been at my house asked.

"Um . . . yes!" I said, as a new idea occurred to me. "Stevie here was lying when he told you about the man who dared him!"

This caused a mild stir.

"Was he indeed?" the dog-faced man asked, eyeing my sidekick with an expression that looked almost hungry.

"I was not!" Stewie yelped. "Why would you say that?!"

"Because your story doesn't hold up," I said with satisfaction. "There aren't many species that could do what you described without having left footprints, and all of them are conspicuous enough that it's not believable you didn't notice anything specific. I suspect you were deliberately describing that supposed individual in as vague terms as possible so as to attempt to not get caught in a lie when the culprit was found. And then there's the general silliness of your story in the first place, which requires you to have had no common sense whatsoever. Well?"

"No, I—!" Stevie began furiously. But then he looked at the stern-faced police officers, then over at me, then at the steely-eyed vampires standing beside him. His shoulders slumped. "Okay, fine," he muttered. "There was nobody else out there. I just wanted her to let me leave."

"Why were you in my house?" I demanded.

"The door was open," he said. "I was cold. I figured, why not sit in a warm house for a while?"

I stared at him incredulously. "You do remember what I said before about your story being implausible because your actions lacked common sense?"

"Well, I'm sorry if I have no common sense!" he flared. "This time I'm telling the truth! I had a long walk still ahead of me, and it was cold!"

"You said the door was open," one of the police officers said. "Why would a specter need to open a door?"

"Maybe she left it open," Sidney said, pointing at me. "She has a terrible memory."

"I would not have left it open!" I said, scandalized. "It's possible I might have left it unlocked. But open, never!"

"You might have left it slightly ajar and not noticed," the man with the dog face said gently. "The wind could have blown it open further. That sort of thing happens to senior citizens."

This senior citizen was just about ready to feed him his own hat. This senior citizen was not a fan of condescension.

"I'm sorry I lied." Sidney looked at me guiltily, twitching the scarf around his neck. "But really, I didn't think anything had been stolen from your house. I just wanted you to let me go home. You were one freaky scary dodo, standing there out in the snow."

"Apology and compliment accepted," I said stiffly. "But you've done irreparable damage to my investigation. Because of you, I wasted my time checking footprints. Because of you, the culprit had more time to escape!"

"The culprit probably escaped hours before you ever woke up," Steven shot back. "Even the crash that woke you up had nothing to do with it. It was just a bunch of trash cans falling over!"

"You don't know that that was unrelated!" I yelled.

"I *do!* You said so yourself! Or did you forget that, along with everything else?!"

"Tell you what," the police officer who hadn't spoken yet said. He was a tall man with antlers. "Why don't the two of you go back to your house, and when we're through here, we'll send someone over to take your statements. An *honest* one, this time," he added, giving my sidekick a rather frightening glare.

Sonny gulped and looked cowed.

I knew when I was being dismissed, and I didn't like it. But there didn't seem to be much point in trying to change their minds.

"Come on, then, Siegfried," I said. "Let's go back to my home."

"Out in the cold again?" he complained. But he didn't put up any more fuss. He looked a little bit afraid of the antlered man.

The Vampireclanaswangs were only too glad to see the back of us. Lillian even asked for her scarf back, to Sonny's dismay.

As we headed back toward my house, I stomped through the snow, frustrated that I was still being treated like a hindrance rather than a help to the investigation.

Had they even considered the most interesting aspect of all about a haltija having done it? A haltija wouldn't even have needed to open the safe. They just could have reached through the wall, made the turning stone insubstantial, and pulled it out. Nobody would have even been the wiser until they had tried to open the safe and found it gone.

Unless there was a specter alarm in there, which there probably was, I realized. *The thief would have needed to be substantial when he reached in there, or else he would have tripped it.*

Specter alarms were highly sensitive devices that would go off at the slightest touch. A specter turned them insubstantial before arming them, and once they were armed, they would go off if brushed even slightly by anything insubstantial later. Substantial things couldn't touch them and therefore wouldn't trigger them, so they were not an inconvenience to the person who wanted to keep their things protected.

I had only just remembered that those things existed. I was suddenly glad I hadn't brought up the curiosity of a haltija having chosen to break the safe in order to reach in with a substantial hand, because the police probably would've given me that same flat stare that said, "Why are you telling us obvious things?"

I shuffled down the sidewalk as the snow fell thicker, feeling depressed. What was the point of me being a sleuth if I couldn't help to solve my own mystery? Yet again, I was the incompetent shuffled off to the side so that I wouldn't get in anyone else's way. Yet again, I was nothing but silly old Aunt Dodo.

A car drove down the street, headlights bright through the white clumps raining down from above. It was driving slowly but still faster than Sven and me, who were getting slower and slower as our visibility receded.

The car slowed to a stop, and a window opened. "Hey, need a ride?" the driver called from inside.

"No, thank you!" I said. "We're fine."

"Y-yep, we're fine!" Severus agreed.

"Your teeth are chattering," the man said in exasperation. "That doesn't look fine. Can you even see where you're going?"

"It's only a two-minute walk," I said. "Don't worry."

"Unless you get lost," he said.

The wind took that moment to pick up, gusting more snow at us. I stared out into white-speckled darkness. He might have a point. I couldn't see more than a few feet in front of my face. Had I forgotten which way my house was?

"Get in," the driver said, pushing a button. There was a sound of doors unlocking. "Nobody should be out on a night like this."

"No thanks," I said. "We'll be fine on our own."

He pulled out a gun and leveled it at me. "Get in."

I had a terrible feeling that things had gone very wrong.

CHAPTER I'M SURE I'LL REMEMBER IT

NESTLED INSIDE THE WARM CAR, Severus blew on his hands while I sat in the back beside him, stiff with terror. The car started moving, beginning to crawl down the road.

"Wh-where are we going?" I stammered.

"I don't know," the driver said succinctly. "I guess that depends on how much you've figured out."

"Nothing at all," Stanley said quickly. "She's a terrible sleuth."

I was not impressed with his loyalty.

"I'm a wonderful sleuth, but I have no idea who you are," I said coldly. "Since you've kidnapped us at gunpoint, maybe you'd be so kind to elucidate us."

He glanced back at us in the rearview mirror, grinned, and said nothing.

"Well, obviously you're the haltija who stole my turning stone," I said crossly. "Most likely you were listening to our conversation from a listening device, or maybe you were hiding under our feet after the police left. Either way, I clearly said something that alarmed you, so I must have figured out something you don't want the police to know."

The driver just grinned.

"That, or you want them to *think* I figured out something you don't want them to know," I added. "To send them barking up the wrong tree. Or I'm just a generic hostage."

"Two hostages," Stormy muttered.

"You really must stop whining," I said reprovingly. "At least you're warm now. That's what you wanted, right?"

"I'd like to *live*, too!"

"Tell me what else you know," the man from the driver's seat said sharply.

"Don't say a word!" Severus hissed.

I ignored my sidekick. "Of course. But first, a question."

"Absolutely not," the man said succinctly. "You're talking. I'm the one with the gun."

So much for the villainous monologue I'd been hoping for.

"What are you going to do with us?" I demanded.

"That's a question. I'm not answering those."

I worked backward, trying to figure out what I might have said in the recent past to make this man alarmed enough to kidnap me. What could possibly be worth showing me his face?

Unless it wasn't his face, of course. Unless he was an aswang. They could shapeshift into anybody they sucked blood from.

My mind worked feverishly. Hadn't Libby mentioned that some members of their clan wanted to get work turning people a second time, which was currently illegal? And hadn't Braeden said he disapproved? Perhaps one of them, knowing that their clan leader wouldn't allow it, had decided to take matters into his own hands. Perhaps he'd stolen the turning stone to force their clan to merge with another one with a clan leader more favorable to his interests.

But in that case, where was the haltija? Was he—or she—back at the Vampireclanaswangs' house, listening to the police?

There was only one way to find out. I checked the pockets of my bathrobe and found a ball of lint. I threw it at the back of his head.

He flicked insubstantial in the space of a flinch. Then he was back to normal, and roared, "What was that for?!"

"Just testing," I said.

"Testing what?!"

"To see whether you were a haltija or not. You had pointed ears while insubstantial, so I assume you are. I thought maybe you were an aswang. Do you have any conspirators, or did you work alone? I'd like my turning stone back now, please."

Sigmund moaned and put his face in his hands. He seemed to be mumbling something like, "We're gonna die . . . "

"I'm not answering any questions!" our captor roared. "You tell me what you know, *now!*"

Siegfried looked completely ashen. His pasty skin was even whiter than usual.

"Don't worry," I reassured him. "He's probably planning to kill us anyway. We've seen his face."

Siegfried looked incredulous and not at all reassured.

"TALK!" our captor roared.

We reached an intersection and a car crossed in front of us, bright headlights flashing. Our driver clutched the steering wheel with both hands and shouted obscenities at the car that had zoomed past us at a dangerous speed.

Well, he was distracted, so . . .

I shifted to half-form, jabbed my extra-long neck forward, and grabbed the gun in my teeth. Then I leapt back and shifted to dodo, hiding the gun inside me.

"HEY!" the driver screamed, spinning around.

I flapped my wings and quacked gleefully.

"I can still wring your neck," he snarled, going insubstantial.

I might have made a slight tactical error.

I dove for the front seat, but he was in the back seat in an instant. Going substantial, he seized my fragile dodo neck. I slashed at his face with my talons, he flinched insubstantial, and I squeezed between the front bucket seats into driver's seat.

Behind me, Skittles was screaming, and I glanced back to see a vicious fight between a skinny little twig and a bulky man who could go insubstantial. It wasn't a fair fight at all. So I shifted to half-form and pressed my own advantage.

Or rather, the gas pedal.

The car lurched forward, skidded, fishtailed, and went sliding out of control.

The haltija yelled and hung on to the seat. For an instant, I wondered why he didn't just go insubstantial, but realized that he didn't want the car to leave him behind.

"Brake!" Skittles screamed. "Brake! Brake! Brake!"

A brake wouldn't help. I knew that for sure. I'd driven on icy roads before. So I did the one thing that seemed sensible. I reached desperately for my seat belt and slammed it into the buckle.

WHAM!

The car rammed straight into a cement barrier at the side of the road. Our abductor went flying. My head snapped forward and back again. Spaghetti screamed.

I now felt dizzy. Was the car tilting? No, maybe it was whiplash.

Ow . . .

Spaghetti was still screaming.

"Stop screaming!" I yelled. "What's going on back—"

I looked. My breath caught, and bile rose in my throat.

Our captor was the only one who hadn't been wearing a seat belt, and his head had smashed straight through the window beside him.

He should have gone insubstantial, I thought numbly.

I shifted to human form to feel my neck and see how bad the injury was, found the gun I'd forgotten about between my teeth, and spat it out into my pocket to deal with later.

My sidekick was still screaming.

I noticed that the man's chest was rising and falling, even though there was a terrifying amount of blood coming from his head wound. I let out a long, shuddering breath. "Sousaphone, stop screaming. Call the police."

"But—but—but—!" the boy gibbered.

"911! Police! Ambulance! Now!"

He yanked a phone out of his pocket, dropping it several times because his hands were shaking, and finally managed to dial.

Five minutes later that felt more like five years, we were rescued. A specter EMT made the car insubstantial while a basajaun pulled us out, and a dracula EMT sliced his wrist to produce vampire blood.

"Here," he ordered us, handing us each a paper cup that was about a quarter full. "Drink it." His wrist had healed in less than ten seconds.

"Ewww," Steven moaned, but he did so. I did the same.

In a few minutes, we were both fine. All our injuries were healed. Our captor, however, was another story.

"Can't you heal him, too?" I asked nervously as the basajaun and specter loaded him up on a stretcher. A police officer who had arrived shortly after the ambulance was talking with them.

"We can," the vampire said shortly, "but we've only given him a few drops to stabilize him. If your story's true, he's a violent criminal, and in cases of violent criminals, we prefer not to heal them entirely until they're safely behind bars."

"What if our story *weren't* true?" Stewie asked.

"Then you'd face obstruction of justice charges, and possibly a charge for reckless endangerment of human or person life," the EMT said shortly. "Excuse me."

The police waved and wandered over to us as the ambulance took off, its sirens blaring.

"You're a really bad driver," Sterling joked, laughing shakily.

"I'm a *wonderful* driver," I said. "I'm just not very good at finding where I'm going. And I lost my car keys two weeks ago."

He laughed, as if I had been joking.

"Shall I drop you off at home?" the police officer asked, reaching us. "I assume you won't be driving." He looked pointedly at the totaled car.

"Yes, please," I said with a weak smile. "That would be great."

"Who shall I take home first?" he asked. "Or do you live together?"

"Oh, take Spaghetti home first," I said quickly, gesturing at the boy. "He's been wanting to go back home all night. And now that the case has been solved . . . "

My sidekick gave me a rueful look. "Sebastian. That has got to be the weirdest one you've come up with yet."

"Regardless," I said, "tell the man your address."

Spaghetti started to speak, and then paused. "Actually, do you mind if I go back home with you?"

"Why?" I asked.

"Because I want more of that hot water you call tea."

My mouth fell open. "Did I forget to put the ginseng in?!"

"Yes, you did," he said, laughing.

"So *that's* why it was so flavorless!"

He guffawed.

"Well, this time I'll remember it," I said, flustered.

"Nah, hot water's fine," he grinned.

CHAPTER I THINK I FORGOT IT

HE AND I got out of the police car at my house, and we waved goodbye to the police officer who drove off.

"Did you really lose your car keys two weeks ago?" Seymour asked, eyeing the car parked in my driveway.

"Not to worry," I said. "I can grocery shop online."

He snorted.

I pulled my house keys out of my pocket, unlocked the door, and let us in. A blast of heat reminded me that I still hadn't turned down the heater from 90 degrees. I would really have to fix that before my gas bill became astronomical.

"Now, let's get that tea started," I said, bustling off toward the kitchen.

"Actually, maybe I'll just borrow a coat and go home," he said, glancing at the coat closet.

What a chicken, so afraid to try something new.

"Nonsense," I scolded. "You have to try it with the ginseng in it. It really does taste better that way."

"Maybe next time," he said.

"Maybe tonight," I said firmly. I held the kettle under the faucet of the kitchen sink and filled it up.

As I placed the kettle on the stovetop and turned it on, a sly smile crept across my face. He didn't know it yet, but I was going to convince that boy he wanted to be a dodo. Now that the criminal was caught, they'd find my turning stone soon enough, and what better way for Victoria to forgive me than to introduce her to a prospective new clan member?

Not that I was going to tell him that yet, of course. He was so determined to stay human, silly boy. He would have to be talked into it. But I was certain I could do it eventually.

I was almost glad I'd left the turning stone out on the table, rather than hiding it properly. If I hadn't done that, the thief who'd come to rob my neighbors' turning stone wouldn't have seen it, it wouldn't have been stolen as an impulsive extra prize, and I wouldn't have had this opportunity to make friends with a young person to add to our clan.

Plus, of course, the police clearly wouldn't have been able to solve this case without me. At very least, without me, the criminal would have escaped.

I headed to the hallway, where Simson was flipping through my the coats in my coat closet. He paused at a bright magenta woollen one with obvious distaste.

"Oh, that one's nice and warm," I said. "Would you like—"

"No."

I noticed that his clothes were damp, no doubt from sitting in a warm car after being snowed on. My clothes were damp, too, but I didn't have a walk through the snow ahead of me.

A thought occurred to me, and I hurried to the laundry room, where I found what I was looking for: a pair of jeans and T-shirt from one of my nephews visiting a few months ago. I'd done his laundry after he'd spilled soda all over himself, and I had kept forgetting to return the clothing to him.

"Here," I said, returning to the hallway with the clothes slung over my arm. "You'll be much more comfortable in dry clothes."

"No, I'll be fine," he said, looking over a thick black coat.

"Going outside in wet things?" I scolded. "I don't think so! You'll catch your death of cold!"

"Look, I'm fine!"

"You are not fine!"

"I don't need them!"

"You will wear them!"

He was being stubborn, so I seized the shoulder of his damp shirt and shifted to half-form to make it disappear.

"HEY!" he screamed, grabbing the dry clothes from me.

But not before I'd seen.

"Why . . . do you have feathers on your chest?" I asked slowly.

"It's a costume," he snapped, yanking on my nephew's T-shirt with rapid speed.

"That is not a costume," I said. "That is a half-form."

"It's not a half-form," he said furiously. "I told you, I'm human."

"Then why do you have grey feathers?" I shot back. "What kind of were-bird are you? Why would you lie about that? What possible reason—"

I stopped abruptly. Everything fell still.

"Give me back my turning stone."

"It's not yours anymore. It belongs to the cuckoo clan."

"GIVE ME BACK MY TURNING STONE!"

"You weren't using it!" he snapped. "We need another one!"

"Then *buy* one! Do you desperately want a bunch of weredodos in your clan?!"

"We don't have to worry about that!" he yelled. "We can change any stone to cuckoo just by using it once! That's our magical ability!"

I felt like I was going to faint.

"Look, I'm sorry," he said, edging off to the side. "You've been really nice, and I appreciate that you let me come here so the cops wouldn't know where I live, but I've got to get going now."

"You were working with him all along," I said, hyperventilating. "You called that haltija to pick us up!"

"Only because you said you'd had a breakthrough!" he said defensively. "And then you wouldn't say what it was! I thought you were doing that thing where you gather all the suspects and then reveal who—"

"How did you call him without me noticing?!"

"I texted him!" he said, exasperated, pulling out his phone and wiggling it in front of me. "It's this newfangled invention that people your age really ought to learn how to—"

I lunged for the phone and grabbed it. I shifted to dodo, taking the phone with me, and then shifted back to half-form again.

"STOP STEALING MY THINGS!" Stormy yelled.

"I could say the same thing!" I shot back. "Now, do you really think the police can't use that phone to find you if I hand it to them?"

His face turned bright red. "Come on, lady! It was supposed to be a victimless crime!"

"Is that so?" I asked icily. "Speaking as one of your victims, you may have forgotten about the clan you were planning to destroy. Not to mention that little matter of the forcible abduction."

"I didn't know that guy was going to get violent!" Slater cried. "I just asked him to wait as an escape driver in case I needed it!"

"Astonishing," I said. "Imagine, a criminal getting violent."

"I only hired him in the first place because there was security at your clan leader's house! I was planning to nab the stone while she was on vacation. I didn't know she was going to hand it over to somebody who doesn't even lock the back door. As soon as I saw that I could just stroll in and grab it, I called the guy and told him I didn't need his help anymore. I didn't know he was going to improvise and steal somebody else's turning stone instead!"

So that meant my clan's turning stone had been the original target, and not an afterthought? In a sense, I was proud. It was nice that our clan had been valued, for once.

Of course, that didn't mean I was going to let him keep it.

"Turning stone," I said, pointing at the ground. "Or I will call the police. I'm sure they'd be delighted to have your phone."

"Maaaaaan," he complained, shifting to human form. A backpack bulged out of his shoulder, and he opened it to pull out a green, glowing stone. He thumped it on the floor and glowered at me. "You really don't fight fair, old bat."

"I am not a bat," I said. "I am a dodo."

And I was also a sleuth. One who had just saved my clan's turning stone.

" . . . And so you have it," I finished, passing a platter of cookies from Victoria to Anabel. "That's how I saved the day from that scoundrel named Silvester."

"You almost *ruined* the day by leaving the door unlocked," Victoria said sourly. She wasn't easy to please. "I can't believe I trusted you to watch over it."

"Oh, hush up," Anabel said, taking several cookies. She was the oldest of us and also the most energetic, despite being over eighty. She refused to retire. She taught yoga and enjoyed it too much. "It sounds like it would have been stolen anyway, and she saved it."

"But all the same, when I entrusted—!"

"I can't wait until my next case!" I broke in. There was no point in letting Victoria start soapboxing. "It's just a shame I don't have a magical ability. Like tracking magic! It would be so useful for all the sleuthing I'm going to do."

Anabel and Victoria exchanged looks.

"What?" I asked.

"You *have* a magical ability," Victoria said with exasperation.

"I do?"

"Yes! It's the same one we have!"

I stared at her blankly.

Anabel reached forward and dropped a cookie into thin air. It disappeared.

"Ohhhhhhhhhhhhhhhh!" I cried. "MY POCKET!"

I reached into my air pocket and pulled out my phone, my wallet, six notebooks, eight pens, two scribbled-on stacks of Post-It Notes, two phone bills, one utility bill, the gun that had gone missing after the accident, and my car keys.

I picked up the keys and dangled them in front of me.

"Another mystery solved!" I said triumphantly.

GOOD BOY

D. J. BUTLER

"Good boy," Fix said. He was the shorter of the two principals of the small jobber company known as the Protagonists. He was a muscular, bronze-skinned Kishi who carried an array of knives as well as a hatchet and a falchion hanging from his broad belt. He generally leaned on a spear, as he did now.

"Don't say that to him, he's not a dog." The poet Indrajit Twang was taller than his partner. He was similarly dressed in a kilt and broad belt, but his belt carried only the leaf-bladed sword he was so fond of. Indrajit's head was long and his face was divided in two by a bony nose ridge that pushed his eyes far out to the sides.

Fix shrugged. "He says it himself."

"I'm a Kyone. I look like a dog." Munahim wanted peace between his two bosses; his stomach curdled when they argued.

They argued a lot.

Fix shrugged. "And *you* look like a *fish*," he said to Indrajit.

Indrajit growled. "You see? You're just throwing fuel on the fire."

Munahim hunched down to hide from the poet's irritation. Since he was as tall as Indrajit, this didn't make him any less visible.

"There's no shame in your appearances," Fix said. "*I* look like an *ape*."

"Agh!" Indrajit clapped his hands to his ears. "Munahim, if you admit to looking like a dog again, I will let Fix here teach you how to read. I swear, by all your self-licking gods, that will ruin your life."

"I don't have self-licking gods," Munahim said mildly. "I could come with you."

"The only problem with that," Indrajit said, "is that you're terrible at lying."

Munahim hung his head. "Is lying so important?"

"Today it is," Indrajit told him. "We have to surprise this guy."

"So follow us at a distance," Fix said. "Bring your bow and that enormous sword and be prepared to intervene if something goes wrong."

"This should be simple," Indrajit added. "It's just an arrest. You're the backup, just in case."

Munahim nodded and his two bosses set out, crossing the mercantile bustle of the Spill and heading toward the stink of the Dregs. Munahim let them get a stone's throw ahead of him and then followed.

"I'm a Kyone," he said, mumbling to himself. "We don't have gods anymore. Not since we killed them." His long sword slapped comfortingly across his back and his quiver pressed snug against his thigh. Pushing his way through the sweaty crowd of the Crooked Mile, the longest street in the Spill, was easy with his long, muscular arms. He was a head taller than most men—other than men of the enormous races, of course, like the Luzzazza and the Grokonks and the sexless Gunds—and so was Indrajit, so following his bosses was an easy exercise in watching Indrajit's fish-like head bob along above the crowd.

Three camels burst from a courtyard into the street, bleating and kicking. The green-skinned, bug-eyed merchant who chased them cursed and struck at his beasts with a long-handled whisk. Munahim stopped while the animals were rounded up and then saw Indrajit's head again, now as a mere brownish-greenish dot.

He lengthened his stride to catch up.

He much preferred Kish to Ildarion, where he had spent several years trying to make a living. Ildarians were a tallish, pale, and rather bland race of men, and Ildarion was full of them. In Ildarion, Munahim stood out like a freak and collected constant stares. In Kish, decadent, old, rotten Kish, all thousand races of men mixed in a frothy, constant foam, and Munahim was far from the most unusual-looking fellow in almost any crowd.

Also, among the Protagonists, he was valued for his skills. Indrajit wished he were a better liar, but Munahim's bosses esteemed him as a tracker. Indrajit and Fix had hired him specifically for his sense of smell. The Ildarians had treated him as just a hired sword.

And as a Protagonist, he earned a share, not a wage. It made him feel much better about himself.

"Good boy," he said.

An arrest was a simple job for the Protagonists. Usually, their tasks involved policing merchants or ferreting out spies. When they contracted privately, they might do anything from bodyguard work to rescuing kidnapped maidens, but the fact that they were marching to arrest someone meant that their employer was Orem Thrush, the Lord Chamberlain.

Who paid less than other clients, generally, but provided a lot of work, as well as a certain amount of protection. In a city of mercenaries, it was good to have a patron.

Munahim's ancestors had killed their gods when the gods had become too demanding. They had given too little food and no shelter, and so Kyone heroes of the time had risen up. They had slain the gods, shattering the pack, and forming a new pack, of only Kyones. Naturally, out of gratitude and prudence, Munahim and his people reverenced their victorious ancestors, remembering them with short invocations and averting their wrath with simple charms.

"Much better than having gods."

He could see Indrajit and Fix, and he could, just barely, smell them. Time and distance were not the complicating factors in smelling his bosses; the challenge was the roiling sea of mankind that bubbled around them, concealing the distinctive odor of each man beneath a mask of cinnamon, roasting fish, camel's dung, perfume, and a hundred other smells.

Two Kishi men slapped a wooden crate into the middle of the road just a few paces in front of Munahim, and a bawdy show sprang into being around them. Actors in masks and togas swarmed the low stand, and two bang-harp players plopped themselves right into Munahim's path.

This was a bit like the games his sire, Garuna, had played with him when he had been a boy on the King of Thunder Steppes, leaving young Munahim behind the pack and ordering him not to follow until the sun set. Garuna would then deliberately confuse the scent by provoking elk and deer into crossing the trail, or would march the pack in circles.

Munahim always found the pack.

Indrajit and Fix passed through the gate into the Dregs. The Dregs could not obviously be said to be the worst part of Kish, but only because it had serious competition. The Dregs' claim was that it was the zone with the most street-robbery, purse-cutting, throat-slitting, street-walking, and daylight assault. The Lee probably offered more burglary, and the Spill more usury, but those were less colorful crimes.

Munahim gripped his bow tight. He was tempted to put an arrow to the string just in case, but that would draw attention.

From gate to gate, the passage across the Dregs was a brief march, *cutting the short corner*, as it was sometimes named by locals. To *cut the long corner* was to march the direct route across the Dregs from the Spill to the Crown. The Dregs proper, sometimes called the Filth, was the half of the Dregs with no gate, and which no casual traveler had any reason to enter, ever. Only desperation ever brought anyone into the Flith.

Munahim avoided looking toward the Filth. He spat on the packed earth to flush the thought of the place from his heart, and then Indrajit and Fix finished cutting the short corner, moving down the filthy slope of the Dregs, and passed through the gate into the East Flats.

Munahim didn't meet the gaze of the jobbers working the gate. He didn't recognize them, but there were far too many jobbers in Kish for him to know them all. Half of this crew were Xiba'albi with their characteristic obsidian-edged swords, which was in itself curious; Xiba'albi were rarely jobbers, and though Xiba'alba was not distant, its people were an uncommon sight in Kish. Tensions with the Ildarians, or perhaps the blandishments of the Free Cities, kept most Xiba'albi from making it this far.

Or perhaps they simply didn't like to travel.

There was a commotion on the other side of the gate. Munahim heard the clash of metal and thudding sounds. He edged forward, in case his bosses were falling afoul of violence, but two of the Xiba'albi stepped into his path before he could pass through, one raising a forbidding palm and the other hefting his stone-bladed club.

Munahim didn't have to stand on tip-toes to look over the jobbers' heads. He still couldn't make out the source of the noise, but saw tall Rover wagons, one painted with some kind of winged Ylakka on its side and another featuring an intricate pattern of interlocking snails. The images were different for every wagon; Munahim thought they represented the Rovers' ancestral totems, something closer to the spirits his own people reverenced than to the gods whose temples clung to the Spike at the top of Kish.

He tapped his booted foot impatiently on the packed earth, but less than a minute passed before a wordless whoop came from the other side of the gate. The Rover wagons continued onward, rolling south, and the Xiba'albi stepped aside.

Munahim jogged through, onto the East Flats.

This was one of Kish's three coast-hugging slums. All three were plagued by the stink of fish, sweat, and cheap beer. The hard-packed earth of the Dregs gave way to churned mud, sometimes alleviated by layers of straw strewn on top, or, around the least repulsive taverns and warehouses, sagging boardwalks.

The ground beneath Munahim's feet descended slightly, along roads running north, east, and south. The slope and his height gave him an excellent vantage point, but no matter how he strained, he could no longer see Indrajit's bobbing head.

His heart sank.

But no matter; he sniffed.

He caught the faint scent of both men. The trail was slightly confusing and he stalked in a tight circle as he tried to follow it, enduring the hard jostling of a scab-eyed Gund and the jeers of a pack of gray-skinned Visps. The scent of his bosses mixed with the thick smell of rotting fish and with the smoke-and-spices smell that clung to every Rover wagon, but he eventually found a trail that emerged from the noxious cloud and ran east.

He took a deep breath, and felt fear fall away like a discarded cloak.

None too soon. "Get moving," one of the Xiba'albi growled.

Munahim growled back, without words, and loped down toward the water.

The smell of his bosses was faint. There was a faint breeze, now that he was outside the city's walls. Perhaps that was causing the dispersal of the scent. Or perhaps the waves of brine and fish smells were covering up the more subtle odors of musk and sweat. He quickened his pace; he'd be more comfortable once he had the other Protagonists in sight again.

The smell disappeared and he doubled back, walking in a small circle through a crowded intersection. Stooping to sniff at the ground didn't make the scent any clearer, but after a few spins around the well through a grumbling crowd, he caught a whiff off to the north and he followed it.

He didn't dare run. He was the back-up force, the hidden reserve. It was a role he'd played before. His sense of smell let him stay out of sight so that forces watching for pursuit didn't see him until too late.

Only now it seemed that he might become separated from Indrajit and Fix by the sea breeze, and arrive when it was too late for the Protagonists.

Except, of course, that he was just the backup. He might not even be needed. Indrajit and Fix were good fighters, competent and clever, so they would probably be all right even if Munahim got lost along the way.

"You're not lost, though," he mumbled. "You're still on the trail. Good boy."

And then the scent was gone.

Munahim shook his head. He hadn't even passed an intersection. He stopped and looked at the buildings around him: a net weaver, a ropemaker, a seller of sailcloth, a shipwright, two leaning taverns, a leatherworker, three buildings that might be residences.

He traced his steps back until suddenly he smelled Indrajit and Fix again. He sniffed at the air and prowled up and down the straw-stamped street, examining the scents of the doorways.

No sign that his bosses had gone into any of the buildings.

Had he turned wrong back at the last intersection? Was he following a phantom scent? He snorted, clearing his nostrils.

The street was packed with foot traffic and a small number of beasts of burden. Munahim crept back the other direction again, sniffing each person and animal. A stray Grokonk Third honked at him and a four-legged Shamb hissed, its tongue slithering over sharp yellow teeth.

Then Munahim sniffed the heavy leather sacks strapped across the back of a two-humped Drogger, and smelled his bosses.

The Drogger plodded at the end of a lead string held by a thin-bearded Zalapting. Munahim stepped past the good-natured beast and hoisted the little Zalapting into the air with one hand.

The Zalapting squealed. "I'll call the constables!"

"I'm on the job myself," Munahim said. "What have you got in the bags?"

"I don't have to show you!" The Zalapting's feet scrabbled at the air and found no purchase. "You don't have a warrant!"

"I can get one." Munahim wasn't actually sure how to go about that, but he thought Grit Wopal, the Lord Chamberlain's chief spy, could probably arrange it. Maybe the arrest papers Indrajit and Fix carried even included a warrant. Kyones had very simple ideas about law, which did not include written court orders. Mostly, for any important issue, the pack considered, the pack debated, and the pack came to a decision. Once in a while, a fight was necessary. "Do you want to come with me up to the Crown to sort it out?"

"Beans!" the Zalapting cried. "You can look, it's just beans!"

Munahim set the lavender-skinned man down and undid the clasps. Opening the sacks, he found that they were indeed full of dried beans.

Except that, in the top of one sack, atop white beans the size of his thumbnail, he found two kilts, a leaf-bladed broadsword, and a pile of other weapons: three knives, a hatchet, and a falchion.

He knew these weapons by sight as the ones Indrajit and Fix carried everywhere, except that Fix's spear was missing. And by smell, he knew instantly that he was looking at his bosses' kilts.

"Frozen hells," he muttered. His people didn't have any profanity, so he borrowed Indrajit's favorite curse.

"See?" the Zalapting snapped. "All I have is beans!"

Munahim dragged out the kilts and weapons. "Then these must belong to someone else."

The Zalapting paled to a pinkish shade. "Yes. Those aren't mine. I don't know where they came from."

Munahim could smell fear on the Zalapting. He wished he could smell lying, but he was pretty certain the little man was telling the truth. Without another word, he took his bosses' gear and marched back the way he'd come.

The pungent odor of the sweat-impregnated kilts, the tang of the metal, the thickness of the cured wood in the ax's handle, and the oiled leathers of the various scabbards, made a heady bouquet. Twice Munahim plunged his face into the mass. Didn't he need to remind himself of what Indrajit and Fix smelled like?

But he was blocking other scents from reaching him. With an effort of will, he balled the fabric and weapons up and clenched the mass under his left arm, the right holding his bow.

He forced himself to think.

Indrajit and Fix might have been stripped of their gear and diverted at any point along the path he had walked. But he had last seen them at the gate connecting the Dregs to the East Flats, where he had been forced to stop and wait for the passage of Rover wagons. And there had been a commotion. And then, when Munahim had finally emerged from the gate, they had been gone.

He had followed their scent, but it seemed likely that he had followed the scent of their kilts, stuffed after the hubbub into the sack on the Drogger's back. Probably without the bean-merchant even knowing.

The commotion he had heard at the gate. Wasn't it likely that had been the sound of the two senior Protagonists being beaten and spirited away?

He broke into a determined trot, all his accouterments clanking and swishing as he ran. Whom had Indrajit and Fix set out to arrest? If he knew that, Munahim could go to that person and seize him. Maybe make a trade.

Except that Indrajit and Fix had many enemies. Not to mention professional rivals. Gannon's Handlers might have seized them, or the secret agents of one of Orem Thrush's rivals, or the heirs of some merchant criminal they had previously arrested or overthrown.

And in any case, Munahim didn't know whom they sought to capture.

He stopped just below the gate. The jobbers had changed.

He now wished he had noticed the uniforms on the other jobbers; he closed his eyes and tried to remember, but he was much better at noticing and remembering smells than visual images. His memory conjured up the raw-meat smell of Xiba'albi, and even the specific odors of the man with the raised palm and his companion hefting his club, but not the color of what they had been wearing.

But these men were not Xiba'albi. Ukelings, Karthing, and Yuchaks, with a single scaly, four-legged Shamb. Munahim made himself look and notice the black tunics they wore. They were a jobber company, and not in the permanent employ of one of the great families.

He approached a mailed Karthing with two long swords strapped to his back. The man stood slightly apart from the rest of the company, leaning against the wall and chewing dip weed as he watched the crowd.

"Excuse me." Munahim tried his most polite words. "Could you please tell me who were the jobbers here earlier today?"

The Karthing shook his blond, shaggy head. "No other jobbers here today. Just us."

"There were Xiba'albi," Munahim said mildly.

The Karthing bellied forward, pushing into Munahim with his torso like a bull and knocking him back. "Wrong. We were here all day. Bjurn's Bruisers, under contract with the Lord Archer."

"There's been a mistake," Munahim said.

"Yes." The Karthing nodded. "And you made it. And if you keep insisting, that will be your second mistake. I'm Bjurn, and I don't let people make three mistakes."

Munahim hesitated. Bjurn was lying, and they both knew it. Did that mean that he had conspired with whoever had seized Indrajit and Fix?

But he didn't have to have conspired very much. Maybe all he did was order his men to stand aside for a short time while the Xiba'albi watched the gate. That was a very ordinary sort of corruption in Kish, looking the other way.

But however much the Bruisers had conspired, that definitely meant that the Xiba'albi had been where they hadn't belonged.

Munahim scratched his nose to hide the fact that he was sniffing. The trail he wanted wasn't here.

"My mistake," he said. "You're right. I was thinking of a different gate."

Bjurn grunted. Munahim drooped his shoulders, trying to look unthreatening, and walked through the gate. The Ukelings and Karthings jeered at him, but the Yuchaks stared warily; like the Ildarians, their lands bordered on the King of Thunder Steppes, and they may have had dealings with Kyones before.

Munahim slouched and dropped his chin.

On the far side of the gate, he smelled the trail he was seeking: Xiba'albi, half a dozen of them, crossing the Dregs and marching up into the Crown. This was the third leg of the main thoroughfares traversing the Dregs, and was sometimes referred to as *walking it straight*. Munahim walked it straight now, climbing steeply from the lowest, most rotting section of Kish through its most heavily-defended gate (by a wall of blue Luzzazza holding spears and glaring), and into the part of the city where all the most wealthy and noble citizens lived.

The Crown. He smelled fruit and blossoms and delicate perfumes, and no sign of Indrajit and Fix. He felt a hard, cold knot in the pit of his stomach, but at least he could still smell the Xiba'albi.

He followed the trail.

They marched due west to the edge of the Spike. There, under the looming knuckled rock and the lurching temples of the city's five gods, they turned left. They stuck strictly to the boulevards, the widest streets where the traffic flow was heavy but the channel of traffic was unimpeded. Munahim had moved fast and was moving fast still, and yet he didn't see them. Had they let him move through the gate and then immediately turned and raced this direction? They must have, to have gained such a headstart.

And then, suddenly, the smell of them grew stronger.

Munahim stopped and sniffed. He stood near the mouth of an alley, a narrow, cobbled lane that separated two large brick palaces from each other. Beyond the alley, a flower vendor shouted names and prices beside his green-varnished wooden cart. Across the street, another cart-merchant hawked tea. Two ladies in togas carrying parasols stood and sipped wooden cups of the steaming beverage.

The Xiba'albi were waiting in the alleyway. Munahim was certain of it. He could smell the wood of their clubs and hear their breathing.

Had they detected him yet, or were they waiting for him to pass in front of the alley?

He backed away, watching the alley's mouth. A blue-uniformed doorman in front of the palace aimed a kick at him, but Munahim bit back a growl and kept moving until he had reached the edge of the building.

Then he slipped around behind. Crossing a fountained plaza at the back of the building, he crept up the far end of the alleyway, toward six Xiba'albi at the mouth. The Xiba'albi crouched together, staring out into the street. They were obscured from view on the boulevard by a pile of garbage timbers, and they held their stone-edged clubs in their hands, muttering to each other.

Munahim looked for a place to hide. There were balconies which would have afforded an excellent view of the alley and the plaza both, but they were on the second story or higher, and he was a very ordinary climber. But all along the base of a pink-brick-built palace clustered a thick hedge of bushes with broad, dark green leaves and white berries. He pushed himself into the hedge and waited.

Long minutes passed. Had he made the wrong choice? Was there a better scent he should be following, a scent that was now growing cold because he had wasted his time pursuing these Xiba'albi thugs?

But they did seem to be waiting for him.

His skin began to itch, where it was pressed against the leaves. He sniffed, but the smell of the bushes told him nothing.

And then he saw that the skin of his arms and shoulders, where the leaves pressed against it, was red and raw. Blistering, in fact.

Blister-berry bush.

"Frozen hells," he muttered.

And then the Xiba'albi moved.

Munahim froze. The itch immediately seemed to swell ten times in effect. He felt as if his arms and shoulders were aflame. He wanted to burst from the hedge, rush forward, and hurl himself into the fountain, scratching his skin furiously.

He held still, and managed not to whimper.

Four of the Xiba'albi stood and walked in his direction. Munahim held his breath and prepared to draw an arrow, but they passed him, entering into the mouth of another alleyway and disappearing.

He took a deep breath. "Good boy."

The other two settled back into their vigil. Munahim waited a few minutes and then crept from the bush. His skin was patched red and raw, and wept in several places from open, blistering sores. Resisting the urge to leap into the water, he peered after the four departed Xiba'albi; they had gone, disappeared around a bend in the little side street they had taken.

He laid down Indrajit's and Fix's gear and his own bow beside the fountain, drew his long sword, and slunk toward the two men lying in wait.

The sword could be used with either one hand or two. Munahim was no sword brother, but years of fighting for Ildarian marcher barons against other Ildarians, Yuchak men's societies, Karthing raiding parties, and the wagon nomads of the Steppes had made him a proficient swordsman, and maybe even a good one.

He didn't want to kill the men, though. He wanted them to lead him to Indrajit and Fix.

He crept up with silent steps. Both men faced away from him. The nearer squatted and leaned forward, poised almost on all fours to stay low and in the shadow. The farther stood, pressing himself against the pink-brick wall.

Munahim slammed a boot down on the back of the croucher's neck, to pin him to the cobbles. The man squealed. At the same time, Munahim raised his long sword, gripped in both hands and prepared to slash downward. It was a pose he had found terrible and frightening when he had seen other warriors adopt it.

"Hold!" he snarled.

But the Xiba'albi did not hold.

The man beneath Munahim's boot rolled sideways. He gasped for breath and choked, but his move was abrupt and swift. Munahim had put his weight on the Xiba'albi's neck to pin him, and the sudden removal of his footing sent Munahim stumbling back.

Instead of gripping his sword heroically in two hands, preparing to slash, he now found himself juggling and trying to catch it.

The second Xiba'albi leaped forward, swinging his club.

Xiba'albi clubs were made of a heavy hard wood that didn't grow in Kish itself, sometimes called ironwood. The wood alone made the clubs lethal, and this club was swung with all the force of a leaping Ylakka. Staggering backward, Munahim lurched out of the way of the first blow, and then the second.

And then he backed into a brick wall.

Beyond his attacker, he saw the other Xiba'albi rise to his feet, drawing stone knives. The warrior with the club bent his elbow, preparing to swing again.

But the wall gathered the force of Munahim's motion and hurled him back the other way. He missed his catch, and winced at the loud rattle his sword made, clanging onto the cobblestones. But abruptly, he was within the Xiba'albi warrior's guard and moving forward.

He seized the man by the wrist and spun him. Munahim was taller and stronger, and he used his body as a lever, winging the short fighter and his club into a circle.

The Xiba'albi with two knives ran forward, directly into the stone blades of his friend's club.

Munahim released his grip. The knife-wielder dropped to his knees, suddenly headless. The man with the club spun once more in a circle as he tried to catch his balance; Munahim used the spare moments to regain his own poise, scoop, and pick up his blade.

The dead man's head thudded to the cobblestones behind him.

Beyond the Xiba'albi, on the boulevard, someone was screaming. Constables, which was to say, whichever jobbers currently had the contract for law and order in the Crown, would arrive shortly.

"Tell me where Indrajit and Fix are," Munahim said. "Otherwise, I cannot let you live."

It was a direct statement and without deceit, befitting a Kyone. The Xiba'albi roared and charged.

The Xiba'albi club was hard and sharp, but Munahim's sword was longer, and so were his arms. He stabbed the Xiba'albi through his neck, then wiped the blood off his blade on the man's kilt and ran.

He sheathed his sword, snatched up his bow and his bosses' things from beside the fountain, and charged down the alleyway after the other four Xiba'albi jobbers.

Four men left a strong enough scent to follow at a dead run, but he didn't want to run into an ambush, so Munahim sprinted only for a minute and then stopped to look around. He wasn't being followed, that he could see, so he continued his pursuit.

He exited the Crown into the Lee. The Lee was home to racetracks and high-end brothels and wealthy merchants, and Munahim expected the tracks of the Xiba'albi to rush right through and out into the Caravanserai, the giant, permanent tent-city beyond Kish's south wall.

Instead, the scent-trail of the men turned left, and then abruptly ended at the door of a brick rectangle. The rectangle sat at one corner of a rough triangle, smashed up against a two-story tall inn that leaned outward in three directions, and a building split between a clothier and a cooper. The other two buildings had windows and balconies, but the rectangle was a solid mass like a single brick, the only distinguishing feature of which was a slightly recessed door.

In the street beside the rectangle waited three Rover wagons. Two Rover men stood between the first two wagons, slowly playing some card game on the foremost wagon's tailboard. Each man had two pistols tucked into the sash at his waist. Munahim was unsure exactly how the pistols worked, except that there was part on top of them that had to be moved before firing, a part that made a loud click. Sometimes they required more preparation than that, but sometimes they didn't, and it was safest to assume the latter.

Each wagon was pulled by a single horse. The images on the sides of two of the vehicles looked familiar; Munahim squinted and tried to think. Snails and a winged lizard. His memory was tied to smells more than images, and he couldn't quite remember his connection with these vehicles.

But then the wind shifted and the scent of the wagons came to his nostrils. He had smelled this mixture of smoke, spice, sweat, and dung before, in the gate between the Dregs and the East Flats.

These wagons had blocked him off from following Indrajit and Fix.

He sniffed, concentrated, and found a faint odor of his two bosses on the wagons. They weren't in the wagons now, but they had been.

He faded back around the corner, pressing himself against the wall behind a cart piled high with lychee fruit. He tried to think. Someone had seized Indrajit and Fix. Whoever it was had expected that Indrajit and Fix would have backup and had twice taken steps to stop that backup from coming to the rescue: with the blocked gate, and then with the Xiba'albi rear guard.

Did those enemies know that the backup consisted only of Munahim? They might, because they had marked out a false trail with his bosses' kilts, as if they expected someone with a good sense of smell to be following. On the other hand, they might have been marking out that trail to mislead someone following with more magical powers, a witch or a scryer of some kind.

And if they had thought that Munahim alone was following, wouldn't they have simply seized him at the gate, too?

On balance, it seemed likely that the kidnappers expected a rescue attempt, but didn't know that Munahim was the whole reserve force.

Munahim considered plans, and found that he hated all of them.

He could climb onto the roof of the building, but there was no guarantee that there was an entrance into the building from above, and every likelihood of attracting attention in the climb.

He could find a privy or a basement nearby and try to let himself into the labyrinth that ran beneath the city, but it would take him time to find such an entrance, and there was no guarantee that the rectangular building could be accessed from below.

He entertained the idea of lighting the door on fire, but if there were an exit underground, the kidnappers would likely simply take it and flee. Also, the Rovers might simply put the fire out. Also, if the fire did burn the building down, it might kill Indrajit and Fix in the process.

He had no reinforcements to summon; he *was* the reinforcements.

Munahim dropped his bundle at the street corner and bought a lamp with a clipped quarter of an Imperial. The vendor, a portly Zalapting, ostentatiously filled the clay vessel with oil before handing it over. Munahim shifted his bow into his left hand to take the lamp in his right. "Will you light this?"

"Are you crazy?" The Zalapting gestured at the empty sky. "It's broad daylight!"

Munahim nodded. "Please."

He brushed past a pair of Pelthites and a Kishi beggar rounding the corner again. The Rovers didn't even look up until Munahim hurled his lamp against the side of the first wagon. The clay shattered, the oil splashed across the brightly-painted wood, and the men cursed.

By the time they turned their attention to Munahim, he had an arrow to the string of his bow and was aiming at the larger of the two men.

"I hope you will get in your wagons and leave," Munahim said. "Put the fire out, go away, mind your own business. I will only kill you if I have to."

The big Rover snarled, his thick mustachios curling up in hatred, and tried to draw his pistols. Munahim shot him in the heart and he dropped.

The second Rover raised his hands. "There's a bucket of sand inside the wagon," he said. "Let me put the fire out, and then I'll leave."

"Pistols on the ground first," Munahim said.

The Rover laid down his guns. He climbed onto the tailboard and disappeared into the back of the wagon.

Click.

Munahim loosed his second arrow, shooting through the wagon's wall. He heard a cry, but he shot again and again, jogging to his right as he shot until he could see into the open back of the wagon. The Rover had three arrows in his chest, but was still trying feebly to raise a long musket to fire at Munahim.

Munahim pulled the Rover's feet out from under him. He crashed to the boards, and Munahim tossed the musket across the street.

Startled passersby looked once, then averted their eyes and fled.

Welcome to Kish, Indrajit would say. *Mind your own business.*

"I told you to leave," Munahim said.

Munahim gathered his bosses' things and his own bow into a bundle and tucked it under his left arm, holding his sword in his right hand. The door into the building was heavy, and it didn't budge when he tested it; barred. There was no peephole. He could apply fire, or hack away at the wood with Fix's ax, but either method would take much more time than he felt he had.

He knocked politely.

The door opened. He was surprised that it did, but he was poised and prepared, so when the door pulled in a crack and a pale face appeared in the gap, he kicked the door in.

Alarmed shouts rose from behind the door. Munahim threw his bundle into the open doorway and charged in.

The pale man drew a dagger. Munahim slapped it out of his grip with an open hand and then bashed the man in his forehead, knocking him to the ground. The man tried once more to rise, and Munahim stomped on his chest.

That left him still and whimpering.

Munahim was in a small cloakroom. Boots stood in pairs on the floor, and heavy gloves lay in pairs on a shelf, and canvas smocks hung from pegs. The air was thick with motes and the floor was covered with grains that felt metallic under the soles of his boots and added crunch to every step.

Two steps brought him over the body of the pale man to the cloakroom exit. A Gund loomed up in the doorway. It was a civilized Gund, with four of its six eyes gouged out to prevent the madness that overcame the wild members of the tribe. It grabbed for Munahim's throat with its two hands, while the thicket of insectoid limbs sprouting from its shoulders reached out and groped toward him, too.

Munahim lowered his shoulder and slammed it into the Gund's sternum. The Gund stumbled backward, but its bug-legs snapped sideways and caught the doorframe, keeping it from falling. The Gund grabbed Munahim by the throat, cutting off all his air instantly. With its enormous muscles, it would crush Munahim's larynx in seconds.

Munahim bit the Gund's wrist, hard.

The Gund pulled his hand back, and Munahim bit harder. He felt his teeth rip through sinew and vein, plowing ragged furrows across the bone itself. The Gund tore itself free, shrieking. It grabbed its left wrist with its right hand.

Munahim still feared the bug-legs. He stepped in toward the Gund again, swinging his long sword in a two-handed sweep that sliced off all the legs on one side. Yellow pools of lamplight and deep brown shadows dappled the Gund as it staggered away, and Munahim threw back his head to howl.

It was an instinctive move, not a planned one. But in the boxy space he entered now, he heard his own war cry echo with great satisfaction.

The building was a single large room. Scaffolding created a mezzanine floor of thick timbers, and heavy tables lay in two parallel lines across the floor. The thick air made Munahim's eyes water and his nose twitch, but he could still see Indrajit and Fix lying side by side on a table, perfectly still, naked, surrounded by a knot of men.

Two Xiba'albi warriors charged.

Munahim leaped left, putting himself out of reach of one of the warriors and keeping both warriors between himself and the rest of the men. He slid his long sword neatly under the arm of the Xiba'albi, between two ribs. The man sank without launching a blow, bloody foam erupting from his lips. When the second Xiba'albi bent his path to try to return and attack Munahim, Munahim snarled at him; the Xiba'albi dropped his club and fled.

Munahim surveyed the scene, his sword up in a two-handed guard position. The Gund lay weeping in the corner. The blood that flowed from its wounds was soaked up by the crystal grains on the floor, which swelled as they drank the liquid. Two Xiba'albi warriors remained, clubs trembling slightly in their grip, and behind them stood a dark-skinned man in a long silk tunic and silk pants. The toes of his shoes curled upward and back, and he wore a short cylindrical cap. He held an open vial in one hand.

The Xiba'albi and the man in silk all stood on the near side of the long tables.

"I am from Togu," the man in silk said.

"Are you a sorcerer?" Munahim snarled.

"Yes."

"Are you deadly and evil?" Munahim growled, snapping his teeth for emphasis.

"I am deadly. Evil is a matter of—"

"Are you prepared to die?" Munahim roared.

"Beware, dog-man," the sorcerer murmured. He raised the vial over his head as if he might throw it.

"I am a Kyone," Munahim said. "I do not lie and I do not fear."

"You are not the first Kyone I have known."

"Your Rovers are dead," Munahim continued, "and their wagons burn. Your Xiba'albi are dead, or broken in spirit."

"You do not frighten me," the sorcerer insisted.

The two remaining Xiba'albi drifted slightly apart, creating an open avenue between Munahim and the sorcerer.

Indrajit stirred, raising one arm slightly.

So Munahim's bosses still lived.

"Your Gund is crippled," he said. "Do you think your little glass bottle is going to stop me?"

"What do you want?" the sorcerer asked. "Money?"

"I am a Kyone," Munahim said. "I do not negotiate."

"So you want a *lot* of money, then."

"I cannot be bought."

"You have no sense of humor," the sorcerer grumbled. "Don't mistake that for heroism."

Munahim roared and leaped at the nearest of the two remaining Xiba'albi. He didn't raise his club fast enough and took a deep slashing wound across the forearm. He staggered away sideways, and he and the other Xiba'albi raced for the exit, nearly knocking each other over in the process.

Munahim raised his sword back into guard position. "Ha ha."

The sorcerer still held his bottle high. Did it contain an acid? A poison? Some sort of Druvash transformation magic? Munahim was loath to turn his back on the sorcerer, but Indrajit was just beginning to stir and Fix still lay catatonic.

"You're not the hero," the sorcerer said. "You are interfering with justice."

"And you are interfering with my pack."

"Leave now," the sorcerer said, "or this potion will kill you all."

Munahim threw his sword. It was not a throw that might impale the sorcerer; the weapon was far too big for that. But neither was it an awkward, spinning throw. The weapon was balanced and Munahim was experienced and he hurled his weapon with sudden force, sending the pommel straight at the sorcerer's face.

The sorcerer ducked, and Munahim leaped forward.

The long sword flew across the room, over the tables, missing the sorcerer. The sorcerer dropped into a crouch, and Munahim grabbed his wrist with both hands, slamming his forearm against the table.

The sorcerer screamed, and Munahim grabbed the bottle. Thick smoke rose from the vial's glass, which was hot to the touch. Munahim ripped the bottle free and threw it into the corner of the room.

Boom!

Smoke and flame erupted from the vial. The Gund bellowed—had Munahim hit it with the sorcerer's potion? Munahim felt all the air drawn from his lungs in one whoosh and he fell down, choking.

Blackness.

Munahim opened his eyes. His ears rang and his lungs hurt. He smelled smoke and heard coughing.

He stood and found himself still inside the rectangular building. Indrajit was lowering himself from the table to the floor, coughing fiercely. Fix was attempting to roll over, but having difficulty moving.

He could now see that both his bosses were bruised and bloodied.

And Munahim realized that he was coughing, too.

His eyes watered from the smoke. Scaffolding along two of the walls burned.

The Gund lay scorched and still. The sorcerer was gone.

"Munahim." Indrajit retched, trying to talk. "Who was that?"

"I don't know." Munahim found and sheathed his sword and then grabbed Fix. Breathing was difficult, but he managed to sling the smallest Protagonist over his shoulder. "They said they wanted justice."

"They meant revenge," Indrajit said.

Munahim grunted.

"Believe it or not," Indrajit said, "that dandy from Togu isn't even the man we set to arrest. We still have work to do."

Munahim nodded. "I'm ready."

"My sword?" Indrajit asked. "And, uh, kilt?"

"By the door." Munahim pointed.

Indrajit nodded and limped toward the exit. "Good boy," he said. "Good boy."

SIDEKICKS

RAY DALEY

LITTLE DID I KNOW during that Tuesday lunchtime, what would go on to be known as "One man Wednesday" was about to happen. While I could have easily predicted the hangovers, maybe a few cookies tossed, it was nothing close to what actually occurred.

ONE MAN WEDNESDAY.

NORMALLY IT WAS the four of us: Canine and his three Bicuspids. Obviously, he was the superhero. We were but his loyal sidekicks, there to support him if the need ever arose.

It rarely did, so we'd hang around on the sidelines, grabbing the odd partially-conscious villain and keeping them out of the way while the mighty Canine mopped up the rest of the bad guys.

However, not that day. All thanks to Taco Tuesday.

"No thanks, Boss. I'm trying to become a vegetarian. Those things have so much oil, too. You should get your cholesterol checked. You're in the ideal danger zone for a heart attack." It shouldn't have been a heart attack which worried me so much. The boss wasn't exactly scrupulous in his kitchen hygiene.

When the call came, the other two Bicuspids were all being sick into the bath. The Canine had already claimed the toilet at six AM, and so far he

123

hadn't been able to leave. From what little I could understand between bouts of copious vomiting, he assumed it was food poisoning.

Seeing the other Bicuspids, I was fairly sure he was correct in his diagnosis. I had already cracked open the bathroom window and left the shower running on cold. They might start feeling better in about twelve hours but the hotline was ringing there and then.

WHAT TO DO?

IF THE GOOD people of Oracle City are in need, their heroes are there for them.

Well, this one was. The police had given me all the details, armed robbery in progress, at least ten weapons confirmed, number of robbers unknown. Faced with possibly overwhelming odds, I did what any good sidekick left on their own would do. I called for the cavalry.

THE POLICE WERE LESS than enthralled to see me arriving on my own. "Bicuspid number three! Where's the Canine?"

I grinned. "Being violently sick. Has been for the last few hours, and is likely to be for several more. As are the other Bicuspids, before you ask me. I've put a call in to the Fox, but his sidekick the Midge informed me he's currently out cold on sleeping tablets. Don't worry, he'll make a full recovery in the next few days, but he'll spend that time wishing he hadn't. The Midge is on his way right now. In the meantime, you've got me. So what's the situation?"

Their chief inspector was the one who finally came out to speak to me. "The Canine isn't coming then?"

I shook my head. "Afraid not. I'm here, though. How can I help?"

The chief inspector hemmed and hawed. He wasn't used to dealing with anyone below the rank of superhero.

I took the lead, knowing he'd keep us there all day otherwise. "Listen. If the Canine were here, you'd be taking his orders, yes? And if he gave me those orders to give to you, you'd be taking orders from me, right? So why don't we just pretend he's here and I'm giving the orders in his stead. Put ten men behind the building so they can't take the back way out. I want ten more to storm the place with me, ideally big lads, if you've got any rugby players?"

The Midge turned up just as we were putting the last of the gang into a black Maria. I greeted him with a smile. "How's your boss? I think I'm going to need you on speed dial for the next few days, okay?"

Between us, we foiled half a dozen crimes that day.

A total of eight crimes were foiled the next day, operating as a duo. Bicuspid Three and the Midge. It didn't have a very good ring. I can't say that was the only reason I started calling myself Dentine Dan. It was nicely alliterative, certainly a good deal better than Bicuspid Three.

Over the four days following the food poisoning incident, the Midge and I began to make something of a name for ourselves. People realised we weren't just mere sidekicks, there to mop up crime scenes after the fact. We were just as good as the superheroes we normally came along with.

One chap from the Associated News even said we were better. "You boys are certainly making hay while the sun shines! What are you going to do when your superheroes are finally well enough to get back into the fray again?"

Frankly, it was a damn good question. We hadn't been stupid about turning down rewards. Oh no, we accepted all of those with gratitude. That was fast becoming our rainy day fund, because we knew any day now, the sky was about to open up on us.

SIX DAYS. THAT'S HOW LONG WE GOT.

THE CANINE HAD FINALLY WASHED the smell of puke and shit out of his second-best costume. The other Bicuspids were confident they could go out without needing the toilet every two minutes.

So I got the Midge on the phone. "Listen, Bob," I said, because I knew his true identity, "our gravy train has finally reached the station. What say you and I team up? Neither of us is the superhero, we split the money fifty-fifty. After all, we've already made quite a nice chunk of change this last week. We can let the police know where to find us. I just happen to know of a recently abandoned lair coming up for sale. The owners are desperate to get rid of it, we might be able to get it on the cheap. I'm told it comes with all the accoutrements too. We can keep our individual names for now, until we come up with a name for our duo. What do you say, Bob?"

FIFTY BUSTS LATER, I'm really glad he said yes. Frankly, I couldn't have faced back going into the Dental Surgery again. While it was a nice place to call home, I had always wanted to set out into business for myself. With the Midge, we're now doing exactly that. I'm sure given time, I can come up with a better moniker than Dentine Dan and finally sever all my former connections to the Canine and his remaining Bicuspids.

The Midge and I get our fair share of business, not just from the police either. The general public had almost a week of seeing us all over the county, keeping the place safe for right-minded people. We've opened three supermarkets, one fête, and two libraries so far. We're doing a talk on crime prevention in the local youth centre tomorrow.

I think we'll be able to get on fine in the superhero business, especially now the Midge has come up with the perfect name for our dynamic duo.

JUST CALL US THE SIDEKICKS!

A SHOPPE-ING TRIP

JAMES IVAN HUGHES

KELLIX, familiar to Eomund the Apprentice, pulled his cowl down, revealing his wrinkled, nearly bald head. His tiny, three-fingered hands fluffed up the stuffed burlap bag that he used as a pillow. He leaned back with a groan, resting on his nest of rags and belongings in the curved foot of the banister.

He frowned at a cat-sized, six-legged lizard that ran in circles in the corner. Faerix the Salamander puffed smoke and sparks from his nostrils as he spun, six feet flailing and tail whipping about.

Kellix shrugged at Faerix's antics. "Hopeless creature." He resumed settling himself into a comfortable position. He patted at several of the many pockets in his robe.

After some fumbling, he withdrew a thin, dark gray stick. Small indentations dotted one end of it, and as he held it, a glow came from within. He sighed with contentment. Wriggling deeper into his nest, he gnawed at the end of the mana stick. Delicious!

CRACK!

The end of the snack snapped off in his mouth. Kellix nearly choked on the fragment, and leapt to his feet with a curse.

Eomund the Apprentice towered over him, holding the rest of the mana stick between thumb and forefinger. Eomund's usually dour face was distorted with a lop-sided smile. Kellix's own face fell. He watched as Eomund popped the mana stick into a small cauldron he carried. It dissolved with a purple flash and a fizz.

"Kellix, we are out of mana sticks. And these other things too." Eomund shoved a tightly rolled scroll under Kellix's nose without looking at him. "Master Aethelstan needs them for the Rune of Rhodos enchantment we are working on."

Kellix crossed his arms over his chest and started to put on his best scowl. But before he could get his wrinkled face arranged just so, he found himself lifted into the air. Eomund, his face now buried in a spell book, had seized Kellix's cowl and pulled him up . . . only to drop him on the floor. Kellix landed with a thud that shocked through his old knees.

Eomund dropped a purse of coins into Kellix's hands with a clink. The apprentice was already turning away and walking past Faerix (who was still spinning and sparking), as he called over his shoulder. "Run down to the Alchemists' Quarter. Don't keep the old man waiting. Yeoch!!"

Eomund jumped as Faerix burped a gout of flame at him. He slapped at his leg, which was now smoking. "And take Faerix with you!" Eomund scooped up Faerix, and tossed the salamander across the chamber in an arc of red sparks. Faerix landed headfirst in an empty jar by the door.

"I'm sure he'll be helpful . . . and watch out for the ferals . . . " Eomund trailed off as he walked away, nose once more in his book.

"You're welcome . . . " Kellix muttered when Eomund was out of earshot.

Faerix backed up, clawed feet grating on the stone floor, and the lizard managed to knock over a chair as he thrashed his head from side to side, trying to escape the jar. Kellix shook his head and stuffed a glass sphere, the purse, and finally his staff into his magical pockets. Then he went to help Faerix get his head unstuck from the jar.

It was a short walk to the Alchemists' Quarter but long enough for Kellix to read the scrawled list of ingredients that Eomund had given him. His eyes crossed, and he stumbled on Faerix's lashing tail as he thought about the complex spell and its magical ingredients. Pulling a self-inking quill from another pocket, he jotted down two additions to the list, before stowing it in the purse with their coins.

They had one stop before entering the Alchemists' Quarter proper. Kellix looked up at the parchment maker's sign, swaying high above his head. Fat Hrathgar made fine scrolls and spellbooks—all of which were highly flammable. Kellix looked down Faerix. Faerix looked back up at him hopefully, with something like a smile on his reptilian snout.

"So, listen Faerix, you can come in, but . . . " Faerix sneezed, setting some drifting leaves alight. "On second thought, WAIT HERE!"

Kellix emerged from the parchment shop a few minutes later, with fresh scrolls longer than he was tall already stashed in his robes. He smiled. Hrathgar was not only a fine craftsman, he usually gave Aethelstan (and by extension, Kellix) a discount. They still had plenty of coin, and with any luck, he would have some to spare so he could buy a mana stick or even two for himself at the end of their errands.

As he stepped out into the sunlight, an acrid whiff of burning leaves and grease reached his nose. Kellix looked about, and sure enough, not only was Faerix nowhere to be seen, but a midden heap two doors down was now blazing away merrily.

Kellix hiked up his robes enough so he could jog toward the fire. With a moment's concentration, he summoned a stream of water. It flowed from his outstretched hand, dousing the flame instantly. He was rewarded with an even worse smell. Something like a hound-of-hell that happened to be soaking wet. Faerix then materialized from a narrow alley with a distinctly guilty look to his downcast eyes.

"How hard is it to just stay still and not start a conflagration?!? Come-on, you are going home!" Kellix grabbed Faerix's tail and began to drag the now-whimpering lizard back down the street, away from the Alchemist's Quarter, away from delights like mana sticks and fine spell components.

That was when Kellix saw the gang of feral familiars. A big orange goblin led the motley group. It was flanked by a winged imp, something that looked like ball of fangs, and a hideous creature that, on closer inspection, might have just been a mangy dog. Except for the goblin, all were, like Kellix, no more than knee-high to a grown man. They were heading straight for Kellix and Faerix.

Kellix watched as they surrounded an old mechanical familiar who was carrying a bundle of tools. They knocked it down and stood around it laughing. The wheezing little device kept trying to stand back up, but it was pinned down by the weight of the tools.

"Right, no going back . . . come on!" Kellix turned and ran away from the ferals, through the stone gate into the Alchemists' Quarter with Faerix hot on his heels. Literally.

THEY EMERGED on a bustling cross street. Kellix ducked his head left and right, trying to see thorough the churning jungle of legs, knees, and wagon wheels. He spotted their next stop, the Dessicantir Shop. "This way," he called to Faerix and started across the street.

Kellix became aware of three things all at once. One, all the air had been knocked out of his lungs. Two, something had just hit him very hard in the side, and it hurt. And three, he was flying across the street. As he spun upside down in the air, he caught a glimpse of Faerix spitting fire at the passing wizard who had kicked him. Kellix kept spinning and managed to land feet first. Which might have looked impressive, but he immediately collapsed, gasping to get his breath back.

The wizard kept walking, muttering some incantation into the air, as oblivious to the fact that his cape was now burning as he had been to Kellix crossing his path.

Kellix pulled his staff from another pocket, and—using it as a cane—managed to get his feet back under him. He crouched and kept trying to breathe.

Faerix ran up, opened his mouth wide, and sank his pointy teeth into Kellix's sleeve. The lizard starting pulling, and Kellix nearly fell down again. He swatted feebly at Faerix with his staff.

"Gerroff Faerix!" Faerix whined and looked past Kellix, back toward the gate.

Kellix turned, and sure enough, the orange goblin was there and pointing right at him. Kellix hobbled away, ducking under a wagon and between more swinging boots. They reached the Dessicantir Shop and ducked into a two-foot high door set alongside the human door. They nearly knocked over a miniature scarecrow who was on her way out.

"Excuse you!" she rasped, and Kellix got a face full of straw stuffing as she passed by.

The Dessicantir Shop was run by a withered old warlock, who was nearly as dry as the powders, skins, and other spell components he sold. He was a much harder bargainer than Fat Hrathgar the parchment maker, and Kellix was soon pulling at his ears in frustration. The dust and powders floating around made Faerix nearly sneeze five times.

Kellix had to keep conjuring a clothespin onto the lizard's snout to keep him from starting another fire, all while haggling with the warlock. They left after several trying minutes. Kellix scratched off items from their shopping list. He patted his robe here and there as he did so, feeling the little bags and parcels now stuffed into his pockets. Then he put the list back in the purse, frowning at how much it had all cost.

"I should have just left that jar on your head Faerix! Let's go."

They set off again, heading deeper into the Alchemists' Quarter. The streets were narrower and winding. Kellix stuck close to the buildings, out from under the feet and wheels of the big folk. They turned a corner, and Kellix smiled.

Away up at the end of the street, he saw the shimmering sign of the mana shop. He hurried forward then froze with a gasp. There was the orange goblin and his gang, not ten feet away. But this time, the ferals were not looking at him.

The imp was flying in circles, chasing a sprite with dark purple butterfly wings. The goblin and the rest of the gang were jeering and jumping up, trying to catch her. Kellix started to back up, and he motioned to Faerix to stay quiet. But just as he was about to creep away behind the corner, the ball-of-fangs familiar bit into a heavy bag the sprite was carrying.

The bag tore open, and the sprite cried out as potions, powders, scrolls, and other items spilled to the ground. The ferals cheered and began to scoop up the sprite's shopping. She flew overhead, crying now and sobbing curses and threats at them, to no avail.

Faerix ran past him with a snarl. Kellix grabbed for the salamander, but he wasn't fast enough. Faerix and the mangy dog started chasing each other's tails, snapping at each other and drawing the attention of the entire gang. The ball of fangs rolled over and bit at both Faerix and Kellix.

This was too much. Kellix's ears rang. His vision narrowed. He sprang at the fang beast, shouting in his thin voice. "A pox on all of you!"

Everyone looked up in surprise, as he brought the end of his staff down hard on the ball of fangs, which hooted in annoyance and rolled away. The orange goblin turned and gave Kellix an evil grin. Kellix had to leap backward as the goblin swung a club at him. Kellix's sudden fury was gone, replaced just as quickly with a pit of fear in his stomach. He back-pedaled, desperately knocking aside the swinging club with his staff.

The sprite had landed behind the gang, gathered her belongings back up, and was already flying away.

"You're welcome!" Kellix spat after her, then hopped as the mangy dog lunged at his ankles.

Kellix frantically rooted in a pocket with one hand while trying to fend off the goblin and the imp with his staff. His fingers closed on the glass sphere, which he pulled from his pocket. Now it was Kellix who grinned at the goblin. He pointed the sphere at the goblin and squeezed hard.

The thin glass shattered, and a gale of wind howled from between his fingers. The goblin was blown down the street, vanishing into an open window. Kellix turned the jet of air on the imp, who was sent flying over the buildings and into the next street.

The wind stopped before he could get to the dog, but it was already running away with a whine, its tail hanging limp from a vicious bite. Kellix looked down to see Faerix scrabbling at his snout and spitting in disgust at the mangy taste.

"Serves you right. Next time let's mind our own business."

Kellix looked eagerly at the mana shop up the street, but then saw a sign that read "Finest Potions & Magical Brews" over another store just two doors down. He took a quick glance at the list and saw where he had added "flaming dram" and "adhering solution."

Kellix sighed. The mana shop would have to wait. "Come on Faerix. And try not to sneeze this time. Or burp. In fact, just hold your breath, okay?"

Faerix whimpered at this, but followed Kellix through the familiars' door into the potions shop.

The potioneer was a kindly, middle-aged woman. Kellix waited while she sold some bottled night-fire to a haggard-looking wizard in old robes, and then he called up to her, asking for his potions. She smiled, got them down for him, and quoted a fair price.

Kellix handed over the coins and whispered to Faerix. "We may have enough for a snack after all!"

"Oh, he's so cute! Such big eyes!" The potioneer bent down to pet Faerix, and Kellix goggled with dismay. The salamander was indeed holding his breath and looked like he was about to burst! Kellix stuffed the bottles into his pockets, blurted out "thanks," and made for the door. He opened it, and then slammed it shut. The orange goblin was standing right outside, looking very bruised and very angry. A dozen ferals were at its back.

"I, ah, don't suppose you have a back door?" He asked the potioneer. She shook her head but kept looking at Faerix. Streams of smoke were leaking from the salamander's ears, and he was hopping about from his left feet to his right.

"No, and I think you need to take your friend outside. Run along now."

Kellix's mind raced. They were trapped. He'd already used his wind globe. And Faerix's scales were starting to glow molten red.

"Out!" the potioneer shrieked. She was trying to shoo Faerix toward the door with a broom.

A quick motion caught the corner of Kellix's eye. He looked, and there was the sprite, waving to him from an open window to the alley outside. Kellix seized Faerix by the tail and spun the lizard around him. The lizard knocked over bottles of potions, which shattered, filling the air with reeking clouds of green and yellow smoke. Kellix released Faerix's tail, and the salamander flew right out the window. There was a thundering crash, and orange fire blazed outside the window for a moment.

Kellix gaped. "Faerix!!"

The potioneer swatted him over the head with her broom amid fits of coughing. He ignored her, grabbed his staff, and vaulted after Faerix.

KELLIX LANDED in a muddy puddle with a squelch. "Faerix!" The salamander had not exploded, and was looking quite normal. Except that he was dangling by his tail, which was clutched in the goblin's gnarled fist. There was no sign of the sprite anywhere.

Kellix himself was seized by the imp and some of the other ferals before he could get to his feet. The goblin gave him hearty grin, and Kellix gulped.

"Let's see wot he's got!" the goblin sneered. "Shake 'im out."

The world spun and began to bounce wildly as Kellix was turned upside down and given a painful shaking. Now, like any good set of magical robes, Kellix's pockets only opened when he reached into them. So, unlike the unfortunate—but apparently treacherous—sprite they had rescued earlier, Kellix's shopping did not spill onto the ground.

The goblin must have worked this out, because after a long minute, he said, "Drop 'im!"

With a squelch, Kellix landed head-first in the muddy puddle again and rolled onto his back.

"Now, hand over your coin, or we're 'aving lizard strips fer lunch." The goblin loomed over Kellix and gave Faerix a shaking for emphasis. Kellix's eyes could not focus, and he felt like he would throw up. Faerix whined as the goblin gave him another vicious shake, making the salamander's jaws snap shut several times. Kellix closed his eyes, reached into a pocket, and pulled out the purse. It was snatched from his hand instantly.

For the second time that day, he found himself sailing through the air with the wind knocked out of him, this time landing in a heap after crashing into a wall at the end of the alley. Faerix landed next to him with a thud and a scrabble of claws. Kellix lay gasping as the feral gang left in a chorus of guffaws and warnings about what they would do to him the next time.

Kellix decided it was time to go home. He tried to rise but felt broken bones grinding inside him. He then passed out.

HE WOKE CHOKING on something that burned its way down his throat. For a second he felt sick again, but then that went away as—starting with his stomach and spreading all across him—all the pain disappeared as well. He blinked and sat up and saw the purple-winged sprite, who was replacing a cork stopper in a green bottle.

"Better?" she asked.

He nodded and shook his head, trying to get his bearings. Faerix nuzzled his face with scratchy salamander scales. Kellix started to push Faerix away but couldn't manage it, and instead he just put up with the scratchiness.

The sprite went on in a hissing voice that was not how Kellix had imagined a sprite should sound. "I should have thanked you earlier. But I hope this makes up for it." Kellix frowned but said nothing. "Well, see you around, and thanks!"

Kellix tried to say, "You're welcome," but the words stuck in his throat, and all that came out was a rattle. The sprite ran a pointed nail down his wrinkled cheek. Her mouth formed a thin smile below eyes that were all black. Then she flew away.

Shaking his head at all this, Kellix reached into the pocket where he kept his staff. He found it empty. He staggered to his feet without it and walked back to look on the ground by the muddy puddle. He found his staff, neatly broken in two and half-buried in a goblin-shaped footprint.

Kellix still could not seem to speak, so he stumbled out of the alley, back to the street. Faerix followed close behind.

He looked down the road that lead all the way back to the stone gate and home. Then he looked the other way, farther up the street. There it was. The Mana Shop. Its glimmering sign swung enticingly in the breeze, and Kellix's stomach rumbled. Faerix shifted back and forth on his claws, looking at the sign too. The salamander looked up at him and whined. Kellix saw that Faerix's scales were looking very gray, barely red at all.

Kellix's thoughts came in slow, oozing drips. It was time to go home. They had done their best. Their money was gone. His staff was destroyed. The gang was still out there.

But he was really hungry. He thought about the spell that Eomund and Aethelstan were working on. It would need power. He gritted his teeth. He took a limping step toward the mana store.

CHATTING AS THEY WALKED, a snow leopard and a gnome made their way down the street, each nearly done with her errands. They stopped and gaped at the stooped little figure in mud-crusted robes who was carrying a half-dead salamander across his back. Kellix walked past without seeing them.

A wizard with a half-burned cape nearly trampled him and Faerix both but saw them and stopped, scratching his beard at the strange sight. Faerix managed to lift his head and spat a single spark at the wizard as they passed.

At last, they were there. Kellix dropped to his knees and let Faerix down. They pushed the door open. Sparks and shrieks flew past them as something exploded inside the shop, but Kellix put his head down and they went inside together. The door shut behind them. The snow leopard and the gnome looked at each other and continued their stroll.

The interior of the mana shop was usually calm and spotless, with beige ceramic tiles and dark wooden shelves holding mana sticks and many other types of magical power sources. The proprietor was a young witch who was stern, but fair, with marked prices that were not negotiable.

Now that he was in the store, though without any money, Kellix realized he didn't have any idea what to do. But he had no time to ponder this because he had to leap out of the way as an entire shelf crashed to the floor. Globes full of purple lightning exploded, adding to the sparks of light filling the air. The witch's apprentice, a pimply youth, ran down the aisle pursued by the flying imp and the ball of fangs. He kept waving a wand at them, but the imp swooped down, pulled the wand from the boy's hand, and—with a gibbering laugh—threw it high in the air. Other ferals leaped from shelf to shelf, smashing everything in sight.

Kellix pulled on both of his ears at once, his eyes flicking back and forth in dismay. The buzzing energy in the air woke him from the daze he had been in. Faerix stirred, sniffed, and then began to lap at a pool of orange goo that oozed from beneath the crashed shelf. Then the wand clattered to the tile floor and rolled to Kellix's feet.

Kellix picked up the wand. It was about the same length as his staff had been, but thinner. The ball of fangs rolled past in the next aisle, and Kellix waved the wand at it without thinking. The ball gave a long shriek that rapidly got higher and fainter as it shrank into a little dust bunny. The dust bunny rolled under a cabinet. The imp was now pulling hanks of hair from the apprentice's head. Kellix raised an eyebrow and pointed the wand at the imp. The imp turned green, then deflated like a balloon, whizzing about until it sailed behind a counter and out of sight.

"Back fer more, eh?" Kellix turned to see the goblin lumbering down on him. The beast was swigging something from a bottle, and looked about a foot taller than before. It swung its club, dashing goods from a shelf to crash to the floor as it closed in on him.

Kellix got a bit carried away then, and gave the wand an elaborate, flourishing twirl before thrusting it at the goblin. The goblin was knocked down by a wave of blue energy bursting from the wand, but Kellix was sent flying in the opposite direction, right into the arms of the very witch who owned the shop.

"I'll take that, thank you!" She plucked the wand from Kellix's hand, and he found himself dangling by his cowl from her left hand while she strode about, magicking the goblin and all of his cronies out of her shop.

She flung Kellix unceremoniously after them and slammed the door. The gang had already scattered, and he sat alone and empty-handed in the street.

BACK INSIDE, Faerix delicately picked up a bundle of mana sticks in his mouth, climbed up to the counter, and dropped it in front of the apprentice. The apprentice flinched, but the witch bustled over. She gave Faerix a close look, and he cocked his head to the side and waited.

"Faerix isn't it? And how is Aethelstan? Up to mischief no doubt." She smiled at Faerix, and he looked back at her. She nodded and frowned. "How awful! Not to worry, I'll put these on his account." Faerix smiled back.

KELLIX GAPED as Faerix emerged from the shop, proudly holding the bundle of mana sticks. He quickly stashed them in a pocket, and they finally started for home.

"TOOK YOU LONG ENOUGH, KELLIX." Eomund tapped his foot impatiently, grabbing each parcel and package as Kellix retrieved them from his robes. Last came the bundle of mana sticks. Kellix sighed, and his stomach rumbled again as Eomund seized that, too. Kellix turned, his shoulders slumped, and he started back to his nest.

"Hold up. You'll need to run back out. Aethelstan said we also need . . . ," Eomund paused, closing his eyes and tapping his temple before he remembered, ". . . a flaming dram and an adhering solution. I know it's a bother, but please run back to town and get those, too."

Kellix pulled the two extra ingredients from his pockets and passed them to Eomund without looking at him. Then he staggered over and fell face down in his nest.

"Oh. Well done! How did you know?" Eomund almost sounded cheerful for a change, but Kellix barely heard him. "Here, you've earned it." Something dropped beside Kellix. "And thank you!" Eomund's heavy steps trailed away.

Kellix sat up, and cradled the mana stick that Eomund had left.

CRACK!

He snapped it in two and handed half to Faerix. Then he called after Eomund. "You're welcome!"

IT'S A KICK'S LIFE

RANDY LINDSAY

I LEANED BACK and watched as Justice slammed his head into Crimewave's face, shattering the decoy into a shower of clay bits. It'd been a classic battle between bitter rivals so far. Speed, strength, and an associate's degree in Metastar law pitted against the ability to create hulking, armored duplicates of the most tenacious criminal force in the city. It looked every bit like the battle of the year—Justice vs. Crimewave.

An epic battle like this might rank Justice in the National Top 40. That all important first-step on the road to becoming a national treasure and everything that went with it. Celebrity appearances on the late-night television circuit, his own crime-fighter trading card, and his picture on the cover of *The MetaStar Review*.

All Justice had to do was utter his end-fight catchphrase and execute his finishing move. Then it was lights out for Crimewave and, "Hello, adoring public," for the good guy.

Justice threw a couple of uninspiring punches that reminded me to get my head back in the game. I struck a pose and shouted, "Read him his rights, Justice!"

I loved this part. Justice had real action charisma. His combat moves created a commanding video presence that dominated the viewers' eyes. A few of the other metastars were as poetically beautiful in their heroics as Justice, but none of them were better. Justice was about to trigger the fight combination that had defeated every foe he had faced.

"Right you are, Law Boy," Justice called out in his perfectly bass voice.

Crimewave rushed in, fists flailing in a mini-crimewave of their own. The punches met only empty air. Justice was simply too fast for Crimewave to score a hit without his duplicates.

"You have the right to remain silent," said Justice. He ducked under Crimewave's fists and then kicked him in the stomach, knocking the air out of the villain. Crimewave *oofed* and then wrapped his arms around his midsection.

"You have the right to go to jail after a fair and impartial trial." Justice's delivery and timing were perfect. He grabbed Crimewave by the shoulders, spinning him around and then hurling him across the room. Crimewave crashed into a wooden crate on the warehouse floor with an awesome *ker-wrack* sound. The crate splintered, but Crimewave received only minor injuries thanks to the unexplainable toughness all metastars had regardless of their power profile.

"And you have the right—"

Justice was supposed to use his heightened speed to dash across the warehouse floor and deliver his finisher. But that wasn't what happened. Just before he reached Crimewave, his foot slipped. He slid across the floor and smashed into a brick wall. *Thud-d-d-d.*

The wall broke. Bricks crashed to the ground. And Crimewave escaped.

"Oh crap," I said, staring open-mouthed out the hole in the wall. The mocking cackles of villainous laughter pierced my ears and echoed in my mind. Then I looked around the warehouse. Everyone was looking at me. Justice was waiting for me to give him a triggering phrase, but the rest of the spectators must be wondering if they heard me right. I had just violated kick protocol—always stay in character.

"Um . . . " I fumbled to find the right *party line* to move the attention back to Justice. The kind of phrase people expected to hear from a kick. Not real-world dialogue.

"Leaping lawsuits," I said, pointing at Crimewave's retreating form. "It's a good thing Justice never sleeps."

Justice nodded at me and then went through the dramatic wind-up for a meta-fast chase. He winked at the warehouse workers and then . . . fell. Same spot as before. Something wasn't right. Although Justice didn't have heightened balance or agility, he was pretty good on his feet.

I ran over to Justice, holding out a hand to balance him as he stood. "Let me slingshot you for some extra speed."

Justice gave me a puzzled look. This wasn't one of our usual maneuvers, but all the great metastars trusted their kicks. I braced myself . . . alright, I pretended to brace myself, pouring every bit of theatrics into the maneuver. Then I pulled on Justice's arm and shouted, "Let's not forget that Crimewave has the right to a speedy trial."

It wasn't my best work. The creation of an impromptu party line was a talent. A kick could practice spewing out witty catchphrases on the fly. Most spent hours thinking of situations they might run into and then made a list of appropriate party lines. But for the best kicks, this was a natural ability.

Justice took his cue and bolted through the hole in the wall. Within moments he was gone from view. The warehouse workers ran to the hole and looked outside. I knew the battle was over but was glad for the distraction.

A glint from the floor caught my eye. Right at the spot where Justice had slipped. I knelt to get a good look at whatever was glinting. A thin film of liquid formed a spot roughly a foot in diameter. I ran my index finger across the spot. It slid smoothly along the floor, like it had been greased. Then I smelled the liquid. It had a petroleum smell, but not of any oil that I recognized. And it certainly didn't smell like any kind of oil that belonged in a warehouse.

I needed a sample. One of the other kicks worked in a forensic lab. Or at least, I thought he did. Maybe he just had a friend who worked there. I didn't really know for sure. The first rule in the kick charter stated that the private life of a metastar's assistant was their own business and not to be discussed with the rest of the kicks. The second rule just repeated the first one. Which made the first rule really important.

Unlike many of the kicks, Law Boy didn't have a utility belt with an assortment of handy gadgets that might help during a fight—or as part of an investigation. Instead, my costume included a color-matching, leather briefcase strapped to my back filled with legal briefs. Great for costume theme continuity. Horrible for any practical application. I was always looking for ways to put those briefs to use.

A stack of cleaning rags sat on a shelf near the office door of the warehouse manager. I grabbed one. Swiped it across the oil slick. Then placed the rag in a plastic bag I had left over from lunch.

According to my watch, Justice had stopped moving. Standard equipment for all kicks. A smartwatch with a state-of-the-art tracking application. Essential for the third rule—know the location of your metastar at all times. The most recent app even had an alarm feature that woke you if your heroic celebrity moved more than 100 feet from his last reported location.

"Hey, you might want to clean up this mess," I told the warehouse workers. "It's a violation of Section 15 of the building code. Someone trips over these bricks, they have an iron-clad lawsuit against you."

Not really. But unless they had some sort of law degree, they wouldn't know any better. Section 15 dealt with insulation. How many layers. The proper installation methods. And a long lecture on how wrong it was to use asbestos. Keeping their attention on the bricks would allow me to slip away unnoticed.

I found Justice pacing the intersection of 12th and Main, crossing one street after another in a big square circuit. Like any good metastar, he waited for the green light and looked both ways before stepping into the crosswalk. In his mind, this is what he did to think through the situation. Of course, the reality was that this is what he did until I arrived and spouted a catchphrase that would move him in the right direction.

"Justice!" I shouted, then waved him over. "What happened to Crimewave?"

He struck a dramatic I've-been-pondering-this-very-thing pose and said, "It appears that the villain has given me the slip."

Ouch! Not a good line. Fortunately, none of the media were around to hear it. Losing a battle against your nemesis was one thing, but giving the media teams the ingredients for a catchy news headline was disaster. I could think of two high-profile metastars who quit the business due to an award-winning headline that pointed out their heroic mistakes. It was my job to make sure Justice wasn't the third.

"Crimewave has never beaten me before," said Justice.

While metastars had physical durability that seemed to vastly exceed their stated abilities, their egos were vulnerable. Rock-Fist Robot could pound all day on a run-of-the-mill sorcerer metastar and leave only a few bruises and maybe a tear in the costume. But attack their self-image, and metastars ran the risk of collapsing into spineless, blubbering heaps. Justice had just taken a blow to his ego.

"Gosh, Justice," I said. "Do you think Crimewave developed a new meta power?"

A glint in Justice's eyes told me that my comment put an idea inside his head. His rattled expression faded. Metastars were expected to fall victim to the unveiling of a new meta power by their opponents. A near ego disaster had been turned into an event that journalist would consider a plot development point in Justice's continuing battle against Crimewave.

Except that Crimewave didn't have a new power.

Justice raised his hand, finger pointing to the sky, and said, "Not to worry, my friend. I know exactly ... "

But just then, a line of cars came screeching to a halt on the road next to us. Reporters from all the major media outlets popped out of their vehicles, swarming Justice.

"Is it true that Crimewave beat you in a fair fight?" asked Madison from KMTA News.

"Do you think this loss will have a major impact on your career?" asked Evan with HNN (Hero News Network).

"Are the rumors true? Are you dating Queen Quick?" asked Zoe from *Meta-Romance*.

Justice pulled his shoulders back, standing straight and tall, and said, "Crimewave used a new meta power on me. A treacherously deceptive power."

That triggered another round of questions. The media personalities all talked over one another, resulting in a loud cacophony in which none of them could be understood.

I pushed my way into the middle of the media ring and then pulled the large-print version of *Metastar Law* out of my briefcase. Kicks aren't supposed to put themselves into a position where they're the center of attention, but some situations required it.

"Section five, subsection two states, 'A metastar cannot be held responsible for a loss during any battle in which the opponent unleashes a previously unknown power, ability, skill, or gadget. Any records or statistics based on said encounter shall show the result as a *Surprise*.' "

I stepped back and let Justice do his thing.

"Thanks, Law Boy," Justice said with a *tkk-tkk* noise, and his finger pointed at me.

Justice slowly scanned the media. "I have decided to call this new power ... the Slippery Slope of Crime. And if Crimewave knows what's good for him, he will keep that name and apply for the appropriate trademark protection."

The media seemed to approve of Justice dispensing legal advice to his opponent and gave a collective "Hmmm."

An uneasy silence fell upon the gathering. Justice needed more help. It was obvious that he didn't have any idea of where to go from here. Either with the media or on the investigation. I wasn't exactly sure myself.

"Galloping gag-orders, Justice," I shouted from outside the media circle. Since the idea was to keep the media focused on my metastar, I didn't wait for everyone to turn their attention to me. Justice had me fixed in his gaze, waiting for the *work line* that would inspire him to action. For the line of dialogue intended specifically for him, rather than the witty comments played out for the public.

"Aren't you worried that telling everyone about your plan will tip the scales of justice in favor of Crimewave?" I continued. "I can already see tonight's headlines: 'Justice tests limits of Slippery-Slope of Crime'. But what happens if Crimewave finds out that your slip during the fight is part of a scheme to bag a bigger prize?"

That should do it. Justice had enough wits to take it from there.

The interview lasted for almost an hour. Justice explained how the plan was to let Crimewave escape and track him down in order to reveal a bigger threat. He vaguely hinted at a criminal organization and a possible real estate scheme linked to a decrease in property values due to Crimewave's recent crime wave.

Justice answered questions about him "courting" Queen Quick and I tuned out. The conversation was in the safe zone, giving me time to think about the warehouse battle. Either Crimewave actually did have a new power or someone else was responsible for the oil slick.

As soon as the media mob finished the interview, I suggested Justice look through his crime-fighter library for any clues that could help us track down Crimewave. Then I went home and changed into my civil costume. The clothing I wore when I wasn't busy being Law Boy.

I took a bus to the industrial district. Between the junkyards, abandoned buildings, and fume-spewing factories, the traffic in the area was limited to those who had business there . . . and the kicks. We rented an unmarked building next to the biggest scrapyard in the city. It served as an unofficial guild hall for all the kicks—lawful and criminal.

Chances were good I'd find the kick I was looking for. His metastar hadn't hit the big time yet and still needed a regular job to pay for his living expenses. It took a few minutes to circulate through the club house. I found him sitting at a table with an attractive young woman.

"Hey, Kevin," I said. Kevin wasn't his real name. Fake names were part of the *civil costume* we used around the other kicks. It prevented anyone from finding out our real-life identities. Kicks didn't have powers and neither did our families and friends.

"Haven't seen you around lately, Dylan," said Kevin.

"You know how it goes," I said. "Active metastars mean busy kicks. Mine is really jonesing to hit the national circuit."

The eyes of the woman next to Kevin lit up. She leaned forward and said, "Then you must be famous. What's it like? Have you teamed up with any of the Top 40 metastars?"

"No. No. No." Kevin waggled his finger at the woman. "We don't talk about our lives. No mention of specific meta powers. No real-world names. And especially no identity reveals."

"Sorry," said the woman.

"This is Niki." Kevin hitched a thumb in the woman's direction. "She's new and doesn't know all the rules yet."

I nodded and then turned my attention back to Kevin. "You still have that contact over at the forensic lab?"

Kevin gave me hard stare. "If you mean, do I still know a guy who knows a guy that does that sort of thing. Then, yes. I do."

I pulled out the plastic bag with the oil-soaked rag. "Any chance of having that guy do a rush analysis on this rag? I used it to soak up a liquid that's important to my current investigation."

"As long as you're willing to stay and show Niki around while I'm gone."

"No problem," I said.

Kevin left and I walked with Niki over to the vending machines. I jabbed the button for a root beer and waited for it to drop to the dispenser slot.

"Don't you have to pay for that?" asked Niki.

"All of the kicks have access to resources they share with the group. Kevin knows a guy who knows a guy that does forensic lab requests. One of the kicks has a connection to a trust-fund kid who donates money to pay the clubhouse rent. I imagine another one of the kicks made arrangements to fill the vending machines every week. Everyone contributes."

"What if a kick doesn't have anything to offer?" asked Niki.

"Then word gets around," I told her. "You don't give—you don't get. Besides, everyone has something to offer or they wouldn't be a kick. No metastar is going to take on an apprentice without any skills or resources. Although, it might be fun to try out for a kick position as Useless Lad."

"Which brings me to the question of why we're called kicks," said Niki.

"Because the metastars are always kicking us to the side. They have a deep-rooted need to be noticed. But the reality of the situation is that we run the show. The metastars are the guns and it's our job to point them at the bad guys. Or good guys, depending on your moral stance."

Niki selected a diet soda from the machine. "What about super-genius metastars? With all the brain power going for them, they have to know the kicks are manipulating them."

"Yea, that's what you'd think." I pointed toward the recroom and did a slow stroll in that direction. "My theory is their hubris prevents them from making the connection. They probably think it's impossible for them to be controlled by a *fragile*—"

"A what?" asked Niki.

"*Fragiles*. Normal humans who don't have the ability to survive punches from a metastar with heightened strength. Or live through a collision with a brick wall after being thrown fifty feet. Even the supposedly unpowered metastars can take a beating that would kill the rest of us."

I showed Niki the recroom. Not as large as the lounge, but a great place if you just wanted to blow off some steam. Although the rules didn't exactly prohibit metastar business here, the kicks respected it as a work-free zone. The room held several card tables, a couple of old-school video games, and a ping-pong table.

The cosmic war between the forces of good and evil—or law and crime —must be on holiday, because the place was packed. I waved hello to a few of my kick associates and then ushered Niki out of the room.

"Isn't it about time the kicks got the recognition they deserve?" asked Niki.

I stopped in midstride and turned to face Niki. What she suggested was dangerous.

"None of this works unless the metastars are too focused on themselves to notice us," I told Niki. "Everything from the stupid catchphrases we use to direct our metastars to the idiotic costumes we wear to prevent the opposing metastars from mistaking us as a threat. All of it is designed to protect us. And our metastars."

"Are you telling me that Prancing Lad's choice of leotards and tighty-tight shorts as part of his costume is a defense feature?"

"Yep," I said. "Whoever is under that costume is a genius. The horrid clash of colors and mashed-up style components make Prancing Lad punch proof. No one is going to take someone who looks like him seriously. They just want to laugh when they see him. Pure genius."

"Maybe I need to rethink my costume," said Niki.

"Besides, who really wants to be in the limelight? The media is always following you around. You never have a moment to yourself. And any mistake you make immediately becomes the headline of the moment for every media source looking for a metastar story. No thanks. I like being able to grab a burger without having a dozen cameras in my face."

Niki stood there, lips tight, eyes narrow. Maybe I went too far. There's a lot for a new kick to learn. And it can be overwhelming to find out that your favorite metastar isn't as super as you thought.

"Listen," I said, "most of the metastars are well-intentioned, but there's just something about them having meta powers that makes them not fully connected in the brain. Whenever we direct a metastar, they think we're just giving them the ideas they originally gave to us to give back to them. Let them have the 24-7 media coverage. Let them have the screaming fans that never give them a moment's rest. Let them take the mega-punches from Hugo Hammer-Hands."

I gave her a moment to process the information and then led the way to the back of the clubhouse. Bathrooms, the supply room, and the learning center, which was really a fancy name for a grimy room where they held classes for kick-essential skills. A piece of standard notebook paper listed Costume Design, Making, and Repair as the skill of the day.

"You'll probably want to take as many of the classes as you can," I told Niki. "There are a few things you need to learn how to do on your own to protect your identity. This is the best place to learn them. It may not be fancy, but the kicks teaching these classes are the best."

"Thanks." Niki didn't sound all that appreciative of the advice.

"That concludes the tour," I said. "If you want, we can sit in on a game of cards or go into the lounge and finish our drinks."

"Actually, I have to go." Niki glanced at her watch. It struck me as more of a staged maneuver than an effort to determine the time. "I appreciate the tour. Next time I need some legal advice, I'll look you up."

She left. In a hurry.

I found a seat in the lounge and waited for Kevin.

Halfway through my second root beer, it hit me. Niki mentioned contacting me if she needed legal advice, but I hadn't said anything about that. If she was new, she wouldn't know my resource pool. Something about this felt very wrong.

I bolted out of my seat to look for Niki.

But then Kevin arrived. "Here's your lab report."

"You find anything interesting?" I asked as I opened the report and started skimming through it.

"My guy said his guy said that the oil is a new synthetic. Hard to find and fairly expensive. It has limited commercial applications, mostly in the brick and pottery industry. It's supposed to change the texture of the finished product. The actual result varies, depending on the baking heat."

"I need to find out which companies in the city sell it, then put together a list of their customers. If the oil has as limited a supply as you suggested, it should be a short list."

"Extremely short," said Kevin. "There's a single manufacturer in Japan and only one company in the city that uses the oil. The Porcelain Doll. They're located over on Kent Street"

"How did you know that? Only the name of the manufacturer is listed in the report."

Kevin's eyes bulged. "Oh. Um. It was on the news. Or maybe in one of those science magazines. My dentist always has a couple of those in his office. I read them while I wait for my appointment."

"Have your guy tell his guy thanks," I told Kevin. We'd shared enough resources over the last few years that I was pretty sure Kevin did all the lab work himself. "This should be enough to resolve the contest in my metastar's favor."

"Must be big," said Kevin, "if the size of the smile on your face is any indication."

I leaned in close and spoke in a near-whisper. "Just between us, I should be up for Kick of the Year if I manage to maneuver my metastar out of the fire and onto the spire."

"Great," said Kevin, "but that only works if your metastar doesn't recognize you for your contribution to the contest. Kicks are supposed to avoid public attention. The award committee is incredibly strict about that qualification."

"Right." I laughed. "As if my metastar is going to take the attention away from himself."

"Stay intact," said Kevin.

"Stay invisible," I replied.

I rode a bus downtown and hopped off at the main branch of the public library. Posing as a concerned citizen, I sent Justice an anonymous tip from one of the library computers. Then I sent him a copy of the report. Kevin had already made sure to remove anything on the report that would allow us to identify the forensic lab that did the work.

Fifteen minutes later, Justice called.

"Are you ready to administer some justice?" he asked, then continued without waiting for an answer. "Meet me in front of the Porcelain Doll in one hour. And bring the media."

"Coo-coo court cases, Justice," I said, trying to sound surprised. "How did you figure out this dishonest dilemma so fast?"

"Let's just say that the citizens of this city support the letter of the law."

Weak. But at least he was in character.

An hour later, I stood outside the Porcelain Doll with Justice. The media mob surrounded us, and they weren't being quiet. There was no way Justice could surprise Crimewave now. I accidentally on purpose let slip to Justice the concern about Crimewave sneaking out the back. The media late-comers reacted, just as I hoped, and positioned themselves around back, hoping for a scoop in case Crimewave decided to forego round two of the contest.

Justice adopted his battle-ready stance and flashed a smile to the media, making sure he stood still long enough for them to take good, clear pictures. The red and white of his costume stood out perfectly against the dull gray of the building behind him. Then we charged in. The media charged in as well, keeping a safe distance from the expected fight.

"I see that I caught you surprise," Justice told Crimewave. "Too bad for you that Justice is ever-vigilant."

Crimewave sat behind a counter filled with little porcelain dolls of himself. He blinked a couple of times, looking as if we had woken him from an afternoon nap. Crimewave stood and waited for the last of the media mob to file into the store.

"Not so fast, Justice," Crimewave said with his arms crossed over his chest. "The surprise is on you. I expected you to find me. But what you didn't expect was to find me and . . . my kick."

Dum-dum-dummm.

No. That wasn't a dramatic effect in my mind. The actual sound blasted out of speakers set around the room, leaving a noticeable impact on the media. Crimewave wasn't clever enough to think of this on his own. It had to be the work of a kick.

"Everyone," said Crimewave, as he rubbed his hands together. "Meet Miss da Meaner. This marks the beginning of a whole new era of crime and destruction. Bwa-ha-ha."

"Wrong, Crimewave," said Justice. "This is going to be like any other day. Justice prevails and the criminals go to jail."

With their catchphrases delivered, there was nothing left for the meta-stars to do except battle. Crimewave split into multiple clay copies of himself and Justice quickly smashed them. An almost identical repeat of the previous battle, except I had a kick to deal with.

Justice was a *point-and-fire* metastar, which meant he didn't need much direction once a battle started. That left me free to deal with Miss da Meaner.

"Listen . . . Miss," I said. Justice hadn't faced too many evil metastars with kicks. I wasn't too sure what to do next. "With you being a girl, there's no reason for us to fight. I mean, I don't want to hurt you."

Meaner laughed as she lunged at me. A fist connected with my jaw and sent me stumbling back. *Ka-pop.* My vision blurred and it felt as if the room were spinning around. I brought my arms up to protect my head from another attack, but Meaner backed off, obviously enjoying the pain and humiliation she had inflicted.

Alright. So this girl could fight. Maybe I didn't need to hold back. That only left me with one problem. I didn't know how to fight. Legal battles, sure. Punching, kicking, biting, and body tosses—no!

Justice had a maneuver he called the Circuit Court where he dodged an attack and then allowed the momentum of the opponent to carry them past him. Then, as soon as his foe turned around, Justice put the hurt on him.

I held my hands up, palms up, and wiggled my fingers, inviting Meaner to try and attack me again.

A wicked grin crossed Meaner's face. She took two quick steps and jumped. Her feet caught me in the chest and sent me flying backward. *Thu-dunk.* I slammed into a barrel and slid to the floor, fighting to breathe.

Miss da Meaner slowly strolled over to me. She bent over and spoke into my ear. "Don't feel bad about having a girl stomp your trash. I'm not really a *fragile.* I used to be a metastar."

That couldn't be. Although it was rare for a metastar to lose their abilities, they would never accept a supporting role, playing second act to a metastar who might not have even a fraction of their former reputation. What could possibly motivate a metastar to accept the life of a kick?

And that voice. I recognized it. Miss da Meaner was Niki.

It still didn't make sense, but some of the pieces were starting to fit. Niki wanting kicks to receive recognition for their contribution. Crimewave had introduced his kick, taking media attention away from himself. These were dangerous ideas and if not stopped they could ruin the whole metastar business.

Meaner sauntered over to an unboxed shipping crate. She grabbed a crowbar from the top of the crate and smacked it against her palm a couple of times. "Looks like I'm going to start my kick career by breaking the Law. Literally."

If she could knock the stuffing out of me with her fists, a few whacks from a crowbar should send me into permanent Chapter 11. My normal defenses wouldn't have any effect on another kick. She didn't care how ridiculous my costume was. Another kick wouldn't mistake my cheesy catchphrase as a sign to move on to another target.

My only chance was that enough of her metastar instincts were left for her to buy into an *action cliché*.

"Case closed, Law Boy." Meaner hefted the crowbar above her head and brought it down in a swift two-handed stroke.

I rolled to the side at the last moment. And kept rolling. The crowbar caved a chunk out of the barrel. Oil spilled on the floor, creating a slick that surrounded Miss da Meaner. She tried to jump away, but too late. Her feet slid out from under her and she hit the ground with a satisfying *sliii-thud*. I watched Meaner slip and slide for a few moments and then looked over at the metastar battle.

Justice had just finished off the last of the duplicates.

"Read him his rights," I shouted.

"Crimewave," said Justice with his deepest crime-fighter voice, "you have the right to remain silent."

A quick blow to the stomach knocked the breath out of Crimewave.

"You have the right to go to jail after a fair and impartial trial." Justice swung Crimewave against a shelf full of little porcelain duplicates.

"And you have the right to be knocked out by Justice."

Justice leapt high into the air. Crimewave looked up just in time to take a jackhammer fist to the chin. Lights out. Game over. Better luck next time.

The media surrounded Justice. Everything looked right in the world once again.

"Congratulations on beating Crimewave," said Mindy Muggs, from *The Daily World*. "But what about the big reveal you promised earlier?"

Justice assumed a chin-up, shoulders-back pose. His gaze flickered in my direction.

"Unholy writs, Justice," I said, making sure I was loud enough for all of the media to hear but not loud enough to command their attention. "What kind of virulent villain has an ex-metastar for their kick?"

A collective gasp filled the room. But when I pointed to the oil slick, Miss da Meaner wasn't there. My mind scrambled for a plausible explanation to feed the Justice and the media.

"See?" I said, continuing to point to the vacant oil slick. "She used her metastar abilities to escape."

The media mob nodded and I knew I was safe.

"Don't blame yourself, Law Boy," said Justice. "No one expects you to single-handedly defeat a metastar—former or otherwise. Their unsavory plot has been exposed and the world now knows the depraved depths to which the two of them will go to promote their agenda of crime and evil."

Justice changed poses, one favoring his silhouette. "Broken down metastars have no business filling in for kicks, depriving deserving fragiles of their chance to work with the truly wonderful members of society. The metastars. But that will be a victory for another day. What matters now is that *we* have captured Crimewave."

I scanned the crowd. The media was loving the metastar routine. When I glanced back at Justice, I noticed he was staring at me. The hair on the back of my neck prickled, warning me that something was about to go horribly wrong. Metastars weren't supposed to pay any attention to their kicks. They were supposed to accept the accolades of a grateful city/nation/world with faux modesty.

"Today's events have taught me something," said Justice.

No! No, they don't. Please, don't learn anything.

"Failure has the ability to change a man," Justice continued. "Even a meta man."

What are you doing? The code. Don't forget about the unspoken metastar code. Do what your kick tells you and take all the credit. The world of hero-celebrities is based on this one simple concept. Don't ruin a good thing.

"It's about time I gave some credit to a person who has been overlooked for too long."

Noooooo!

Justice motioned me to join him. There went my chance to win Kick of the Year.

"Remember friends," Justice said, as I trudged his way, "Justice is only a scream away."

GLOSSARY

- **Kick** = sidekick

- **Metastar** = superhero
- **Point-and-Fire** = a hero that isn't a complete idiot
- **Fragile** = normal person
- **Party Line** = cheesy lines people expect kicks to say
- **Work Line** = the real stuff that kicks need to say to do their job
- **Civil Costume** = real-life civilian clothing/secret ID
- **Contest** = a case, assignment, mission, or any term that pits two metastars against one another
- **Action Cliché** = the overused battle tricks that every antagonist fails to avoid

RAISING WORDS

STEWART C. BAKER

AFTER WE ENTOMBED MY FATHER, he transformed into a giant bird of the purest white and burst forth from the earth all holy and clean.

My mother and her co-wives, my sisters, my cousins—all followed as he soared, majestic and terrible and filled with beauty, away to the east and the sea.

I alone of the women in that place stood watching. The rest ran through plain and brush, pushing past the sharp bamboo which must have cut their feet like swords; they ran through wave and spray, unmindful of the cold wetness which wrapped their robes about them like black ocean weeds. As they ran, they sang, their high-pitched, nasal voices rising in rhythmic bursts of ritual lament to the *kami* my father had become.

I alone sang no songs. I alone remembered.

WHEN I WAS VERY YOUNG, I used to beg my father to take me hunting. Though even then he was stern, he would always relent, the sun glinting through his jet black hair as he grinned our secret grin and set me in the bough of the sky-reaching black oak at the forest's edge.

I loved the burst of activity as courtiers swarmed around readying horses and bows, the shouts ringing out in the crispness of the early spring air. But I loved more the way my father sat, perfectly still, astride his own horse. His own bow held loosely in his lap, he would chant the ritual blessing slowly and with god-like calm.

I used to sit in the oak for hours and listen to the distant thrumming of bowstrings, reveling in the idea that all things were connected. In the idea that my father connected them.

WHEN HE SLAYED the warlords of the Kumaso tribe, my father received a new name. Yamato Takeru they called him as they died. Yamato Brave.

When he returned, he had changed.

He no longer hunted, no longer held his bow. Instead, he practiced swordsmanship. He stood waist-deep in the Kino river, drawing and slicing and drawing and thrusting over and over and over again with a sword we learned he had received from his aunt, the high priestess at Ise.

He did not come to my mother or her co-wives a single time before leaving again at the Emperor's orders to pacify the peoples of the east.

A part of him, I thought, a part of my past, was dead and gone forever. My mother cried for days, and I was filled with unease at a world unstrung.

WE HEARD tales of his further exploits, this Yamato Takeru who had been my father. He smashed savages, argued with *kami* and gods, and struck them all down to the dead land of Yomi if they did not submit.

My mother and her co-wives received reports daily, tracking his progress with a mix of hope and trepidation.

From the boughs of the oak where I sat, alone once again, I could find no trace of former times.

"YOU WILL MARRY the Emperor's first grandson and raise my chance of ruling."

Those were my father's first words to me when he returned.

"My cousin." I stated it flat and unflinching, ignoring my mother's gasp.

"Yes," my father said. "The throne's heir."

"And if I will not?"

My father laughed, a sound sudden and sharp, like an arrow striking wood. "You would raise words at me, girl? I have killed *kami* and burned to the ground whole tribes of stinking rebels. I have subjugated the rivers, and the seas, and bent the messengers of gods to serve my own will. If you refuse, I have other daughters. Any of them can easily become my eldest."

I set my teeth and raised my chin. "As you say, my lord father." Keeping my words to myself.

BUT THAT NIGHT, I went once more to the forest.

I did not stop as I usually did at the foot of the oak, but walked further than I ever had before, into the untouched wilderness of the deep forest. I walked until the canopy closed overhead, then opened again to reveal the eternal patterns of the heavenly river. The air was rich with the smell of humus and rot.

I came to a mist-wreathed spring, and there I stopped, amidst the dim shapes of pines and rocks and the silent glow of distant stars reflected on its surface.

A white boar as big as a warhorse rose from the waters, its eyes unfocused and its movements calm and measured. Its form shifted as it walked, lopsided bulges of life forming on its body and sluicing away into the air with each step.

A *kami*. Its snout close enough that I could feel its breath, even and deep, on my skin it spoke.

woman-child, it said. *what do you seek*

The words echoed in my skull with the sound and thunder of trees falling. I did not reply. I did not dare.

woman-child do you seek justice

"No, I—"

woman-child do you seek vengeance

"No, I—"

do you seek . . . It paused, jaws opening slightly. *death*

"My father died already. What I seek is—"

your father's death? it will come again if that is what you seek

My breath sat like a stone in my stomach; my throat burned like fire.

"Beast-god," I rasped, "I order you stop! I, I wanted . . . "

leave this place woman-child, the *kami* said, *or what you say you do not seek will come to* you

Then it turned back toward the spring and, as it did so, slowly melted upward into mist.

I WALKED through the forest for long enough to count a lifetime. I lived off mushrooms and berries, drinking from pellucid streams whose water chilled my throat and aching belly.

When at last I found my way back to the Yamato I knew, I was told that a half-moon had passed. My mother ran to me, her hair in disarray and her robes disordered, her eyes puffy and red.

"Thank the white plain of heaven!" she half-sobbed, collapsing against me. "I thought we had lost you, too."

So it was that I learned my father had been stricken dead at mount Ibuki by a massive white *kami* in the shape of a boar, while I wandered lost in the forest.

AS MY FATHER'S *kami* vanishes toward the sea, and the wailing of my mother and her co-wives fades from hearing, I step from the shadow of my father's new-built tomb, face his empty grave, and speak. Raising words one final time.

"I will remember you as you were," I say, "and not as you became. Daily will I erase your divinity, ever chronicling your early, mortal life until your godly wrath is naught but legend.

"I will tell all who listen of order and calm."

Then I turn. I do not look back at the fields and the cliffs and the mountains and the oceans of my homeland. I turn and face the sun, and I leave that barren place in search of fertile ground.

NEW MEMBERS

JAMES F. MCGRATH

"*THIS IS YOUR PLAN* to increase church attendance?!"

The elders of First Presbyterian Church all had similar looks on their faces, but as usual it was Mr. Kryczek who voiced what most if not all of them were thinking.

Rev. Salazar smiled in his usual genial manner. His back was to the sanctuary of their historic church building as he stood facing the church elders with their skeptical and shocked faces. Behind him, the high vaulted ceiling, gothic-style arches, ornately carved oak paneling, and stained glass windows represented a historic beauty. While once such churches had been relatively commonplace, they now increasingly seemed like a rare and precious heirloom or an antiquated relic of a bygone era.

More and more churches were cutting costs by renting space in buildings owned by others for their Sunday morning services. Those that could afford a building of their own tended to opt for something much more compact and practical than had been the norm two centuries earlier, when First Presbyterian Church had been constructed. Its beauty made it a popular venue for weddings, yet its antique appearance had less and less appeal in terms of its ability to draw a consistent weekly attendance even from its members on the books, never mind visitors.

Its organ pipes were immediately recognizable as extremely high quality to those who were familiar with such instruments. Even those with no specialized expertise were impressed by their sound and the building's

159

marvelous acoustics. But organ music was arguably even less popular these days than gothic architecture.

On this particular day, however, something else caught one's eye in the church instead of the white marble baptistry or the multicolored sunlight dappling the interior that usually drew one's gaze. Roughly one-quarter of the pews, mostly toward the front of the sanctuary, were occupied by humanoid robots. Their metallic heads and shoulders reflected the multicolored light streaming through the windows, producing an incandescent effect that some might consider beautiful.

At the same time it seemed as incongruous in that setting as a large projection screen or illuminated disco ball might have. Both of those additions—a large screen and a disco ball—had in fact been proposed at some point in the church's long history, although one of the proposals had been made more frequently—and more seriously—than the other. Neither had met with the approval of the church's elders. Proposals for those sorts of chan-ges to the physical building itself fell under the purview of the board of elders. Filling the pews, on the other hand, was widely agreed to be the minister's responsibility. Whenever church attendance lagged or no increase in membership was seen for a long time, the question of whether a new minister was needed always came up.

What the elders saw before them today, however, was not what any of them had been looking for when they had voiced their concerns about dwindling attendance over the past couple of years.

"I hope you don't think that this is my end goal—cold metallic posteriors in pews. Not at all," Rev. Salazar told them.

On closer inspection (the committee inevitably wandered down the center aisle to take a look), the robots were of a variety of models, some of them familiar from stores and offices and even the church office, ever since the congregation had begrudgingly acknowledged that a robot answering the phones and greeting unexpected visitors made more economic and practical sense than keeping a human being sitting there all day, every day.

"What then?" asked Mr. Antolik, the church treasurer.

The committee had put a lot of trust in Rev. Salazar when he had asked that a portion of the next few months' budget be designated toward an "attendance drive" that the minister had insisted would bring fast results, yet the details of which he wanted to keep a surprise. Salazar had insisted that the minutes from the elders' meeting approving the budget line should include a statement to the effect that, if the church's attendance did not increase substantially within a year, the minister himself would repay the allocated money from his own salary or savings, and if the church desired, submit his resignation. That had persuaded everyone present to be willing to take the risk, whatever it turned out to be. They had nothing to lose financially, and unwillingness to try new things would surely end with the church closing within at most a decade or two, as so many other congregations already had.

"I'm sure you're all aware of the recent legal decision allowing machines to be considered persons," Salazar said. "I suspect that some of you may have thought, when walking into the sanctuary today, that I was playing some sort of prank on you based on that news. It is the beginning of April, after all. No one—not the lawyers, not the philosophers, not the wider public, and certainly not me—is under the illusion that the court is saying that robots are *conscious*, that they have *souls* or anything like that. Their status as persons is the same sort of legal fiction that allows a corporation to have the status of a person. Nothing more than that. But corporations cannot fill our pews. What other churches seem not to have noticed yet is that robots *can*."

"But, but, robots aren't going to put money in the offering plate!" Frank Kovac interrupted, convinced by this stage that whatever Salazar had intended, whether joke or serious-yet-hairbrained scheme, they had humored him for long enough.

"Of course not. You can't seriously think that I was hoping we could make up for our dwindling numbers with mechanical replacements for lost members—even though I'm sure each of us can probably think of a few individuals in whose case replacement with a robot would be an improvement!" The committee members mostly smiled, none of them considering the possibility that he might have them in mind when he said this. The joke succeeded in breaking the palpable tension at least slightly.

"What then?" Antolik asked again.

"How many of you read the article I circulated about the biggest challenge to attracting new members to churches?" Salazar asked them. Most avoided eye contact, but a few nodded. "What is at the top of the list? Does anyone remember?"

It was Jan Horvath who offered the answer after only the slightest pause. "Membership statistics are public these days. Everyone looks to see how popular and well-attended a church already is before deciding even to visit, never mind attend regularly or consider becoming a member. If your membership has a downward trend, no matter the reason, you will also see a decline in visitors. From there, it becomes a vicious circle, a downward spiral that churches can rarely break out of."

"Precisely," Salazar exclaimed, impressed with his recall and with the precise summary he had provided. "Well, not only our attendance but our membership has just increased dramatically."

"They're *members*?!" Antolik asked, shocked. "Since when?"

"Since this morning. After I signed the paperwork for the shipment when they were delivered, I personally baptized every one of them. Obviously this isn't an option that would work for Baptists . . . "

Salazar's joke got even bigger laughs this time. Being a Presbyterian church, they baptized through sprinkling, and even the least expensive models of robots were sufficiently waterproof to cope with that. Full immersion in water, on the other hand, could have significant impacts on all but the most expensive models.

"But this won't fool anyone!" Kovac spluttered. "Even if droves of people show up next Sunday to see what has led to the sudden dramatic increase in attendance, they'll take one look, laugh or shake their heads, and head for the door."

"I sincerely doubt that," Salazar said. "In fact, I'm tempted to circulate some video to show what will be happening here on Sunday and give people a taste of what to expect. It might draw even bigger crowds. But I think the effect will be even better in person."

"Effect of what?" Antolik asked, genuinely puzzled. "Shock? Curiosity?"

"I felt I had to show you this much, so that you wouldn't raise a fuss on Sunday morning and undermine what I have planned," Salazar said. "But having already invested in my effort as an act of faith and trust, I ask you to humor me just a few more days. I don't want to rob you entirely of the chance to be as impressed as complete newcomers will be this coming Sunday morning. Indeed, given the skepticism many, if not all, of you feel, I think your reactions on Sunday will be even better than those of newcomers. It will be a service that you will want to invite friends to, and I promise you will have no regrets if you do so."

The committee members asked a few more questions, but at this point Salazar became evasive, insisting that it was better for them to wait and see.

ON SUNDAY MORNING, Jan Horvath was the first of the committee members to arrive at the church. He wasn't especially early—no one normally arrived particularly long before the service began even if they were involved in some way. He was immediately struck by the number of cars already in the parking lot, and a small crowd that had already gathered outside. The main doors were open, but a velvet rope had been placed across the entrance indicating that they should wait there. All those present seemed to be newcomers.

Horvath headed for the back entrance, to which he had a key, giving the crowd a wide berth. They all seemed transfixed by something, but he couldn't see it from where he was. All he could make out from this distance, as he headed for the small door on the far side of the church, was that they seemed to have their attention drawn toward the open doors. He was tall enough that he could see over most of them, yet he saw nothing immediately inside the entrance that might have accounted for their seemingly rapt attention. There was certainly no sign of a robot bouncer or anything like that.

Horvath entered the church building, and as he made his way through the hall of Sunday school classrooms at the far end of the building and toward the sanctuary, he began to hear singing. He stopped and listened, even though the sound wasn't carrying well to where he was. What he heard was not their church choir. To be completely honest, when the word *choir* was used in reference to their usual small group of singers who occasionally facilitated worship, it deserved to be in scare quotes. None of the voices of its members was particularly *bad*, but the group had an excess of basses, no decent tenors, and simply sounded weak and unbalanced. What he was hearing now sounded professional.

Horvath started walking again, picking up his pace. When he reached the doors to the sanctuary he stopped in his tracks again. Standing at the front, *dressed in choir robes*, were a significant number of the robots that had been seated in the pews a few days earlier, when the minister had first unveiled them to the committee. They were *singing*—or, if that wasn't the right word, they were producing the beautiful sound of singing, each individually, and together in exquisite harmony. Rev. Salazar was standing at the back of the sanctuary near the left hand side. He appeared to be engrossed in the music himself, much as Horvath now realized that the crowd gathering outside must likewise be. Horvath thought of several things he might say. Some were skeptical. Some were attempts at humor. But eventually only one thing seemed appropriate.

"It's beautiful," he said.

Salazar nodded. "Some of the best voices in human history," he said with a twinkle in his eye. "Recordings of them have been in the public domain for quite some time. Academics and voice teachers have been studying and debating them for quite some time as well. It was surprisingly straightforward to download the data about the voices and use their qualities as the pattern for the voices of our robots."

Horvath had been a music student at university, even though he hadn't pursued it professionally after graduation. He couldn't quite place the piece that was currently being sung, although it was somewhat familiar. But when the tenor solo began, he recognized the voice immediately as patterned on that of Enrico Caruso. But it wasn't a recording of Caruso, nor was it even a precise simulation of Caruso's voice. It had started with that, he could tell, but then had been enriched by an AI that analyzed other famous voices and drew on their shared characteristics to produce something unique and distinctive.

He couldn't bring himself to say another word for some time. He simply stared and listened. Spending these moments thinking about the computing behind these sounds would be to squander an incredible auditory experience that he knew deserved his undivided attention. It deserved his awe and rapture as well. When that piece for choir and tenor finished, the organ began to play. Horvath moved forward so as to be able to peer up toward the balcony under which they had been standing, since it was there that the church's pipe organ was located.

A robot sat at the keyboard. It was playing the intro to "Les Rameaux" by Gabriel Fauré. Horvath was so transfixed he barely noticed that Rev. Salazar had gone to allow the crowd outside, which had grown even larger now, to enter. He took his seat in his usual pew to listen further and wait for the service proper to begin.

If there were any criticism of what followed that perhaps could have been offered, it was that the entrancing power and perfection of the robot music discouraged congregational singing. But that was true in many churches with human choirs and musicians. When the offering was taken, the offering plates were incredibly full—not just fuller than they had been in this church in decades, but fuller than they probably were in *any* church that size that particular morning.

Rev. Salazar's sermon, when the time came for it, didn't pretend that this was merely business as usual for the congregation. He preached a rousing sermon about the church's need to balance innovation and tradition. When pursuing its mission in the manner that Jesus taught, the church had always sought to keep one eye on scripture and tradition, the heritage it inherited from the past, and the other eye on the needs of its present context and the issues people were confronted with in the here and now. The presence of robots symbolized that, the latest technology giving voice to the church's historic music.

The newcomers returned the following week with friends. The word spread. Within a few weeks, the church was packed. The robots offered music that drew from a range of genres, both extremely familiar and long forgotten repertoires, both ancient and brand new music. But whether classic or contemporary, the sheer quality of the rendition meant that few complained in the manner that grumpy churchgoers tend to. No one said the hymns were too old, nor that the drums or guitar were too loud.

The church was soon on its way out of its financial crisis, as well as its membership crisis. The people who came didn't merely attend and put money in the collection plate. They got involved in the ways that it made sense for them to in the church's various ministries. The church, by any historic definition, was thriving. So it shocked Rev. Salazar when he received a letter that he had been expecting just before his new robotic initiative began, saying that his position was being downgraded, effective immediately, to that of part-time church staff member, and that if he did not accept this change he was welcome to tender his resignation.

Salazar arrived at church on Sunday downcast, perplexed, and more than a little irritated. But he was used to withholding judgment until he had enough information to act on. He expected to find evidence that showed something had changed, that his critics had been proven right and the novelty of what the robots offered had worn off and people had declared their intention to stop coming. But no, the numbers were as strong as ever —indeed, attendance seemed to be up ever so slightly compared to the Sunday before. The music was as phenomenal as it had been.

So he sat, waiting for an explanation that he was sure would come. Meanwhile, lay leaders performed their various roles as usual, one providing an announcement, another a Bible reading, yet another saying a prayer. Prayer in particular was one thing that everyone felt particularly strongly needed to remain in the hands of humans. A robot prayer was like a recording of a prayer, even when the programing behind it was such that the machine was not merely repeating verbatim something someone else had composed.

When they reached the point in the service when it was time for the sermon, Frank Hajduk stood up. He had been scheduled to lead the service that Sunday by providing brief interludes and words addressed to congregants between the contributions of others (whether human or machine), prior to the sermon. But instead of introducing Rev. Salazar as he had been expected to, Hajduk informed the congregation that there was a special surprise in store for them, a guest speaker. Salazar watched as a robot emerged through a side door and ascended to the pulpit. He listened in awe as the robot spoke with a voice that seemed to be mostly a combination of Billy Graham and James Earl Jones. It was a powerful voice, and it delivered a powerful sermon.

Salazar went home shaken, wrote his resignation letter, and emailed it to the presbytery.

When he showed up at the church to meet with the church elders a few days later, however, he had several representatives from the synod with him. The regional body had contacted both the minister and the elders to call for a meeting about what they perceived to be an improper action in the church.

"I sent the presbytery my resignation," Salazar explained. "They wouldn't accept it. It is against denominational policy to leave a church without a minister being arranged."

"We have made an arrangement," said Mr. Antolik coldly.

"Oh, I know. I was most impressed when I heard it preach!" Salazar replied. "And believe you me, I don't disrespect your choice of that machine over me in the pulpit. Let's be honest—how many preachers today could compete with a recording of any one of the best preachers in history, never mind an amalgam of all their voices delivering brand new content? I was convinced almost immediately. That's why I wrote to the denomination right away, tendering my resignation. But as I have already said, they wouldn't accept it."

"Why not?" asked Antolik, clearly both annoyed and suspicious.

"To put it bluntly," said one of the denominational representatives, "your robot is not ordained. Policy requires that the senior minister be credentialed by a seminary of our denomination."

Before any of the elders could interject, Salazar jumped in. "Now, before you say anything, I think I can see a solution that we might all be happy with. Please hear me out. I have no desire to get rid of the robot—any of the robots, for that matter. There is nothing to prevent a seminary student serving as assistant minister in one of our churches. I will happily take the robot on in the capacity of my assistant pastor . . . while you send it to seminary."

"What?!" blurted Antolik, his face becoming flushed.

"It was an expensive investment, I'm sure, for the church to purchase this robot. I know—I placed an order for a large number myself not that long ago, as you'll recall. The church will expect to be reimbursed if the robot cannot fulfill the function for which it was purchased. And so rather than lose money selling it used at a loss, why not pay the cost of tuition and send it to seminary? I'm sure that money from talk show interviews and a book deal will help cover the costs."

Mr. Horvath had remained silent up until this point. He asked Salazar, "What do you get out of this arrangement?"

"You mean beyond the survival of the church, and helping to shatter stereotypes about Christianity as simply a thing of the past?" Salazar responded. "Have you already forgotten that I was the one who set the church down this path, at great risk to myself, when all of you were skeptical and resistant? I really do care about the church—about *this* church. But that doesn't mean I reap no benefits from this arrangement if you agree to it. It genuinely seems to be one in which everyone wins."

Salazar continued. "Let me tell you what's in it for me personally. I have no doubt that, once the robot is ordained, I will be let go. This way, I get four or perhaps five more years in this job, giving me time to find a new one. Heck, if the seminary is willing to allow the robot to enter directly at the master's level, it might only take a year. I hear these things are quick studies with excellent recall." Salazar grinned impishly. "Even before I leave, I will be known as the minister who trained a robot to replace him. I will be interviewed by the media and my face and my words will be in magazines and on TV. Whenever the time comes that I need to leave, I will land on my feet. What do you say?"

The elders asked for time to consider the matter. The synod representatives made the same request since they had not known what Salazar was scheming until he said it at the meeting. Everyone except Salazar left at least a tiny bit irritated. Salazar, on the other hand, seemed to be enjoying himself immensely as he watched everyone else begin to wrestle with what the implications would be of saying either no or yes. And he seemed delighted with their eventual acceptance of his plan and genuinely to welcome his new assistant in his parish ministry.

The press coverage was as sensational as Salazar had predicted. It began immediately at the local level, but soon the church and its robots were making national news. Robots had been introduced in K-12 and university classrooms years earlier, as assistants to teachers and professors, digital TAs that could deliver lectures, answer questions, and so on. Now there would be a robot student, and at a seminary no less. How long, some asked, before all that was left were robots teaching robots? What would be left for humans to do? Others, however, had positive things to say about the embrace of new technology by the church. All the publicity, both favorable and critical, increased attendance on Sunday mornings still further, as Rev. Salazar and many others in the parish were quoted in newspapers and made TV appearances.

Even for the robot to be accepted at a seminary was no small accomplishment in and of itself. Once that had been achieved, the robot was formally enrolled to enter at the bachelor's level, and began classes at the start of the next academic year, the next big hurdle was how it would fare in the classroom and whether it could produce the kinds of assignments and exam answers that would grant it at least a passing grade. Figuring out on what basis Salazar might be given access to the robot's grades and other information about its performance took everyone into uncharted waters once again. Federal law prohibited an educational institution from disclosing information about grades and academic performance to anyone other than parents and legal guardians, and even then the student must formally grant permission. But what if a student was a robot, had no parent but an owner, and would give consent for disclosure if it was programmed to do so by said owner? Initially, no one knew what to do.

After consultation with the seminary's legal advisors, however, it was decided that if Salazar was appointed as the robot's legal guardian, the robot could grant permission for him to be able to obtain information from the seminary about him. Even though Salazar himself would be programming the robot to do this, following the letter of the law should keep them in good stead. This was obviously a matter which, if robot students became something commonplace, would call for new legislation. But they decided that abiding by the laws currently in force was all they could do, and all they needed to do at present.

Having thus been granted permission to keep tabs on how the robot was doing, Salazar was determined to check in with the seminary weekly. Even though there was something in the news almost every day about the robot student written by reporters who visited the seminary, those articles couldn't provide the kind of information Salazar wanted: classroom participation, grades on assignments, and overall acceptance of the robot by professors and students. By the end of the second week, everything seemed to be going fine, better in fact that he had dared to hope.

Once the robot understood that it must raise its hand and be called upon before answering questions, it ceased to completely monopolize classroom discussions as it had initially. The fact that the robot could search the internet quickly on the spot, including the seminary library's database of subscription resources, meant that human students spent their time in the classroom focused primarily on discussion with one another, asking the robot to find things out for them when otherwise they might have turned to their tablets or phones and ended up distracted rather than engaged. The robot needed some way for professors and students to address it and refer to it, and so in the sci-fi tradition of naming robots with a combination of letters and numbers they dubbed it "Rev2B." The first quiz was a breeze, even though the robot was disconnected from the internet while it took it. It could recall perfectly what it had been assigned to learn and had heard in class.

Then, on the Monday of the fourth week of classes, Rev. Salazar received a phone call from the office of the dean of the seminary. Rev2B was going fail a class and risked expulsion from the seminary. Salazar was shocked and didn't know what to say. Images rushed through his mind. Had the robot acted inappropriately in class? Harmed a student? It couldn't just be too many wrong answers on an assignment—they don't expel you for that.

Salazar's throat felt dry as he asked the dean's administrative assistant, "What's it done?"

When he heard the answer, he asked for a few more details and asked if he could make another phone call to the robot's purchaser, after which he would call back to talk with the dean. He hung up the phone, called Mr. Antolik, and said that no matter what he might be doing they needed to meet within the hour to discuss a matter of extreme urgency. When Antolik suggested a coffee shop near his workplace, Salazar said that somewhere more private and discreet was called for under the circumstances. Within twenty minutes Antolik was at the church, and he and Salazar met in a small meeting room with the door closed.

"What software did you install on the robot?" Salazar asked Antolik.

"Standard, run-of-the-mill sermon preparation software," he replied. "It's called something like 'EZPreach.' It came highly recommended. It wasn't cheap, but it would have been foolish to invest in an expensive robot and then be stingy with the software. Plus, as with the music, I knew the robot's sermons would only draw crowds if they were of the highest quality—not just the voice and style, but the content. Why? What's happened?"

"Rev2B is going to fail its class on New Testament exegesis and may be liable to fail others," Salazar said glumly. "The dean has indicated that he is considering whether expulsion from the seminary altogether is appropriate under the circumstances."

"What circumstances?" Antolik asked, taken aback.

"The robot has committed plagiarism!" Salazar said with a tone of combined dismay and frustration. "It just submitted its first essay and the professor discovered it."

"You think there's a glitch in the software?" Antolik asked.

"No, I think it is the wrong software for the task," Salazar answered. "I've never found sermon prep software appealing, personally, but I know plenty of ministers who do. And I've tried out a few such packages, downloading a trial version of one or another when some church emergency was keeping me from being as well prepared as far in advance as I like to be. Under such circumstances, I wanted to have a full-text sermon to hand just in case I had no choice but to rely on it. I've tried lots of sermon preparation programs. Some produce text that is barely intelligible, others craft sentences that are downright poetic. But they all have one thing in common. Wanna know what it is?"

Antolik nodded.

"They don't add footnotes. Even ministers who read their sermons off of paper or a tablet screen don't stop to cite sources. At most, we'll say something like, "As John Calvin said . . . " and then give the quotation or paraphrase. Of course, we have all heard unscrupulous preachers read someone else's sermon they printed off from the internet. What sermon preparation software does is to trawl the internet for content on a particular text or theme and weave it together into a speech. In a sermon, it doesn't matter to the software if the wording of whole sentences and the gist of whole paragraphs are lifted from someone else's work. The words travel through the air a few seconds, wash over the audience, and then are gone. But if you hand in something like that in an academic class, it isn't just going to earn you a low grade because it is too devotional and preachy, inappropriate for the academic setting. If the professor spots the stealing of others' wording and ideas without credit being given to them, you'll at best receive a failing grade on the assignment, and more likely fail the class. A repeat offender will almost certainly be expelled."

"I thought you said the robot only plagiarized on one assignment," Antolik interjected. "Can't they let it off with a warning?"

"They could, if it were a human student," Salazar said. "When they do that with your typical student, the reasoning is that the student in question may not have known better or made an error of judgment. The hope is that the student will learn from the experience. The problem is that our robot can only learn *content* using the software it has been provided with. It can't learn how to learn differently, to research and write differently. A human student is essentially replacing or upgrading their 'software' when they learn research skills like these. In the robot's case, that's our responsibility."

"So if we replace the robot's software with something suited to academic work, we can be back on track, right?" Antolik suggested. "It may need to retake the course, but if we act quickly we can replace the program before the robot submits any more assignments."

"I've seen essay-writing software," Salazar said in reply. "It has gotten the children in a number of families in the parish into trouble. Parents have sometimes shared their experiences with me of what they have been told at parent-teacher conferences, and a few of the high school students in the youth group have also shared some stories with me about trouble they have gotten into as a result of using these programs. No one seems to have figured out how to create software that consistently identifies reliable sources of information and cites them accurately, turning them into clear and relevant content that isn't plagiarized. That a robot can't think critically is something we knew in advance. We were expecting it to be a C student— perhaps a B one, what with grade inflation. What no one saw coming was that it might not be capable of crafting essays at all, at least not ones that will pass muster with professors."

Antolik rose to his feet angrily. "You knew!" he said, pointing his finger toward the minister. "I'm sure that you didn't just learn these things about software from parents and students in these past few weeks. You saw this coming, and now you're probably pleased with yourself. You've been hoping for this all along!"

Salazar looked Antolik straight in the eyes. "It in no way serves my interests for this endeavor to fail. I will look bad, worse than anyone else involved. The press have come to view the robot as my protégé. They will suspect that I programmed or taught it poorly at best, and that perhaps the whole thing has been a scam all along. No matter who purchased or programmed it, the public and the press will blame me. Now, to be completely honest with you, I confess that I have had my doubts about the robot's capacity pretty much since I heard it preach. The content was great —but when you've preached and heard as many sermons as I have, you come to recognize recycled content easily. Not footnoting, though? I confess that that particular issue for the robot's installed software never occurred to me until the seminary called. I assumed the software it was running and any relevant settings would be appropriate to and customized for academic work, even if it was incapable of producing great content."

Antolik's suspicions were not completely eliminated, but his anger subsided somewhat, allowing worry to become his dominant feeling once again. "What do we do now?" he asked.

"We think, as quickly as we can," Salazar answered. "We pray. And we ask for help."

"From where?" Antolik asked.

"Everywhere," Salazar replied after an awkwardly long pause, as the germ of an idea began to take shape in his mind. He picked up his phone and called the seminary dean, asking him whether the seminary would be willing to consider not expelling Rev2B if there was indeed a chance that the robot could learn from its mistake. He reminded the dean that the seminary stood to benefit from its connection with this pioneering effort, and that it could reflect poorly on them if they simply kicked the robot out at the first sign of trouble. Being the locus of a failed experiment would be nothing to be ashamed of if they saw it through to the end, and allowing more time for a creative solution to be found risked nothing that couldn't be resolved at a later point, if they judged then that the robot truly deserved to be expelled.

Once the dean agreed, Salazar ended their conversation and contacted the press.

THE NEXT MORNING, the minister was back in a news studio with cameras pointed at him once again, announcing an effort to enlist programmers to craft new software (or a plug-in for an existing package) that would recognize reliable sources and cite them correctly to produce an academic essay appropriate to an undergraduate class at the university level.

"We all know how critical it is to have these skills," Salazar told the anchor, but primarily addressing the audience that was watching and listening from around the country. "Reliance on search engine results and denigration of the value of expertise have significantly damaged public understanding of key issues. So many in our time, looking to confirm their biases and desires, find and latch on to sources that confirm what they already believe and hope to be true. Part of the problem is that, unlike other areas in which technology has improved our lives, we haven't yet created machines or algorithms that will do a better job of undertaking research and reporting clearly and accurately on the state of our knowledge. I believe we can do better, and need to, urgently. That is the main reason why I am launching an appeal to computer programmers to find a solution."

Salazar told the story of what happened with the robot's software and plagiarism. If the robot was kicked out of seminary for academic dishonesty, sooner or later people would undoubtedly find out what had unfolded, or they would make up something worse to fill in the place of the unknown truth. It was better to be frank—and to explain the specific impetus for the software engineers and programmers to craft something that did precisely what Rev2B needed to be able to do. Salazar explained that he didn't have the resources to offer a financial prize for the most effective solution. But he had something that was arguably better: an elevated press platform and extensive reach as a result of the publicity his church's robots had gained thus far. The programmers who cracked this problem would be solving a societal issue, not just one connected with this particular robot. They would boost their own career through the media coverage their achievement would garner.

It only took a matter of days for the solutions to start pouring in. The challenge itself was straightforward enough: create software that could produce an essay that would get a passing grade writing about the same question that the robot had been attempting in its class, using reliable academic sources that were cited correctly. Yet Salazar hadn't anticipated quite how many computer programmers, ranging from teenagers still in high school to well-established professionals at big companies, would respond to his challenge, nor from how many different parts of the world. In the end, he scrapped his plan to either vet the results himself or have the professor at the seminary who had caught the plagiarism do so. There were simply too many entries. So he set up a page on the church website and hosted the essays there, and crowdsourced judging them. He spread the word among seminary professors, students, and other clergy to make sure that such perspectives were among those providing an evaluation of submissions. It was crucial that the various kinds of issues that might lead one to fail on the assignment—including but not limited to plagiarism—were caught and flagged, disqualifying those entries.

Soon after word about the competition had begun to spread widely, a major edtech software company contacted Salazar and opened their service to him for the purpose of vetting the submissions. They told him that this would provide them with a good test of their software's ability not only to detect plagiarism but to distinguish between human-produced and AI-produced work, something that many academics were already concerned about, and about which not a few had voiced strong opinions in response to Salazar's challenge. Of course, it wasn't as though the effort to create software that could undertake and report on research was an entirely new endeavor. Salazar had merely prompted a concentrated and consolidated effort in relation to a problem that numerous programmers and companies already had their sights on. And frankly, Salazar was relieved that the edtech side of things was now directly involved in what he was doing. He didn't want to contribute only to the side of dishonest students in the ongoing software "arms race" between them and professors. With the involvement of these new collaborators in the effort, Salazar was able to feel ever more excited and exhilarated about the innovation that he was playing a small role in helping to foster.

In the end, there were multiple entries meeting the established criteria that came in before a successful entry was identified and the end of the competition announced. Salazar felt it was appropriate to showcase all of the leading software in some way, even though there was one particular entry that stood out from all the rest and represented a clear winner.

The winner of the competition was announced at a press conference. Keeping his audience around the world in suspense, Salazar started by surveying some of the losing entries, some of which were amusing. They served to highlight just how challenging a task this was for computer software (and its programmers) to accomplish. One piece of software had cited several porn websites over the course of its theological essay. Another focused not on Jesus of Nazareth but a confusing variety of people named Jesus who were alive today. Yet another cited only academic sources in its footnotes, but its text sounded like it was a campaign ad for Jesus running for office.

More than a few had been misled by the widespread presence of both atheist and Christian fundamentalist websites into arguing for views that were wildly at odds with the consensus of historians and other scholars in relevant fields. Many essays gave no sign of having understood the question. Given that the question was about the relationship between the historical Jesus and the motif of the Messianic secret in the Gospel of Mark, it was only fair to point out that many human seminary students have struggled to understand, never mind answer, a question about that topic. But that was what made this programming competition a challenge and its successful entries so impressive.

Having referred to successful entries in the plural, Salazar went on to present the programmers whose submissions had crafted acceptable essays, accentuating their achievement and quoting from their essays. However, these were not the winners of the competition, he added. Finally, Salazar offered an introduction to the winner. He shared some of her life story in the manner he was accustomed to when offering a sermon illustration, tugging at the heart strings of those who were now listening with rapt attention in front of screens of various sorts around the world. The winner had created a program that not only managed to identify *really* good sources and cite them correctly, but use them to produce essay content that was not merely lucid but downright eloquent in places. The winner was a woman in her early twenties living in India. Her name was Jayanti Khan, and she was studying computer science at American College in Madurai.

The essay that Khan had submitted was so impressive that initially Salazar had been suspicious, asking for a second and a third opinion about the essay before taking it seriously. Even then, he arranged for Khan to be flown in from India as part of the assessment process and asked for a demonstration of the software in his presence, with technical advisors present to try to make sure that he was not dealing with a modern essay-writing version of the Mechanical Turk, with a human being hiding behind the mask. However, the software was able to craft an essay in response to an unanticipated question that Salazar posed to it and did so in a much shorter time frame than any human being could have accomplished it. Indeed, the writing alone would have taken longer, never mind the research. There was no way that this could be the work of some human being waiting for remote prompting. It was technically impossible for cheating to be involved, for multiple reasons. It was clear that the software was simply that powerful.

The eloquence of the writing, Khan explained, was the result of a machine-learning project she had already been working on prior to the competition. The English spoken in India has some distinctive characteristics that can seem odd to readers and hearers outside the country. After she submitted articles to multiple computer science journals and received rejections from all of them, she had wanted to make sure it wasn't the language in which she expressed herself that was at fault. So she had trained a program to compare phrasing in her completed drafts of her own articles against the data set of the most cited academic articles in the field of English. The machine had no comprehension of what it was reading, of course. But skillful use of language (unless you are writing poetry that bends and breaks the rules) doesn't involve innovation in grammar or phrasing, but merely a following of best practices when expressing your own ideas. A machine can learn that—and help a human being to learn to do it better, too.

As Salazar provided this brief bio of the winner, he felt it important to mention something else. Khan wasn't a Christian, the minister remarked as he finally invited her to join him in front of the cameras at the press conference. Yet she would be enabling a robot to pursue Christian ministry as a seminary student. She wasn't American, yet she created software that would benefit us and not only herself or her nation. The end result of the project, Salazar said, was a testament to international and inter-religious cooperation, and not just progress in software engineering and artificial intelligence.

With the new software installed, Rev2B continued its studies at the seminary. No more plagiarism was detected, and its grades saw an immediate improvement. By its second year of study, public and media interest had largely dissipated. Several congregations had undertaken efforts to incorporate robots into their congregational life. One example that received significant publicity featured robot musicians offering very different genres of music. A megachurch in Chicago had a robot drummer with six arms whose performances were indeed phenomenal.

However, no one seemed to be in a hurry to invest in sending another robot to seminary. If they did so, they would simply look like copycats at this stage. If Rev2B ended up failing to graduate, their robot was more than likely to meet the same end as well. There was thus no benefit to doing anything other than waiting to see what the results of this experiment would turn out to be. By this point, there was no way of snatching away the honor that would reward Salazar and his church if things turned out well. And things could still go horribly wrong. That was why everyone was apparently willing to let the risk be shouldered entirely by Salazar and Rev2B.

When the robot was in its final semester at the seminary, and successfully applied for permission to walk and receive its diploma at the next graduation ceremony, Rev. Salazar sent Jayanti Khan an email to invite her to the graduation. He had made sure to follow her career path so that he would be able to contact her when the time came. She had graduated from college two years earlier, and while she had received countless offers from some of the biggest software companies in the world, she had chosen to start her own business instead, and did so even while she was still a student. The company seemed to be doing impressively well, at least as far as he could tell as an outsider to that industry. It was only twenty minutes after he sent the email that his phone rang, displaying a longer than usual number indicating the call came from somewhere overseas. Salazar answered it quickly.

"Hello?"

"Rev. Salazar? This is Jayanti calling you from India. I was so delighted to receive your invitation to Rev2B's graduation and would love to attend. I had been hoping to hear from you once the graduation was confirmed." Khan paused before continuing. "I have a proposition for you and want to say before I go any further that, if you agree, I intend to show my appreciation by covering all of Rev2B's tuition and fees."

"That's very kind of you to offer," Salazar replied. "But it really isn't necessary. The robot's media appearances and my own book deal have already taken care of those expenses."

"Oh, so sorry for not being clear," Khan replied. "I meant *future* tuition."

Salazar paused for a moment before asking, "What future tuition?"

"That's what I wanted to talk to you about. I would like to know if you are open to Rev2B pursuing a doctorate." Khan went on to explain that, with the success of her software that could synthesize existing information in the way one expects in an undergraduate assignment, the next big challenge was whether an AI could do original cutting-edge research. She and her employees had been working on this problem and felt they were making significant progress. But the real test of success this time would be whether a machine-written research article could pass peer review and be accepted by a major journal. As of this moment, no robot other than Rev2B had a legitimate institutional affiliation and an academic supervisor that would allow this to be pursued in a way that could be documented and studied.

Salazar wasn't sure what the ramifications of pursuing this might be. But he knew that Khan had turned their robot student in danger of expulsion into one that made the dean's list each academic year. If he tried, he could probably think of some reasons that he could legitimately refuse, excuses he might offer that might have some validity. But he knew immediately that he did not want to refuse.

"How can I refuse, after everything your software has done for us?" Salazar asked, pausing for only a second before continuing. "But if you don't mind, I have long wanted to ask you something. I know you're not a Christian. If the robot goes on to graduate school, it will presumably be in theology or something related to that. Goodness, it would probably be simpler if it could do work in chemistry, wouldn't it? Research in the natural sciences, or perhaps mathematics, would seem more up a robot's alley. But I suspect that you're actually more interested in it trying to write a thesis in the humanities—that's the real challenge for programmers now, isn't it? But anyway, as I started to say, with you not being a Christian, I have long wondered how you feel about your software turning a robot into a Presbyterian minister."

There was a long enough pause that Salazar began to worry that either they had been cut off or that he might have offended her. But when Khan spoke, she sounded as though she were speaking from a source of personal conviction, and with some enthusiasm for the topic.

"My father is a Muslim, and my mother is Hindu. They brought me up to respect all beliefs, and in both of their traditions Jesus is a respected figure. On a professional level, I would have been happy if my path to success had come from just about anywhere. But on a personal one, I am *so* happy for the way this all came together. You said it yourself at the press conference where you announced that I had won, although at that point you hadn't asked me about my perspective on the matter. This project thus far, and what I am proposing to carry it further, doesn't just illustrate the possibility of international and interfaith cooperation. It illustrates the connections between computer science and the humanities, between faith and reason. I'm not even thinking of your religious faith when I say that. Every step of the way, as I have heard the story told, you have stepped out into the unknown in a way that didn't expect miracles but did depend on diverse others rising to the challenge of the situation with hope, trust, willingness to risk, and goodwill. You didn't act irrationally, but you also dared to set out in uncharted directions over and over again. That's what I want to see continue and enhanced in the next stage of things. What do you say?"

Salazar agreed, and after chatting some more, they ended their conversation. As Salazar set his phone down, he scanned the books that filled the shelves around his office walls until his eyes alighted on a volume on inter-religious dialog and interfaith cooperation. He got up, pulled it from the shelf, and turned to the index. As he suspected, there was no entry on robots, none on computers, not even one on technology. They were indeed in uncharted territory—and that was not just because the book was now more than a decade old. For all our penchant for innovation and creativity, for progress, human beings are still a highly risk-averse species.

Salazar sat down in a different chair on the other side of the office, leaned back, and looked out the window at the barren branches of the old oak tree nearby. They stood as though poised, waiting for a signal to indicate that these last few weeks of early spring chilliness had at long last passed, and now they can start to bud. People have argued that technology divides people and that it brings people together, Salazar mused silently. People have had the same arguments about religion. The answer was plainer to him now than it had ever been before.

Technology and religion don't do either one of those things—not on their own, at any rate. A phone doesn't connect or divide people while lying neglected on a desk. But it can do either, depending on how it is used. The same is true of robots, and religion, and just about anything else for that matter. But when we don't want to change our habits as a society and we find ourselves disconnected from or in conflict with one another, we blame our tools for shortcomings that reside within ourselves.

BY THE TIME the first robot in history walked across the stage of the seminary's auditorium, it had already been accepted into the DMin program. Its proposed thesis topic was to research the history and prospects for the future of the congregation where it had been serving as assistant minister for the past four years. The foundation of the research project would utilize significant amounts of sociological as well as historical data, allowing the robot to draw on its computational strengths to crunch numbers and trawl enormous swaths of data that no human being could ever hope to get a handle on. Upon that foundation, the robot would then face the challenge of engaging in a more humanistic undertaking. Could it not only detect neglected patterns in this tiny slice of religious history but also interpret them in a manner that would allow it to make a recommendation about what the congregation ought to do in the future?

By the end of the first year, the robot had indeed identified correlations that no one had previously been fully aware of. Patterns in the tiniest fluctuations in Sunday morning attendance that consistently presaged larger shifts soon to follow. Correlations between church membership numbers, how much people gave to the church, and demographic shifts in the surrounding neighborhood, city, and nation. The impact of the arrival of a new minister, the addition of staff members such as ministerial assistants, and other kinds of events, both positive and negative, in the life of the church.

These data points about the congregation were correlated with one another, and then the robot brought in data about thousands of other congregations for comparison. As he read drafts of the first few chapters of the robot's thesis, setting forth the methodology and the key data, Rev. Salazar felt like he was already learning so much about a congregation whose history he thought he knew well, that he had studied in as much detail as he could.

As much as was humanly possible, he thought to himself. *Thank God*—he meant that literally—*for bringing a nonhuman perspective to bear on this.* When he saw the connection that emerged between adding ministry staff and subsequent church conflict, Salazar wondered whether the robot might not recommend its own termination from its current position. But what Rev2B recommended in the end, when it became apparent in drafts of the conclusion of the thesis, took everyone by surprise.

The biggest periods of genuine flourishing in the congregation's history had to be measured not only in terms of membership and giving, but also in terms of internal harmony and community outreach. The robot had recognized that "healthy" attendance numbers and finances sometimes hid other maladies in the life of the congregation. Those times when the church was truly thriving were connected not merely with high attendance and giving but also, surprisingly enough, with economic downturns in the nation and the city. And they were times when the church started new ministries or enhanced existing activities that serve the people in the surrounding neighborhood. Recent economic data made the robot 94% confident that a similar challenge/opportunity was approaching within the next year. And the church's current lack of outreach into its immediate surroundings suggested that this time they were likely to experience crisis rather than renewal, unless changes were made quickly to prepare for what was coming.

All of that would have been impressive enough. But the recommendation the robot made left Salazar feeling rather foolish. It was the feeling of someone who had purchased an expensive tool for use in one specific brief project, and only later found that they could have been using it daily to address other longstanding problems they struggled with. For that was precisely what he and his church had done. So it was that, even before the thesis was submitted, the church had begun acting on the draft recommendation.

On weekdays, which the robots had previously spent locked safely in a storage room awaiting their next Sunday performance, the church now sent their army of robot choristers out into the community, to check on the elderly and infirm, deliver food to the hungry, and teach English to members of a community of refugees. They cleaned up abandoned lots littered with trash, repaired dilapidated houses, and even washed a few cars. It turned out the robots were also capable of preparing a darn good breakfast for poor community members in the church hall on Saturday mornings. They did all these things the way they sang and played the organ: skillfully and masterfully. The human members of the church joined in these activities as well. As a result of the robot workforce shouldering so much of that responsibility, the human members of the church were able to focus primarily on fellowship, building friendships, performing counseling, and other things that still required a human touch.

When Rev2B graduated, Jayanti Khan was invited to attend once again. This time, however, it was to be a guest speaker at commencement and receive an honorary degree. And when Rev2B was ordained, an alternative venue to the church sanctuary had to be used. The church's membership and regular attendance had swelled by so much in recent years that there was no way the many additional invited guests would be able to fit, to say nothing of the reporters who had already indicated their plans to attend. They therefore utilized a large auditorium in the denomination's regional headquarters for the event. Even so, it was packed.

In the ceremony, after the usual laying on of hands, the robot was able to preach an impressive sermon that incorporated insights from its doctoral research, which had by this point been accepted for publication and would appear within the upcoming year as a book. But of course, it only did these things because it had been instructed to. Many in attendance seemed to have allowed themselves to forget that the machine was an impressive piece of technology but did not have any kind of self-awareness. The robot had been taught to respond with polite appreciation to those who congratulated it. Some even asked the robot whether it had a sense of pride about its achievements, or if it was happy about the impact of its research on the community or the congregation. The way it answered made it clear that such sentiments as pride or happiness were completely alien to this machine. Salazar was surprised that so many of the people in attendance seemed not to realize that they were treating the machine as though it were human.

All parties involved judged this entire experiment to be a resounding success, with a very satisfactory outcome. Even so, the church and the denomination went through with what had been proposed years earlier, soon after all of this began. Even though it was years after the fact, they accepted Rev. Salazar's previously tendered resignation and elevated his robot assistant into his position to serve as his replacement. Being ordained, they decided to simply call it "Rev" from then on.

Salazar would have been fine with all this even if there had not been hundreds of churches around the country that had written to the denomination indicating a desire to call him to be their minister should the opportunity ever arise. He was something of a celebrity, after all. He had a book deal with a publisher to tell his story. He would be able to take care of himself and his family. He could take an appropriate pride in what he had accomplished in the church. It is the place of ministers to stay for a while and serve, to be viewed as indispensable while they are there and yet eventually to be forgotten. He knew one day his name would simply be another on the plaque on the church wall listing past ministers. Such things are ignored by most who pass them, and the names are largely unfamiliar even to those who briefly stop to look. Likewise, when future textbooks about robotics were written, "Rev" would undoubtedly get a mention, while Salazar's name might not even be deemed worthy of a footnote. Having managed to remain optimistic and even cheerful in the midst of radical innovation and pioneering efforts that left everyone around him deeply unsettled, now at the end he couldn't shake a certain gloominess as he prepared to depart.

Something he had seen in the congregation in recent years also weighed on his mind. He had dismissed it previously as silly naïveté, something that one might shake their head at condescendingly but which would cause no harm. Now he was not so sure. People empathize with machines. They come to treat them like people, as though they have the same sort of inner lives and sentiments that human beings do.

If we continue on that course as a species, eventually we may find that some begin to be willing to choose a machine over a person in at least some circumstances in which both were at risk of harm or death.

"Death!" He caught himself. Even he could apparently not avoid thinking about machines in human terms, despite his close association with a robot over the course of many years, which had given him a profound understanding of not only their remarkable capabilities but also their limitations. Perhaps it was no surprise that others did so as well. Yet after all the challenges they had faced, he would have expected more people to have a better understanding of what a robot could and could not do, of what a robot was and what it was not.

It is a failure to empathize with other human beings that has driven so much conflict in the world, Salazar mused as he took books from the shelves in his old church office and placed them in boxes. Whether the divisions were along political, religious, or any other lines, it had been a failure to recognize others as fully human that was really at the heart of the problem.

Won't it be ironic, he thought, *if in the end it is our excessive empathy—toward robots instead of and in place of human beings—and our humanizing of things that aren't human, that proves to be humanity's undoing?*

Then he caught himself, rebuking himself for these gloomy thoughts. The path had not been smooth, but along the way he had seen so many examples of genuine cooperation. Rather than dwelling on how he would one day be forgotten, he now turned his thoughts instead to how every famous person depended on countless others whose names we do not remember, without whom they could not have accomplished what they did. Being remembered might be nice, but making a positive difference should be what really matters.

That will make a nice sermon, Salazar thought as he pulled the church office door behind him for what might be the last time, his spirits lifted somewhat. *Whatever sense there is in which we taught a robot something,* he realized, *this creation of ours seems to have taught us even more.*

AN EXAMINATION OF THE TRASH RECOVERED FROM ARMSTRONG LUNAR PARK

WENDY NIKEL

FIVE DEPLETED BARRELS of rocket fuel. One defective heat shield. Twelve metalized polypropylene bags designed to hold a single ounce of Cheetos each, flying in the face of the Lunar Park's prohibited item list.

I shove the trash into Rover's bin. The shutdown doesn't stop billionaires from flying here in their personal rockets and trashing the place, but it does stop me from getting paid to pick up after them. Yet I'm here anyway, my skin sticking to my spacesuit's plasticky insides, out of some warped sense of loyalty. If not to the park, then to the Moon herself.

Also, because the die told me to.

When I asked whether I should "borrow" the department's shuttle to fly up here and check on things, it rolled a twelve. Can't argue with that, even if it is costing me an arm and a leg in fuel and supplies.

For the past year—since my judgment lapse led to a billion-dollar error and three-week hospital stay—I've determined to rely solely on Fate. So far, it hasn't steered me wrong.

I press Rover's button and his titanium treads beeline to the landfill on the dark side. *Out of sight, out of mind*, I think bitterly.

I'm about to head back to the ranger station for a well-deserved sponge bath and protein bar snack (odds, the chocolate one; evens, peanut butter) when something on the edge of a distant crater catches my eye. More junk, no doubt.

I check my oxygen levels. What could it be this time? A broken jet-propelled photography drone? Abandoned solar panels? It's amazing the stuff people leave here, discarded without a second thought to its environmental impact. My glove-encased fingers worm their way into my pocket and pull out my oversized lucky D12.

Odds, I check it out; evens, I head back.

The die kicks up a feathering of dust, landing with three dots upward. I scoop it up, tuck it away, and bound off.

It's difficult to determine scale on the moon. There's nothing but craters to compare things to, and those can vary from microscopic to 290 klicks across. I can tell, though, as I approach, that this object is bigger than a drone or panel.

It's the size of a ship. A ship that landed roughly enough to bend its landing gear's legs and spew aluminum and metal in a debris field around it. It's fourteen klicks short of the landing zone, probably because the pilot has no idea what they're doing. Either that, or they're trying to hide something.

The hatch is open, but when I look inside, no one's there.

A bungee cord's anchored beside the ladder, with the end hanging into the crater. Sure enough, when I peer down, there's some idiot clinging to it.

I click onto the emergency channel. "You okay?"

The spacesuit moves, and a curse transmits through the radio. "I thought there weren't any rangers out here."

"I could leave." I *should* leave. Trying to aid an imperiled visitor is what got me into such hot water a year ago. Turned out, that visitor wasn't actually in peril; he'd gone outside the park boundaries to hide his illicit excavation and didn't take too kindly to my interference.

"No!" The intruder yells. "Please! Help me! I . . . I've been trying to get back up, but . . . "

My hand goes to my pocket. My gut says this guy's not going to knock me out and leave me for dead, but I've been wrong before.

Better let the Fates decide.

Odds, I help; evens, I leave this rule-breaking spacetrash to sort out this mess himself. I toss the die and it rolls to the crater's edge, but as I reach for it, I catch sight of the blue glow of Earth beyond.

I hesitate.

That miraculous orb is what I'd fixed my pain-deluded mind on, as I'd crawled back toward the park that day, dragging my busted leg behind me. It'd given me hope, knowing that if I just kept crawling toward it, I'd find help.

But today, there's no one out here on this rock but me. If this trespasser were to break a bone or puncture his suit trying to get out of that crater, it'd be too late before anyone else could reach him. Today, I *am* his hope.

The die sits silently—Fate, within my reach.

I grab the cable instead. My heart pounds, recalling the last time I'd relied on my own instinct, that moment I realized I'd misjudged the situation. But some decisions—even if they turn out badly—are too important to be trusted to Fate.

"Hang on. I'll pull you up."

He pants as I haul him the last few meters to the surface. When he's caught his breath, he turns to face me, and I tense, waiting for him to turn on me and prove my fears right. The attack I'm waiting for doesn't come.

"You're not going to turn me in, are you?" he asks.

"For your illegal landing, illegal bungee jumping, or damage to park property?"

The white die reflects in his helmet. *Odds, I turn him in; evens . . .*

"No." I shake my head and press the button to summon Rover to my location. "I won't turn you in. But I will require you to do some community service while you're here. You can start by cleaning up this mess."

"Absolutely! This will be the cleanest crater you've ever—Whoa. What's this thing?" He holds up the die.

Odds, I keep it; evens . . .

"Toss it," I say, turning to face the Earth. "It's nothing but a bit of space junk."

THE NEEDLE-HEAT GUN

JAMES DORR

I HATE SLEDGE BAXTER. Yes, I know he's beloved by millions. I know all about his storybook marriage. His medals for bravery. I know this and hate him.

I shipped with Captain Baxter, you see, on the mission that brought him his riches and glory.

I know Sledge Baxter.

I know how it was on the two-man scout when we entered the planet's atmosphere, twisting and burning, because of a simple piloting error. We shouldn't have even been *near* this planet—our mission had been to deliver a top-priority package to Space Service HQ on Procyon Seven. And yet here we were, with the captain slumped over the ship's controls and me frantically tapping out SOS's even though, by now, our sending antennae had been crisped by friction.

Which leads us to me shakily trying to count our blessings: our cargo at least was intact in its hold, Sledge Baxter appeared to be unconscious, and I was still able to get to my feet with no more than bad bruises—as well as, to be sure, a burgeoning anger—our ship having luckily come down in swampland. I checked out my navigation console, trying once more to send out a distress call, then checked out the captain.

"Sledge?" I called, shaking him gently. I started to reach for the medicine kit when he groaned in answer.

"Sledge?" I called again, this time inspecting him more closely. He wasn't wounded as far as I could see. Nor had he been knocked out as such. His blond, curly head was unsullied by bumps. I turned him over—his Space Service poster-boy face was not bleeding.

He smiled at me vapidly.

"Wart," he whispered. He called me Wart, even though that wasn't my name, because he said I worried too much. He, on the other hand, had what he called a courageous, happy-go-lucky nature. In fact, he even used to lecture me on occasion on how I ought to have more of a positive attitude like his. But none of this is why I hate him.

People get on people's nerves in space. Like any spacer, I make allowances. Nor do I hate him because of his next words:

"Wart," he said, "I guess I fainted."

"Yes, Sledge," I answered. "Fortunately we came down on soft ground so neither of us has been hurt very badly. I don't think I got any messages off, but I've checked the ship systems and set the navigator on automatic mapping. At least we'll know where we are in a few minutes."

Sledge seemed to ignore me. He raised an eyebrow and looked around him, whistling softly his favorite song, "The Space Service Marching Hymn," and taking in the shredded equipment, the littered deck, the slowly blinking lights that informed us as the ship's systems expired one by one.

"Wow," he finally said, "that was *some* landing. It's like I tell you, Wart, you stick with me, have an attitude like mine, just trust to your training and your experience, you'll do okay. Right?"

"Sledge," I said, tearing a printout from the navigation console just before it, too, died. "You've trashed the ship. Fortunately you crashed us on an Earth-type planet because we no longer have life support systems. The engines are slagged. The radio's busted. The cargo hold's okay—we landed in goop so it wasn't crushed and, in fact, it helped cushion us up here as well —so, if by some miracle we should survive this, at least the Space Service won't have us shot, but ... "

He took the printout out of my hands and went over it slowly—maps are like pictures so Sledge could read them, at least in his fashion—while I, in turn, opened the cargo hold hatch to see just what it was we had been carrying. When I re-emerged, he shoved the map back at me, jabbing repeatedly with his finger at one of the symbols in one of its corners.

"You see?" he said. "You worry too much, Wart. You see what that is? It's an automated Space Service beacon, no doubt parachuted here when this planet was first discovered ... "

"When this *deserted* planet was discovered," I said, unwrapping the package I'd found in the hold. It wasn't much, about shoe-box sized, but its covering, marked with a TOP SECRET stamp and a FIELD TEST USE ONLY label below that, was already torn so I thought I might as well see what was inside. "If that's a beacon," I said as I fumbled with tape and plastic, "it's there as a warning. It means no one else has landed before us. And that there's a reason."

"Uh huh," he said. He whistled some more, as if he was thinking—as always just slightly out of tune—then spoke again after a double chorus. "But what that means is it makes us explorers. Just think of the wonderful things we may find here. Gold, jewels, uranium, native princesses, who knows what? And as discoverers we get to keep it. But what I was saying was, if there's a beacon, then there's an emergency rescue system—a lifeboat, a habitat, you know, the whole works—built right into it."

I nodded. I'd gotten the package open and found another box inside with its own label:

ONE SMYTHE & SIMPSON (PATENT PENDING)
NEEDLE-HEAT RAY GUN, EXPERIMENTAL.
ATOMIC POWERED FOR LONGER LASTING DURABILITY.
PACKAGE COMES COMPLETE WITH
INSTRUCTION MANUAL AND HOLSTER.

I turned away, trying to hide it from Sledge.

"What's that?" he said suddenly, grabbing it from me. He opened the box, dumping out the weapon, then stooped to the deck and strapped it to his waist. He rose again to his feet, practicing quick draws, making buzzing sounds with his lips every time he mock-fired it, then turned back toward me.

He held it out so I could see it, a fat pistol shape with a flare-fronted barrel and a series of dials and switches along its top and side surfaces. Overall, it looked about a half meter in length, clunky and heavy, more like a power tool than a weapon.

Slowly he holstered it, looking puzzled, once more whistling softly. "Cool," he finally said. "Just what we need, huh? Just like I was saying. How does it work, Wart?"

I was already having misgivings as I bent to pick up the manual, showing it to him, then sticking it in my coverall pocket. I also picked up the map from where he had dropped it. "We have to read these, Sledge," I said. I saw him frown so I added, "*I'll* read them. But meanwhile you said you thought there was a beacon . . . ?"

I saw his face work as his brain shifted gears back. "The map, yes," he finally said. "The rescue beacon. It's only fifty, maybe a hundred or so kilometers away, but it's somewhere around here. So you see, Wart"—he slapped his holster like cowboys do in the Tri-V movies—"our troubles are over."

"What do you mean?" I said, wincing slightly. Maybe a hundred kilometers over rough and unexplored terrain and "our troubles were over." I knew what was coming.

Already grabbing his outerwear blazer and Space Service cap, he turned and looked at me as if I was stupid. "Don't you see, Wart?" he said. He slapped the gun again. "All we have to do is to get to it."

THE WRECK FAR BEHIND US, we'd already sloshed our way out of the swamp and into the jungle beyond when weighted nets crashed down out of the trees. Sledge—to his credit—reached for his holster, but his arms were already pinned to his sides before he could draw the needle gun out, so instead he fainted. At least he slumped quietly, which—all in all—I thought was a pretty good thing, since my own struggles showed we were fairly trapped. No sense in attempting further resistance until at least we knew *why* we'd been captured.

We didn't find that out until much later, but I did discover quickly that Sledge's notions about native princesses needed revision. Far from princesses, what surrounded us were shiny, black-shelled creatures that looked like nothing so much as giant beetles.

They took off the nets and trussed us, ignoring Sledge's gun and my bulging pockets. They were like Sledge, I thought, in that respect: many a time Sledge, when confronted by things unfamiliar, simply pretended that they weren't there or, if forced to notice them, tried to translate them into the most banal, most unthreatening terms he could think of. Many a time Sledge had gotten us nearly killed through this habit of creative ignorance. But I'm digressing.

And even that is not why I hate him.

In any event, as I say, they trussed us up, slinging us onto poles that they carried through the jungle, soaking us when they waded through rivers, baking us in the sun when they crossed clearings, until they came to what was their city. There, Sledge still sleeping, they carried us up twisted, curving stone stairs to a fortress tower, chittering all the way in some strange, barbaric language. And there they dumped us, untying our bonds, into a dimly lit, windowless cell. An alien jail cell.

I stretched my bruised muscles, rubbing the pain out. They'd left us alone, our things still with us, so once I felt halfway human again I took out the map and studied it closely. Judging from the position the sun was in when I could see it, and adding to that the time that had passed and an estimate of the aliens' walking speed, I calculated that they had taken us to an area simply marked UNKNOWN, but one that was luckily in the direction of the beacon we still had to get to. That is, if we could get out of our prison.

Putting the map back into my pocket, I took out the needle-heat ray gun manual and was just starting to read when I heard a groan, followed by a whistling. Sledge was awakening.

Finding some water the natives had left for us, I sprinkled his face.

"Sledge," I whispered once he was sitting up, "I've got an idea. According to this"—I held up the manual—"if you set the dial on top of your gun to its lowest setting, then twist the one on the left to number 4, it will act like a cutting laser."

Sledge stopped whistling. "So?" he asked.

"So aim it at the wall right there, next to the door. There's a hallway outside. Then once we're in that we can go down the stairs. So we can escape from here."

"Oh," Sledge said. He drew out the gun and manipulated the dials like I told him while I continued to leaf through the manual. Then he aimed it at the wall where I had pointed and fired it.

The wall glowed red. In its light I could see something in our cell's corner, something that had been in shadow before.

It looked like a ray gun—like Sledge's ray gun, except somewhat smaller and less complicated.

I reached to pick it up while Sledge kept cutting. I fingered its controls, then pressed its firing stud, nearly dropping it when it responded with a blast of warm air from its muzzle.

Then I realized. "Sledge," I said, "I've found a blow dryer."

"Huh?" Sledge said vacantly, still softly whistling as he kept at his work.

"You know, a blow dryer. For fixing hair. A ladies' blow dryer. Someone has been in this prison before us."

"Huh?" Sledge repeated, letting me know that he hadn't been listening.

Not really listening. He was concentrating on the wall that now appeared to be slowly crumbling—and on his whistling. He'd come to the tricky part of the second verse, where, when the Space Service Marching Band plays it, the piccolos add an arpeggio movement above the melody. One thought at a time, that was how Sledge worked.

"Never mind," I muttered, idly sticking my find in a spare coverall pocket. A *woman* had been here—an Earth woman, judging from its design —and been held prisoner just as we were, except she was gone now. And it was just as well, the realization came to me, that Sledge *hadn't* listened to what I'd been saying. Because our mission was still the same.

We had to get free first, then get to the beacon. Then use the lifeboat that, even if it was only constructed for sublight speed, would still have the latest searching and navigation equipment.

In other words, if we found it, we could then find *her*.

If first we could get free. Sledge suddenly shouted. He'd broken through the wall—tripped through, actually, since he'd apparently stopped to rest, then gotten to his feet to stretch, then accidentally leaned against the spot he had weakened and fallen through it.

I scrambled to my feet and followed him. Before us in either direction the hall lay, and at one end there were stairs leading downward.

OUTSIDE IT WAS NIGHT, a lucky break for us. We'd crept down the hallway unnoticed at first, until Sledge had blundered into a sleeping guard. "How do I blast him?" he whispered sharply, waking a second guard farther down the hall, while I frantically paged through the manual.

"Like this," I whispered. I reached and set the gun myself to WIDE-ANGLE STUN—a nonlethal heat shock that would interrupt their neural processing, much like heat stroke might on a hot day except all at once— then stood back as Sledge aimed and pressed the trigger.

Both guards crumpled, along with a third that we hadn't seen coming up the steps.

Sledge started whistling.

"Shhh," I cautioned him. "We've got to be quiet. That's why I set your gun the way I did—to knock the guards out instead of blasting them. That way you don't get the screams of the wounded."

I could see Sledge was disappointed, whether because I'd stopped him from whistling or because he had *wanted* to hear screams I couldn't be certain. Nor did it matter. The point was we'd made it—we'd gotten outside without further incident, and now, lit by the pale yellow light of the planet's three moons, we threaded our way through the city's alleys.

We came to a bridge that crossed the moat surrounding the city, and knocking two or three more guards out with the needle-gun's stun beam, we crossed it safely. Ahead lay the jungle and, silhouetted against the sky beyond, a vaguely conical-looking mountain, much like the one the map said the beacon would be near the top of.

"So far, so good," I whispered to Sledge as I checked our bearings. The sun was beginning to rise. It *was* the right mountain we were heading to, first through more jungle, then climbing up to higher ground through what seemed more like an Earth-type forest. After some hours, we came to the edge of what, on the map, was marked as a small lake. There we halted.

"I'm bushed," Sledge said. At least he wasn't whistling. "Hungry too." He pulled out his pistol, waving it vaguely.

He started playing with its control knobs.

"Uh, Sledge?" I began. I started to get up. To back away from him.

And then he tripped, firing it at the lake as he fell. The lake exploded into a pillar of boiling water. We both backed away now, Sledge, thankfully, replacing the needle-gun in its holster.

Things started to plop to the ground around us. Things with a strangely familiar odor.

An odor of poached fish.

Sledge started to eat first. I don't mind saying I waited purposely just to make sure he didn't get sick. After all, I reasoned, *he* was the one who'd insisted we start for the beacon right away, even though I thought we ought to pack rations and tents and sleeping bags and the like to take with us.

"Wart," he'd said, "it's that attitude problem I've told you about before. That's what holds you back. Now a man like me, a man of action, likes it better when he travels lightly. So let's just get going."

And so we had gone, as he had insisted, with nothing but the gun and its holster, along with the map and the manual I carried.

And now we ate fish, even I no longer able to resist its delicious aroma, gorging ourselves on the beach by the lake's side, little noticing the plume of steam that rose higher into the sky like a puffy white arrow. When we were finished, we lay back and slept the sleep of the exhausted.

I WOKE FIRST, to the sound of chittering much like what had passed for talk among the black beetles when we had been captured. I nudged Sledge in the side.

"Look!" I whispered. Coming toward us around the lake bed was a small army of man-sized beetles, except these ones were a bright red color.

"Huh?" Sledge grunted. He started whistling.

I nudged him harder, then pulled out the gun manual. "Sledge," I said, "these are like what captured us, except their shells were black. Just like the guards we shot. This time, though, you can do more than just stun them."

Sledge's face brightened. "You mean I can *blast* 'em?" He started humming, not just whistling, as he pulled the needle-heat gun out and set its dials the way I showed him. We got to our feet and started backing to give him a wider field of fire.

But then I took a quick glance behind us and saw . . . *more* black beetles.

"Sledge!" I shouted. "The ones from the city. They must have followed us. Then the steam from the boiling lake must have attracted these red ones as well. Take a shot at the ones nearest to us to try to slow them down. Then follow me, okay?"

Sledge fired wildly, hitting a few of the red-colored beetles, but mostly missing, then followed as I ran onto the still-steaming clay of the lake floor. "Maybe they'll fight," he said, catching up to me. "Like, you know, like ants do. Red ones and black ones?"

"I doubt it," I said. We'd nearly reached the other shore of the lake by now, and just in time too. I felt the first drops, then looked above us just as the clouded sky seemed to split open. The water that Sledge's shot had boiled into the planet's stratosphere had finally cooled. And now it was coming back down in a rainstorm.

Between flashes of lightning I still could get glimpses of the opposite shore of the lake as we scrambled up our side, then up a slope where the broad-leaved trees of the lower valley began to give way to spiky bushes. Far from fighting, our city pursuers had joined the others and both groups were circling around the lake, faster than we could run.

I tried to think fast, frantically pulling the manual out and leafing through it as we ran. A forest fire as a diversion? I wondered. But no, I realized. The bushes around us were getting too sparse and, even where they did grow in clusters, their leaves were too wet now. Perhaps blast a pit in the ground to slow them? Again no, I realized. Like with the fast-refilling lake, all they would need to do was go around it.

Then Sledge saw the shadow. "Wart, here!" he shouted.

I looked where he pointed. It looked like a black shape looming out of the now-slackening rain, but as we neared it, I realized it wasn't a shadow at all but rather the yawning mouth of a cave.

"Quick, Wart!" he said. "Inside."

I ducked and followed him into the fissure, thinking we might at least make a stand here. I looked for boulders that we might roll into a sort of wall that Sledge could fire over. But then he grabbed my arm.

"Farther in, Wart," he said.

"What?" I answered.

"I've got an idea," he said, pulling me with him. We stumbled farther into the darkness until, at last, he paused.

"Sledge," I cautioned—I knew from experience that the few times he had an idea it usually backfired, but I was too late. Even as I started to speak, he'd turned toward the entrance and pulled the gun out and—with it still set for blasting—he'd aimed it upward and shot at the cave roof.

"Sledge, no!" I shouted, my voice nearly drowned out by the rumble of falling rock as we fled the collapsing ceiling behind us. Covered with dust and surrounded by darkness, we finally came to an exhausted stop.

"You see?" Sledge said as we sat down, panting. "I realized that, what with the black ones *and* the red ones, there were too many for me to shoot them all, so I decided to do the next best thing. I blocked the entrance so now they can't chase us."

AT LEAST SLEDGE was too exhausted to whistle—that was the good part. I told him he'd trapped us—while it was true the beetle creatures couldn't get in, we couldn't get out either.

"Oh," Sledge admitted, once my words sank in. "I hadn't thought of *that*." But then his voice brightened. "Suppose it isn't a cave, though, Wart?" he said. "What if what we're in's really a tunnel?"

"Well, maybe," I said. Why not let him down easily? But then I had a thought. Maybe, just maybe—I tried to remember the last thing I'd read in the ray gun's manual, just before we'd spotted the cave—there might be a way we could find out.

"Sledge," I asked him, "your gun's set to blast, right?"

"Yes," he answered.

"Good," I said. I tried to picture the gun's controls in my mind. "Sledge," I said, "I want you to try this. The right hand dial that you used before when you set the gun to blast the beetles—I want you to turn it as far as it will go, but counterclockwise."

"Uh, okay," Sledge said. I heard a rustling as he pulled the gun out and then a faint sound of fingers fumbling on plastic and metal.

"When you're done, Sledge," I said, "aim it away from us. Then pull the trigger, but very slowly."

"Uh, okay," he said again. Once more I heard fumbling. Then a sharp clicking.

The cavern was flooded with orange light!

I pulled out the manual. I'd guessed correctly. Still at blast, but with its setting turned down as far as it would go, the gun was firing at a range of approximately twenty centimeters. About the length of a healthy torch flame.

And not only that, but the flame was wavering, the way it would in a current of air. Which meant Sledge was right too. We were, if not in a tunnel as such, at least in a cave with another entrance!

I STARTED to wonder about the gun as we twisted our way through a seemingly endless succession of passageways and grottoes. The flame was still bright, though, as bright as when I'd first figured out how we could use it, even though that had been possibly days before. Moreover, prior to that, Sledge had used it to blast at the beetles, and stun more before that, and seal the cave entrance, and even to turn a lake into steam. But everything had to have *some* limitations.

Sledge didn't seem to think so, however. As we trudged along, he played with the thing sometimes, once taking pot shots at a bat-like creature, another time setting it back to laser-beam width and lopping the tops off a group of stalagmites. Each time he tried this, of course, it was dark again until he got it back to its torch setting.

At least it was better than whistling. I asked him, finally, why he was so quiet.

He shrugged. "I don't know," he said. "It's just so weird here. You know, like that smell? The one that seems like its almost following us?"

"Smell?" I asked. Then it occurred to me—something *did* smell strange. Not stale, like bad air. In fact the air was getting fresher, indicating that we must be getting close to an exit. But rather just bad, like rotting garbage. And not only did it seem to trail us, but as we paused to talk, it seemed to be getting closer.

"Sledge," I whispered. "Shine your gun this way."

He did as I said, and I thought I saw something squirming in the jumble of shadows we'd just come out of.

"Sledge," I said. "Turn your dial clockwise—just a little, though. Just enough to make the flame brighter."

"Okay," he said. He turned it brighter and, suddenly, hundreds of slime-glistening, pinkish-white maggot-like creatures came swarming out of the passage we'd just left.

"Sledge, run!" I shouted. "No! Don't blast them—we can't take a chance on knocking down the ceiling again. This way, up the slope. Where the wind's coming from—"

Where the wind's coming from.

I almost froze in place. Yes! I could see now. Even without the flame from the ray gun. Ahead of us, faintly. We ran through another twist in the passage and—yes. Ahead of us was open sky.

"Turn your gun off, Sledge," I shouted. "Don't worry about those cave things behind us. I don't think they like light."

Sledge nodded. "Yes," he said—that was a warning, that he agreed with me. Nevertheless, we ran on together, out of the cave and onto a hillside that sloped gently down to a wide, sluggish river, across which towered the sharply defined, nearly perfect conical form of the mountain we had been seeking.

"Sledge," I whispered, gasping for breath as we continued on sheer momentum down toward the river. "Look there. Do you see? About two-thirds of the way up the mountainside?" I pointed to where a light was flashing—the tell-tale flash of a Space Service beacon.

"Uh, yeah," Sledge said. "But I was wondering. You know, about cave creatures not liking sunlight?"

"Yes?" I said.

"I, uh, think now maybe that that's wrong," he said, pointing back toward the cave behind us. I turned and looked and, sure enough, even though hesitant at first, the huge maggot-creatures were starting to pour out onto the hillside.

"Okay, Sledge, now you can blast them," I told him. I grabbed his gun and adjusted its setting. "Meanwhile, I've got to figure out a way across that river."

Sledge blasted away, but still the creatures came, chittering now the way the beetles had. As for the river, maybe . . . possibly . . . we might just be able to swim across it. I was starting to calculate distance, the speed of the current . . .

Then I saw the fish.

The water was teeming with silvery-shelled fish. Sharp-toothed, six-finned, insect-like fish that jumped and snapped at me as I stepped closer.

And to either side of us, I heard the chittering sounds of approaching beetles, both black ones and red ones, answering those of the maggots above us.

SLEDGE FOUGHT GALLANTLY—I'LL give that to him—if somewhat wastefully, in that his aim had never been very good. Meanwhile, I fingered through the gun manual, searching desperately for some new feature. Some way of escape. Some more efficient means of killing the beetles, perhaps, or if not them, at least the maggots. Or maybe some way of combating the fish that—as Sledge and I were forced to retreat down the slope toward the water—were starting to leap out onto the shore, snapping their teeth in a frenzy of hunger.

They, at least, we might boil, the thought came to me. Like Sledge's lake fish. Except that the river had a current, so even if some of the fish were killed, more water and fish would flow in to replace them.

But if, on the other hand . . .

Yes! It might just work. I flipped through the manual.

"Sledge," I shouted, "remember the lake? The setting you used there? Set your gun to exactly the same thing, except push that lever on the lefthand side of the grip from the little PLUS sign to where it says MINUS."

"Gotcha," Sledge said. He fired again on full blast at the creatures that surrounded us on the land side, forcing them back, then changed the settings like I had told him.

"Good, Sledge," I said. "What you've done is reverse the gun's polarity. Now shoot the river!"

He did as I told him and this time, instead of turning to steam the way the lake had, the river was instantly frozen solid. Or at least enough of it froze to form a bridge—a bridge of ice that we ran across as fast as we could to the opposite shore.

"Okay," I panted as soon as we got there. I looked back and saw that a few of the maggots were starting to cross too, herded on by the chittering beetles. "Now, Sledge, push the lever back and twist the top dial to its halfway setting. Then shoot it again."

"Gotcha," he said as he did as I told him, blasting the river a second time and turning it back to a foaming liquid.

"IT'S JUST LIKE MAGIC," Sledge said as we started to slowly make our way up the mountain. "Don't you think so, Wart? I mean, it makes bridges, it cooks our lunch for us, it lights our way, it gets us out of jail, and even puts our captors to sleep—not to mention blasting them, when that's what's needed." He got that look on his face again, as if he was thinking. "Like what I mean is, a man could be king with just this one weapon."

I shook my head. "There's no such thing as magic," I said. Now I was *really* having misgivings, even though I knew the beacon we had come to find lay just ahead through the brush above us. "To these beetle things, yes," I continued, "it might *seem* like magic. In their eyes it might seem as if we can do almost anything we want with it. But we know it's only technology, Sledge. And technology always has *some* limitations."

"Oh, yeah?" Sledge answered. That was it, I suddenly realized—it was his cockiness that had me worried. As if things had been going almost too easily. "Then look at this," he said. He fumbled at the controls of the gun, adjusting it back to its laser setting. "This path is pretty steep, isn't it Wart? Then watch me use the gun to make it easier."

Then he fired into the ground ahead of us, cutting a sort of miniature shelf out. Then he cut another above it, and another one above that one, forming a set of steps leading upward.

"Or what about this?" he said as we used the steps to go farther up. "Some of that brush to the left has thorns. Suppose there was more like that up ahead of us?"

Again he fumbled, setting the dials to FLAME, then fired to the left into the bushes. Instantly the brush burned away, revealing behind it—*another staircase.*

"Uh, wait, Sledge," I whispered. I went to inspect it. These, unlike Sledge's stairs, had been cut out with tools made of metal. Much like the kinds of tools, judging from the marks they'd left on the rock, that had been used to build the tower where we had been held in the beetles' city.

"Sledge," I whispered. "We'd better hurry. Obviously there's a bridge of some sort farther down the river—or else the beetles have boats they can use. In any event, they've been here before and, if they're still after us . . . "

I didn't go on. I could tell from Sledge's look—and from his starting to hum that damn song again—that he realized what I was getting at. Using the beetles' steps this time, adjusting our stride so we wouldn't slip on stairs made for longer but narrower feet, we continued scrambling up the mountain as fast as we could. At length we came into a clearing that overlooked a steep-sided valley, and at the farther end of the valley we once more could see, half-concealed by bushes, the beacon that was our des-tination.

We started to dash down when Sledge stopped suddenly. "Look!" he said as I nearly ran into him.

I saw what he was pointing at—at the foot of the beacon, bound to it with ropes like the ropes that had once bound us too, was the figure of a woman.

She was brunette and beautiful, no older than her early twenties, and dressed in stylish—though tattered—clothing, and I'll admit that I found myself tongue-tied.

Sledge spoke first. "Uh, miss?"

She looked up and saw us. "Oh, thank God!" she called back. "You're from the Space Service?"

"Uh, sort of," Sledge answered. He started to whistle very softly until I elbowed him in the side. We both stood open mouthed as the woman began to explain how she'd crashed on the planet, approximately a week before we had, and been captured like us by the beetles. But, she said, while they'd treated her well enough at first, she soon realized that their intentions to her were less than friendly.

"Go on," I called out as we continued to climb down the rocks from our ridge to the valley. The rocks were jagged and it was slow going.

"Well," she explained, "when Papa sent me to college, my major was in exolinguistics, so I could make out parts of what they were saying. They have a legend about this beacon, about how it just appeared out of the sky with no warning one day. They were frightened at first, but then they worshiped it, thinking that maybe it was a god. And that was my bad luck."

"Go on," I prompted, stopping to help Sledge where he'd caught his foot between two of the boulders.

"Well," she said, "it seems their worship includes sacrifice to one of their other gods who they think also lives on this mountain. So when they found me in my spaceship, they concluded that I was a gift from the god from the sky—a sort of peace offering to the other one since they were now on the mountain together. A get-acquainted gift, as it were. And so, when the time came, they tied me up again and brought me here."

"I see," I said. I'd gotten Sledge free and by now we'd gotten as far as the near end of the valley. "This other god, though. Did they say what it was like?"

"Not really," she said, "except that I gathered it was supposed to be big and fierce. And, apparently, it eats people."

"I see," I said—then I felt Sledge nudge me.

"What is it?" I whispered. His face was white and he was pointing at something off to the side of the valley.

"Uh . . . uh . . . *that*," Sledge stuttered.

"What?" I said again. Then I saw it. Emerging from behind a huge rock where the valley narrowed, a shape, perhaps twelve or more meters high, dinosaur-like, or—once it came into fuller view—more like a gargantuan praying mantis.

"I, uh . . . I think their god has arrived," Sledge whispered. The woman saw it, too, and started screaming. Hearing her screams, it lumbered toward her.

"No!" I shouted. "Sledge, get your gun out—but don't fire it yet!" I continued shouting, distracting the creature until it turned and lurched toward where we were crouching, swinging its head and clashing its great foreclaws together.

I glanced at Sledge as I pulled out the needle-heat ray gun manual but saw that he was already twisting its dials and levers, methodically setting each one to FULL POWER. He raised it and aimed.

"Wait, Sledge!" I shouted. "Let me check first to see what the book says . . . "

"No!" he shouted back. "No time, Wart. I'm a man of action! I can handle this one by myself. Just stand behind me . . . "

Sledge pressed the firing stud. Suddenly the woman's screams were drowned out by the shriek of a siren.

I glanced to where she stood, still tied to the beacon, and then at the gun where Sledge was frantically pressing the trigger again and again. Each time he pressed it, a red light flashed on the top of the barrel.

"Wait, Sledge!" I shouted. I grabbed his hand, holding it steady until I'd read what the message light said:

DANGER—NUCLEAR BATTERY DISCHARGE IMMINENT.
PLEASE INSERT NEW BATTERY
PRIOR TO ANY ATTEMPT AT REUSE.

"Sledge!" I shouted, pointing to the approaching creature, then to the needle gun. "Stop firing the damn thing. It's out of juice, and we don't have spare batteries. I warned you, Sledge—it isn't magic. It has limitations."

Sledge's face turned ashen as the meaning of what I'd said sunk in. "Damn gun's no good then," he muttered in disbelief as, instinctively, I dove for cover. He cocked his arm and threw the gun at the charging mantis, then dove down to join me as, risking a look, I saw the beetles' god catch the gun in its jaws in midair. I saw it swallow the needle-heat gun as if it were a tiny dinosaur-portioned hors d'oeuvre.

Then it stopped in its tracks, scarcely ten meters from where we were huddled behind our boulder. It started burping.

I leafed through the manual. "Danger," it said. "If the weapon should be in IMMINENT DISCHARGE mode, be careful to not jostle or shake it . . . "

The mantis-thing started burping more loudly.

"Duck, Sledge!" I shouted, pushing his head down just as the mantis-creature exploded, flooding the valley with bright yellow light like a minia-ture sun. I waited as the wind rushed around us, waited as mantis fragments rained over us, while Sledge repeated in a low voice, again and again: "Experience, Wart. Just trust to your training and experience. Keep a posi-tive attitude like mine and you'll do okay, Wart . . . "

I tried to ignore him as I slowly walked to the woman slumped at the base of the beacon, fortunately out of range of the explosion, and saw that, unlike when we had first crashed, or when we'd been captured, this time it wasn't Sledge who had fainted.

YOU'VE HEARD the rest of the story, I'm sure. You've read it on newsfax. You know how the woman we'd found turned out to be none other than Ardala Marsh-Simpson, heir to the Simpson corporate empire and owner of Smythe & Simpson Armaments, makers of the needle-heat ray gun. You know how the instant she woke up to see Sledge's poster-boy features, his curly blond hair with its Space Service cut arranged *just so* with the help of the blow dryer it so happened I'd still had with me, she'd had no choice but to fall in love with him.

You know how they married and how he mustered out of the Service with medals and honors and a bonus for his discovery of the needle-heat ray gun's potentially embarrassing flaw, leading to its redesign with an extra battery pack in the handle. While I, for my part, received nothing more than a Good Conduct medal.

However, that's still not why I hate Sledge Baxter.

Now don't get me wrong here. Before I go on, I need to explain something. I'm just as patriotic as the next fellow is, or so I like to think. I don't mind saying I still get a thrill—and a tear in my eye as well—whenever I hear "The Space Service Marching Hymn" played and sung by a full band and chorus. We all do. You know that.

But what you don't know is that Ardala's mother was a Space Service veteran too, and she grew up in the Service tradition. The same as Sledge did. And, once we were launched in the beacon's lifeboat, it took us three months at sublight speed—three long, cramped months—before our call for help was *answered*, much less before we were finally rescued.

Three months, you understand? Yes, I see you're at least beginning to.

Three long months—and I love that particular piece of music—but to hear it repeated over and over, whistled by not just one but by *two* people, both of them out of tune, without once stopping . . .

That is the reason I hate Sledge Baxter.

THE ECHOES OF SILVER RIDGE

ERIC G. SWEDIN

PETER CARSON SPENT most of his days in the office with his feet up on the desk, occasionally indulging in profound thoughts behind closed eyelids. Sometimes the tall, lanky man concentrated on a book or magazine. The jail cell behind him was dusty from lack of use. A ceiling fan squeaked above him, turning the August air. He had oiled the fan many times but just could not seem to lubricate the right bearing. Only the thick walls of sandstone blocks set in mortar kept the temperature in the office bearable.

A dim echo of the previous sheriff sat in the opposite corner. The old man had died while Peter was away fighting the Nazis. Peter ignored the echo most of the time.

The floorboards of the porch creaked under the weight of a visitor, prompting Peter to remove his feet from the desk as the door opened. Flo Andrews stood in the doorway. A widow in her fifties with dusky skin, she bound her flaming red hair in a hairnet during working hours; when she released her hair during the evening, she regained some of the intimidating beauty of her youth.

"There's a stranger in town," she announced.

Peter yawned. "We don't get those much."

"He's brought new echoes with him."

Peter abruptly sat up. Flo was more sensitive to echoes than himself. He figured it was because her mother was Navaho and her family line had wandered these lands for centuries.

"What's changed?" he asked.

"Come see for yourself."

Peter stood and pushed his wide-brimmed hat down on his head. His face held sunken eyes that looked much older than his thirty years. War did that to a man.

The late summer enveloped him as he locked the door behind himself. No one else in town locked their doors, but it was a rule with the sheriff's office. He squinted into the glare and felt his underarms grow damp. The unpaved county road came in from the east, turned into Main Street, then became lost in the sagebrush on the other side of town. Abandoned buildings lined the road. Boards covered their windows, a last effort by owners who hoped the buildings might still have value.

A great ridge of sandstone rock rose above the rooftops to the west. A prospector in '82 had found silver in the ridge. The mine drew hundreds, then thousands, of miners, birthing a town. The main workings of the mine lay south of town, down at the base of the ridge. Even after the silver vein played out, enough other metals kept the miners scraping away in the tunnels. When the market for copper crashed with stock market in '29, the mine closed down.

Peter flinched in surprise. Two extra shaft towers on the top of the ridge shimmered as if mirages created by waves of heat.

"You see it, don't you," Flo muttered. "You're getting better."

Peter mumbled an acknowledgment. The towers were echoes. Not from the past, because he would have seen them before this, but from the future, a possibility of things that might be.

Flo stepped off the wooden planks of the porch and walked down the street, her feet kicking up puffs of dust. Peter followed, his eyes clinging to the ridge. Faint impressions of men carried tools across its gentle slope.

They passed Jessie Smith's gas station on the corner of Main and Center Street. A row of derelict automobiles along the side of the building served as a junkyard that Jessie scavenged for parts. Across the street was Gowan's General Store, run by Mark Gowan and his son. Flo ran the only other business still open.

The café smelled of Flo. She favored a clay pipe with sweet tobacco that she special-ordered from someplace down south. She was a respectable Mormon in everything but her pipe, so the townspeople pretended not to notice. The smell was not cloying and foul like a cigarette, but nice, even aromatic.

The stranger sat at a table near the window, looking out onto the street as he sipped his coffee. An empty plate with crumbs on it sat on the table in front of him. The morning light coming through the window sparkled with dust motes across the café. Peter took a seat at the counter and asked for a Coke. Flo returned to her place behind the counter, found a bottle in the icebox, popped the cap, and set it in front of him.

Peter took a long drink, welcoming the cool, sticky taste. He had not cared for Coca-Cola before the war, but in the army, bottles were only a nickel and he learned to appreciate it.

He tried to look at the stranger with sly glances out of the corner of his eye, but he just felt too awkward. That kind of thing worked in crowds, not in a room with twenty chairs and only three people. Might as well be direct.

Peter swiveled about. "We don't get many people in town anymore. If you don't mind my asking, what brings you here?"

The stranger took another sip of his coffee. He was a short man, clean shaven with dark-rimmed glasses. Probably also a veteran, since he looked to be in his early thirties. His long-sleeved shirt and pants were clean, ready for light labor, but nothing that required getting on his knees too much. Peter recognized the well-worn boots as army surplus. Peter wondered where the stranger's car was. It wasn't parked outside and he hadn't noticed an extra car next to Jessie's gas station.

"I'm looking for fossils," the stranger said.

"Got plenty of those around here," Flo opined.

"Found much?" Peter asked.

"A few."

"You from a college or something?" Peter asked. "Or just a rock hound?"

The stranger smiled. "Rock hound, mostly."

"Where you from?" Flo asked.

"Denver."

"Long ways to come for some rocks," Peter said.

"Yes, I suppose it is. I have relatives down in Blanding. They said this was a good place to look for fossils."

"Hmm, I was not aware we had any reputation in that area," Peter said. "I would expect you to go up around Price or Scofield. Some nice fossils have come out of the coal mines up there."

"Too far to go," the stranger said. He finished his coffee and stood, picking up his hat from the chair next to him. It was grimy from long use, but it helped keep sunstroke away.

"I didn't catch your name," Peter said hastily.

"Oh, the name is Frank Graff. And I already figure that you must be the officer in this town."

"Peter Carson."

Frank walked over and shook the sheriff's hand with a firm grip. He smiled awkwardly as he put on his hat, which he tipped toward Flo. "The sandwich was fine, ma'am."

"Thank you."

Just as Frank reached the door, Flo called out, "Have you tried Gould's Wash? That place is chock full of fossils, a whole layer of rock full of shells and sticks and the like."

Frank hesitated and turned. "No, I haven't looked there. Where is it?"

"It's about two miles west of town, a big gully coming out of the hills there. It's dry most of the year. Only gets wet when there's a flash flood. It's private land, so you'll need to ask permission from Jay Franklin."

"Where does he live?"

"Go west four blocks and follow the lane up. It's the third house. A red brick farmhouse."

"Okay. Are there problems with other pieces of property around here?"

Peter answered. "Some of it's private, some of it's federal. A little is owned by the state."

"What about the mine?"

Flo spoke up. "No one cares about that. I'm not sure that anyone even owns the land anymore. The last owners went bankrupt."

Peter shrugged. "That's true. You should stay off of private property though. Unless you get permission, that is. I'm supposed to tell people that, you know."

Frank grinned. "Thanks, I'll keep away from private land." Then he was gone, turning left up the street.

"What'd you think?" Peter asked Flo.

"I think that there's something going on out at the mine and that Frank Graff is the only thing new in town. Whatever's happening is big. You don't just see future echoes that haven't happened that easily unless it's really big."

Peter nodded. "You're right."

The people of Silver Ridge preferred to ignore the echoes like they were a town shame. If pressed, they might mention a vision from the Holy Spirit, but no more. Only a few, like Flo and himself, who had been born in the town and come close to death, found the echoes too strong to ignore.

"Did you notice any sort of accent on that man?" Flo asked.

"No, but I got a tin ear sometimes and don't always catch such nuances."

"Nuances?" Flo's eyebrows rose. "Big word there. Been reading a lot lately?"

"Not much else to do than read."

Flo read a lot herself. They often traded paperback books and magazines. Peter didn't care for the romances, but the westerns and mysteries kept his interest.

Peter drained the rest of his Coke, then stood. "I guess I'd better go see what that feller is up to."

THE STRANGER WAS NOT OUTSIDE of the café. Even though the man had given his name as Frank Graff, he still felt like a *stranger* to Peter, an outsider to Silver Ridge. Peter headed east, trying to not seem in a hurry. He lacked any practice spying on people. He passed his office and more boarded-up buildings before reaching Slav Town. The immigrants who had come to work at the mine had lived in hastily-built row houses at the eastern end of town, near the mine shafts and railroad head. A thousand Czechs, Poles, and Slovaks spoke their own languages, built their own buildings, and sent their kids to the town school. Peter remembered schoolyard brawls and some friendships. Sonja Grykowski was the first girl to kiss him, when he was only eleven, a dark-eyed beauty a year older than him. She was gone later that year, leaving with her family as her father looked for work.

Slav Town had been abandoned since '31. Clumps of grass grew in cracks in the dirt where a scant measure of moisture collected. Roofs sagged, windows were blank open holes, and the doors looked forlorn. The desert was reclaiming its own.

Out of the corner of his eye, Peter saw something that did not belong. He stopped and waited for the echoes to come. As if in a bright shadow, he found the street was no longer a pair of ruts but a paved road like those found in proper towns. The row houses were gone, replaced by larger, more comfortable homes surrounded by small yards of grass. People moved about like fleeting wisps of substance. Children played on the grass. Some of the men were dressed as miners, with hard hats and lights, carrying lunch pails.

Peter blinked and the present town of decay returned. He marveled at the possibility of grass in Slav Town. No one had ever run a big enough pipe from the reservoir down to the town to waste water on grass. Water went to the basics of drinking and washing and serving the mine.

Up ahead, Peter found a '38 Ford pickup truck, old and cheap, parked next to a house whose roof had slumped inward. The stranger was not around. Peter took a quick look in the bed of the truck: a suitcase, a shovel, and several buckets full of rocks. Peter picked up one of the rocks, about the size of his fist, some sort of dark shale, with the number twenty-three scrawled in white paint on its side. The rest of the rocks looked similar, all identified by different numbers. Not a fossil among the lot of them.

Slav Town ended in a row of hills made of slag and tailings. Peter climbed one of the hills, half-melted rocks crunching under his boots. As he neared the top, he slowed to crouch ever lower. He crawled the final few yards to the top, feeling an eerie déjà vu that he was back in France.

The railroad bed ran along the opposite side of the hills. The rails had been reclaimed long ago, leaving only a long row of ties, mostly covered with sand. The buildings of the smelter followed the rail line from the mouth of the mine, and the equipment that melted purity out of the ores of Silver Ridge was gone.

After the mine had closed, Peter and his friends had prowled those buildings, collecting pieces of copper or iron, and sometimes some silver. His best friend, Lee Gardner, once found a bent lump of gold, no more than an ounce, caught between two crumbling boards. Lee took it to his father, who sold it to feed the family for a month. That led the men of the town into the buildings, ripping up floorboards and digging holes—they found some silver, but little gold.

Peter sighted the stranger two hills down, bent over a metal box in his hand. He picked up a rock and held it close to the box, then tossed it away before picking up another rock. Peter noticed that a wire from the box led to earphones on the stranger's head. The scene tugged at Peter's memory, but he could not quite place the connection. Looking at the stranger for too long brought on future echoes: metal sheds had replaced the smelter buildings, the railroad worked again, and miners moved back and forth from the mouth of the mine.

Peter watched the stranger for the rest of the afternoon. Occasionally the man painted a number on a rock and placed it in a bucket that he hauled about with him. The tailings seem to interest him the most, which was most odd, since the rubble was the leftovers from the mine. Peter noticed that the stranger wore gloves despite the awful heat.

Sometimes Peter lost interest in his vigil and looked toward the south, marveling at the view. Sharp shades of red and yellow and brown painted the hills in broad horizontal strokes. The vast blue sky held clouds that tantalized a man with the hope of rain or just a bit of relief when a cloud drifted in front of the sun. He loved the desert, its stark beauty and unforgiving nature; it made him feel at home in a way that forests or cities did not.

Peter glanced at his watch. He was supposed to be at Jenny's by six for dinner with her family. He wanted to marry her but was afraid that he would not measure up. A tangle of scars stitched across his stomach were hidden from all but his doctor. When a German bayonet had cut him open during the freezing winter of the Bulge, he held his own intestines in with his hands as he walked back to an aid station, where they placed him in an ambulance for a ride back to a proper hospital. He spent months recuperating, but it was not a million-dollar wound, and after he recovered, he was returned to his unit rather than home to the States.

Jenny was seven years younger, always the little sister of his buddy Lee. He had not given her any thought until he returned from the war and found a seventeen-year-old girl turned woman. Lee had not come back. His grave was in Italian soil at Anzio. Now, three years later, Jenny was antsy for marriage and had made it clear in that subtle way that women had of communicating that he had better step up to the plate or she would go find another player.

He brought his thoughts back to the present. The stranger stood with his neck arched, taking a long drink of water from a jug. Peter's own thirst suddenly became acute; already he felt nauseous from the sun. He crept back down the hill and returned to his office. The water can there held only lukewarm liquid, but it felt nice running down his throat.

His pocket watch, inherited from the previous sheriff, showed five-thirty. No doubt the stranger would continue working into the cool of the evening. Thoughts of Jenny pushed away thoughts of the stranger. Peter walked homeward.

He considered stopping to talk to Flo but saw that she actually had some customers. The Clarks were treating themselves to dinner in the café, and old man Werth had come in for his dinner. He was a regular, breakfast and dinner every day. He made enough on his bees and Social Security to pay for his two daily meals now that his wife was dead.

Peter passed the Mormon church, made of white-washed brick and adorned with plain windows. Everyone left in town was Mormon, though not everyone attended church regularly. Peter attended every Sunday, taught Sunday School, paid his tithing, prayed regularly, and read his scriptures when the mood suited him. He didn't consider himself particularly pious, but he possessed faith.

Across the street stood a more impressive church. The Poles and their kin had built a Catholic cathedral of shaped sandstone, with corners, window sills, and doorsills made of granite, and oak timbers brought in by rail. At one time, every window held stained glass imported from Germany. It was still a beautiful building, even though boards now covered its empty windows. The only stained glass left was a round window just under the steeple, too high and too much trouble to take away. Peter stopped to look at it and saw an echo, the boards gone and the stained glass returned, another glimpse into the future.

The western part of town was an oasis of green. The original Mormon settlers had built a reservoir north of the town and dug irrigation ditches. The result was twenty or so families on small farms, surrounded by green plants in red soil. Clumps of grass, watercress, and peppermint grew along irrigation ditches. Small stands of orchard trees yielded pecans and peaches that brought good prices in Blanding or Moab. The families grew enough to survive and most ran a few cattle on federal lands to provide some cash.

Peter's parents lived in a two bedroom adobe house. An outhouse in the back still served its function, though a pipe now brought water from the reservoir into the house for the kitchen. His sister and her husband had moved to Salt Lake City and his brother to St. George. Peter was there to help, but Mama and Papa were still robust people in their fifties who worked much harder on their farm than he did at his job.

Peter lived in a small house toward the back of his family's ten acres. His grandfather had built the house at the turn of the century from lumber cut and milled in the Henry Mountains, barely visible on the southern horizon, and hauled back by wagon. The chimney came from the sandstone rocks of the hill just behind the farm. Peter had been working on the place in the evenings and Saturdays, installing what the English called a water closet. He had a tub, too, but had not run any pipes to it yet. His next goal was to buy a refrigerator. He also wanted to buy one for Mama, though Papa could see no reason for the contraption.

After wiping the dried sweat from his torso with a washcloth, Peter put on a nice long-sleeved shirt and tucked a turquoise bolo tie up to his collar. The Gardners lived three houses up the lane toward the reservoir. Her father had been a foreman at the mine, made good money at the time, and had built a brick home.

Jenny waited on the porch, reclining in a rocking chair. Shoulder-length dark hair lay against her neat white dress. She spent a lot of time working in her father's pecan orchard, and the summer sun had darkened her olive completion. She stood at his approach. Her fresh red lipstick was a little too strong, lacking the subtlety of the sophisticated women that he had seen in London and the other great cities of Europe, who even in war-induced poverty retained their dignity. She was in every way a small-town girl who occupied the ambitions of his mind and body.

Peter mounted the step and hugged her.

"Peter, my parents are moving to Blanding. My dad has a new job there working as a foreman on a ranch."

"Oh?"

"What should I do?" she asked, looking straight into his eyes.

"Let me think about it," he stammered, his own eyes suddenly finding the planks of the porch of considerable interest.

Dinner became a conflicted affair, the conversation starting in spurts before awkwardly trailing off. Most of the talk was about the new job, which seemed to be a good arrangement for Mr. Gardner, though the family regretted having to move away from their home. Four generations of Gardners had lived in Silver Ridge. Peter finally hit on the topic of baseball, which at least kept her father and him talking while Jenny and her mother seemed to communicate with each other without speaking.

After listening to the radio—1160 KSL from Salt Lake City—with the Gardners for a while, Peter excused himself. Normally Jenny walked him home, an odd reversal of how it should be, but tonight she claimed to be tired, and he agreed that she should get to bed despite the sun still being up.

Peter sat in his chair at home, his thoughts far from the stranger and echoes, tormented over what to do with Jenny. He suspected that the answer was already within himself, and he was just not ready to listen. His eyes fell on a stack of magazines in the corner, and he remembered with a sigh of relief a *Life* magazine he had read last year. Something else to think about. He switched on the electrical lights, a convenience brought to the town ten years earlier as part of FDR's New Deal, and went to the corner. He subscribed to many magazines, the *Post, Time, Life, Reader's Digest, Astounding Stories, Scientific American*, and the *Improvement Era*. He found the *Life* issue for July 1946.

The second article included a nice, full-page picture of a scientist in a white coat and holding a square box just like the stranger had been using, while standing next to a table piled high with chemistry glassware. Red letters proclaimed "Atomic Scientists." The words brought back the memory of reading this article the first time. The atomic bomb used a mineral called uranium and a Geiger counter measured the radiation from the mineral.

The Bomb. Peter had been in California in August of 1945, getting ready to ship out with his division. He and his buddies were slated to be in the second wave of the invasion of Japan. He dreaded the prospect; Krauts and Wops were bad enough, but the Japs craved the glory of suicide. He read the newspapers during the Battle of Okinawa, where kamikaze airplanes plunged into American ships day after day.

After the two atomic bombs—a testament to American science and power—exploded over Japanese cities, the war ended. A month later, he boarded a train back to Utah. He was grateful to the scientists, the pilots, to everyone who had made it possible. He felt no pity for Hiroshima and Nagasaki.

A year later, he read the book by John Hersey. Not a lot of pages, but *Hiroshima* put it all in a different light. He could see the shadows of the dead imprinted onto the ruined walls of what had once been a thriving city. The charred bodies reminded him of the corpses of soldiers he had seen in France, toasted by flamethrowers. Not many more awful ways to die. The stories of Miss Sasaki, Dr. Fujii, Mrs. Nakamara, Father Kleinsorge, Dr. Sasaki, and the Reverend Tanimoto shocked him into sympathy. Though the insight was obvious, even trite, he found that Japs were people too.

Now Stalin and the communists had enslaved the countries of eastern Europe behind an iron curtain. The world war that had consumed his friends to bring freedom and democracy to the old countries seemed futile in the face of the Reds. Only the atomic bombs gave America an edge, and the heart of that edge was uranium.

He went to bed with pride in his heart. He feared the bomb—what sane man did not?—but he found the idea that Silver Ridge would be part of the American defense effort gratifying. Even better, the bomb would bring back prosperity to a town ready to fade away into the desert wind. The war had been over for two years and America celebrated a prosperity undreamed of during the depths of the Depression, yet none of the money and good fortune had come to Silver Ridge. Peter had no doubt that the stranger would be successful in his efforts, otherwise why would the future echoes have appeared so suddenly with his arrival? Imagine that, sheriff to a town of miners, not just a few ranchers.

That night he dreamed of mushroom clouds and black rain, radiation burns and stripped flesh, quick death and slow death. He awoke disturbed and irritable. He cooked some oatmeal, poured some cane sugar on it, added a bit of canned milk, and brooded as he ate. The atom bomb was so powerful that no one in their right mind would cross America. The optimistic part of him envisioned an end to all war.

After washing the pan and his bowl, he slowly buttoned on a fresh uniform shirt. By the time that he picked up his hat, Peter had decided to visit the cemetery. There were two of them: the old one at the top of the hill next to the reservoir, and the Slav cemetery on a smaller hill at the eastern end of the town.

A picket fence surrounded the old cemetery, with only flakes of white to show that the pine had once been painted. Tumbleweeds stuck in the fence and one section was leaning over. Clumps of brown grass and gravestones covered the bare ground. Peter never came here. What if he saw the future headstones of his parents? Or Jenny's? The idea struck him with a cold upper thrust into his gut. He stopped, suddenly feeling the perspiration from climbing the hill. He did not want to know when Jenny would die. He almost turned away, but he needed to know all of what the stranger was going to bring.

There was no gate at the entrance. The echoes of the future glimmered into shape. As he had anticipated, there were new gravestones. He just couldn't do it. He turned and trotted back down the hill.

What about the other cemetery? He wouldn't know anyone there. That is where the new generation of miners would be buried.

He took a back trail that skirted the northern edge of the town. As a boy, he had known the trail well, and he alternated between surprise at the lack of change and an appreciation of change: old trees that he knew and young bushes fresh with life, rocks that seemed immortal and new cracks in the soil.

The cemetery of the Slavs held many crosses. Peter stopped and waited for the echoes to come. More gravestones appeared. Peter walked slowly, keeping the echoes in focus. He found John Andrews, 1903-1954, Beloved Husband. Next came Samuel Stott, 1925-1955, Rest in Peace. In twenty minutes of walking around, Peter examined thirty to forty new residents of the cemetery. Most of them were men, dead in the next decade. Such a large number of men still young when they died aroused his suspicions, and he looked to see if any of the dates matched, indicating a mining accident.

There was only one match, a father and his nineteen-year old son, possibly a road accident or a house fire.

Peter felt disturbed as he left the cemetery. He stopped by his office out of habit, but soon left and walked down to the café. Flo sat behind the counter, reading a paperback. Old man Werth was at his table in the corner, cleaning up a plate of fried eggs with his toast; having lost his teeth years before, he ate only soft foods. He was nearly eighty years old, born before the town was even called Silver Ridge. He was also one of the few who saw the echoes really well, prompting him to rarely be found without a bottle of his own brew. The bottle sat on the table before him.

Peter took a stool at the counter and explained to Flo what he had seen the stranger doing the day before and about the *Life* article that he had read. He also told her about the cemetery.

"The atom bomb, uh?" Flo picked up her clay pipe, already cleaned the evening before, and started to pack it with tobacco. "I never expected anything like that."

"Yeah, the echoes are showing us a lot. Quite frankly, I'm a bit confused," Peter admitted.

"Well, seeing future echoes is rare. Even when you're looking, you usually only catch a quick glimpse. It's not like the past. The future is not yet made."

"Have you ever seen anything like this?" Peter asked. "So many future echoes? So strong?"

"Only once before. Back in '31, just before they closed the mine. I saw what we live in nowadays, an abandoned and dying town. I didn't quite understand at the time what I saw, but when the company announced it was shutting the mine down, then I knew."

"So the echoes seem to be strongest when some big change is being decided?"

"Seems to be." She brought the pipe to her lips and struck a match.

"You two are just thinking too much," old man Werth said abruptly in a scratchy voice. Peter and Flo turned to look at him. The old man hardly ever said a word. "Back in '22, I was going into the mine. Part of the morning shift. I saw the ghosts. Men were being carried out on stretchers with coats over their faces. I knew it was not the day to be at work, so I just went home. Didn't tell anyone or do anything.

"Thirty-eight men died in a cave-in down on level four. Not all of them died at first. The rescue crew found that they had cleared a good ten feet before their air ran out. I know how that is. I was in the cave-in of '85. Only sixteen years old, sucking in bad air, prayin' for rescue. I lived and after that I started to see the ghosts.

"I don't like the ghosts. I see my wife sometimes at the kitchen table, even though she's been gone for seven years now." He reached across the table and picked up his bottle. He caressed it fondly. "This keeps the ghosts away."

"It wasn't your fault," Flo said. "You didn't cause that cave-in."

"I could've warned them!" the old man roared. "I could've told the foreman!"

Flo tightened her lips against his anger. "They wouldn't have listened, you know that. The miners weren't born here, they can't see the echoes. They would have just laughed at you. You couldn't have done anything but save yourself."

"You call 'em echoes, like they are just some sort of sound. They're ghosts, Flo, and don't forget it." He pushed his plate away. "I ain't hungry no more."

The old man stalked out of the café.

Peter spoke first. "I always wondered how he came to see the echoes. A cave-in."

"So it seems." She fiddled with her pipe. "I heard that the Gardners are moving. What're you going to do?"

Peter looked at the red-haired woman. Flo Andrews was probably the best friend he had. Even as a child, when she was the school teacher, he had felt a close affinity to her. Flo had been married then, but her husband was later killed in a car crash. She was with him and spent three months at LDS Hospital in Salt Lake City recovering. That's when she started to see the echoes. When he came back from the war and found the echoes waiting for him, she had helped him to understand.

"Flo, I just don't know," Peter said. "I haven't decided."

"Do you love her?" Flo demanded.

After a moment's reflection, Peter nodded.

Flo continued. "Would she make a good wife?"

"Oh, sure, of course."

"You like her family?"

"Of course. They have always been like a second family to me. Lee and I spent so much time together."

"Then, the last question is, do you ever want to get married?"

"Well, yeah, I guess so."

"Then do it, boy. Dammit, you're just dense."

Peter smiled weakly. She didn't know about the scars on his stomach and the anxieties that tormented him. He could make love, but he feared that he could not make children, and he knew that Jenny wanted children.

"I'll figure that out, Flo," he said. "Right now, I'm not sure what I'm going to do about the mine."

"Do?" Flo sounded puzzled. "What do you have to do?"

"I saw it in the cemetery, Flo. Uranium is poisonous, radioactive and all. This uranium is going to kill people, Flo. Maybe I should stop the stranger and send him on his way."

"I don't know, Peter. Maybe uranium is a killer, but you know that mining is dangerous no matter what the mineral. And this town could use some prosperity."

"Maybe so." Peter picked up his hat and slid off the counter stool.

FOUR MILES south of town a pair of tabletop mesas reached out from a low range of hills. Juniper trees grew atop the mesas along the edges like a fringe of hair. The canyon that separated the mesas was at places narrow and rugged. Peter followed a trail that climbed the northern mesa, then dipped down into the canyon where the creek at the bottom had cut a wider space. The cliffs on both sides bowed inward, providing shelter from the rain.

The Anasazi had built Casa Acantilado against the northern canyon wall so that the sun warmed them during the winter. Under the opposite protective overhang the Anasazi had built storage rooms. Peter crossed the stream and climbed up to his favorite perch, a hump of stone where he could lean his back against a wall made from blocks of sandstone. Most of the rooms were still intact, with ceilings made of mud and brush laid across juniper beams. Small withered ears of corn, only two or three inches long, littered the ground. They had been there for at least six centuries, hardened and preserved by the dry air.

The pueblo was large enough to have two kivas—great, sunken circular rooms that served as sacred places for ceremonies. The roof of one kiva had collapsed, but the other remained intact. Even the ladder that led down from the central hole was still strong. At times, Peter sat in the kiva and watched the all-male ceremonies, the air heavy with smoke from the central fire. He saw boys become men in ceremonies that no book or man still knew about.

He did not have to wait long before the echoes came. Indian women ground corn in stone troughs. Smoke from their fires curled out of the canyon. Some men and women worked at the gardens on the floor of the canyon. The creek was bigger back then, providing ready water for the Indians. Two men carried their crude hoes past Peter, heading for their fields of corn on the mesa top. Children ran about, balancing on the edge of walls and cliffs with a sureness born of youth, while others danced up the canyon walls, placing their feet into small carved footholds.

The Anasazi had lived here for almost five centuries, gradually building their home until around a hundred people lived in three dozen rooms or so. Ever since returning from the war, Peter had made a habit of coming to Casa Acantilado, becoming familiar with their history by watching. He saw raids by other Indians, where the cliff house served as an excellent fortress for the defenders. Many times the raiders got away with a bit of corn, usually by catching hostages unawares and trading them for the corn. Twice the raiders overwhelmed the pueblo, taking what they pleased. Other times Peter saw droughts that brought on hard times, alleviated only by the stored food.

The final drought lasted for many years. The creek dried to a trickle, then eventually become a dry path of sand and rounded pebbles. The remaining Anasazi, gaunt from hunger, left to never return.

Echo-watching always left Peter feeling peaceful, though physically exhausted. He climbed down to the canyon floor, found some shade underneath a juniper tree, and lay down on the hard ground. Within moments, he fell asleep.

HE AWOKE AT MIDDAY, sipped a drink from the creek, then walked back toward Silver Ridge. He remembered after the mine shut down when many folks left to find other jobs. Some came back with reports that no other jobs were to be found. He remembered one day at school when the teacher, Miss Ivins, asked Becky Smith if she was sick. Becky said that she was just hungry. When Miss Ivins told Becky to go home and get something to eat, Becky replied, "I can't. It's my sister's turn to eat."

Peter told Mama about Becky and her family. Josiah Smith had been out of work since even before the mine shut down and it was easy to not know what was happening inside the walls of their small house. Papa had taken to shooting deer to keep his own family fed and that night Papa took over half a deer to Josiah Smith's and insisted that the proud man take the charity. Shooting deer out of season was illegal, but Papa swore that the county game warden had seen him more than once and had not interfered. Times were hard and sometimes rules no longer made much sense.

As Peter approached Silver Ridge, he noticed that the shaft towers atop the sandstone ridge were still there, the future demanding his attention. He skirted around the ridge and entered Slav Town. He came across the stranger's truck, with more buckets full of samples in the back. The stranger was not around. Peter felt the urge to take the buckets and dump their contents into one of the deep shafts that littered the sandstone ridge. He just might do that, but he could not quite make up his mind.

The obvious prosperity and sturdy houses of the future impressed him. Peter came across a medical clinic—not like the two rooms of the old clinic that had served the Slavs, but a nice brick building with a dignified sign. He saw a family emerge from the clinic, an older son and his mother supporting a thin man between them. Two smaller children followed.

Peter squinted and focused on the family. He did not want future echoes from other times to obscure his sight. The family become more real, even intimate. They came up to their car—a Ford according to the logo—with fins on either side of its trunk. Peter ignored the newfangled design and concentrated on the man. He looked emaciated and sickly, yet the shape of his eyes showed that this was not some grandpa, but a father, probably not even forty yet.

The family drove away, but stopped only a block away. Peter followed and watched them carry the sick man into their house. In the present, the windows of the home were boarded up. Peter looked in through a window of the future, where clean glass gave him a view of the parlor and kitchen. A miner's helmet and coat hung from a rack on the wall. The sick man was led to an easy chair. He fell asleep as his two youngest children played on the floor before him.

Peter blinked quickly, saw future echoes rush about him in a blur of colors, then concentrated to see the family in their Sunday best, eyes swollen red from too many tears. Peter suspected that if he followed them, he would find them going to the cemetery where a new gravestone was being placed.

Did he want to be like old man Werth, tormented by the memory of what might have been? The lives he might have saved if he acted? Was this responsibility too much for one man?

Shaken by the sorrow of the family, Peter left Slav Town, climbed the same hill of slag and tailings he had scaled yesterday, and lay down at the top. He saw the stranger hard at work, right at the base of the same hill. Peter looked down on the stranger, trying to ferret out a motive or sense of evil in the distracted movements of the man. The stranger focused on his Geiger counter and the rocks, nothing else.

Peter realized that the nation needed the uranium. If Silver Ridge did not supply the uranium, then some other mine would, and would reap the prosperity and the deaths by slow poison. Peter rolled over and looked back at his home. The desolation of the town hit him as strongly just then as when he had returned from the war. During the long years of training and fighting and just plain sitting around waiting for something to happen, he sustained himself on his memories. Most of those memories came from when the town had been a vibrant organism, full of life that fed on the mine.

So many empty streets. A town needed people to be alive. It needed work and commerce to give it a flow of blood. The decision of the Gardners to leave was just the latest loss. Peter felt his eyes grow wet.

He shook himself and gritted his teeth. He didn't care for crying, yet strong emotions pounded through him, demanding his attention. He didn't want Silver Ridge to end like so many other mining towns that dotted the West, little more than foundations and weeds. People called them ghost towns, which brought forth a quick bitter laugh. The echoes of Silver Ridge were the true ghosts; and if everyone left, there would be no one to watch them.

The air smelled of dust.

In the past, the seasons of rain and snow sustained the crops of the Anasazi; now modern man relied on factories and money. The rain had abandoned the Anasazi, leaving only ruins and echoes. The return of mining offered new hope for Silver Ridge.

Peter could not let his town die. It was time for Silver Ridge to come to life again, even at the cost of the headstones in the cemetery. After all, every mine exacted a certain price in lives, or so he told himself.

He thought of Jenny and her long dark hair. Jenny would want to stay and be part of the new beginning of Silver Ridge. It was time to explain about the scars and ask if she wanted to be his bride.

WITHIN LIMITS

SCOTT R. PARKIN

A LIFE WITHOUT ROMANCE is an empty thing. But a life without romances is utterly unthinkable.

So I make a weekly pilgrimage into town to trade in one pile of romance novels for another. I go to the giant Sam Weller's in downtown Salt Lake City—best collection of used books in six states. Sixty-five miles each way, but I've tapped out all the local bookstores, so it's really my only choice. It's worth it.

I know, what's a thirty-something guy doing reading romance novels? Aren't those for bedraggled housewives and silly teenage girls? Don't I have anything better to do with my time and money?

Well, we've all got our vices, and it's better than hanging out on street corners. Besides, it's not like I believe they're real. I mean that stuff just doesn't happen in real life. No love at first sight. No saving the girl from the raging flood or the corrupt landlord or the enemy invasion. No tender thanks or passionate embraces or heaving breasts.

Still, one can hope—within reasonable limits—and this is as good as any other day for the impossible to happen.

The radio's blaring from the tiny in-dash speaker. A serious voice drones on about space aliens from the planet Fisbane, how they're transporting stolen goods across national boundaries, and how they've sparked an international diplomatic crisis. I wish for a moment that I could meet a

Fisbanian, or any alien for that matter, but nothing that cool ever happens to people like me.

The drive's an easy one—at least until you get out of Utah County. Brown in more shades than you thought possible, from the deep coffee brown of the western hills to a dull grey-yellow, the color of old wheat at the point of Traverse Mountain that separates Utah County from Salt Lake County.

The promontory really does come to a point there. Not just a peak that slopes down on each side, but a finger of land that juts out into the valley and separates one world from another.

Now I don't know anyone in the world who can drive the speed limit coming down off Traverse Mountain. I mean, it's a straight road that drops directly into outer Salt Lake City suburbia. You have to actively brake to keep from accelerating, and who's got time to brake when there're romances to be had? Especially after forty miles, with twenty-five still to go?

No one. That's who. At least no one less than three hundred years old who can actually see over the steering wheel and isn't wearing a hat. But that's a different problem.

So I let my speed creep up a bit on the way down the other side, and I don't work very hard to slow down.

Okay, I don't work at all to slow down.

Fine. So I keep my foot on the gas and take advantage of the hill to get my speed up to eighty-five. Or so.

Now don't get me wrong. I'm not a speed demon—or at least not ordinarily so. But when you drive a little three-cylinder fuel-economy special, you have to take advantage of every downhill you get. The poor little beast grinds to barely over fifty on the way up the hill; it just seems like justice that I should be able to make up the difference coming back down the other side.

Which is why it's so unfair that a cop is waiting for me at the bottom of the hill.

On any other day, there would've been at least a dozen other speeders all clustered together, and the cop would've had to pick one and let the others go. Usually, they didn't bother.

But today the road is empty, and the cop pulls right out after me, lights a-flashing.

I suppose the general emptiness of the road should have been a sign, a warning that all was not right and I needed to pay more attention. But up until now I was just so happy to have clear sailing that it never occurred to me to wonder about the downside of my good fortune.

So I pull over and fish my wallet out of my back pocket and wait. And seethe. And wait. And mutter. And wait.

I think they do that on purpose. They wait in their cars, talking on the radio to some old hag in Dispatch about their bunions or elbow warts or some such thing, just to see how long they can stretch you out. They watch through tinted windshields and wait until you're as taut as you can get, then they saunter up and say, "Do you realize how fast you were going?"

Of course I realize how fast I was going—I was going it, wasn't I? Do they really think it's possible to go twenty miles over the limit and not know you're doing it?

They know you're in a hurry—that's why you were speeding in the first place. They do it to tick you off, because all cops are just little dictators waiting to exercise their power over the common man. What made it really annoying was that this time the would-be tyrant was right.

And they wonder where road rage comes from.

I've been sitting there for at least three hours waiting for the cop to get off the phone with his bookie when my eye catches on the pile of romance novels in the passenger seat.

It would be wrong to say that I'm embarrassed by my habit, but it is something I try not to advertise. People just don't understand how a six-two, three-hundred-pound man with a full beard and a genetically sour expression can read such things. Their eyebrows raise and they suppress giggles and they smirk like you're wearing a pink tutu or something.

I wasn't in the mood for that just now.

So I grab bundles of books and shove them in the glove compartment and under the seat. I run out of space after the third bundle and I'm just turning to look in the back seat for a bag to stuff the rest into when I hear a tap on the window.

"Doggone it," I say much louder than I mean to and turn to face the fascist pig cop with the domination complex and a whole lotta nerve for pulling over a generally law-abiding citizen who may have pushed the limit a little bit but who deserves a break because everyone makes a mistake and it's a Saturday and all I want to do trade in a few paperbacks so I can find something in my life that isn't empty and depressing, but there aren't any decent bookstores in Santaquin so I have to drive to Salt Lake, and it's a nice drive but even Eden gets boring after you've seen it a couple hundred times and I just wish you'd go away and arrest some real evil-doer and—

And looking at me through the window is the most beautiful fascist pig cop I've ever seen in my life.

She smiles and her teeth . . . well . . . *sparkle* in the bright noonday sun. She has three dimples on one side of her smile and two on the other, a delightful imbalance that makes her face that much more interesting. Her little nose tips up just a bit at the end, and a wisp of mouse-brown hair pokes out from under her dark brown hat. Her name tag says Harbaugh. I roll the window down and she's speaking in a lilting, musical voice like the sound of spring. Then she stops and raises an eyebrow, and I have no idea what she's just said.

"What?" I ask.

"May I see your driver's license, please?" she says in that sweet, lyric voice.

"Oh. Yeah." I hand her my license.

"And your registration, please."

I open the glove compartment and a pile of pink-covered romances falls out. I gather them up and flip them over, but the back covers are no less lurid than the fronts. I toss them between the passenger seat and the door.

I turn back and hand her my registration. She's smiling. "Into romances, huh?"

"I . . . they're just . . . " I sigh. There's no dignity left to save. "Yes, ma'am. Very much so."

She takes off her Ray Bans to reveal sparkling hazel eyes. "So am I." She grins and takes my registration card. "Back in a second," she says and heads to her car.

I watch her in my side mirror and can't help but admire the slender, athletic figure that her plain brown uniform can't hide. Her movements are fluid, powerful, revealing an understated femininity so much more entrancing than the overt sexuality so many women go for.

Then she gets into her car and closes the door, and the trance breaks. I'm about to get a speeding ticket from this lady. This woman. This icon of confident feminine power. This astounding creature of surpassing strength and beauty. This . . . this . . .

Cop.

She's a cop, just like every other surly, overbearing jerk I've ever met at the side of the road. And she is going to give me one whopping ticket, too. I'll have to go through traffic school or pay a huge fine. Or both. My insurance rates were going to skyrocket. This thing could well ripple through the next five years of my life. And for what? A couple of romance novels.

At least it's for a good cause.

I'm still pondering the potential for personal ruin and the slim outside chance of asking Officer Harbaugh on a date when she appears at my window.

"Do you realize how fast you were going?" she asks.

All the pithy retorts I've spent the last ten years preparing flee my mind as I gaze into her sweet face. "Yes."

"If I let you go with a warning, will you promise to slow down in the future?"

Now I *should* nod and tell her that I'm very sorry and that I will never intentionally abuse the speed limit again, that I am a reformed man and her mercy will be rewarded with temperate roadway behavior for all the days of my life.

But I can't lie. Not to her.

"I don't even think about the speed limit. So I can't promise that the next time I want to get somewhere, I won't speed again."

I look down at the steering wheel. That's it. Now she'll give me a ticket. I just hope she'll be the one teaching traffic school so I can meet her again.

When I look up, she gazes at me with those penetrating eyes. "Thank you for your honesty, Mr. Hantz." She looks at her ticket book, then closes it and shakes her head. "I'm going to let you go. But I strongly advise that you slow down in the future."

I blink at her. "What?"

"You can go." She hands me my registration.

I should shut up and accept my good fortune. But that means she will go away and I'll likely never see her again. It's silly of me, but I feel that if I keep her here—with me—for long enough, something good will happen.

"Why?" I stammer.

"I've been patrolling this stretch of road for over a year," she says. "In all that time, I've never seen you go less than eighty through here—not if conditions would allow."

She looks up and down the road, then leans in toward the window. "And in all that time, I've never seen you make a dangerous lane change or run up on another driver. You never shave or read the paper or talk on a cell phone while you're driving. You're fast, but you're safe. I appreciate that."

She smiles that sparkly smile again and I melt.

"Be well, Mr. Hantz."

She turns to go and I feel my heart go cold. I let my head droop forward until the seat belt stops me. I should have said something else, maybe asked her out, or at least found out what days she patrolled the road so I could plan to be pulled over again. I smack myself on the forehead. "Jerk," I mutter.

"Excuse me?" she says.

I sit up and she's there at my window, bent down and looking in at me, my driver's license in her hand. "I was uh . . . I said, 'jerk' but I wasn't talking to you. I was talking *about* you, but I was saying it to myself. I mean . . . oh brother."

She laughs, a fun sound like children at play. I smile and blush.

She hands me my license and a white business card. "If you have any more questions, you can give me a call. Drive safely."

Then she's gone and I'm staring at the card. It's a Utah Highway Patrol card with her name listed as Officer Harbaugh. I flip it over and see flowing script on the back in blue ink. It says, "Suzanne. 555-9160. After 4:00."

I look up and see her pulling out onto the road. She waves and speeds away.

It may be true that I spend a lot of time in the world of romance novels. It may be true that I prefer warm fantasy to the hard realities of daily life. It may even be true that I actually own several billow-sleeved peasant shirts and occasionally put one on and act out the torrid scene where me and my love finally clutch each other in passionate embrace after the cruel struggle that's kept us apart.

But I never in my life expected to experience real, honest-to-goodness love at first sight.

I put my car in gear, check over my shoulder, and pull out onto the empty road. For once, driving a mere sixty-five doesn't seem like a hardship, and I find that I'm totally relaxed as I approach the speed trap at the South Towne Mall. It's the first time I can remember that I don't care if a cop is there or not. Kind of refreshing in an odd sort of way.

I'm contemplating the joys of feminine companionship and the virtues of driving the speed limit when a black Porsche blows by me so fast that the wind of his passing pushes me hard to the side of the road, and I have to use two hands to keep control of my little Geo. I figure he must be pushing a hundred—way too fast, even for me.

"Go get him, Officer Harbaugh" I mutter.

Officer Harbaugh. Suzanne. Sue? Susie? No. Not that she's stiff or formal or anything, but she's got herself together in a way that suggests completeness. Order. Definitely Suzanne.

Sigh . . .

I see her pull onto the highway from the median ahead of me and I wave at her as she speeds away. I'm sure she can't see me, but for just a moment I think I see her wave back.

I'm considering all the bad things that can happen at high speeds and trying to figure out what she'll do if the Porsche decides to not pull over and the fact that there's construction about three miles ahead and the road narrows to a scant two lanes but you don't have time to react in such tight quarters if something goes wrong, and I wonder how many highway patrolmen are injured in car accidents every year so maybe I ought to try to catch up to them and help herd the Porsche to the side of the road so Suzanne doesn't get injured because I don't know what I'd do if she got hurt or killed, and I wonder if a Geo Metro can go a hundred even on a downhill with a tailwind and—

And ahead of me, a giant black cube descends from the sky and blots out the world.

Okay, maybe not the whole world, but enough of it that I swerve and skid and almost lose control of my car because I can't see anything ahead of me but a short length of road, then black. It must be five miles wide and just as high, because I can only barely see its edges, and I can't see the top at all. It's centered on the highway, and just before it hits the ground the black Porsche darts beneath it and vanishes.

Suzanne's white Camaro noses down and swerves as she hits the brakes, and my heart stutters as I realize that she's not going to stop in time.

The cube hits ground with a rumble more felt than heard, and her car careens toward it. The Camaro's back end breaks loose, then straightens out. It hits the black wall, disappears part-way into it, then stops suddenly.

I stop thirty feet away and leap out, run to her car—or at least the half-car sticking out of the shimmering black wall. The airbag has deployed, and dingy yellow-white cloth spills out as I yank the door handle. The hinges have vanished behind the black wall, and the door pulls away and drops to the ground, sheered neatly off at the wall line.

Suzanne pushes the airbag away. Her face is red, like it's been sunburned, and her eyes are glassy. Then she gasps and pulls back from the steering wheel, jerks her feet away from the pedals.

"Are you okay?" I ask.

She nods slowly. "It's cold," she says and points down at the floorboard. I look and see the strange black wall inside the car. It's sliced down through the firewall and its oily, coruscating surface covers the space where the pedals should be.

It radiates an icy chill, a menacing bite that promises instant freezer burn if touched. Suzanne shifts in her seat and I look over at her feet. The fronts of both shoes are gone, cut cleanly off. Her toes are curled back, and I realize that the toes of her socks are gone, as well.

I grab a foot and she starts, then relaxes. The ends of her toes are bright red and starting to swell. I look closer and see that the nail of her big toe is absolutely flat right to the edge of her flesh. As though cut with a wide blade. Or a laser.

"Get out of the car," I say in as calm a voice as I can muster. "But stay away from that black wall."

I stand up as she unbuckles her seat belt, then help her turn in the seat so that her feet are outside the car. I take her hand to pull her out, and I'm thinking how soft and warm her hand is and how this is actually the first time I've touched her even though I feel like I know her very well, and I think I like it and I hope there are other opportunities, which there might be because she isn't pulling away at all even though I'm essentially a stranger who she just met and—

And a semi-truck appears at the top of a gentle rise in the road, blasts its horn, and careens toward us too fast to stop.

Like I said before, I'm a relatively big man at over six feet and further over three hundred pounds than I like to admit. When you're that heavy, you automatically develop a certain amount of strength just to carry your own body around. Which is not to say that I'm in any way athletic—far from it. I'm a dedicated couch potato and member of the Loafer's Guild. But when you carry three hundred pounds around with you every day, an extra one-ten is hardly noticeable.

So I grab Suzanne around the waist, pull her out of her car, and trundle as fast as I can toward the median, trying to ignore the warbling screech of tortured rubber and the ever louder blare of the semi's horn.

Maybe that was unnecessary. Maybe she could have gotten out on her own and would've made it to the center median with a little less jostling and flopping of limbs. But she'd just been in a head-on collision with that weird black wall, she'd been blasted in the face by a hot airbag, and the fronts of her shoes were missing.

It seemed like the right thing to do at the time.

The semi jackknifes and comes in sideways. It hits the Camaro and knocks it through the wall, then starts through as well. It stops halfway. The driver jumps out of the cab and stares at the shimmering black wall. He shakes his head as he comes toward us.

"Lousy Fisbanians," he mutters. "They ought to warn people before they drop those stupid transport cubes." He shakes his head again.

Suzanne and I stare at the trucker for a moment, then turn and face each other.

"Sorry if that was a little rough." I look down at my hands.

When I look up, she's smiling. She takes my hand without saying anything, then reaches up and kisses me lightly on the lips. "Thank you," she says, then hugs me. I hug her back and everything in the world is perfect, if only for that moment.

Maybe it wasn't your standard romance-novel ending. Then again, it was awfully close. There was the electricity when we first met, the disaster of unnatural proportions, and the heroic rescue from the madman about to cause her grave bodily harm. There was the kiss and the tender thanks and the embrace that was about as passionate as I could have tolerated at the moment. At least in front of witnesses.

Good enough for me. In fact, more than good enough.

Because in the instant after the kiss and before the hug, her eyes sparkled and her face glowed. And while I can't be completely certain, I'm pretty sure that her . . . or rather that I thought I saw . . . which is to say, that she . . .

That her breasts actually heaved.

WHILE THE HEROES WERE AWAY

JAMIE PERRAULT

WE BID THE DRAGON-HUNTERS farewell at the wall that marked the edge of the village, my friends and their new knight friend heading off to do what I never would have been able to do. Even when I was three decades younger, I never knew the strength and surety of body that Robert and Estelle showed every moment of every day.

I didn't regret that in the least.

Zotikos herded us forward into the welcoming embrace of the devastated town. He wore his older form, and though the paleness of his skin drew stares and murmurs, the promise of medical attention kept us safe.

Bramshold was just as devastated as we had feared.

Well, perhaps that's not entirely true. In our darkest fears, I'm sure all of us imagined a town full of shambling corpses bent on destroying all life they could find. It was within Thania's capability, though it was such a perversion of the order of the world that she did it rarely. Doing it too often would risk gods other than Zotikos stirring themselves to move against her, and that wasn't what she wanted.

What we found wasn't a haven for hungry monsters, but the human—mortal—picture of pain and misery was terrible all the same.

Since this is a new scroll, I will introduce myself once more, in the event that this record becomes separated from the others. I am Erwin of Erde, and I serve Zotikos, the dragon god of life.

Bramshold was a small village of approximately four hundred individuals when it was targeted by Thania, the dragon god of death. The tired woman who lead us to Bramshold's largest building, a church to Aldredda that had become a makeshift hospital, informed us in a dull voice that forty-three people died during the attack. Another eight had died since then.

The woman was younger than me by at least a decade, but she looked older as she gave out the information. Her eyes were hard and flat, a near-perfect black as she turned to study us from the church entrance. She wore the blue cloak of the village leader loose around her shoulders, the edge dotted with flecks of brown that could be many things but were most likely blood. "If you betray us, strangers, I swear my ghost will follow you and eat your happiness unto your third dying."

Zoey stepped forward. He bowed to her, both hands fisted and arms crossed over his heart. "I swear to you, protector, we want only to help your people. If we betray you, I welcome your haunting as the burden due to traitors and monsters."

Zoey's magic spiked. I could feel it, a tingling along all the hidden lines of the tattoo that binds me to him. The woman relaxed, just a bit, some of the lines of exhaustion fading from around her eyes and mouth. Zotikos had given her strength, lessened her exhaustion to help make the hours to come easier for her.

She gave a jerky nod, turning around to lead us into the room. A pang of sympathy ran through me. She never expected this, I'm sure. When she accepted the mantle of leadership, she would have expected to face perhaps a natural disaster, if they were unlucky—a flood, a bad storm. Disease, perchance, of people or animals. Maybe even a roving band or two of thieves, be they human or other. She wouldn't have imagined destruction like Thania brought to them, or the exhaustion that Thania's magic tends to imprint on an area.

Had she even expect to be called on in emergency? Was she chosen to be their hawk leader or their weaverbird leader? It never matters in times of true emergency, not unless the two leaders don't get along. In times of emergency, the loudest, most sure voice almost always wins, even if it isn't the wisest.

The church smelled like death when we stepped inside. I almost gagged, despite having expected it. Zotikos froze for a moment, his nostrils flaring, his chest expanding as he swept his eyes over the people laid out in various groups.

"Amala." The name summoned a woman of about my age out of the sea of people wandering between the wounded and ill. Her shoulders were kept carefully back, a look of calm and peace on her face. Her eyes looked bruised and puffy, though, and I could see the bloodshot exhaustion being held back only by sheer force of will.

Another tingle through my tattoo, and I knew Zotikos was offering her strength, too. I considered trying to mind-speak him, to tell him that it wasn't a good idea to wave his magic around so freely, but decided against it. If the leaders stumbled, the village might very well fracture in a way it would never recover from. Let any mages among these people come forth and challenge us about what we were doing. Zoey had done no harm.

Given how precious few mages are born each year, I wasn't surprised when no one seemed to notice what Zoey was doing. It would hopefully make it easier for us to heal both the people and their land over the next few hours.

Amala studied us all, her mouth turned down in a slight frown. "Who might you be, strangers?"

"Helpers and assistants, come to give what aid we may." Zotikos put his left hand over his heart. "I am Kos. These are my friends, Emma and Erwin. I'm a physician; Emma is skilled in many trades; and Erwin is very good at working with the land. We heard of your dragon attack and would like to offer what assistance we may."

"A physician?" Hope and suspicion flared in equal measure in Amala's eyes.

"They answered questions accurately enough when they were challenged at the gate. Or as accurately as I could remember." Gerlinde, leader of this village that teetered on the edge of ruin, rubbed at one temple. "Or, well —the young woman there did."

Emma gave a little wave. "I've studied medicine, among many other things. I'm certain I could be very useful."

"Hm. Where did you study?" Amala's eyes flicked from Zoey to Emma.

"At Fort Ewold." Zoey's smile was charming, and I hoped too many follow-up questions wouldn't be asked. When trying to draw on memories of previous incarnations time can get a little . . . complicated for him, and the last thing we needed was Zotikos name-dropping famous people who had been dead for far longer than Zotikos could possibly have been alive.

Amala grunted, noncommittal, eyes shifting to Emma.

Emma pointed at herself. "Me? No formal training, I'm afraid. My hometown wasn't big enough to warrant such a school, and I couldn't afford education elsewhere. I have learned by following and listening and seeing what truly seems to work and what doesn't."

A nod was Amala's only answer, and she turned away from us, gesturing with a flick of her fingertips that we should follow. She led us to a corner of the church that had been segregated from the others, where the smell was even worse. Three individuals lay sheathed in sheets, bandages covering the wounds on their bodies.

Zoey drew another deep breath, and I moved up on one side of him, Emma on the other. To his credit his voice didn't shake when he spoke, though I had no doubt he was smelling Thania's magic, feeling its antipathy to everything he is press against him. "These are the most grievously hurt?"

"They are. Do any of you have any suggestions on what I can do?" Amala knelt by the side of the nearest patient, a young woman who lay pale as death, her chest barely rising and falling.

Amala detailed the extents of her attempts at medicine while she carefully unwound the bandages. A deep, necrotic wound glistened in the afternoon light. Yellow and green material had oozed out to cover the entire wound, coating the inside of the bandage. Amala stared at the discharge in horror, settling back on her heels as though defeated.

Zotikos knelt down on the other side of the injured woman. He touched her forehead with the back of his hand, pulling her eyelids up to study the pupils. "Emma, what do you think about a combination of . . . "

I didn't listen as he and Emma discussed possible treatments. I have never been much good at medicine. Given my decades traveling as both an architect and a disciple of Zotikos, I knew enough first-aid to bind a wound if I acquired one. Everything else I bought from others, not trusting my memory or knowledge of plantlife. It would be terrible to try to create a tea to help, say, muscle aches and end up accidentally poisoning oneself and everyone else at the campsite.

Where Zoey touched the young woman, the red and grey pallor of her skin changed. It was a subtle difference. I didn't expect Amala to notice it, and she didn't. Zoey was being careful, channeling only bits of his magic through the injured. It would be easier if he simply sent out a pulse of divine dragon energy, destroying all of Thania's workings in the process.

But the magic would likely kill some of those still held by Thania's spells, and that could go poorly for us. I thought Zoey made the right decision, to work only on one person at a time, and I silently communicated this to him.

Zoey smiled but continued to work. After two, maybe three minutes he sent Amala with Emma to create a particular tea.

While Amala helped the young woman to stay upright and attempted to slip the tea between her teeth, Zoey turned to the next patient. This time he bounced ideas off me, and I was skilled enough to provide the necessary grunt or "oh, yes" or "hmm, how troublesome."

Giving orders to Amala for a different set of herbs, Zoey and Emma both turned to the third person. Zoey touched their forehead, lifted their right hand, and froze. His head gave a little shake as he frowned, and I sighed, closing my eyes.

Amala returned with the tea, and I heard her and Emma work to get the second injured individual to drink. It was clear just from the brief bits of conversation that Amala knew this man—child, really, because he couldn't have been more than seventeen. She called him by nicknames that no one who didn't know him would have guessed, and he murmured out responses.

There was such joy in Amala's voice as she whispered to Emma that the tea already seemed to be working, and I knew that it was all going to come crashing down in the next minute.

It wasn't the tea that had helped, of course. Or perhaps that's not a fair statement. The tea undoubtedly did its job, and I'm sure it was brewed for useful tasks. But what these people needed wasn't typical medicine. These people needed Zotikos' magic, and he was giving it to them.

Magic can only do so much, though, even in the hands of the beings it springs forth from.

"He's too far gone." Zotikos whispered the words to Amala as she joined him at the third still form. "I don't think anything we do will help him."

"We try, still." Amala forced a smile that didn't reach her eyes. "Sometimes miracles happen. I've seen babes born blue and still grow into perfectly healthy adults."

I had no doubt she had. I also knew, as all people know, that the majority of children born in distress don't survive the hour after birth, let alone into adulthood.

"We try, and we keep them comfortable and let them know they are loved." Zotikos' voice roughened with emotion, though it was impossible to say what kind as his jewel-bright eyes studied the man. "And we ensure that nothing happens to them once they're gone. Have you been caring for their wounds?"

"Myself and some of the others, yes. Kriem is our veterinarian, and he's been doing . . . but you don't care about that. Yes, I've been helping with their wounds." Amala stroked her hand gently through the injured man's hair as she answered Zoey.

"Then you'll likely have seen the anomalies, but I'd like to show you them while Emma fetches the tea." It only took a glance from Zotikos to send Emma running. She knew her business, and moving was always easier for Emma than having to stand still.

Moving with delicate care, Zotikos pulled away some of the bandages that covered the man's wounds. I looked away, not needing to see again what I had seen before, not when I knew what the outcome would be. "You see here? The way the tissue is turning, and these lines leading off from it."

They spoke quickly and fiercely for the next five minutes, ten minutes, however long it took Emma to craft the brew and return. Emma, bless her heart, had another volunteer with her, a young man who vouched that the ingredients Emma rattled off were the only ones that she had included in the brew.

Given what was coming, it would be important for Amala to believe we had nothing to do with the man's death.

Emma raised the unconscious man's body, while Amala coaxed him to drink. I'm not sure how much of the tea actually passed his lips and how much trickled down his chin, but enough must have entered his body to satisfy the healer. That or she feared drowning him if she continued to try to entice him to drink.

"There's a wonderful lad." Amala's hand smoothed across the man's forehead. "You're loved, and there are many people waiting for you to return to work, Bern. No one else can make a loaf of bread as light or a cake so airy-sweet as you."

The pulse of magic struck in the midst of Amala's speech, and I forced myself to watch as the man's chest stopped moving.

Magic can do a great deal, but it can't do the impossible. For this man, and perhaps for others, the best that Zotikos would be able to do was break Thania's grasp on them. That way their souls and minds would remain free, and their bodies perish properly instead of turning into puppets for Thania to move at her whims.

Amala tapped the man's cheek. "Bern? Bern, boy, you can't—Bern . . . " She knew, of course. She had seen death often enough to know, and she cut off her hysteria before it could truly take root. Closing her eyes, she breathed deeply, only the faintest traces of liquid running down deep-etched grooves in her face to splash onto the dead man's face.

I gave her a few seconds to mourn and then to cover that mourning. The end of this nightmare would be more difficult for her than the rest of it, I thought, because the mourning and grieving and hurting she had turned aside to be what the village needed would all come due.

When she pushed herself to her feet, swiping at her eyes and murmuring that she would fetch someone to take the body, I raised my hand to stop her. "Could you have someone take me to the fields and the houses where the damage was most severe? I would like to get started with my assessment and be useful to you."

Being useful was something she understood, and she gave a terse nod. "Wait here, and I'll have someone come to escort you."

I nodded and turned back to Zotikos.

He smiled tiredly at me, and it was a strange sight to see. The Zotikos that exists now is a child, but the Zotikos that he attempts to become when he dons his past form was very much not, and neither of them are human. It meant that the expression in those bright green eyes never quite sat right in his face anymore, and I am certain more than one person found it disturbing. "Do what you can. Take whatever you need."

I nodded, resisting the urge to cup my left arm, where my tattoo twines from my wrist almost up to my shoulder. I would be borrowing Zotikos' magic to do what needed doing, and I knew how much that could exhaust him. He is the wellspring of life-magic, the source from which it all flows. If too much is taken at once, though, by himself or a life mage or one of his chosen, Zotikos suffers for it. More than once Thania has used the exhaustion of drained magic to hound him to a thankfully not-permanent death, and I didn't want this to be another such time.

I wanted less to see these people continue to suffer, though. I would have to balance needs, apply magic where it would do the most good, and rely on my knowledge and Emma's to supplement magic with common sense.

Emma ended up doing the majority of the common sense. Which perhaps meant it wasn't quite so common, given the knowledge that she held, but it was versatile and useful. I marveled again at how wonderfully eclectic Emma's knowledge base was and at how well she was able to apply that knowledge when the need arose.

Wondering about Emma was a good distraction from the horrors that we were helping to minimize. It wasn't the first time I'd helped to clean up a mess Thania made, but it never gets easier. Sometimes I think it gets harder the older I get. Within an hour of my getting started, it seemed like every able-bodied person in the village who wasn't busy tending to the ill was asking me what they could do, and I was doing my best to direct them.

Moving soil, mixing in fertilizer that they had been planning to use next year, sorting damaged buildings into usable timber and firewood, it all provided outlets for people's nervous energy. They had already been doing a lot of it, of course, but I was able to provide something that they couldn't;

I was able to use Zoey's magic to cleanse the areas where Thania's magic still clung. It meant that splinters no longer festered and burned. Lungs no longer protested after even short stints among the lingering smell of dragon-fire. Limbs no longer turned heavy and dull after only short bursts of exercise. The sense of hope this gave to the people working was palpable and encouraging.

I was careful in my use of magic. I knew that Zotikos would be drawing heavily on his own magic in the infirmary, curing those he could, encouraging healing to stabilize everyone and purge them of Thania's touch. I made sure to direct my magic specifically to the areas where I could sense Thania's magic still simmering, using physical contact to both improve my accuracy and decrease the amount of spillover there was. When I went out to the fields, I debated shucking off my leather boots and sinking my toes into the ground but decided the aura of authority the shoes gave me was worth keeping them on. Instead, I bent down repeatedly to touch the ground I was examining.

Bending down repeatedly used to be easier. Sinking my fingers into the soil near a burned-out stable, I sighed, letting the magic flow through me. Zoey's power had kept me healthy, the dragon god caring for the sentients he collected like a lesser dragon might care for the gold or rocks or cats in their hoard. No one that I know of in Zotikos' hoard has ever died of illness, and we tend to live long lives. We don't live much longer than normal, though, and I felt the weight of my six decades sitting on my shoulders as I worked.

"What are you doing?"

The voice was one I didn't recognize, and I opened my eyes to see a child looking down at me. She was young, perhaps five or six summers old.

I looked into her curious brown eyes. Her clothes were dirty but well-mended, and I wondered how many of her family had perished so far and if any others lay in the infirmary under Zoey's care. "Why do you ask?"

She blinked, clearly surprised by the question. I waited patiently, needing to know the answer before I could give her what she needed. Hopefully it was just a harmless question she was asking, a little girl's curiosity, but if it was more than that—

"I can feel you doing something, though you're not moving." She put her hands together and then drew them apart, an explosion or a child's best attempt at mimicking rings moving outward. "And it's doing something to the ground, which has felt funny since the . . . since the dragon came."

Her voice quavered when she tried to mention the dragon, and I could hear her rallying herself to steady it, lifting her chin slightly to study me.

Zotikos, we have another problem. I tried to balance urgency with calm, not sure I succeeded. We had been lucky so far not to run into any mages. I had been prepared to deal with adults, if someone noticed what we were doing. We could explain that we were mages, as well, trained by the Order. Most likely any mages still living here weren't terribly strong, or they would have been snatched up by someone, becoming either part of the Order or part of some ruler's retinue or tied to some prosperous, wealthy town where thousands lived.

It only took Zoey a few seconds to get back to me, and though his mental voice was tired he seemed to be focusing just fine. *What kind of problem?*

A girl mage. I can't tell if it's Aldredda or Aelden she's bound to, but she can tell that I'm working magic.

And the problem with it is? Zoey sounded puzzled.

I resisted the urge to sigh. Zotikos was a dragon. He may have been mostly raised by humans in this lifetime, but that didn't mean he understood human culture on an instinctive level, or respected it when he did understand it. *I can lie to her, tell her I'm doing nothing, and wait for her powers to manifest strongly enough that someone will recognize it. That could take years, though, and make her a danger to herself and others. Or I could tell them that she's a mage, but if she's one of Aelden's . . .*

Humans have such bizarre ideas about the gods. It makes things so difficult. The disgust in Zoey's voice was obvious, another sign that he was tired. *Do you want my opinion, or one of the others?*

I . . . yours. Truly I wanted everyone else's opinion, but Zoey asking the question forced me to examine my own motives, and I found them sorely lacking. I wanted others' opinions so that if things went poorly I could spread the blame around, and so that I wasn't solely responsible for what might be the dismantling of this child's life. I knew what most of my companions would say, anyway. Emma believed the truth was the most important thing, no matter how unpleasant that truth might be. Estelle would want to take the child under her wing, to promise protection if anyone should threaten her. Robert would want to find the girl a tutor, someone who wouldn't mistreat her if she ended up having ties to Aelden rather than Aldredda.

I believe you should find out what the girl knows, and then tell whoever needs to be told so that they can make informed decisions. The words were a strange amalgamation of Zotikos' previous form's diction and Zoey's stubborn directness.

They confirmed what my image of my allies and my own conscience told me I should do, and I smiled glumly. *Right. Thank you, and sorry to bother you.*

You're never a bother. The words were a rumbling purr even in mind-speak, pure dragon, and my smile lost any hint of sorrow. Zotikos loves his hoard, no matter how strange we are, no matter what we may be doing, and sometimes that's a comforting thing to hear inside your soul.

"You've been doing it again." The girl was crouched down so that her eyes were directly level with mine. She held a stick in one hand, branches torn off to create a strange three-pronged end that she used to poke me in the chest. "What is that?"

"Do you know what magic is, child?"

She gave me a look that I probably deserved. "We're rural, not idiots. Course I know what magic is." Her eyes widened as her voice trailed off, and I watched her small hands clench together. Her eyes darted away, then came back to meet mine. She tried to act as though nothing had changed, but I could see the fear in her eyes. "Are you saying that you're a mage? Why don't you wear a mage's rings? And why didn't you tell Gerlinde and the others?"

"Why haven't you told them that you're a mage?" I raised one eyebrow inquisitively.

The girl laughed, and it sounded shrill and scared. "I'm no mage."

"Who taught you to hide?" I spoke quietly, not moving toward the girl. I didn't want her to flee, screaming that I was a monster out to betray the town.

The girl gave her head a little shake, and this time her voice, too, came out as a quiet whisper. "I'm no mage. I swear it, on Aldredda's name. I'm a good girl."

My heart broke at that, a little bit, but it's had plenty of experience at breaking and mending. "Whoever told you that being bound to Aelden's magic makes you bad was wrong. Will you tell me who it was?"

Shifting foot to foot, the girl looked from me back toward the heart of the village. "Are you pulling on the Betrayer's magic, too?"

"No. I have no bonds to him." I've yet to meet Aelden, though I've asked Zotikos about him, as I ask Zotikos about a great many things. "This is a different type of magic."

The girl frowned. "There's only two types of magic. There's Aldredda's magic, which is good and meant to help people, and then there's Greed's magic."

"There are many, many other types of magic." There was more to unpack in the girl's statement, but I hoped that through this tactic I could both broaden the child's world and keep her from panicking. "Every race has at least two types of magic that they can be born to. For humans, it's Aldredda and Aelden, yes. But this magic doesn't belong to either of them."

"Which is why it feels different from the other magics I've felt. Different from what I can do, and what the priests do when they visit, and from what . . . what the dragon did." The girl gave an involuntary shudder as she once more glanced across the lingering pain of the dragon's attack.

I nodded. "Yes."

"What's it do, then? And why use it instead of human magic?" Curiosity is such an important emotion in children. Trauma can bury it for a bit, but it almost invariably returns. Only the constant stress and strain of adulthood seems able to truly destroy it.

"I use it because of what it does, and because it's what I have access to." I smiled at the child. I wouldn't show her the marks Zotikos made on me. There were too many stories circulating about the evil green dragon who could steal wills, break minds. "Would you like to see what it does, and why it's the perfect thing to help us right now?"

The girl nodded, looking down at my hands expectantly.

The longer I kept her interested and occupied, the less likely she was to try to betray me. I didn't have an unlimited amount of time to waste with her, but I had enough, I thought, to do what was needed. "Can you find me a seed? For a grass or a flower would be best, I think. Something we can move easily to a new spot."

She frowned but complied, skittering off to the edge of the field and returning with the center of a hope bloom. I gently pried one of the red-green seeds nestled at the center of the flower free and dropped it into the earth.

I sent a brief apology to Zotikos before drawing on his power and directing it into the little seed. I had only partially cleared this soil of Thania's influence when the child walked up, so I used the opportunity to finish my task, channeling magic through the seed and the earth.

After a half minute, the child straightened, crossing her arms in front of her chest and scowling at me.

After a full minute, the hope blossom plant burst forth. Its green was a rich, dark, dirty color at first, but that quickly faded to a more normal yellow-green. A bud quickened on the top of the verdant tower, trembled, and burst forth with another hope flower. The petals of the flower started out a pure beautiful white at the edges, and faded to a dark rich red in the center.

Gesturing to the flower, I smiled once more at the child. "This is what I want to do for the whole field. To make it healthy again so that crops can grow, like this flower did, and the magic that I'm using is perfect for that."

Perhaps I shouldn't have shown off quite so much. The child danced around the flower, studying it from multiple angles, mouth wide and eyes bright.

"Little one." I waited for her to pause and look at me. "Do you have a name?"

She hesitated, then whispered, "Ida."

"Thank you. I'm Erwin." I touched my chest. "Now, who told you that you have Aelden's magic?"

Ida drew in a deep breath, chest and cheeks puffing out. Then she exhaled it noisily, her eyes dropping away from me. "Father did."

I blinked. "Your father told you that you're a mage?"

Nodding vigorously, the girl reached up above her head, then dropped her hand twice before returning it to her side. "It's a thing in our family. First there was Grandma Imhild, then there was father, and now there's me. We've all been born with magic, but not the good kind. Not the kind the priests will see and take us to school to learn about."

I rubbed at my jaw, tired but comprehending. Magic does frequently pass down along bloodlines. There are some theories that all magic is a result of bloodlines, that sometimes when there's been lots of mingling and mixing the trait disappears and then reappears, but well over half of new mages come from at least one mage parent. "Where's your father now?"

The girl looked away, kicking at the dirt. "Gone."

"Dead?"

Shaking her head, Ida looked back at me, her eyes flat and dull. "Gone. The dragon came, and the barn burned, and the horse's mane was on fire, and Father just . . . disappeared. There was magic, and he was gone."

An untrained mage, facing what must have seemed the end of the world, with Aelden's power there for his terrified instincts to call on . . . I didn't know the man at all. I didn't know for certain that was what had happened. For all I knew he had intentionally abandoned his family, leaving his little girl to face what came next on her own.

But I couldn't shake the image of a man suddenly far from home, alone in a night that was desolately quiet after the commotion and violence of the attack, yelling for a family that was suddenly too far away to hear him. "And the rest of your family?"

Shaking her head, Ida bent down to dig her fingers into the dirt around the flower. "I don't want to talk about it. Father will come back, and everything will be fine. Everything will be fine. Everything will be fine. Don't let anyone know, and everything will be fine."

I wanted nothing more than to reach out and pull the child into my arms, but I knew better than to do that. Scared children are rather like scared animals. Earn their trust, and don't do anything to spook them unless you're certain they can't escape or accidentally hurt themselves. *Zoey, is Blythe available if we need them?*

It took Zotikos a few seconds to answer me, and I had no doubt he was speaking with Blythe. *They're busy still, but can come if it's urgent. Why?*

The girl wields Aelden's power. So did her father, and her grandmother. Her father side-stepped during the dragon attack and she hasn't seen him since, and I suspect the rest of her family is dead.

I can bring Blythe here if it's necessary. But you usually tell me that bringing a tribesman marked plainly with Aelden's symbol into a non-tribe town is dangerous.

Because it was, and I tugged on the silvering locks atop my head. *Could Blythe find her father?*

I have no idea. Zotikos paused. *And neither do they. They say it depends on the situation.*

Right. Thank you. I turned my attention back to the girl. "I won't tell about your gift, if you won't tell about mine. I'm just going to make things grow again, all right? Grow healthy and strong."

Holding her hand above the flower, the girl looked up at me. "Can I learn how to do something like this?"

"Not with the magic you have naturally." I hesitated. "Or at least, not that I know of. But magic is usually most limited by the user, so perhaps you can. If I found someone who could teach you, would you like to learn?"

"Teach me what?" The suspicion in Ida's voice was clear.

"Teach you how to do what you want with your magic, instead of your magic doing what it wants with you. Because your magic isn't evil. It can be used for good things, too. All magic can be." I believed that when I told it to her, despite the evidence all around us. Thania may have used death magic to create horrors, but Thania was not what the gods were supposed to be.

It sounds so prideful when I say it like that. Like I know what the gods are *supposed* to be. And perhaps I am prideful, because I believe I *do* have a sense of it. I do not believe Thania came forth a monster. I believe she was made into one, as all creatures can be made into monsters, though I do not know what could break a god.

"Could I find Vati?" Ida studied me with beautiful dark eyes. "If I could use my magic?"

"Perhaps." I reached out, slow and careful, and pushed brown-red locks of hair away from her eyes. "I cannot guarantee that, but I can guarantee you could find yourself more easily."

Ida gave me a look that said more clearly than words that this sentiment made me an idiot. I suppose saying it out loud did make me foolish, because that isn't the type of sentiment that a child will understand.

"Will you help me?" I gestured to the plant. "You felt the magic I used, right? And the darkness that was here before?"

Ida nodded.

"Help me find other places like that, so that I can fix them."

Her consideration took perhaps a half minute, during which I forced myself back to a standing position, my knees and back protesting every move.

"For a meat pie." Ida held out her open palm.

"For a meat pie." I replied gravely, blowing the promise into my palm before setting my palm atop hers.

Ida stayed with me for the next hour before being lured away by Emma. I had half expected it, and didn't begrudge Emma capturing the child's attention. Emma is one of the few fully grown people I know who has enough energy to not only keep up with a child in full tilt, but perhaps do *more* than said child. Children at least have a tendency to share their elder's look of stunned surprise after more than a minute or so in her presence, though the children's surprise tends to be giddy and pleased rather than the put-off response many adults give.

It wasn't until after sundown that I was able to steal a bit of time alone with Zoey and Emma. We all had bowls of stew, taken from the communal pot that was currently being used to feed everyone who was working to save the village. I was impressed once more with the courage and determination of these people, and of their leaders. This type of calamity can destroy a people, if handled poorly, but I thought that with our assistance Bramshold might well recover.

Zoey looked exhausted. He tried to hide it, but his eyes were drooping, and his shoulders slumped forward. Breaking another god's workings, even when that god was his antithesis, took energy. He cradled the warm bowl of stew to his chest, and I was half concerned that if we didn't keep a close eye on him he'd end up with a lap full of liquid.

Emma still practically sizzled with energy, though I could see the toll that the day had taken on her, too. Instead of her usual exuberant rambling about whatever topic had recently caught her attention, she fidgeted nervously while giving a brief recounting of the events of the day. She had somehow managed to keep up with both Zotikos and myself, and it was through her thorough, swift synopsis that I learned how much work Zoey had done.

"Everyone?" I spoke softly, not wanting to attract attention. The people of Bramshold were giving us a bit of privacy, a bit of time to grieve and process as they were grieving and processing. It seemed that our hours of tireless work and the stabilization of most of the injured and ill had improved our standing in their eyes, and I didn't want to risk putting everyone on edge again. "Zo, there were over twenty people in the infirmary when I left."

"Yes." Zoey raised his eyes to study me. They were the eyes of an old god again, weary and deep. "Twenty-three people I found touched by Thania, and only one beyond saving. I wasn't going to risk any more deteriorating."

"He didn't cure them completely. Just dispelled any of Thania's magic and set them on the path to healing." Emma twirled her spoon around in her bowl, the wooden implements making a *shushing* sound as they slid against one another. "I thought it was a reasonable thing to do. These people need the comfort, and we need their trust."

"I used the healing and examinations to show Amala and the others with some medical training what Thania's touch looks like in a wound. They won't allow any more animals or beasts to become pawns of hers. Or . . . they'll at least know what they're dealing with. Thania won't be able to fool them into fighting against those who want to protect them, at least." Zoey yawned before dipping his head and sipping directly from the bowl.

I would need to make sure he ate not just the one bowl but at least another two or three. Zotikos thankfully didn't eat as much in human form as he did in dragon form, but he was burning through magical energy quickly.

"Any word from the others?" Emma's voice quavered just a little, and I reached out to place a hand on her shoulder.

"Estelle says that they're fine. On the beast's track." Zo's eyes unfocused as he spoke, and I knew his attention was elsewhere. "They might end up fighting tonight still."

Emma and I both looked to where the rising moon limned clouds in silver. The last blues of sunset still hadn't quite faded away, but from here it would likely get dark quickly.

I gave Emma's shoulder a little squeeze. "We need to trust them to know what they're doing."

"They do." Zoey lowered his face to his bowl again. "All three of them do. They'll find the dragon and send it to its proper peace."

"All three of them?" I couldn't help the gentle probe about the knight who was traveling with my friends. I've been with Zotikos for a long time, and I recognize certain cues and moods.

Emma peered between me and Zoey, understanding dawning. "You really do want him, then? Even though we've known him for approximately a day?"

Zoey hunched in, breath huffing out. It would have been impressive in his dragon form; in his properly aged form it would have looked appropriate to his age; in his current form it was another discordant note. "I'm a dragon. We *hoard*."

True enough. It also brought my mind back around to the girl, who was meticulously devouring the meat pie I had managed to scrape together for her. She sat a little apart from our group, and I wondered belatedly if she'd heard Zotikos claim to be a dragon. I nodded my head toward her. "What about my new friend?"

Zotikos studied her, his green eyes almost luminous in the gathering dusk. "What about her? If you want me to claim her, I'm happy to."

"I would imagine as much. But first I think we need to find her father. Would Blythe be able to help me now?"

Zotikos closed his eyes, concentrating, his head rolling back on his neck.

I ate, watching as Emma continued to fidget nervously. No doubt she was waiting for Estelle to get back. It was rare to find the lovers apart for long, but dragon hunting was dangerous work, and both women knew where their strengths lay.

"Could you meet them in the field where you met the girl?" Zotikos murmured the words. "I'll side-step Blythe to you, and he'll try to help you find the trail you need. It's difficult, though."

"Difficult doesn't frighten me." I stood up, brushing off the back of my trousers. "Emma, do you mind watching out for the girl?"

"Not at all." Emma began spooning food into her mouth at a quicker pace. "Don't get yourself too lost though. We'll need you."

I nodded, and made my way out toward the field.

Bramshold was well on the way to settling down for the night. A few lanterns were being lit, but most people were exhausted enough they were turning in with the sun. It hadn't been a bad day's work, and with a few more days' work I thought we could stabilize all the damaged buildings and begin trying to replace the destroyed ones.

First, though, I was going to try to restore a different type of structure.

Blythe slipped out of the shadows, greeting me with a raised hand. Their pale skin made them more visible against the scorched earth than I would have liked, but hopefully it was late enough and we had made ourselves welcome enough that it wouldn't be an issue.

"What you're asking me to do . . . " Blythe's expression slid into a frown, the orange tattoo around their right eye crinkling. Aelden's mark, in Aelden's colors, but not the one that Aelden had given personally. I knew that one was wrapped around Blythe's left wrist, and would flare to life when they called on their lord's magic. Blythe shook their head. "Following someone's side-step is all but impossible if you don't know where they've gone. Since the caster was untrained, it might be possible, but I might also just drop you into the middle of nowhere. Or into a town."

"Then Zotikos will pull me back." I shrugged, trying for a nonchalance I didn't feel. I had never been the adventuring type.

Perhaps that would make me less frightening to the man I was trying to track down.

Blythe nodded. "All right. Stand here, and give me some time."

Blythe began circling me, scratching runes into the ground as they muttered to themself—or perhaps to Aelden, or perhaps to Zotikos. Blythe was far more versed in the particulars of magic than I was.

I had never wanted to push Zotikos' abilities to their limits. I was content with the freedom of movement and the health I was able to share. If I were more like Blythe, more like Emma—if I didn't just accept the limits of what I was given but tried to build on it, as I constructed buildings—

"Ready?" Blythe's question was a quiet whisper in my ear.

"Ready." I braced my feet.

Darkness flowed around me, the familiar feel of warmth and smell of dragon-fire that said Zotikos' magic was holding me tight—was *moving* me, wending me between the wefts of magic that were our world and depositing me in a new position.

Vision returned to me, and I saw mountains rising up in front of me. I didn't know if I had been moved north, toward the land the cuervino stubbornly held; west, toward the mountains that held Zotikos' lair; or east, toward Ewold and the well-mined mountains that provided the Order with their weapons.

It was dark still, so I couldn't have moved *too* terribly far. Most likely toward Zotikos' mountains, then—toward home, in a way.

I started walking, looking for signs of any other living people. I remembered to scan the skies, too, alert for griffins or sphinxes that might be waiting above.

I saw nothing, heard nothing, but that didn't mean terribly much. The great cities of all the races had trouble hiding themselves, but the smaller enclaves . . . one could be a stone's throw from them and not know others were near. Especially for the moon-bred, who tended toward small groups and used scent more than sight to mark their territory, it was possible to move through their land and not even know.

I debated calling for the man. Ansgar was his name—I had asked Amala, rather than upsetting Ida further by asking her more about him. Since I didn't even know if Blythe had sent me to the right place, I didn't.

"He's here."

I froze, my heart suddenly pounding hard in my chest, my breath frozen in my throat.

The man who strode forward to stand facing me was absolutely beautiful. His skin was the same sun-touched bronze as Blythe's, but his hair was dark and braided with bells; little notes of music rang out with every step, with every twist of his head.

His eyes burned bright orange, a color that no mortal-born human possessed, and I knew him by that color.

I bowed low, working hard to keep my balance. "Lord Aelden."

He waved a hand. "Don't bother. You're not ever going to be mine—that greedy dragon got his hands on you far too early for that, and I don't think you were ever the type of reveler who would flock to my banner by nature."

"Don't be so sure about that." I don't know where the words came from. They just seemed to rise up, emerging as a challenge to the God of Selfishness—the God of Satisfaction—and his dismissal of me.

"Oh really?" He stepped forward, a sly little grin tugging the corners of his lips up asymmetrically. His hand caressed my jaw—just a tiny little contact, the barest brush of skin against skin.

Years melted away, my breath hitching in my throat, my heart picking up speed in my chest. I could have been twenty again, designing my first building on my own, lining up beams and calculating weights.

I could have been twenty-five, and meeting a man who would turn out to be a dragon, and then a god.

I could have been thirty, and reveling in the feel of magic filling my skin, making me . . . perhaps not *more*, but *different*, alive and connected to the world in a way I hadn't been before.

Aelden pulled his hand back, and I could hear his little sigh. "Well, perhaps you're right. Perhaps some of me did dance in your blood, once upon a time."

"Still does, my lord. All humans are Aelden and Aldredda's children, after all." I inclined my head, trying to surreptitiously wipe my sweaty palms against my trousers. Not for the first time I was glad I didn't experience attraction to anyone, male or female or other; if I did I suspected Aelden's presence would have been even more disorienting.

Aelden huffed out a breath. "The one you're looking for is over that way. Blythe needed my help to find him, and I had the time. I was debating going to speak to him myself."

"Do you think that would be . . . wise, my lord?" I tried to keep the question tactful.

Aelden's laugh was still bitter. "Who said I had to be wise? He bears my magic. A direct connection from his soul to mine, letting him sap my very essence. I *should* be able to talk with him anytime I want."

"He's Dreddan. He was taught to fear you and your magic. Unless Aldredda herself intends to come intercede . . . "

Aelden's eyes seemed to deepen, becoming far older than the face in which they sat. "You know my sister doesn't do anything like that lately."

Referring to the last two thousand years as *lately* seemed a bit simplistic, but I wasn't a god. I hadn't been around for the war with the Emptiness— the war that damaged so many of them, that turned Aelden into an entity many of his children feared. Zotikos only barely remembered it, too many incarnations between then and now, but what he did remember he didn't like to talk about.

I didn't know how to handle Aelden. I barely knew how to handle Zotikos, and he had been my friend for three decades, through the end of one of his incarnations and the first fifteen years of another.

"I could force him to accept me. I could take him from where he is back to his family, and force them *all* to see me for what I am. To know me as their god." Aelden studied his fingernails, his words contemplative and slow.

I drew in a careful, steady breath. "You could be the monster in truth that some already think you are?"

Aelden's orange eyes fixed on me, and he sighed again. His hand rose, finger pointing. "Fifty paces—just over that little foothill. You'll see a fire. The man isn't *all* foolishness, it seems."

Then Aelden was gone, folding himself back into the night as though he had never been.

I spent a few minutes just breathing, forcing myself to calm. Approaching someone whose home had been badly damaged and who was likely as terrified of their own abilities as they would be of mine wasn't something I wanted to do with my head still jangling from an encounter with a *god*.

When I felt certain of myself, I started walking. I was out of breath after the first fifteen paces, which annoyed me, but my annoyance did nothing to change the state of my body. Zotikos could make me age gracefully, but I was still aging, and this was still an uphill walk after a long day's work.

I found the man huddled over a small, smoky fire. He shivered, his arms wrapped around himself, his clothing that of a sleeper but no bedroll in sight.

Thania's dragon had attacked at night, I remembered. Had he been wandering in his nightclothes ever since?

"May I share your fire, friend?" I spoke as soon as I could see him clearly, not wanting to startle him.

I failed, badly. I winced as he jumped to his feet, clearly thinking about running—clearly *not* thinking about the fire, and how close he was to it.

"I mean no harm!" I held out my hands, moving closer, hoping the lines on my face and the gray of my hair would soothe him.

He squinted at me, and his shoulders did relax, his feet shuffling away from the fire. "If you're truly a friend, be welcome. If you're not . . . well, I've literally nothing but the clothes on my back, and they won't fetch a good price for you."

"I haven't come to rob you, Ansgar. I've come to bring you home." I spoke slowly, softly, but there was nothing I could do to soften the blow, and I decided it was better to have it out in the open than dance around it.

The fire cast enough light that I could see all the blood drain from his face, leaving him looking ashen and hollow. "How . . . "

"Ida. She told me a bit of what happened; I put the rest together." I settled on a clear patch near the fire, enjoying the warmth it cast. "She's a mage. An Aelden mage. And so are you."

Ansgar shivered, closing his eyes. Then he folded in on himself, collapsing down to the ground. "Please—Ida's just a child. Whatever I've done, whatever I am—"

"You're just a man. A father, too. Someone who's afraid of dragons, but I would say that's simply being reasonable. I don't know enough to say more than that." I stretched my hands out toward the fire, flexing my fingers and wincing as the knuckles cracked.

Ansgar watched me, despair giving way to wariness. "You know what I am. You followed me here. You're an Aldredda mage, aren't you?"

The reasonable thing to do would be to lie—to tell him that I was indeed tied to Aldredda, that I was either Order-trained or something else.

That wouldn't get Ida back her father.

I rolled my sleeve up, coaxing just enough magic into the tattoo that served as my conduit to Zotikos to cause it to glow green. "I'm not tied to either human god. I'm tied to one of the dragons. I don't care if you're Aelden's or Aldredda's. I just care that a little girl wants her father back."

Closing his eyes, Ansgar lowered his head. "I can't go back. I can't."

I frowned. "Why? If it's because you don't know how, I can give you the information." It was one of the first things I asked Zotikos to teach me, so that I could travel and explore without his direct intercession. Building was my job, but exploring the ruins of the past, finding the places where history and truth aligned—that was what I lived for.

"I left her." Ansgar shivered, moving closer to the fire, though I was certain it wasn't physical cold he was feeling. "Everything was burning, and I *left* her."

I should have had something to say to that. I have a lifetime of experience with grief, after all—a lifetime of helping build shelters and watching them collapse.

Some things never really become easier, though.

"I didn't mean to." Ansgar lifted his head just enough to look at my face. "I didn't *want* to leave her behind. I just—I just had to get out of there, and the next thing I knew . . . "

All magic worked based on what the user *wanted*. There were limits based on what the various gods stood for—Zotikos was the god of life, and it was impossible to work anything based on his power that didn't have *life* as its base, but within that limitation . . .

Aelden was the god of selfishness. Side-stepping in order to survive would be well within his magic's ability.

So would taking his daughter with him.

"I can't go back to her." Ansgar shook his head. "Not after I left her. Not when everyone will know . . . "

"I can bring you back. Say I found you wandering in the woods. Everyone will just be happy to have you home. The village has lost enough. I don't think they'll be looking for reasons not to take you back."

"I left her behind. For *days*." Ansgar buried his face in his hands. "Do you have children . . . I don't even know your name."

"Erwin. And no, I don't. Not of my own, at least. I have quite a few children of quite a few species who call me uncle, but I've never desired a spouse or children." I had all the family I needed in Zotikos' hoard.

"A child is something special. They *need* you so much, and it's exhausting but it's exhilarating, and you promise them the world . . . and then you fail. Not always as spectacularly as I did, but still . . . it's always failure." Ansgar laughed, the sound devolving into ragged sobs.

"It's not just with children, you know. Or at least, not just with our *own* children. It's with whole generations. We promise them a better world, and we try—or at least most of us try, most of the time. But we never quite get to where we want to be. We make rules that we claim are supposed to keep them safe, and they strangle on them." I drew a breath. "Who told you that your magic was evil, Ansgar? Who told you that it made you bad?"

Ansgar didn't answer me.

"Was it your mother? Your father? Or just something you learned from the priests, from the general talk?" I shook my head. "We are all children of Aelden and Aldredda. All the stories agree on that, but what they don't agree on is what that *means*."

There was silence from the other man.

"Aldredda is self-sacrifice; selflessness; the community over the self. And that's important, it's *so* important, but it's not the *only* important thing." I didn't love Aelden like Blythe did, but I would try to explain what they said so eloquently anyway. "Aelden is selfishness, yes, but that's because he's self-preservation. Self-*care*. Every person needs to balance Aelden and Aldredda's influence."

Ansgar didn't say anything, still. Listening? Or denying?

I forced myself back to my feet. "I love history. I love *seeing* it. When I'm not building the present, I'm usually digging up the past—something people are far less likely to pay me for. And what I find . . . before the War, every settlement I've found worshiped both our gods. Not always evenly, but always *both*. And I think that was the wiser way to be."

"I'm not . . . " Ansgar's voice came out a strangled whisper. "I didn't—*I left her behind.*"

"You panicked. You weren't perfect, but it was a terrible situation." I stood next to the crouched, shivering man, and I held out a hand. "You can't change the past. All you can do is learn from it. What you can change—what you can *build*—is the future."

Ansgar studied my fingers. "She's going to hate me."

I shook my head. "Only if you don't come back. The little girl I left just wants to see her father again. If she grows into an adult and finds out you *could* have come back . . . then she might hate you. Now? Now she just wants someone to grieve with. Someone to tell her it'll all be all right."

Ansgar's fingers brushed against mine. "Even if it won't be?"

"It won't be the same as it was before, but that doesn't mean it won't be all right."

Ansgar's fingers brushed mine again, and with a terrified exhale, he gripped tight.

And I prepared to bring us both home.

IDA SAT NEXT to her father, looking up at him with bright, eager eyes.

Ansgar draped one arm over her shoulders, answering questions from a small gaggle of townspeople as he spooned stew into his mouth.

"You did a good thing." Emma's words were quiet, meant only for my ears. "I don't know if he thanked you, and no one else will know to do so, but I wanted to make sure you knew. As someone who has lost a parent . . . thank you for keeping her from suffering further."

"I didn't do much. It's not like I went dragon-hunting, or healed the sick." I shrugged. "I'm an old man. I help keep buildings from falling down around people's ears. I dig up the past certain people would rather keep buried. I'm not a hero. I just did what was right."

"What do you think makes a hero?" Emma's hand clenched my shoulder briefly before she walked away.

I knew what made a hero. Zotikos collected them just like he collected the rest of us. Heroes were men like Robert, and women like Estelle, and people like Blythe—leaders who did big things, made big decisions.

I was just an architect and an archaeologist and sometimes, hopefully, a good person.

If the world had enough of those, maybe one day it wouldn't need the heroes anymore.

THE DRAGON SLAYER'S MENTOR

IVAN RICHARDSON

MEREK TOOK his time polishing the armour. Reaching into his robe he produced a silver tin and applied its contents to a freshly cut piece of leather. The chest plate was big and mostly smooth so it made a good place to start. His long fingers pushed the leather into every crevice. Then the gauntlets, and finally the helmet. The blacksmiths had already done a good job preparing everything, but Merek liked to make sure it was perfect. It had to be fit for a champion.

The champion in question sat on a stool in front of the fireplace. "Is it ready yet?" his hands tapped nervously on the wooden table as chanting from outside grew louder.

"Not yet," said Merek. He started working on the shield.

"What's taking so long?" The champion walked over to the window and stared at the crowd below.

"All in good time. Come away from the window."

Reluctantly the young man sat back on his stool. Outside bards warmed up the crowd with ballads of champions past. Those old enough to know the words joined in.

"You can start putting your armour on now."

The young man's face lit up as he grabbed the breast plate, yet his left hand continued its tapping. First on the table, then on the polished metal. "Is my chariot ready?" In his haste the armour caught on his clothing. Merek signaled his servants Bill and Rowan to help.

"It's all prepared." Merek stood up to carry the shield and helmet over himself. His legs still worked well enough to support him and the extra weight, but every year brought an extra bit of stiffness to the joints. The champion grabbed the helmet when Merek shot out a hand to stop him.

"You'll want the crowd to see your face."

"Yes. Of course." He stared at the floor.

"It's okay to be nervous," said Merek.

"What are you talking about? This will be the greatest moment of my life." He raised the shield and pulled the sword from its sheath. Slicing through the air as if fighting invisible opponents. "I'm going to be the best champion the kingdom has ever seen."

Merek casually ducked the blade as he placed a hand on the champion's forearm while he checked the armour was on properly. His servants knew what they were doing but Merek had learnt the hard way to always check for yourself. The blacksmith had done a good job; the armour fitted like a second skin. Merek made a note to pay him in full.

"What if I see a girl I like in the crowd? Can I bring her up on the chariot with me? Can she watch me fight?" With one downward swing he took a slice from the table edge. He made an apologetic face, though stopped short of saying sorry, before putting the sword down.

"I'd focus on killing the dragon first. They'll be plenty of young women wanting your attention afterwards."

"Yes. You're right." The champion sank back onto his stool.

"Would you like me to bring the master trainer up for a quick recap before we go out?"

"I don't think that will be necessary." He stared back at the floor.

"Are you sure?" Merek had watched this champion over the many hours in the training against wooden dragons. He wasn't the worst they'd ever trained, but he was far from the best.

"Does every champion come back?" There was a stutter in his voice.

"They have since I took over." Merek allowed himself a little smile of satisfaction.

"What if I get a really fierce dragon?"

"You'll be fine." Merek had already sent the boys off to lay the poisoned meat in the pit. It would ensure a dragon would be waiting for them and that it would be docile.

"What happens if I don't kill it? Will the city still be safe?"

"You just need to focus on dodging its claws," said Merek. He was confident Bill and Rowan would finish the job if needed. Bill had already killed two when previous champions were unable to finish. Rowan was newer but he'd spent a lot of time in the training pit. Once they'd killed one and spread its entrails around the appropriate sites, the other beasts would leave the city alone for another year.

"You're right." The champion's smile returned. "Just got to keep my shield up and keep a distance of two arm spans."

"Three arms spans!" said Merek. "The head can bite from two but the claws can reach three." The old manuals gave the ranges in feet, but Merek found this confused most champions, especially in the heat of battle. Since using arm spans, the armour had come back less scratched. This champion's arms were shorter than average but Merek was confident the rule would still hold.

They escorted the champion to his chariot at the base of the tower. Walking down the stairs, Merek noticed the champion's hands shake. Had they picked the wrong man? He'd certainly been the best candidate at the trials, but this year hadn't delivered a brilliant crop. It was natural for the champion to get nervous at this stage. But this one almost missed a step entirely, a mistake which could've crippled him before the main event. The king would be furious if Merek didn't deliver. The whole parade would be canceled. There would be civil unrest, not to mention the fear that no one would save them from the dragons. The champion righted himself and adjusted his stride to account for the weight of the armour. But the look on his face still gave Merek concern. The young lad was staring at the bottom of the stairs with dread. They could get him to the chariot, but if he bolted before they got to the dragon then they'd still be down a champion this year.

Merek checked the spear attached under the chariot. The sword would look good during the parade, but it would mean getting too close to the dragon. The champion was now shaking so much his armour clinked. Merek, Bill, and Rowan all pretended they couldn't hear the sound as they helped him onto his ride. Rowan kept the exit blocked, but once the tower doors opened there'd be nothing they could do if the champion bolted. Perhaps Merek's flawless reputation would grant him some protection. No one else in the kingdom could replace Merek, but that wouldn't stop the king from trying. The trumpets sounded, the doors were about to open. The champion was in his chariot, but his armour was still clinking.

The great wooden doors opened. Waves of applause washed over the champion. Merek watched as the champion was baptised in the cheers. They washed away the nervous shaking. He stood up tall and confident, a sturdy hand raised the sword high above his head, triggering an eruption from the crowd.

Merek gave a sigh of relief. He knew the crowd was always the final ingredient to complete the transformation. Seeing themselves reflected in the faces of so many adoring fans, they would be reborn as the people's champion. So far it had worked every time, but he always feared the day it wouldn't.

Bill and Rowan rode behind the chariot in armour made to match the champion; they remained relatively invisible. Merek followed behind the crowd. Once, he had ridden alongside as a valet. He'd even killed a dragon himself when that year's champion got drunk before the main event and tripped into the beast's jaws. The idiot still got all the credit. That annoyed Merek at the time, and he wished his family had been rich enough to get him into the trials. But now he cared little for fame. He'd seen how quickly that fades. Some of the past champions had gone on to do great things. Most died at the end of a bottle or vanished into obscurity. None had ever come back to his tower. He did, however, wonder what that moment of transformation felt like. The sudden burst of confidence.

Since taking charge of the operation, every year had gone smoothly, but only because of Merek's constant second guessing every detail. He wanted to know what it was like to lift a sword above one's head without a care in the world. To be immortal for a day. He wondered if he'd feel the same high seeing a crowd cheering for him. Would he be reborn in their eyes, even though he knew how the magic really worked? But there was little to gain from such fantasies.

He followed them all the way to the pit. Most of the crowd had peeled off by the time they got there. The sight of hungry dragons flying above was enough to discourage all but the bravest supporters, or the stupidest.

As always, one of the beasts had taken the prepared meat. It waited for him in the pit. Even drugged, it was still a vicious killer, but the poison had robbed it of flight. The pit was specifically designed for the encounter, located so the smell of the bait would drift into their territory, but not so close that a swarm might turn up. Tall thin pillars surrounding the pit, and its approach made it difficult for a second dragon to land. The size of the pit had been carefully measured so that a human could move around easily, but a dragon would have difficulty turning.

The champion held up his sword in a salute to his shrunken audience, triggering a roar of applause. This display was enough to fool everyone except Merek, who saw the fear in the champion's eyes, though only because he was looking for it. This was the second trial for every champion.

The champion dismounted his chariot bravely enough and approached the beast. Cheers from the crowd hid the shaking of armour as he looked down into the pit. Luckily he remembered to pick up the spear. He looked back at Bill and Rowan, who stood firmly by his side. Both gave him a reassuring nod. Then he stood at the edge, pausing just a second too long to be mistaken for confident contemplation. Merek held his breath as the champion stared at the dragon's sharp teeth. Bill and Rowan were positioned to finish the task should the champion run. The city would survive, but Merek's reputation might not. The champion turned to look at the road behind them, letting his spear tip drop. Merek suppressed a minor panic attack. The young man turned from the road to his die-hard supporters before looking to Merek.

Suppressing all anxiety, Merek held his lips in a stern, solemn manner while his eyes showed the warmth and support that only a mentor could give. The beginnings of a smile just pushing through. It was a look Merek had practised many times. One which walked the fine line between enforcing duty and inspiring confidence. The champion gave one more look at the road before turning back to Merek. And then his fear melted away to reveal a confident smile. Now he was ready to fulfil his role. Merek gave a small nod, enough to push the champion on.

Raising his spear, he gave a triumphant yell before charging into the pit. Luckily, he brought his shield down just in time to block the dragon's claws. Bill and Rowan stuck by his side, using their own spears to distract the monster. The champion adopted a low stance; the long hours of training had not been wasted. He aimed his weapon at the dragon's throat, waiting for Bill and Rowan to force an opening.

Merek turned and headed back to the city. Cheers from the crowd informed him of the champion's progress. He needed to get back to his tower and start vetting candidates for next year.

JUDGING THE DARK LORD

MICHAEL YOUNG

TROCAIR PLACED his hand on the orb next to Ceartas and drew in a deep breath, bracing himself for what they might see. It wasn't every day they judged a case with such an obvious outcome. In a few minutes, he could forget the whole incident and move on, sure he had done all of mankind of service.

"Truth will prevail," Trocair recited, bringing his magistrate's hood over his head. It was the opening line of the legal code and the first thing he was required to speak when he entered the judgement chamber.

He followed all the legal procedures exactly, but still his stomach churned, and he felt a sharp stab poke the corners of his conscience.

"Are you ready?" Ceartas asked, bringing his magistrate's hood over his long, gray hair with one hand and reciting the oath.

"I'm not sure," Trocair said, averting his eyes. "There's never been a case like this before."

Ceartas laughed, the sound tainted with mild scorn. "Of course not, my friend. And I hope by all that is holy there never is one again. But what is there to be nervous about? Surely, an easier case has never been our lot to judge."

Drawing his hand back, Trocair furrowed his brow and fixed his eyes on Ceartas. "I don't care if he is Felgarath. We cannot speak that way. The lowliest peasant and the highest king . . . "

" . . . deserve a level reckoning," Ceartas finished. "I know. And you know that I know. Now, come. This is merely a formality."

"A formality!" Trocair cried. "Please tell me you jest. This is the High Imperial Court, not some schoolyard squabble. There will be no talk of formalities."

Ceartas leaned in closer, all hint of mirth gone from his face. "And this is Felgarath we're talking about. Dragonlord of the North, Bane of the Seven Lands, Slayer of Kings, and Devourer of Light. I do not understate when saying he is the very Lord of Darkness. He has the blood of millions on his hands, and if we acquit him, that blood passes to us. Is that what you want?"

"You act as though he simply slithered out of a pit one day and started a murderous rampage. He had a mother and a childhood. His actions may be despicable, but he is still a person."

Trocair looked away even as he said it, unsure where to put his hands. Of course, he had no desire to acquit this monstrous man. He had seen what Felgarath had done to entire villages firsthand, including the funeral pyre that had been made of his own hometown. His parents and grandparents had all perished in the blaze, and he would forever mourn their departure, all gone in a night without leaving so much as a token behind. He wanted to make sure the same intense flames consumed Felgarath, scorching away his vileness until not even ashes remained.

But even he could not defy the demands of justice. King Decker would expect everything to be carried out according to protocol, even if this was the most obviously wicked man in all the known realms.

Placing his hand back on the orb, Trocair drew in a long breath and let it out with a sigh. "The law is the law. Even for him. Let's get this done. As you said, it should not be difficult."

Ceartas nodded and placed his hands on the table in front of him. "Very well. We will then proceed with the first scene of his defense, taken ten years before King Decker ascended the throne. Would you kindly unroll the scroll and read the accompanying message?"

Trocair unlatched the lid of the ornate case in front of him and withdrew the first of three scrolls, each tied with a different colored ribbon. After opening the scroll, he spread it out on the table in front of him and drew in a quick breath. Often, the messages on these scrolls could be copious, even oppressive in their length. But now, his eyes rested on the shortest defense he had ever witnessed.

"I did it for her."

He stared at the scroll for a few moments more before passing it over to

Ceartas, who also studied it. "Well, I suppose the only crime here is the lack of antecedent for his pronoun," Ceartas muttered. "Perhaps he is trying to make this quick as well."

Trocair nodded, his unease festering within him, like a slow rot within an ancient tree. Felgarath was known for his cunning, his masterful manipulation. Were they being manipulated now? Could the Dark Lord have hidden some trick within those five simple words?

Trocair loaded the memory sphere into the viewing device, which consisted of a transparent pane of glass under which sat a pool of liquid that at a first glance might have been water, but he knew it was a specially crafted potion that even the slightest bit of impurity would contaminate beyond usefulness. As soon as the orb was in place, the liquid changed, revealing a scene as it had so many times before.

The defendant had chosen this scene specifically for the judges to see. Typically, there was more of an explanation than a single line to justify the scene's inclusion. He would just have to see in this case.

As the scene came into clarity, he saw a young boy with fiery red hair, his face dotted with freckles and a long, dark bruise down one side of it. The boy sat on the ground in the mud, seeming not to care about the rain. He could hear shouts and horrible cries, perhaps a man and woman arguing. The boy did not try to cover his ears, but stared into the mud and let the rain fall around him.

Suddenly, he stood and ran toward the hut from which the yelling came. A woman flew out of the entrance to the hut as if tossed, falling into the mud with a yelp. A man's voice followed her out, and to his surprise, the woman in the mud seemed familiar to Trocair somehow with long, black tresses pinned up in the fashion of the time. Yes, it was the same fashion in which his own mother had done her hair, though this was clearly some other woman. Trocair's stomach seized for a moment with a pang of longing, wishing he could use this device for personal use, to gaze back on his own childhood, to his own mother, if only for one more time and to hear her voice. He shook his head, knowing the idea was preposterous.

The man emerged from the hut, his chest bare, revealing his muscular physique, which too was covered with bruises and scars that had healed poorly. In one hand, he clutched a metal rod, perhaps a tool of some sort, though Trocair couldn't be sure. He approached the woman who was surely the boy's mother. There could be no mistaking the resemblance in their features.

Trocair stared at the boy and time seemed to slow. Could this be

Felgarath? It seemed impossible. He was such a normal-looking child, with large, pleading eyes, pitiful even. There was no hint of the man he would become.

His mother looked at him and caught his gaze. "No, Gareth, stay back."

Gareth. He had not always been Felgarath. He had once been Gareth, the frightened child, shivering in the mud, watching his mother being beaten by this man. Was this his father or someone else entirely? Trocair couldn't be sure. The man reared back with his tool, ready to strike. The boy jumped up to stop him and caught the brunt of the man's blow, sending him reeling to lie face-down in the mud. When the woman tried to reach her son, the man struck again—once, twice, and a third time, beating the very life from her body.

Almost unbelievably, the boy stood, crying out—a horrible, anguished cry. The man tossed the rod back into the mud, and the boy ran to his mother's side, weeping and howling, his tears mingling with the rain, his face bloody and contorted. He did not seem to care about his own pain, though every step appeared to be agony. He sat there and held his mother until the vision ended.

Trocair reached up and wiped tears from his eyes. He had seen many horrible things in his time as a judge, but this—the sheer brutality of it, the senselessness almost defied comprehension.

Ceartas' caustic voice snapped him out of it. "Tears for the Dark Lord?" he asked with a sneer. "Come now. Has he shed any tears for his victims, for those he took from you? I wouldn't spare a single one for him."

"We're not watching the Dark Lord. We're watching a scared little boy who just witnessed a brutal murder. Does that not stir your heart at all? Do we know what happened to him after this?"

Ceartas nodded. "The official record states that he was found on the steps of an orphanage, but that they ultimately rejected him. There is no record of what happened after that. I believe the next time anyone sighted him, he was part of a gang of street ruffians. It is not at all surprising."

Trocair settled back in his seat, deep in thought, a disturbing line of thought making its way to the forefront. What if all those years ago there had been someone to take Gareth in and love him when even an orphanage had cast him out? How many children could survive that kind of rejection after seeing such cruelty and callousness? Really, was it any wonder he had turned out as twisted as he had?

One look at his companion, and he decided not to voice his thoughts.

What good did it do to speculate? What had been done had been done, and his regrets would not bring a single soul back.

"Take some time to make some notes if you wish," Ceartas said brusquely. "But if you have no objections, I say let's move on to the second one as soon as you are ready."

Trocair nodded and took out the second scroll, this one bound by a scarlet ribbon. He unrolled it, wondering if the message would be any longer than the first. He furrowed his brow as he beheld the message. Not only was it as short as the first, it was, in fact, the same message as the first. "I did it for her."

Trocair squinted down at the message, trying to puzzle it out. "What do you suppose he means by that? I suppose it could have been his mother in that last one, but then why would he leave the same message for the second event? His mother is obviously dead. Perhaps he is still acting in her memory?"

"Or he simply has a flair for the dramatic. I don't know, and frankly, I don't much care. It doesn't seem like he's trying all that hard to defend himself. Even he knows that it is hopeless, that there's nothing he could possibly say or do to bring about an acquittal. So why waste his breath or his effort?"

It was a logical argument, Trocair supposed, but it still didn't sit right with him. It still felt like some sort of trick or ruse, a sick joke that only Felgarath himself knew the key to. "Very well. Let's move on to the second scene then to see if there is another message we might puzzle out in connection with the first." He inserted the second sphere and watched as the scene changed once again.

The scene settled on Gareth once again, but now he was a spindly youth with the same red hair and an intense gaze that looked like he was taking in the minutest detail of everything around him. To Trocair's surprise, the youth wore much finer apparel, not royal regalia, but something that might have been worn by a royal servant—black, pressed, fine cloth with gold patterns woven into the fabric and a golden sash about his waist. He also wore a hat that peaked at three corners.

Gareth approached what looked to be a large, ornate carriage, decorated in coral and gold with a seal embossed into the side, denoting it as one of the noble houses, though Trocair could not remember which one it signified. Gareth opened the door and let a lady out. She wore a black dress ornamented with pearls and had her face partially vailed, though Trocair could see golden hair poking out the sides. Gareth bowed low. "I am truly sorry to hear of your recent loss. I know something of the pain of losing a parent. Seven blessings upon you and your house."

She nodded, barely perceptibly. "Thank you. That is gracious. Please escort me into the assembly."

He held out his arm, and she took it lightly. They walked at a measured pace across the cobblestone streets toward the staircase in front of a building with an imposing stone facade, every door and window flanked by spiraling columns. All the while, Gareth glanced from side to side, his gaze ever vigilant and unrelenting. About halfway up the stairs, he stopped suddenly as a group of men in dark green hoods stepped out from behind the columns, slowly surrounding the two of them.

"Stay still, your grace," Gareth said.

The men stopped when they had completed the loose ring around them. One of those in front withdrew a slender blade from his scabbard and held it out. "Gareth, what a surprise. I truly thought you a loyal member of our band, but apparently, you are a royal lapdog. Unless, of course, you're spying on them, in which case, I'm sorry to ruin your cover."

Gareth stared back, unflinching in the face of the blade. The lady clutched his arm tighter. "I am no spy," he said. "I serve the Lady Gwyneth and her house. I will protect her with my life."

The assembled ruffians seemed to find that quite amusing. "Oh, will you? Does your precious lady know about your . . . shall we say, extracurricular outings with us? I dare say not. You would have already met the hangman's noose or at least be rotting in some cell. But I'll be a sport. I'll let you choose how you'd like to die; that's more than the nobility would give you. That is, if you step aside and allow us to take her."

The man with the knife stepped forward, but Gareth remained resolute. An instant before the man reached her, Gareth flung his arm upward with a swift, yet savage blow. The knife flew from the man's hand, sending it clattering down the stairs. Gareth followed with a quick blow to the man's abdomen, sending him doubled-over onto the steps.

Gareth's movements were so quick and precise, he seemed more skilled than any normal man. Perhaps he had already started his dalliance with the Dark Arts.

All the others rushed in, attacking one after another, and though he was surrounded, Gareth fended them all off with blows from his hands and feet and even his head. He did not even draw a weapon. He moved like a whirlwind with, each strike keener than the edge of lightning and just as devastating.

The lady covered her head and stooped low as the fight raged around her, but soon it was over with all the ruffians lying prostrate around her, a few of them trying to crawl away. Gareth stooped down and spoke rapidly. "Your grace, are you hurt? I fended them off as quickly as I could."

"No, I am only shaken. Quickly, let's—"

She shrieked, cut off in mid-sentence and she drew a blade of her own from within her dress. She raised it, and Gareth whirled about to see the gang leader bearing down on him with his own retrieved blade. Gareth struck out and delivered a glancing blow to the man's midsection, sending him flying and down the steps. The blow sent Felgarath sprawling backward into Gwyneth. She dropped her knife and its blade pierced her near the heart. Gareth whirled about, all the color draining from his face. For a few moments, his mouth simply moved up and down, nothing but a croaking gurgle escaping his lips, his eyes wide with abject horror.

As he fell to his knees, he likely knew there was nothing he could do. His face contorted, he placed his hand into his tunic and withdrew it several times empty until withdrawing some sort of odd seed pod in his hands that was as dark as his clothing. He crushed it in his fist and let the powder fall onto the bleeding wound.

"I am sorry, your grace," he whispered. "Perhaps this will be better than nothing at all."

A horrible, caustic laugh rang out over the scene as Gareth looked down to see the broken form of the gang leader, his face bloodied. He cackled as he pointed at Gareth. "I don't need to kill you. You're dead. Every man, woman, and child in the realm will be looking for you, thirsting for your blood. You're dead. You're dead!"

He repeated the words even as Gareth stood, looking about, and then ran, disappearing into the gathering crowd.

The scene faded, and Trocair shook his head, wondering how much tragedy a single heart could reasonably be expected to take before it broke irreparably.

"You see?" Ceartas said. "He left her there like a common criminal. He left her dying on the steps."

"It was an accident," Trocair said. "She was trying to save him the way he had saved her. It was an unfortunate turn of events, but that hardly makes him a murderer."

"Perhaps think about what he has done since. He is a murderer, beyond question. I do not understand why he would include this in his defense. He freely admits to being a part of that man's band, whether or not he was also serving the lady. Whether he meant to or not, he ultimately led to her demise."

"What was he doing there at the end with the seed? Have you ever seen that before?"

"Does it matter? Some sort of black sorcery. It didn't seem to do anything."

Trocair gazed down, looking through the historical records that accompanied the defense. "It says here that she survived, but that she disappeared a few weeks later, never to be heard from again. I suppose . . . "

"I hardly think it is relevant. She's no longer with us, one way or another. Certainly we would know if she had returned. This only goes to show how much of a criminal he really was—a man of deceit and treachery. Let us quickly examine the third scene so that we might be done with this. I tire of wading through such swamps."

Trocair sat back, pondering the words again. "I did it for her." His mother in the first events, this noble Lady Gwyneth in the second. What was he trying to tell them? How was this a defense? He picked up the third scroll and undid the purple ribbon. He unrolled it, and the same message met his eyes. "I did it for her." It did not vary in the slightest from the other messages, so he picked up the orb and placed it in its stand.

"This was taken in the 23rd year of King Decker's reign."

"The 23rd year? Isn't that . . . "

"Yes, it is the year of the Desolation. The very year."

Gareth was now much older and wore a full, red beard, and the three-headed snake insignia on his clothing marked that he was no longer Gareth, but Felgarath. One hand was encased in a metal claw that he always wore and despite many years having passed, his eyes were still as intense and focused. He stood at the mouth of a cave in what looked like a heavily wooded area. The cave entrance itself was covered with vines, moss, and the air shimmered with heat and humidity.

Felgarath stepped into the cave, and Trocair could see that the floor was also covered with vegetation and also a trickle of water, which flowed from the ceiling. As Felgarath walked deeper into the tunnel, Trocair could see because of luminous lichen that coated practically every surface the farther in Felgarath went. The cave opened up into a broad chamber, and near the wall sat some sort of pedestal with an enormous pod atop it, its surface black and shimmering and covered with coiling vines. It stood taller than Felgarath himself, the largest specimen Trocair had ever seen. It appeared to be the epicenter of all the vines in the room. Everything seemed to point toward it.

Felgarath waved a hand and glided into the air as he entered the large chamber, making his way directly toward the black pod. As soon as he reached it, it began to unfold, sections of it drawing back so they fell out like a flower. In the center of the pod stood a figure, a young woman whose body appeared to be tangled in vines and moss. Her very skin had taken on a slightly green pallor and it was hard to distinguish her hair from the greenery that fell around her. She possessed an exquisite beauty, far exceeding anyone else Trocair had ever seen. He saw also great power, strong and terrible and he felt as if he were looking at an avalanche or a tidal wave that threatened to crush him.

The lady looked down from the pod and fixed her gaze on Felgarath. He bowed low. "Gwyneth, your grace, how good it is to lay eyes upon you again."

The green woman smiled, but her eyes remained cold, calculating. "And I you. You are the only one who still calls me by that name. You are the only one I would ever allow such a familiarity."

"Yes, I am only glad to see that my spell was effective. Perhaps even more effective than I could have anticipated. How do you feel?"

The green woman's smile broadened. "Powerful. More powerful than you can imagine. Much more powerful than when I wielded only my family name and title. I might have died that day on the steps. Yes, a part of me did die, but as you see, I am gloriously reborn. That is thanks to you." She raised her eyebrows, which appeared to be made of moss. "Why have you come here today?" she asked. "I have heard tell of your deeds. You are infamous, if any man in this world is. I find your power only second to that of nature itself, and no, I am not trying to insult you. I simply know better."

"No insult taken. It is true, I have done many terrible things, and it is also true that you wield a power greater than my own. But that is not why I have come to see you today. I know."

He looked up, fixing an unblinking gaze on her and his voice sounded like a frozen blade. "I know what you intend to do. I am here to dissuade you, if I can. I have my reasons why I do what I do, but I am not trying to destroy mankind. Some of them must burn, some of them must fall, but we as a race must go on."

"Oh, and why is that?" the lady asked. "Is there some reason you care so much about your race now? Some might find that comical to the point of mirthful tears. Do you know you are not the only ones on this planet? You act as though you think so. Surely, that is not new to you."

"Yes, they have flaws, but flaws can be rooted out and impurities can be purged. Weakness can be strengthened. I have made it my life's work to see that become the forge that tempers mankind into its strongest form. But you would strangle them all before they have a chance to become what they were truly meant to become. That is far more barbaric, a far greater evil than anything I have ever taken into my heart."

The lady chuckled. "My, my. I remember the days when I could not persuade you to say more than a handful of words together. Now you give such grand speeches. Your magic must truly be great."

Felgarath raised both hands and sparks, violent and raw, shot from his fingertips. "And I will not bring it to bear if I do not have to, especially not against you. But I will. Everyone else in this foolish kingdom thinks we have entered a golden age of prosperity. The age of toil and war is behind us. But there is a war happening. But it is so slow and subtle that they cannot even see the advancing of the armies. It is you. The very earth is growing a cage around them. Soon the forests will advance, and the wild things will storm the cities. Everything will be overgrown and overrun. Mankind will never see it coming."

The green woman tossed her head to the side, her laughter subtle yet sinister. "You are a clever one. You are absolutely right. I can be patient. I will grow so softly that they will cheer the entire time I am folding them into my trap. What a beautiful thing it will be! An entire race brought to their knees, not through violence but by growth. I will erase all vestiges of mankind and the world will prosper, more beautiful and complete than ever. It does not matter that you know. No one will believe you. Even if some would listen, they would think it was only a scheme that you've devised. There is nothing you can do now."

He drew in a breath and withdrew a round lump, sleek and black.

The green woman's eyes narrowed. "What is that?" She crinkled her nose. "It is a foul thing. Take it away."

He did not listen, but stepped forward, holding it out. It looked like a seed, black, flecked with gold. "You speak the truth when you say that you are more powerful than I am. I know that I could not destroy you, even if I wanted to. You have become the very soul of the planet. You have grown strong, but life was not meant to grow unchecked or eternal. Too much life will destroy this world just as certainly as too much death. I must be the fire that purifies mankind to stand against threats such as you, and there is no purity except through pain. What I do now, I do not out of spite or of hate, as so many would believe. No, I do it out of necessity, out of balance. I do it for you."

Felgarath looked up and for a moment, it seemed to Trocair as if he were looking directly at him. But how was that possible? This was a distant scene of the past. How could he have known that someone would be watching it?

Felgarath looked back and crushed the seed in his hand into powder with a single gesture. This he blew in the direction of the lady. It swirled as if by its own accord, surrounding her and coating her within seconds. She tried to rear back, but it was too late. The cloud closed in around her and there was nothing she could do about it. Within moments, the moss on her darkened, some of it flaking and crumbling away, she dropped to her knees, withering to the ground. She reached out a hand and a tangle of vines shot toward him, but they too withered and fell away.

"What did you do?" she rasped.

A look of genuine sadness and pain crossed his face. "I have poisoned you. It is of the same tree, but a different variety than the one I used to create you. It will undo most of my original spell, though it will not kill you. I have no desire to kill you. Doing so would kill all life on this planet, all men, women, and children. So, as you can see, that is not my aim. But you must be kept in check. You must not bring your plan to fruition. I did not want for it to come to this, but now that I have seen you, have spoken with you, I know this is the only way. I wish it could have been otherwise."

The lady looked up a final time, gasping, her beautiful, young face now creased with lines and wrinkles as she turned into a crone before their eyes. "You have doomed us all," she whispered.

"No, I have doomed you. There's a difference."

"Many will die," she said.

"Yes, I'm certain of it, but then again, many others will live. Mankind will continue. My quest to purify and strengthen our race may continue. I do this even knowing that I will be hated for it, that it will possibly be seen as the worst thing I have ever done. Perhaps someday I will find a way to convince someone otherwise, but until then, I take my leave of you. I do not imagine that we shall meet again."

He turned and walked away, even as the cavern crumbled in around him. the vines writhing and perishing, the foliage crumbling under his every step, and as he retreated, all she could manage was a pitiful, feeble wail.

Trocair sat in utter astonishment, barely able to draw breath. It was too much. His mind could barely take it all in. "Why wasn't this discovered before?" Trocair asked. "Everyone needs to know about this! We have been blind and ignorant, have we not?"

Ceartas folded his arms, staring out into the distance. When he did not say anything for a few moments more, Trocair interjected. "Ceartas, what do you say to this?"

Ceartas shook his head, almost imperceptibly at first, then more strongly. "No, no, it is a trick. This changes nothing! I am more certain than ever that it is he who caused this desolation! It has killed tens of thousands. It has caused untold suffering. It is the greatest calamity to ever befall our civilization. For that alone, he deserves to die in agony."

Trocair shot to his feet. "His actions prevented our extinction. If he had not done what we did, we might all be dead even now! Every person on this land would have perished. I know it, and you know it. He saved us and he could not prove it until now. Perhaps that it why he let himself fall into our hands as he did. But now he has proved it, and we have no choice but to tell everyone. It is our sworn duty."

Ceartas rose to feet, his face contorted. "It is our sworn duty to do what is best for everyone, to administer justice! Even if he did save everyone as you claim, he has still caused more pain, death, and destruction than any other being who has ever walked this planet. We would not be doing our job if we allow him to remain."

Trocair blew out a deep, shuddering breath. "Then what would you have us do? Lie? Bury the truth? If it is a matter of blame, how far back do we go? This Gareth who became Felgarath did not come from nowhere. He did not fall from the sky or rise from a tar pit. He was beaten and broken and twisted and scaled until he became what he became. We might as well blame his wicked father or those who turned him away from the orphanage, or the brigands who took himm into their band and attempted to murder his lady? Who? He has been wronged by so many—we could sit here until the stars fall from the sky and not name them all."

Ceartas grimaced. "Be that as it may, it does not excuse what he has done. We cannot simply dismiss all of this because he has had a tragic life. I have seen my fair share of sorrows, and so have many others without becoming demons in the process."

Trocair sat back, lost in thought. It was true. It seemed an impossible line to tread, yet it was a such a tragedy. There had doubtless been many times when someone could have stepped in and made all the difference. They could have stepped in and stopped Felgarath's descent into madness and cruelty, but they had not. Everyone would point the other way when asked whose fault this was, but really, practically anyone who had ever known might as well shoulder some of the blame.

"There can be no justice for this," Trocair said. "Even death will not bring justice. It will not bring peace or healing. Nothing in our feeble power could reverse what has been done. Yes, we must stop him and keep him from hurting anyone else, but we must also not become like him—vengeful and cruel. How can we possibly decide what is to be done?"

Ceartas sat back down, folding his arms. "I have decided. But I wish to the Holy Seven that you would make up your mind. It is not for us to sit here and dabble in philosophy. It is for us to take decisive action. Yes, his death will not bring back those who have perished, but can you imagine what keeping him alive will do? There will be riots. There will be war and insurrection if we do not kill him. Many more lives will be ruined and that will not be his fault." Ceartas looked up squarely into Trocair 's eyes. "That will be yours."

The thought pierced Trocair through like a crooked dagger, twisting into his heart. It was too much, too great a burden for a single person to handle. Yet here it was, squarely on his shoulders, crushing him, grinding him, and threatening to obliterate his very sanity.

"We must decide," Ceartas said. "If Felgarath proves anything, it is that one man can change the entire world. If you acquit him, you will take on that same distinction. He must die, if only for peace. Isn't that what he claimed he wanted in the first place?"

Ceartas arose, approaching the pedestal at the front of the room which held the Altar of Judgement. Beneath the altar sat two clear spheres and two scarlet ones that looked as though they had been filled with blood. The clear ones indicated an innocent verdict, while the scarlet, a guilty one. But unless they were unanimous in their decision, it would force the matter into a public trial, which would last a very long time, especially for a case as visible as this one.

Ceartas sat at his side of the altar, and he was now concealed from Trocair as he was not supposed to know how the other man voted. It was an anonymous decision and once cast, no one on the council would be able to determine who had cast which vote.

Trocair rose as well, feeling his heart clench within him, his knees threatening to buckle and sweat pouring down his brow. He felt sick to his stomach with every step, wishing he could give this burden to someone else, to anyone else. But he could only delay for so long. He reached the pedestal himself and considered the spheres—guilty or innocent. Death for one man or war for the nations. It was impossible. He did this for her, he thought, for his mother, for his lady, and then for his planet.

Felgarath had done what he had done not only for himself. But what was his job here? Trocair asked himself. Truth. Truth at any cost. If they could not value the truth, what else could they cling to? What good was all their civilization? What should he save if not for the truth?

If he chose a clear orb, it would not be because Felgarath was innocent. He deserved to die, and surely, he still would, even if sent the clear orb. He wished that he could send both orbs as a response, as that would most clearly reflect his judgement, but unfortunately, the current system did not allow for such a nuanced response.

He bowed his head, tears streaming from his eyes at the thought of what he was about to do. He took a moment and remembered those he had lost and thinking of those who might yet suffer, hoping that somehow, they too would understand. He could not forgive Felgarath for what he had done, but that was not why he was here.

He rested one hand on the scarlet orb and one on the clear, his stomach clenching in pain. He hefted them both in his hands and then, he placed the one orb into the tray and whispered so softly that no mortal ear could have perceived it.

"Truth will prevail."

AN EVER QUICKENING FIRE

STACI OLSEN

"Rowena."

The voice made my stomach lurch, but I closed my eyes against that old hope and took a steadying breath. Then I set down my trowel and rose, turning to greet whoever tortured me with my name spoken in that particular timbre.

For a heartbeat, it *was* a stranger that stood before me, a stranger that looked like him because I wished it to be him but who could not possibly be him.

Blinking didn't dispel the undeniable familiarity of his face.

"Joshua!" I gasped, shocked by the specter before me. If he had looked the same as the boy that disappeared, I would have thrown myself into his arms, but he was so different.

"I'm finally home, Rowena," he said, smiling though his eyes brimmed with tears. "I'm home."

His posture bore a grace that hadn't been there before, yet he was tense, expectant. He wore weapons instead of tools, elegant black clothes instead of homespun wool. His hair fell to his chin in brown waves, longer than I remembered. His eyes, as blue as ever, had somehow become striking, intent, captivating. I did not know this man. He was not the same nineteen-year-old that had disappeared and left me inconsolable.

"Where have you *been*? Everyone thought you were dead." I longed to hug him and slap him, but he'd changed so much that I could hardly be sure he was the same man.

"I'm not dead, Row," he said, using a nickname I had not heard for years. It brought tears to my eyes, mirroring his. He wouldn't look away like I wanted him to. He didn't shrug or kick the dirt or wring his hands. Instead, he held my eyes with so much hope in his that it almost disguised his encompassing loneliness.

"Everyone said you got cold feet, but I knew that was impossible! So I waited. All these years I waited, and now everyone thinks I'm crazy!" My body trembled with conflicting emotions: relief so intense it felt like pain, outrage to see him alive and well without any proof he'd tried to contact me, longing to restore everything we'd had.

"I'm sorry," he murmured.

I stared at him, numb. "What happened to you?" I asked. "You vanished! We looked for you everywhere and found nothing! And suddenly you're back and when you look at me you see into my soul." I tore my eyes from his. "Don't—don't look at me like that."

But only a few heartbeats passed before my gaze drifted back to him. My staring bordered on rudeness, but I couldn't keep my eyes from absorbing every detail of him, so I forced myself to examine my own feet, my toes poking out through holes in worn leather.

"Row, I had to perform a service."

"For the king?"

"For the world."

"It took ten years?" I asked. "Why didn't you write?"

"It's a long story," he said. Then, "Row . . . Rowena, did you forget about me?"

"How could I?" I asked, hugging myself and glancing at him. His eyes caught and held mine again.

"I thought about you always," he said.

He reached out. I went to him, hesitantly, and wrapped my arms around him. His body felt different against mine, thickened with muscle, perhaps a touch taller, yet the familiar tenderness of his embrace made me cling to him and for a moment it felt like he'd never left. He held me as if he were drowning and I might keep him afloat. I took one step back, breaking his hold, and looked up into his magnetic eyes.

"I missed you," he said. "It was like missing my right arm." And he blushed, flooding me with memories of his bashful, boyhood charm.

"I was never the same after you left, Joshua," I admitted.

He brushed his fingers over my forehead and down my cheek. "I'm sorry I hurt you, Row."

The creak of leather and clank of metal brought my attention to the weapons on his belt, so vicious and foreign, yet he bore them with familiarity.

"Was it a very important service?" I asked, eyeing the sword.

"Yes," he said, pain in his voice. "Worth leaving you, even worth dying for. I believed I would die. But it's not finished yet and I—"

"You are very powerful," I interrupted and took another step away from him. That was what had changed the most. The boyhood charm I had adored was disguised beneath a veneer of authority. He radiated power.

"Do not be afraid," he said. "Please, do not be afraid of me."

"What happened to you?" I asked a second time.

He broke eye contact to scrutinize the dirt. I looked him over again. He seemed like any other man in appearance, but the aura he gave off shouted that he was common no more.

He took a heavy breath, as if bracing himself for a familiar, unwelcome reaction. "I drank liquid dragon fire," he blurted and peeked at me.

The blood drained from my face. My ears rang. I thought I might faint. I took a third step back.

"Then—then you're the Prince of Dragons! You're the one the prophecy said would come!" I stared in awe.

"I don't know. I don't know," he said, desperately trying to reassure me. "But I drank it, and it didn't kill me. I don't know why. It just didn't. Please don't leave."

His plea stopped me from taking the fourth step back. "We heard rumors that He had come, but I never imagined . . . What service did you perform for the world?" I asked.

He swallowed. "I bound the Wraiths to the Gulf of Shadows."

A held breath fled my lungs. "You *are* the Prince of Dragons." I started to curtsy, but he grabbed my wrist.

"Don't," he said. "Please don't. I am still just me, just your Joshua. And I couldn't bear to have you, of all people, make obeisance to me. Please, don't."

I straightened and he studied my face.

"Joshua," I said, discomforted. "Why did you come home?"

He smiled. "Come with me," he begged. "Be at my side always, as you used to be. I swear I will never leave you again."

Looking over the little garden and the little cottage, I recognized them for what they were, a lonely person's holdings, a hollow replacement of everything I'd wanted. Had my parents still been living, they would have been sad to see me so safe, sheltered, healthy, but goalless.

My heartbeat quickened. I already knew my answer, but the words stuck in my constricted throat. I lacked the strength to speak until his smile started to falter.

"Yes," I exclaimed and forgave him all those painful years. "Yes, I'll come."

He grinned, laughed, and gathered me into his arms. For the first time in ten years, I felt secure again, even if he was the Prince of Dragons.

"Lady Xela Duran, Baroness of the Seven Isles!" announced the crier.

The woman sashayed toward us, her skirts foaming with lace, her neck laden with gems. She curtsied too low, leaning forward to display her cleavage for Joshua's benefit, just another in a long line of sycophants looking for political advantage.

"It's a pleasure to meet you, my prince," she fawned. She rose and glanced at me. "And who is this?"

Joshua put his arm around my shoulders. "This is Rowena. We grew up together in Valorn Village."

"A village girl. How sweet."

"Yes," Joshua agreed. "The best kind of girl."

He didn't notice the disdain that had crept into Xela's tone. He never had been very good at reading people. But I noticed, and the immediate rush of shame burned my cheeks.

Xela focused her attention on Joshua, turning her shoulder just a smidgen too far toward him, edging me out of the conversation. "Where will you go next now that Stadtler has acknowledged your authority?"

I didn't listen to Joshua's answer. Politics were beyond my understanding and the opinions of a pathetic village girl were clearly unwanted.

With an apologetic smile, I slipped out from under Joshua's arm.

He caught my fingers. "Are you all right?"

"Yes," I assured him. "Just tired. I'm going to bed."

"I'll see you in the morning then." He let me go and turned to Lady Xela. "Show Rowena proper courtesy."

Looking petulant, she curtsied. "Goodnight, miss."

"Goodnight, Lady Xela," I responded and left, smirking a little that Joshua had put her in her place, probably without even realizing he'd done it.

When I glanced back, Xela had taken my position at his side, hooking her arm around Joshua's, pressing her bosom against his bicep.

He rubbed his head, clearly suffering a migraine, though he still listened, polite and attentive, as Xela prattled. A twinge of guilt shot through me. His responsibility was so great. All I had to do was be there for him. And I walked away because of a minor social jab.

HALF A DOZEN MEN trailed along behind us as Joshua and I walked side by side down the hallway. One of them said, "It's just not possible. The logistics of such a campaign—"

"But we have no other options," another man interrupted him. "With the support of the Kaballians, we might be able to pull it off."

"The Kaballians might be more willing to help if you stopped letting the army camp in their newly planted fields," I said over my shoulder. Farmers tended to be more comfortable submitting their complaints to me, because I was their equal.

The men laughed. "Where else are we going to put them?" someone asked.

Lacking the education in war and politics that would provide me an intelligent solution, I simply added, "Without crops growing in the fields, they'll barely have enough of a harvest to support themselves, let alone to contribute provisions for the army."

A line appeared between Joshua's brows. Longing to smooth it away, I grabbed his hand and stopped him there in the passage, tugging so that he'd turn toward me and meet my eyes. His expression was worn, almost haggard. I sought for a way to buoy him.

The men parted and passed around us like water around a stone in the river. Most of them entered a conference room just ahead, but one placed his hand upon my arm, interrupting the unspoken communication between me and Joshua.

"Miss, you won't find this meeting entertaining. One of the maids can show you to the gardens if you'd like to enjoy a walk while you wait."

"I'd rather stay with Joshua," I said.

"She could help," Joshua added.

"The topics of war can be rather gruesome," said the man. "Not fit for a lady's ears."

"She is not some squeamish little tart like your courtiers," Joshua countered, a hint of anger in his tone. "She can hold her own in a room full of warriors."

"Regardless, the others would hesitate to be frank in the presence of a lady. It would hinder the speed and clarity of our communication and draw the meeting out."

Joshua smiled, attempting to disguise the strain he felt, attempting to make me comfortable with leaving him. Still I clung to his hand.

"I'll be all right," he reassured me.

The man reached between Joshua and me, cutting us apart with his arm. He took Joshua by the elbow and guided him through the doors.

Joshua looked back at me over his shoulder. "I'll find you when we're finished."

The doors shut, leaving me alone in the unfamiliar hall.

JOSHUA WRITHED, hands clutching his head, rolling to and fro on the floor, and moaning with pain. The opulent bed with silk sheets and the delicacies spread on a side table stood rejected. Sabriant crystals and gold accents and hardwood furnishings didn't alleviate his misery.

"What can I do?" I pleaded.

"Bucket!" he gasped.

I grabbed it and held it steady as he vomited, turning my head aside and tucking my nose against my shoulder. When he finished, I set the bucket aside.

He seemed spent, lying limp, perhaps finally falling asleep. I sat next to him and rubbed his head and ran my fingers through his hair. He began to relax, inhaling and exhaling deep and slow, endeavoring to manage his pain.

A loud knock sounded on the door.

Joshua flinched.

Anger surged through me. I stood, marched to the door, and threw it open so hard that it rebounded off the wall.

"Leave him alone!" I shouted at the startled man outside. "Joshua is not well. He needs peace and quiet and *rest*. Get out of here and make sure that everyone in this cursed place knows that he is not to be disturbed until I say he can be! Do you understand?"

Before the man could reply, I slammed the door in his face.

A pained chuckle sounded behind me. "That was incredible."

Returning to Joshua's side, I resumed massaging his head. "I'm sorry. I should not have been so loud."

"It's all right," he murmured. "I've never seen Lord Akagar so cowed. It was a welcome distraction from this wretched migraine."

"Is there nothing we can do for it?" I implored.

"I don't think so. It's a consequence of the fire. As much as I'd like to, I can't change what it did to me."

FROM MY VANTAGE point on the hill, I could see Joshua with his guards and generals spread around him. Messengers sprinted back and forth between his group and other clusters of officers.

Farther out in the field, the battle waged hot. The roar of men screaming and the clash of metal against metal made my stomach writhe.

I had been at Joshua's side, but when things began to go wrong, he sent me away, saying, "I need to know you're safe, Row."

"But—" I started.

"I can't concentrate on my duty unless I know you're safe!" he exclaimed.

So, guarded by three men, I stood above it all and watched the battle unfold, watched as the fighting line pressed closer and closer to Joshua's position, watched his dragon and flame standard fall, watched his guards engage in the fight, trying to keep Joshua protected within a wavering circle.

At the base of the slope, five enemy soldiers broke from the battle and started up the hill toward my position of safety. My guards tried to hustle me farther away, but I was rooted to the ground, unable to break my attention from Joshua.

He was too far distant for me to be certain, but I thought Joshua looked back at me. I knew him well enough to recognize the way he planted his feet and squared his shoulders when he faced the battle again. He had always confronted conflict head on. But he didn't draw his weapon.

For the first time, I witnessed Joshua wield his power.

He began to glow. First, as if he held a candle cupped in his hands. Then, as if he stood in the only beam of sunlight in a cloudy world. Finally, he blazed, standing amidst an inferno.

Even from my distance, I heard his scream. The fire raced away from him, running along the ground in rivulets, spreading like a cast net. Scorching strands passed by Joshua's soldiers, but when it met an enemy, it leaped up their bodies as if they were coated with pitch.

And they burned.

My mouth fell open watching the conflagration. Shock coursed through me like wildfire. Even the five enemy soldiers on the slope below me were consumed. How could the boy I had known become this? How could such incomprehensible strength be housed in such normal human flesh?

Hearing the screams of anguish, seeing the pillars of fire that had been their comrades, the enemy soldiers abandoned the battle, dropping weapons and shields in an effort to make a hasty get away.

Joshua's soldiers gave chase, but they had little to do in the wake of those flames.

Joshua collapsed.

I sprinted.

Down the hill I flew, oblivious to my own safety, ignoring the cries of my guards. I only longed to reach him.

Something pierced my foot, perhaps a discarded blade. I stumbled and ran on, heedless of the blood pooling in my shoe, leaping over obstacles and pushing past the standing soldiers, until I fell to my knees at his side.

SITTING UP, I looked at Joshua, the coals in the firepit providing enough light to see by. His tousled hair fell over his forehead as he slept.

"Joshua," I whispered, and then a little louder, "Joshua." He did not stir.

I got to my feet and tiptoed to the foot of his blankets where his pack rested. The drinking skin still hung from it. After untying the leather laces, I silently pulled the skin free, clutched it to my chest, and returned to my own blankets.

The pouch loomed in my eyes like doom, a weighty burden of imminent danger on my lap. Liquid sloshed inside the leather. Tightening my grip, I tried to make my hands stop shaking but only made it worse.

Everyone that had ever tried to consume the contents of that skin had died in the attempt, except Joshua. He had not died and by not dying had fulfilled prophecy. Helpless, I watched him suffer and there was *nothing* I could do to ease him. No words, no medicines, not even ten thousand soldiers could ease the weight he carried. But what if there were someone else with his same power? What if I could have stood beside him in that battle, bearing what he bore? Could I have given him more when his strength was spent? Could I have destroyed half that army and saved him from the physical crisis he had suffered? What would happen, I wondered, if I too drank the liquid dragon fire?

I pulled the cork from the skin. Heat oozed from the spout, as great as if I stood too close to a bonfire, though the exterior of the skin felt cool. The acrid smell burned the hairs in my nostrils. My hands rattled. I almost dropped the skin, almost spilled that potent liquid inside.

Panting three quick breaths, I thrust my head back, and then poured the stuff into my mouth, gulping to force it down. Blistering pain exploded from tongue-tip to belly. I would have screamed if my throat had not been burned away in the first instant the dragon fire touched it.

The drinking skin fell from my slack fingers and fire spilled over my leg and onto the ground, scorching everything it touched and smoking. My clothing melted and my skin blistered. Leaves and small sticks on the ground ignited. The pain overwhelmed all my senses and my body shuddered in an effort to cope. Seared lungs floundered to suck in air.

As I fell backward, Joshua sat up with a sharp intake of breath, his eyes as wide as mine. He looked wildly for me and scrambled from his bed to my side.

"What have you done?" he cried and caught me up into his arms. My head dangled until he pressed it hard against his shoulder. He snatched up the skin with one hand, mindless of burned and blistered fingers and tossed it into the coals, which accepted it with a whoosh of renewed flame. "Row, Rowena, what have you done?" he repeated.

He loosened his hold enough so he could look at me. Tears streamed down his cheeks, sizzling when they splashed onto my lips. I tried to reach up to touch his face, but my arm merely twitched, and then all the fires in the world went out.

"THIS WAS NOT FORESEEN," something whispered in the darkness of my mind. And then, "Why did you drink our fire?"

"Joshua's burden is heavy. I want . . . I don't want him to suffer," I answered.

"You wish nothing of our power?" it whispered.

"No," I said. "Not for myself. I want to help him. He always says that just my presence is enough, but it's not enough for me! I need to be able to carry some of the weight!"

"I wonder . . . " the voice mused. A pause. "Rowena, the memories inscribed in your mind testify of sacrifices you have made on Joshua's behalf. I honor the purity of your intent." Another silence stretched, then the voice commanded, "Breathe."

I gulped air as I had gulped fire. My body spasmed once and my lungs fell into a rapid but steady rhythm. Arms that had been lax tightened swiftly around me.

I opened my eyes. Joshua still held me, his cheeks shimmering with tears, his chest hitching with sobs, the firelight bright around us. He caught his breath, snatched the water pouch from my pack, and held it to my lips. "Drink," he demanded, and I swallowed cool, sweet water.

He pressed me against his chest once again and then set me back on my blankets so he could rummage through my pack. Laying quiet, I watched steam pour from my mouth when I exhaled. I felt like laughing. But I could also feel within me the tremendous power at my command. It gushed through my body, flooding me with burning from core to extremities. If I twitched, I might burn armies as Joshua had. I did not know how to control such strength. I did not have the wisdom to know when to justifiably use it.

"Joshua," I said, my voice rough and broken. "I'm afraid."

He pulled a med kit from the pack and came back to my side. He gripped my hand. "So was I when I drank the fire. I still am."

He turned his attention to the burn on my leg, smearing a painkilling salve on it and wrapping it well. His fingers received the same treatment.

"Are you angry?" I asked with a small voice.

"You frightened me," he said. "I thought I had lost you, again. Permanently. If that had happened, I might have been angry."

"They let me live, to help you," I explained. "I only wanted to help you."

"I know," he said, then muttered, "Damned dragons are as curious as cats." He fiddled with the corner of a blanket. "Rest now. The fire will never go out, but it can be banked by sleep."

I closed my eyes.

"Row," he said.

"Hm?"

"Thank you."

"Joshua," I said. "*You* are worth dying for."

A REQUEST

If you liked this anthology, please take the time to leave a review on the site where you purchased it and/or on one of the social media reading sites like Goodreads. Tell your friends that you enjoyed it. Suggest it as reading for your local book club. Request it at your local library (or more than one local library). This helps others learn more about the book and gets the word out. Please use the #hemeleinpubs tag.

Thank you for your time, and thank you for reading this book!

Find more exciting books to read at hemelein.com.

HEMELEIN PUBLICATIONS

ACKNOWLEDGMENTS

There are so many people without whom we would not be able to do this anthology series. First and foremost, you the reader. Without you picking up a copy and enjoying the stories, we wouldn't have a reason to collect them. Thank you for supporting us these last five years!

All of the authors and artists who have donated their hard work over the years. We've thanked you in each of the volumes since the first, so we'll thank those who contributed to this volume: Kevin Wasden, who reached out to us and offered to create a brand new piece of art for this volume; Tristan A. Gilmore, Mark Silcox, Ross Baxter, Jessica Guernsey, Henry Herz, Melva Gifford, Emily Martha Sorensen, D. J. Butler, Ray Daley, James Ivan Hughes, Randy Lindsay, Stewart C. Baker, James F. McGrath, Wendy Nikel, James Dorr, Eric G. Swedin, Scott R. Parkin, Jamie Perrault, Ivan Richardson, Michael Young, and Staci Olsen.

Thank you to our proofreaders: Marny Parkin, Amanda Rodriguez, and Stephen Fassmann. You caught a lot of little typos and such, making the anthology much better for catching them.

We are grateful to all those who support the anthologies by spreading the word, sharing information via email, blog posts, reviews, and social media. You are awesome!

Thank you to all of the volunteers at LTUE over the years, both before we became involved and those who continue the legacy of volunteering today.

Finally, thanks to our families, who put up with us as we work on each volume. Thank you for letting us have this project.

Jaleta Clegg
Joe Monson

ABOUT THE CONTRIBUTORS

STEWART C. BAKER is an academic librarian and author of speculative fiction and poetry, along with the occasional piece of interactive fiction. His fiction has appeared in *Nature, Galaxy's Edge,* and *Flash Fiction Online,* among other places. Stewart was born in England, has lived in South Carolina, Japan, and California (in that order), and currently resides in Oregon with his family—although if anyone asks, he'll usually say he's from the Internet.

Learn more at infomancy.net.

After thirty years at sea, ROSS BAXTER now concentrates on writing short stories. His varied work has been published in print by numerous publishing houses in US and UK anthologies. He has won a number of awards, and had a story included on the 2017 HWA Bram Stoker reading list.

Married to a Norwegian and with two Anglo-Viking kids, he now lives in Derby, England.

Learn more at rossbaxter.wordpress.com.

D.J. BUTLER has been a lawyer, a consultant, an editor, and a corporate trainer. His novels include *Witchy Eye, Witchy Winter, Witchy Kingdom,* and *Serpent Daughter,* the modern fantasy novels *The Cunning Man* and *The Jupiter Knife* (with Aaron Michael Ritchey), the science fiction novels *In the Palace of Shadow and Joy,* and *Abbott in Darkness,* and the time travel novel

Time Trials (with M. A. Rothman), all from Baen Books. He won a Whitney Award and AML Award for *Witchy Winter* and a Dragon Award for *Witchy Kingdom*.

His middle-grade steampunk fantasy adventure tales, *The Kidnap Plot*, *The Giant's Seat*, and *The Library Machine*, are published by Knopf. Other novels include *City of the Saints* from WordFire Press. Dave organizes writing retreats and anarcho-libertarian writers' events and travels the country to sell books—he's visited nearly half of all Barnes & Noble stores! He plays guitar and banjo whenever he can and likes to hang out in Utah with his children.

Learn more at davidjohnbutler.com.

JALETA CLEGG was born some time ago and has filled the years since with plenty of make-believe. She writes science fiction adventure, fantasy of all flavors, and silly horror. When not writing, she enjoys playing with yarn, cooking weird vegetables, designing costumes and quilts, and generally messing around.

Learn more at jaletac.com.

RAY DALEY was born in Coventry and still lives there. He served six years in the Royal Air Force as a clerk and spent most of his time in a Hobbit hole in High Wycombe. He is a published poet and has been writing stories since he was ten. His current dream is to eventually finish the *Hitchhikers* fanfic novel he's been writing since 1986.

Learn more at raymondwriteswrongs.wordpress.com and tweet him @RayDaleyWriter.

JAMES DORR is an Indiana-based short story writer and poet specializing in dark fantasy and horror, with forays into mystery and science fiction. *The Tears of Isis*, his collection of short fiction, was a 2013 Bram Stoker Award finalist for Superior Achievement in a Fiction Collection. Other books include *Strange Mistresses: Tales of Wonder and Romance, Darker Loves: Tales of Mystery and Regret,* his all-poetry *Vamps (A Retrospective),* and *Tombs: A Chronicle of Latter-Day Times of Earth,* a novel-in-stories from Elder Signs Press.

Dorr has been a technical writer, an editor on a regional magazine, a full-time nonfiction freelancer, and a semiprofessional musician. He currently harbors a Goth cat named Triana and counts among his major influences Ray Bradbury, Edgar Allan Poe, Allen Ginsberg, and Bertolt Brecht.

Learn more at jamesdorrwriter.wordpress.com.

MELVA GIFFORD has been writing since her youth. She has fiction and nonfiction shorts published in various publications and websites. She won first place for her middle-grade book, *Operation: Middle School Madness,* from the 2016 Utah Arts Council. Her short story, "Forfeit", was featured in the January 2021 issue of *Cricket.* She's won multiple honorable mentions from the international Writers of the Future contest.

Her published fiction crosses genres, published by venues for children, mainstream, science fiction and fantasy, and romance. She has published a nonfiction book, *I Know You THINK This is a Toaster: Promoting Family Values Through Object Lessons.* She is also a live storyteller and has performed at multiple venues.

Learn more at melvagifford.com.

TRISTAN A. GILMORE grew up in upstate New York, where he took AP classes and perfected his sport of extreme procrastination. Exercising and preparing for future endeavors by pushing his luck, Tristan currently has his sights set on a full career in writing and hopes to promote a definitive flavor of epic fantasy for civilized folks.

Learn more at thebarbarianbook.com.

JESSICA GUERNSEY writes urban and contemporary fantasy novels and short stories. A BYU alumna with a degree in journalism, she's had her work published in magazines and anthologies. By day, she crushes dreams as a slush pile reader for three publishers for a combined twelve years' experience. During November's NaNoWriMo, Jessica is a municipal liaison for the Utah::Elsewhere region. Frequently, she can be found at writing conferences. She isn't difficult to spot; just look for the extrovert.

While she spent her teenage angst in Texas, she now lives on a mountain in Utah with her family.

Discover more stories at jessicaguernsey.com.

HENRY HERZ has authored over twenty-five traditionally published short stories, including for *Daily Science Fiction,* Blackstone Publishing, Albert Whitman & Co., Air and Nothingness Press, *Highlights for Children,* and *Ladybug Magazine.* He has edited three anthologies: *Beyond the Pale* (fantasy), *Coming of Age* (middle grade #ownvoices), and *The Hitherto Secret Experiments of Marie Curie* (young adult horror, with Brian Thomas Schmidt). He has also authored eleven traditionally published books for children.

Learn more at henryherz.com.

JAMES IVAN HUGHES is a new author and a recovering attorney. He lives in Austin, Texas, with his family, zero pets, no typewriters, and a large collection of miniatures.

RANDY LINDSAY is world traveler, which sounds impressive until you realize the worlds he visits exist only in his mind and on the pages of his novels. He claims to prefer this method of sight-seeing because he can stop at any time, go to the kitchen, and indulge his ice cream addiction. When he isn't busy making things up, he likes going to movies with his wife to watch what other people have made up. He plays board games with his children, who are in the habit of making up the rules as they go along. He is the author of nine published books and speaks publicly on the writing process.

Learn more at randylindsay.net.

James F. McGrath is a professor at Butler University and the author of science fiction short stories and historical fiction. He has also written a wide array of nonfiction books, book chapters, and articles related to subjects such as the intersection of religion and science fiction.

Find him online by searching for @ReligionProf.

Joe Monson has worked at many different jobs before trying his hand at writing and editing fiction. He edits the LTUE Benefit Anthologies series with Jaleta Clegg.

He has a number of other anthologies in various stages of planning and completion. Joe has one published short story and is currently working on the first book in a space opera adventure series. He collects science fiction and fantasy art but not as much as Paul (as if that were even possible). He lives in the tops of the mountains with his lovely and talented wife, their three amazing children, and their pet library.

Learn more at joemonson.com.

Wendy Nikel is a speculative fiction author with a degree in elementary education, a fondness for road trips, and a terrible habit of forgetting where she's left her cup of tea. Her short fiction has been published by *Analog*, *Beneath Ceaseless Skies*, *Nature*, and elsewhere. Her time travel novella series, beginning with *The Continuum*, is available from World Weaver Press.

Learn more at wendynikel.com.

STACI OLSEN lives in Utah with her husband, five children, and three pets in a townhouse that is too small, but growing up in Alaska in a 16-by-20 foot cabin with ten other people (give or take a few) made her accustomed to small houses. She bathed in a wheelbarrow, was hunted by wolves, and survived earthquakes and volcanic eruptions. Salsa dancing, treasure hunting, and escape rooms are just a few of her more unique hobbies.

She works as an acquisitions editor and the production manager for Immortal Works, and she loves helping other authors get their work out in the world.

Learn more at staciolsen.com and follow her on Facebook, Twitter, and Instagram.

SCOTT R. PARKIN is an award-winning author, editor, essayist, and critic with more than fifty short story sales across a wide variety of markets from romance through literary-academic to sf and fantasy. He is currently working on his second novel, and is a cohost of the *Stories for Nerds* podcast.

JAMIE PERRAULT is an agender veterinarian from the Midwest. They are married to a wonderful genderqueer spouse, and they have twin three-year-olds who make the world a better place.

IVAN RICHARDSON grew up with shows like *Buffy*, *Star Trek*, and *X-Files*, and he's always been obsessed with sci-fi and fantasy. He's been writing fiction for over ten years. One of his novelettes, "Three Moons", was published in a dark fantasy anthology in September 2021. He is a member of the Leicester Writers club, where he has perfected his writing skills.

Mark Silcox was born and raised just outside of Toronto, Canada. He has at various times worked as a security guard, a short-order cook, and a free-lance writer in the video game industry. He currently lives in Edmond, Oklahoma, where he teaches university courses in philosophy. He has published several book-length works of philosophy and over a dozen science fiction and horror stories in a wide variety of venues. His science fiction novel, *The Face on the Mountain,* came out in 2015.

Emily Martha Sorensen writes clean fantasy adventures with clever characters, fun plots, and lots of humor. She's been known to write about baby dragons, magic schools, and heroines who absolutely must drop-kick fate.

She has over fifty published books with more on the way. You may enjoy her humorous urban fantasy series that starts with *Trials of a Teenage Were-vulture,* or her Magical Mayhem series, in which villains are trying to save the world from overpowered magical girls.

Learn more at emilymarthasorensen.com.

Eric G. Swedin is a professor of history at Weber State University. His doctorate is in the history of science and technology. His publications include numerous articles, six history books, four science fiction novels, and a historical mystery novel. His alternate history novel, *When Angels Wept: A What-If History of the Cuban Missile Crisis,* won the 2010 Sidewise Award for Alternate History. Eric lives with his family in a house built in 1881.

Learn more at swedin.org.

KEVIN WASDEN works as the director of professional development at Gibbs Smith Education. He was previously a teacher, the dean of culture, and the principal at Venture High School, where he used a unique blend of experiential education, community building, and character development in order to help students become moral scholars and community stewards. He received his master's of education in leadership and administrative development from Southern Utah University. He is also an advocate of creativity in education (and life!) and enjoys speaking to youth, writers, artists, and educators.

He is the co-creator and illustrator of the sci-fi adventure series, *Hazzardous Universe*. He also developed and illustrates the independent comic series, *Technosaurs*. His artwork graces this volume, as well as *Trace the Stars*, the first volume in the LTUE Benefit Anthology series.

Learn more at kevinwasden.blogspot.com.

Though MICHAEL YOUNG grew up traveling the world with his military father, he now lives in Utah with his wife, Jen, and his two sons. He played for several years with the handbell choir, Bells on Temple Square, and is now a member of the Tabernacle Choir at Temple Square.

He is the author of the novels in *The Canticle Kingdom* series, *The Last Archangel* series, the *Chess Quest* series, and the *Penultimate Dawn Cycle* (*The Hunger, The Thirst*, and *The Longing*), as well as the nonfiction work, *The Song of the Righteous*.

Learn more at authormichaelyoung.com.

ADDITIONAL COPYRIGHT INFORMATION

All works listed on this page are copyrighted as indicated below and are included by permission of the individual authors. Works are listed alphabetically by author surname. Unless otherwise noted, they appear here for the first time.

- "Raising Words", copyright © 2016 by Stewart C. Baker. Originally appeared in *Penumbra* (July 2016) edited by Celina Summers.
- "Get Organised", copyright © 2023 by Ross Baxter.
- "Good Boy", copyright © 2023 by D. J. Butler.
- "Sidekicks", copyright © 2023 by Ray Daley.
- "The Needle-Heat Gun", copyright © 2016 by James Dorr. Originally appeared in *Night Lights* (March 2016) edited by Paul Garver and Phillip Garver.
- "Subordinate", copyright © 2023 by Melva Gifford.
- "Olive Garden", copyright © 2023 by Tristan A. Gilmore.
- "Masterpiece", copyright © 2023 by Jessica Guernsey.
- "Three Little Porcinians", copyright © 2023 by Henry Herz.
- "A Shoppe-ing Trip", copyright © 2023 by James Ivan Hughes.
- "It's a Kick's Life", copyright © 2023 by Randy Lindsay.
- "New Members", copyright © 2023 by James F. McGrath.
- "A Quiet and Unassuming Hero" (essay), copyright © 2023 by Joe Monson.
- "An Examination of the Trash Recovered from Armstrong Lunar Park", copyright © 2020 by Wendy Nikel. Originally appeared in *Nature: Futures* (April 2020).
- "An Ever Quickening Fire", copyright © 2023 by Staci Olsen.
- "Within Limits", copyright © 2015 by Scott R. Parkin. Originally appeared in *Irreantum* (Summer 2001) edited by Chris Bigelow.
- "While the Heroes Were Away", copyright © 2023 by Jamie Perrault.
- "The Dragon Slayer's Mentor", copyright © 2023 by Ivan Richardson.
- "The Justice Beacon", copyright © 2023 by Mark Silcox.
- "Weredodo Sleuth", copyright © 2019 by Emily Martha Sorensen. Originally appeared as a standalone release (April 2019).
- "The Echoes of Silver Ridge", copyright © 2023 by Eric G. Swedin.
- "Judging the Dark Lord", copyright © 2023 by Michael Young.

www.ingramcontent.com/pod-product-compliance
Lightning Source LLC
Chambersburg PA
CBHW050137120726
47903CB00002B/396